THE FLINT ANCHOR

THE
FLINT
ANCHOR

A NOVEL BY

Sylvia Townsend Warner

New York · 1954

THE VIKING PRESS

Library of Congress catalog card number: 54-8615

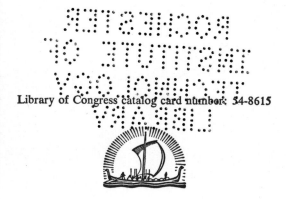

Printed in U.S.A. by The Colonial Press Inc.

To Anne Parrish

THE FLINT ANCHOR

PART ONE

1.

THIS TABLET

WAS ERECTED IN MEMORY OF

JOHN BARNARD

SON OF JOSEPH BARNARD

OF THIS PARISH,

born 20th February 1790, died 23rd December, 1863.
Deeply conscientious in the performance of every Christian
and social duty, he was a devoted Husband and Father, an
example of industry, enterprise, and benevolence to his
native town, and for seventy years a regular worshipper
in this Church.

"In life beloved, in death lamented."

Loseby parish church is in the diocese of Norwich. The
county guidebook remarks that it is notable for its flintwork,
and well worth a visit. During the years when John Barnard
knew it, it was notable for its funerals. As saints get a name
for particular miracles, churches become renowned for par-

3

ticular functions, and people would come from miles away whenever there was going to be an outstanding funeral at Loseby: a shipwreck, a deathbed repentance, or the father of a large family. There are still people in Loseby—in Old Loseby, that is, of the narrow streets and flights of cobble steps twisting down to the harbour, who remember hearing about the funeral of the unknown seaman who was cast up on the frozen beach, rigidly clasping a copy of the Swedish New Testament. And they remember too, by hearsay, John Barnard's funeral, when the snow had to be shovelled out of the grave to make room for the coffin. It had not the emotional intensity of the other, but it had a solemn quality of its own. Those who attended it knew in some occult way that it was the last of the real Loseby funerals, and that more than he was being buried with John Barnard.

Anchor House, where he lived, still stands, and is still called by its old name, though now it houses the Loseby Rural District Council. Visitors to the bracing east coast resort of New Loseby recognize it as Georgian and admire it accordingly. It is brick-built, with long narrow windows and stone coigns. Centred between the first-floor windows there is a representation of an anchor, made of cut flints embedded in the brickwork. The house is set back from the road, which gives it an air of repose and dignity, and the architect of the Rural District Council has emphasized this by fencing it with a row of little posts and chains swinging between them. At the time when John Barnard inherited Anchor House from his father, Joseph Barnard, its appearance was less pleasing. The forecourt was surrounded by a wall of dark flint, twelve feet high, surmounted by a criss-cross of iron spikes. The ironwork gates were spiked also, with bars so close set that a hand could not pass between them. These prison-like protections were put up by Joseph Barnard as a retort to the Jacobins in Paris, and as a deterrent to any Jacobins who might happen to be plotting in Loseby. Similar walls enclosed the garden at the back of the house, and

4

a similar pair of gates closed the stable yard where the property ran out into Back Lane. Joseph Barnard was a man of independent spirit. He feared nothing but God. His fortifications were a manifesto of disapproval. They darkened the front rooms on the ground floor, and soured the garden; but he had allowed for this, and discounted it. One must be prepared to pay something for the expression of one's opinions.

The first Barnard had come to Loseby wheeling a barrow before him, which was loaded with nets of his own making. A generation later there was a shed on the quayside where a Barnard family mended nets and made lobster pots, crans, and kegs. By the fourth generation there was a thriving quayside business, which imported tar and hemp and fats from the Baltic, packed and exported herrings, and supplied ship's chandlery; and when Joseph Barnard married his second wife he bought the house and had the flintwork anchor set into it as a boast and commercial blazon. At the same time he laid down a cellar of port wine, for he intended to get more than daughters in his second match. One cannot manage a business without becoming literate; one cannot become literate without exposing oneself to the culture of one's day. Joseph Barnard read Burke on the Sublime, bought a Dutch canvas of Boors Carousing, installed Rumford grates, and sent his elder son to Harrow and Cambridge. The boy was nervous, slow in learning, and spoke with an accent. His schooldays were torment to him. At Cambridge he suddenly bloomed into good looks and sensibility. He had a room of his own, he was treated like a gentleman, he was personally dear to his Maker. The college was Evangelical and vibrated with prayer meetings, experiences, and convictions of salvation; it was as though Jesus, detaching himself from that awful and mysterious Trinity, had stepped forward in all the sweetness of flesh and blood to walk with John Barnard on the Gog Magog hills. In an amazement of gratitude at feeling so happy, he resolved to devote his life to some lofty purpose; perhaps he would take holy orders and convert the Jews, per-

5

haps he would live in a cottage in Devonshire and write hymns. He was nerving himself for the interview in which, strengthened by divine aid, he would persuade his earthly father to leave the family business to Daniel, the younger son, when Joseph Barnard dropped dead in Loseby High Street. Thankful that he had been withheld from causing his father pain, John Barnard went back to Loseby. But, however difficult it might have been to persuade his father to leave the business to Daniel, it proved impossible to persuade Daniel to consider giving up his career in the Navy. Daniel had already served four years as a midshipman, he was confident of his lieutenancy, and his only thought as a co-inheritor was a delighted astonishment at the amount of the family fortune, coupled with a conviction that as there was so much more money than they had supposed, all that need be done was to put a head clerk in charge.

From feeling that an intolerable burden had been cast upon him, John Barnard presently came to feel that he had been called in the nick of time. He was shocked to find that the business rested on such haphazard foundations (they were, in fact, those which it had grown up from). The father, who living had been so terrible and so venerable, reappeared as an object lesson against financial levity. Practically nothing was insured. Mr. Powles, the family lawyer, was much impressed by his co-executor—so clear-headed, so painstaking, and so prudent. Daniel went to sea; John Barnard settled down in his father's place. He was well into his new life, sleeping in the best bedroom, reading family prayers, writing letters of good advice to Daniel, and enforcing a proper system of bookkeeping in the business, when his twenty-first birthday rose up before him. Mr. Powles asked what he proposed to do about it.

"Let it pass," was the reply. "It can only remind me that I am an orphan. Anything like a celebration would be painful to me."

"The men will expect something, you know—a dinner, at least, and some speeches, and a tea-drinking for their wives."

"They cannot expect me to make a speech while I am still wearing mourning for my father."

"They expect to make speeches themselves. I happen to know that Job Ransom is rehearsing one already."

"I am thinking of dismissing Ransom. I have found him in liquor more than once."

"Don't dismiss him until he's drunk your health, at any rate. You don't want a hornet's nest round your ears. Touch one, touch all. You know what Loseby is like."

John Barnard knew very well what Loseby was like. His knowledge dated from a foggy November evening fifteen years before, when the captain of the press-gang was killed. A girl had lured him down to the beach (she knew what was coming and had her own grievance to avenge, for the press-gang had taken her lover some months earlier). The Loseby boys had followed, barefoot and unseen, till she got him to where the freshet running out to sea made a quicksand. Then she leaped away with a yell of signal, and while he floundered in the quicksand the boys emerged from the fog and stoned him to death.

Sitting in the warm nursery with his bowl of bread and milk, he had heard the tumult, the voices hot with slaughter. "They're mobbing a seal," the nursemaid told him. She was a Loseby girl and in the secret.

Everyone below the authorities was in the secret, and no one disclosed it. When the body was thrown back by the sea and the Coroner's Court brought in a verdict of Murder by Persons Unknown, Loseby had its alibi. On the night of the uproar the boys had found a seal on the beach, and were pelting it. Seals spoil the nets and rob men of their livelihood, and a stranded seal was always stoned. Daniel, a pet among the servants, had learned the true story and told his brother, defying him to repeat it, or he, Daniel, would be whipped as never before for knowing and not telling Papa. From that hour the elder brother had a trammelled conscience. It was his duty to tell, and he had not told.

7

At the coming-of-age dinner he made a speech, referring to his inadequacy to take his father's place, and announcing an intention to devote the rest of his life (he managed as only a young man can do to imply that there was not much left of it) to the improvement, moral and material, of his native town. Neither the lawyer nor the parson thought much of John Barnard's speech: the lawyer thought it impolitic, the clergyman considered that the morality of Loseby might well be left to those appointed by God and the bishop to look after it. But his work-people clapped and cheered—not for what he said, but for how he looked while saying it. They had not realized till now what a handsome young man they had got. Under the stimulus of a public appearance, attention, applause, and a little wine, he was revealed as very handsome indeed, romantically handsome, with such glossy dark hair, such large bright eyes, and such well-made legs. Among Loseby fishermen it was taken as a matter of course that men should feel amorously towards a handsome young man. John Barnard on his twenty-first birthday was the image of a man's young man (women might feel that his forehead was too narrow and his nose too sharp), and Job Ransom, bellowing out his toast of "Mr. Barnard—bless his flesh!" summed up the mood of the occasion.

Not since leaving Cambridge had he felt such pleasurable emotions, and that night he seriously considered pulling down the wall, or at any rate removing the spikes. But the project remained a project. It was overlaid by other considerations, chief among them a danger from which no wall and no spikes could protect him. Try as he might, he could not evade noticing that the mothers of Loseby families were continually jostling their daughters against him. Then there were the maidservants. Though they did not directly menace his chastity, they exercised an oblique pressure against his bachelor quiet. He did not altogether trust his housekeeper to control them; if she failed to do so he would have to do something himself—whereas, if he took a wife it would be her responsibility. *I am a wall, and my breasts like towers*. . . . That was the voice of the church, declaring her wifely functions in The Song of Solomon. Casting about for a wall that would not be so exuberant, he remembered that he had two stepsisters, daughters of his father's first marriage. He did not know much about them, for his father had quarrelled with them; but he knew that Hannah was a spinster, and that Selina, deserted by her husband, was tantamount to a widow, and that they had very little money and lived together at Broadstairs. He invited them to Anchor House. They came, and his housekeeper left. A few months later the husband of the tantamount widow turned up in Loseby, forced himself and a reconciliation on the fluttered Selina, and moved from the Half Moon Inn to Anchor House for what he said would be a week.

Six months later he was still there, and John Barnard was lying awake night after night, trying to strengthen himself to turn them all out. It had to be all or none, for Hartley would not leave Selina, and Selina would not be parted from Hannah. The truth was, they were all very comfortable and did not mean to go. Hannah and Selina saw that he was becoming restive. They countered by putting him into a rapid decline. Those bad nights, that nervous irritability, that fitful appetite, and those suddenly flushed cheeks—it was all too plain, it reminded them only too sharply of their dear and joint Aunt Gore, whose lungs would certainly have carried her off if a jaundice had not intervened. Hannah and Selina took increasing care of their stepbrother. They made him flannel waistcoats, flannel nightcaps, and water gruel, they gave him calves'-foot jellies because meat would be too great a tax on his digestion, they allowed him nothing that might excite or exhaust him; while Hartley proffered lozenges and recommended a little, a very little Marsala, because the vines grow on a volcanic soil. Having failed to get rid of them, John Barnard turned to the notion of departing himself. At no time had he intended to live much beyond thirty, so the prospect of dying rather

9

sooner than he intended was only momentarily startling. Reconciled to an early death, and permanently underfed and overmuffled, he began to feel quite ill. Feeling ill, he began to find his stepsisters' attentions convenient; presently he was even grateful for them. Things were at this pass when a post-chaise drew up before Anchor House, the bell rang, and in came Daniel with a young woman on either arm. Daniel had just got married. One of the young women was his bride; the other was the bridesmaid who was accompanying her on the wedding tour.

While Hannah and Selina were upstairs helping the young women to take off their wraps and Hartley with the utmost readiness had consented to go to the kitchen to order a reviving supper, the brothers had a few words together.

"Isn't she a charmer? Isn't she a sweet creature?" asked Daniel. "I came on shore less than a fortnight ago; we met at a ball. One waltz—she waltzes divinely, but the reel suits her best of all, she's Scotch, you know, Dumfriesshire—and there we were! Her father approved, her mother approved, and three days ago we were married. They're Presbyterian, so all we needed was a parlour. Goodness, John, how ill you look! Been overdoing it with the ledgers, I suppose. Have you ever seen such a picture of health, such a bloom? I expect she'll get fat later on—all Scotchwomen do. Her mother weighs fourteen stone and carries a bosom like Britannia on a figurehead. But I'd rather have *her* than those frights Hannah and Selina. What on earth are they doing here? And who's the seedy customer?"

"Hartley. Selina's husband."

"I wish they weren't here. I don't want Beenie to think she's married into Rag Fair. She has a nice little fortune too. Mr. Black is shrewd, very shrewd. A property in Dumfriesshire. Well, well, Johnnie, I'm glad to see you again, even though you have filled the house with such odd beings. Whatever made you do it? I don't know what Beenie will make of it. I told her you were a handsome young man, brimful of sentiment, and living alone in bachelor meditation, fancy-free. Are you fancy-

10

free? If not, it don't agree with you, you know. You're not poxed, by the way?"

To hear such a thing spoken in his father's dining parlour brought it home to John Barnard that the dining parlour was in fact his, and that he was not getting the credit of it. Hannah, Selina, Hartley, Daniel, and probably those two young women upstairs, all slighted him and treated him as a nobody. He flushed, and straightened himself. "Daniel, that's going too far. I won't have such talk in my house."

"Oh, very well. I'm sorry I offended you. But I wish you'd tell me why they are here. I keep on asking you, and you always turn it off."

"I invited Hannah and Selina to come and make their home with me. I have a great deal to do in the business. The Trading Acts give me a great deal of anxiety, I cannot be responsible for a household into the bargain. Besides, the maidservants were entertaining young men in the kitchen."

"They always did," said Daniel. "They call them cousins."

"Whatever they did in the past, what they do now is my responsibility. I felt it my duty to invite Hannah and Selina here. Ladies can manage these things better than we can, Daniel."

"And did you invite Hartley to keep an eye on the stable boy?"

"Hartley came uninvited. Selina should have repulsed him. But she was weak. As for Hannah, Hannah is shortsighted; she thinks too much of Selina's feelings and not enough of Selina's real welfare. But I must say, Hannah is devoted to my health. She sat up for three nights when I had a quinsy."

"You're in a devilish fix with them, I can see that. They'll stay here forever if you don't do something about it soon."

"No!"

"They will, though."

"But what can I do, Daniel? It's very difficult. You must see how difficult it is."

"No difficulty at all. Marry and set up a family. Get a pair of

11

bawling twins, and you'll soon see Hannah and Hartley and Selina pack off. Marry, John! That's the answer. Marry Robina's bridesmaid, the girl that came with us. She's Scotch too. She's an orphan and lives with an old aunt near Peebles. Beenie will be delighted, and so will I."

"But—"

"She'll get rid of them before a week's out. Here they come! Now, you look at her and see if she won't do."

The suggestion was barely decent, and ridiculous. But John Barnard went so far as to say, "The one with blue eyes?"

"No, that's Beenie. T'other one."

It was out of the question; but for all that, he felt a momentary regret that it was not the one with blue eyes. She was small and slender and ladylike. The other one had a great deal of colour, a great deal of bosom, a large wanton mouth, and no conversation. By the end of the evening he was thinking of her very warmly. It is not conversation that one wants in a wife. Her name was Julia.

2.

Julia Smith had more to say for herself when she was alone with Robina, but it was mostly to the tune that she would never marry an Englishman. The aunt who had brought her up, Mrs. Maxwell of Phawhope, was second cousin once removed to Mrs. Boswell of Auchinleck and had many stories of Jamey B.'s coarse old Englishman, who wrote the dictionary and was worse than a pig in a parlour. But this one, Robina explained, was something quite different; she pointed out his classical features, his interesting pallor. Julia merely granted the pallor, remarking that it was no wonder the man looked like a sprouted potato in a cellar—what else could be expected in such a house, cold as a jail, dark as a coalpit, and everything so horridly formal except the fat man who tried to feel her leg?

12

"Marry him? Because you've married Daniel? Friendship goes far, Beenie, but not so far as that. I'd rather not marry at all than marry a man with two mothers and a father like a pug dog. Yes, I know they are all stepsisters, but at that age where's the difference? Two mothers telling him to mind his chest, and goggling Puggy pulling out his watch to see when it will be dinnertime."

"They'd go off like the morning dew once you set foot in the house. Whoever would think such a big strong girl as you would be afraid of marrying! But wait till he comes to see us. I've invited him. And he'll come."

"He'll not come! His mothers won't let him. And he'd be loth to leave Puggy with the wine-cellar key."

This conversation took place a fortnight later, when Daniel had rejoined his ship and Robina was in country lodgings near Portsmouth with Julia keeping her company. The landlady couldn't cook, but the lodgings were charming, with a bright fire in the grate, wedding trifles scattered about, and the ribbons sparkling on Robina's guitar. The two young women had never been so happy in their lives, eating boiled eggs for supper and wearing out their kid boots in scrambling walks. Laughing over past suitors—Geordie Biddle's anxiety about his buttons, Alexander Moir who fell into the cascade looking handsome as an angel—they were abashed when John Barnard came up the stairs. Business, he said, had brought him to Portsmouth. Business did not prevent him from putting up at the inn and spending three days in their company. But conversation was hard going. Robina could not be forever playing her guitar or asking what Daniel had been like as a little boy. Julia developed a spot on her chin and was mortified by a suspicion that John Barnard's feet were smaller than her own. She sat on a low chair, looking like a turned-out pudding, and glancing from his boots to her slippers. To distract the eye from the spot on her chin she wore her ferronnière, a rust-coloured cairngorm set in gold and bound to her forehead by a ribbon. It was a

13

fine large stone, but it did not make her face seem less fat, and as for countering the spot, it appeared on the contrary to be holding out an example to it. Conversation and the cairngorm drove Robina to suggest walking. It was December; the hollies glittered in the brakes, sheep moped on the frosty downs. John Barnard remembered how Daniel had arrived so unforeseenly with a young woman on either arm, one wearing a crimson pelisse and the other in bottle green with a fur muff and tippet. Now it was he who walked between them and supported them over the rough places, the tippet so sprightly, the crimson pelisse so pensive—the *Allegro* and the *Penseroso,* as in Milton. Daniel had asked him to be a brother to Robina, Robina had invited him, and both had insinuated that Julia also would be pleased to see him; but he did not really know why he was there. Soon he must go back, and on his return he would be welcomed to his own house and given calves'-foot jelly. Renunciation now, and shortly, death: it was the lot appointed him by an all-wise Creator, and he must not rebel at it.

"Oh, do look at that sheep! Isn't it exactly like Mr. Frazer giving out the psalm?"

She was a Presbyterian too. Another difficulty.

On the last day of his visit the weather changed. Rain drove them back from their afternoon walk. "We can't have Mr. Barnard catching cold," Robina said. A bottle of port was fetched from the inn, the landlady supplied a little saucepan, sugar, and a spicebox, and Robina brewed a bishop. Suddenly they became gay, intimate, intensely amusing. They sang "The Merry, Merry Christchurch Bells," "London's Burning," and "Three Blind Mice." They played the paper game called Heads and Bodies, and Julia drew a sideways camel below John's classical head of Minerva. Finally John and Julia pursued each other round a chair to the music of Robina's guitar. It was the little chair on which Julia had sat looking like a turned-out pudding, but one would never think it now. The saucepan was left too long on the hob and scorched. Mrs. Darby removed it uncomplainingly,

14

remarking to Mr. Darby in the back kitchen that we are only young once.

The next morning Robina turned green and was sick. She was sick again on the morning after, and the morning after that. She was with child.

She was eight months gone, unrecognizably majestic, her blue eyes starting from her face, her white throat distended, when she attended the wedding. John Barnard had not seen her for a couple of months. Her appearance terrified him. No amount of common sense, no degree of submission to the laws of God and of nature, could abate his horror. Was this what women were really like? Was this what marriage created them into? He could not believe that this stately monstrosity had been expanded from Robina who played the guitar and brewed the bishop. And he would have to do it to Julia.

So far, all that he had had to do to Julia had proved much easier than he had dared expect. But now the speed and smoothness of his courtship, the marriage settlements' going through so satisfactorily, Aunt Maxwell's blessing, Julia's acceptance of the Church of England, the delightful sensation of buying clothes for himself and pearls for Julia, with everybody in such good humour because of the end of the fighting and Napoleon disposed of on the island of Elba—all this that had been so smiling seemed positively sinister. It was the honey that gilds the wasp-trap, it was the broad leafage that conceals the serpent. He had not thought enough of what he was undertaking. Marriage is an arduous thing, and fraught with perils; if it were not so the church would not have made a sacrament of it. Even the ease with which Hannah, Selina, and Hartley had been dispatched seemed ominous. Julia had said she would do it, and a couple of days later it was done. When he inquired what methods she had employed, she laughed and told him that women have their own way of managing such things. No doubt of it, Julia had a strong character. Probably it was stronger than Robina's, just as she was taller than Robina and more robust. Yet she was not unwomanly; he could not have fallen in love with an unwomanly woman; and her methods, whatever they were, had not been quite all she supposed, for he had had to pay a considerable sum to Hartley. This reflection comforted him. All the same, he wished that he had thought more attentively about the state of matrimony, and he wished that he had someone older than himself, a father who partook also of the milder nature of a mother, to whom he could turn for advice, and he very nearly wished that he had not got to pluck that priceless jewel, a maidenhead, from Julia. Would it or would it not be made easier by going to Paris? For Julia and he were going to Paris. He could not speak French.

Julia's French was perhaps not quite so good as she supposed, but it enabled her to buy gloves and laced handkerchiefs, and to be assured that she spoke it like a native. She and her cousin, Baby Logan, who supplied the obligatory female companionship, took to Paris like ducks to water. They adored the ices, they adored the Cossacks, they adored being splashed by the spray from the fountains. John Barnard was less impetuous. It was hard to assimilate a town so unlike Loseby or even Cambridge, and it perplexed his sense of justice that the city which until a few months before had been the seat of iniquity, first worshipping the Goddess of Reason and then glorifying the Corsican Ogre, should look so totally unrepentant and so very prosperous. Yet after a night of love with Julia it was wonderfully pleasant to go riding in the Bois. He felt so well, the horse was so shiny, he knew himself handsome and desirable, and the avenue seemed to dapple him with approval. He consented readily enough when Julia said that they must revisit Paris in the spring.

This proved impossible. For one thing, Napoleon had escaped from Elba. For another, Julia was about to lie in. Baby Logan's sweetheart was killed at Quatre Bras, Geordie Biddle was mortally wounded at Waterloo, Napoleon was finally put down, the Allied sovereigns met all over again to congratulate themselves, Britannia was Triumphant and Peace Restored, as it said on the mugs that sold in such quantities at Loseby Fair; but Mr. and Mrs. Barnard never revisited Paris. The first child was a boy, named Joseph. A year later a girl was born, and named Euphemia, after Aunt Maxwell. Then came George, and after George, Susan. Both were remarkably promising infants, but later they dwindled and were snuffed out by the whooping-cough. Then came Mary, followed by twin boys, Samuel and Julius. The next child, a boy, died at birth. After this Julia gave birth to a fourth daughter, Ellen. She had intended to call this child, if a girl, Robina, but the baby's face was blemished with such a large port-wine stain that Robina was out of the question. Then came a daughter, who lived just long enough to be christened Robina. The boy born after her was christened Wilberforce, and survived. After that there were nothing but a few miscarriages.

It was after Ellen that Julia took to a sofa and to Madeira. It was called keeping her strength up. Knowing how necessary it is for the mother of a family to keep her strength up, John Barnard thought the Madeira laudable rather than otherwise, an aspect of the general vinosity of fruitful wives, twining like fruitful vines over the dwelling of the man whom the Lord has blessed with increase. He was more inclined to be critical about the sofa. A wife on a sofa can so easily give an impression of ill health, whereas Julia's health was excellent. Dr. Kitter said so, expatiating on the number of teeth she had retained. Teeth are useful, but there is not much consolation in them. Lying on her sofa, her powers of self-criticism increasingly clouded by Madeira, Julia cast a backward look towards her youth: towards Paris, towards the first years of her maternity, when little Joseph was so wonderful and little Euphemia so amusing, and the current suckling at her breast so touchingly weak and dependent (after the first four babies, she ceased to think of them as weak or dependent—they were trampling

17

tyrants); above all, to those airy few weeks in the lodgings near Portsmouth, before Robina began being sick. Now she was half as old again as she had been in the lodgings, and almost twice as heavy. Children die, teeth decay. Only weight accumulates and faithfully remains. It was a providence, after all, that her feet were large; if they had been as small as she then wished them, they could not have borne the matron Julia, she would not have been able to get off her sofa at all—not to meals, not to church, not to bed. Her pleasure in bed had outlasted her pleasure in maternity. Even now there seemed to be wistful sparks of it about her, lurking somewhere inside her sheer bulk.

"Here, a sheer bulk, lies poor Tom Bo–ow–ling." . . . Lying on her soaf, lit by the summer sun and wrapped in a Paisley shawl (for as well as being perpetually fat she was almost perpetually cold), Julia sang the first line of Dibdin's ballad in a husky voice, and laughed at her poor little joke till tears ran down her cheeks; and after that wept, touched by finding herself amusing. No one else in the house would have been amused.

Perhaps it was the wall, perhaps it was her husband, so serious and so very sensitive—none of her children laughed at unexpected jokes. A joke had to be prepared, introduced, and sanctioned before they could laugh at it. She sometimes thought it was a pity that the wall should be so very high, so high that even in the garden there was always a territory of shadow. From the day they left the nursery and came downstairs to begin lessons, and to be held responsible for their actions, and to remember their Creator in the days of their youth, the children came under the domination of the wall and began to stammer, and to be dainty about their food, and to scream at night. After the deaths of George and Susan, who seemed in their coffins almost like deformed children, their heads being so much too large for their narrow bodies, the robust symmetry of their babyhood an incompatible memory, she had spoken out about the wall. Barnard replied that the wall could be pulled down if she wished: its removal would give work to local

18

men who needed it; but that to expect anything more than that would be idle. He too, once out of babyhood, had begun to stammer, to scream at night, to be dainty and peevish and sullen. It was not the wall, but the children's common inheritance from Adam that brought about these changes in them.

"But the wall was there then," she said. "You and Daniel grew up inside it." He gave a sad shrug. The mention of Daniel brought Daniel before her eyes, romping with his children as though they were his cubs, and she said no more about the wall.

3.

If she had spoken a few years sooner she would have met a warmer response. In the early 1820s John Barnard had half a mind to pull down the wall, which had become odious to him, both for what it contained and for what it kept out. The speed with which Julia had made him a husband had been matched by the speed with which she was making him a patriarch, and a further process, as swift and compelling, turned babies, who were charming, into growing boys and girls who were naughty, noisy, and malodorous, who snatched one another's toys and scratched one another's faces, and then suddenly fell sick and re-arrayed themselves in the piteousness of infancy. His father's house, which he had grown up to revere as a variety of temple, was turned into a mart of procreation, where he was jostled by midwives, wet-nurses, dry-nurses, nursery maids, and Julia's breeding acquaintances. Escaping to his office, he passed through the iron gate to the farther side of the wall, and there too was disillusionment. Britannia was Triumphant and Peace Restored. At every public dinner some well-fed person rose up to say that England had saved Europe by her example. Europe had exchanged Bonaparte for the Papacy, and England was starving. Every day as he walked to his office some beggar came up and

19

implored him; and these were not the established Loseby un-
fortunates, whose circumstances he knew and whose pleas he
could decide on, but desperate vagrants, weavers from Norwich thrown out of work by the new manufactories in the North
of England, or cottagers dispossessed by an Act of Enclosure.
The weavers were burning with religion and rebellion, and at
first he was shocked to hear Saving Grace and living wages
tossed up together; but as he listened he recognized the evangelical fervour which had thrilled him at Cambridge. Inflamed
by this discovery, he said and did things that Loseby found
unaccountable. Mr. Powles began to eat his words about John
Barnard. High-minded and gentlemanly—yes, no one denied
it. Open-handed? Yes, and rather too much so. Godfearing?
Undoubtedly, but scarcely fitted to be a churchwarden. A good
employer? Well, yes, it was an old established business; he
would not care to say what Mr. Barnard would have made of it
in ten years' time, unless he gave up some of his present opinions. But just as Mr. Powles was about to use the word "democrat," the fever burned out. John Barnard returned to his
senses, and the wall ceased to be a symbol of social injustice
and was no more than the wall put up by Joseph Barnard—
possibly a protection against thieves, and certainly a protection
against watchdogs; for if it had come down there would have
had to be a dog in a kennel, and John Barnard disliked dogs.

This change of mind had not come about because he was
happier, or the world less full of misery. People were still
workless and starving, and in his own heart he was still intimidated by being the father of a family, and irked by a sense that
in some way he had been wronged. But a new ingredient
had been thrown into his ferment of anxiety, conscience, and
idealism. The new ingredient was love, passionate, romantic
love, and its object was his third daughter, Mary. Such a love
does not cast out fear. It invites and fattens it. Trembling with
prudence, he looked round on a world of dangers, and looking
up to heaven for help, saw, eyeing him out of infinity, that

20

other father, the father in heaven. His liberalism shrivelled and fell away. It was no more than a gown he had worn at Cambridge, the apparel of a young man. And, just as in Europe the republics and the brief mild monarchies had been swept away, and the old regime reinstated, the brief mild Jesus was supplanted by the God of Abraham sacrificing Isaac, the God who visits the sins of the fathers upon the children and is not mocked. Charity is a christian duty, and he continued to help the poor; but now his charity came from a well-ordered conscience, there was no threat to society in it, and Mr. Powles could praise him without reservation.

Under the eye of this reinstated God, John Barnard applied himself more zealously to his obligations as a father—the father of a family, not only the father of Mary Barnard. Mary would not be spoiled by over-indulgence or made vain by being singled out from the rest; he was too much afraid of the God of Abraham for that. Besides, what he felt for her was nothing so weak as preference; it was passion, a thing incompatible with choice or comparison. But as the gardener, for the rose's sake, appears to ignore the rose while searching the rose tree for greenfly to be sprayed and small grubs to be nipped between the nails of finger and thumb, Mary's father now took particular pains to oversee the development of her brothers and sisters. Loseby parents were of the opinion that whatever the little Barnards might lack through Mrs. Barnard's being so continually poorly was more than made up to them by having such a devoted father. Where else in Loseby, it was asked, would you find such a handsome apartment as Mr. Barnard's own study given over to the boys' lessons?

It was this privilege which had made Julia ask if the wall could not be pulled down, for the handsome apartment gave on to the forecourt, and no sunlight came into it. But John Barnard had a purpose in choosing it as the room where his sons did their lessons with Mr. Moore, the tutor, and prepared their work in the evenings, while he made the best he could of the small morning room at the back; he chose it so that his children should realize the importance of education. For the same reason, no change was made in the furniture. A cheap deal table only promotes the trick of spilling the ink. Joseph and George, and afterwards Samuel and Julius, sat, each in studious isolation, at a vast mahogany table, on chairs whose polished legs recorded the slightest inclination to kick; and if they raised their eyes from their books the walls admonished them with Flaxman's illustrations to the plays of Æschylus— Orestes the suppliant, naked, classically unprotected by a slight cloak, and the Furies coldly, classically furious, with blindly rolling eyes and whips of serpents. These last were theoretical. The Barnard children were never whipped. Careful thought had convinced John Barnard that his own frequent whippings had done him no real good; the pain was so pre-occupying that one tried to forget it, instead of concentrating one's faculties on the sense of being in fault. Censure and ostracism were more likely to be effective. Censure and ostracism had seemed to be working very well on George until he died, but failed with Joseph. Perhaps Joseph was an exceptionally frivolous child, or perhaps his father was not so skilful in the application of censure and ostracism when he first began to lay them on. Whatever the reason, Joseph did better after he was sent to Harrow, where old-fashioned methods were used. After the first few terms (which are inevitably disconcerting for those brought up in christian homes) he came back for the holidays looking—not personable, for he was lankily built with a foolish freckled face, but agile and popular, like a mongrel dog that has found a kind master.

On each return Joseph would ask Euphemia as soon as he could get her alone if Mary was as good as ever, and on Euphemia's affirmative he gave a sigh of relief. By the word "good" he did not mean moral goodness. It was Mary's efficacy he inquired after—did Mary still retain her halcyon-like quality of soothing Papa when he was vexed? Sailors are a superstitious race. No doubt there were always some who during the profoundest of halcyon calms remained on their guard, looked with dubious eyes on the long cloudless sunsets, and forbade any whistling on board. Joseph and Euphemia had already learned by experience and observation how babies, which are helpless and blameless, grow into boys and girls and become reasons for anxiety and even disappointment. There was no envy in their minds as they saw Mary's exemption from the common lot. They were far too much obliged to her to feel envy, just as they were too well-schooled in their own inferiority to attempt emulation. But they did sometimes wonder what it was about Mary, and they wondered with trembling concern how much longer it could last out. For her part, Mary felt neither conceit nor speculation. From her earliest recollections poor Brothers and Sisters had been naughty children and often a grief to Papa, and she had been Papa's dear open-hearted child. She took such a state of things for granted, like the greenness of trees in summer and the bareness of trees in winter; greenness was pretty, and bareness was not pretty, and one and the other were aspects of the universe.

Mary's placid disposition had been apparent while she was yet in the womb, and Julia said to herself that after so many pregnancies, one on the heels of the other, she was really getting into the way of it. But the birth had been appalling.

She fell into labour on an April evening; the night and the day went by, and it was night again. By then she had ceased to demand a surgeon. "Now, dear, make an effort, do! Bounce yourself, give one good push." So at intervals the midwife implored her. And obstinately she continued to answer, "I'm dying." On the red sweating face that hung over her, breathing out a strong smell of cloves, she saw to her despair the persisting expression of knowing better. But sooner or later it would be true; she would be dying; she would be dead. Either the pains would be too much for her, or, after the child was out, a flooding would carry her away, as slops emptied into the gutter sweep off a

23

dead kitten. She must wait, that was all. She felt the midwife's sweat falling on her face, servants came to the door with trays, and in the dressing room her husband was walking up and down in creaking slippers. Later she heard him praying. The thought of his prayers oppressed her—there was already wasted effort enough without praying to deaf ears. "Tell him to go and have breakfast," she gasped, and the midwife replied that it was three in the morning. Timelessly later she felt the child wrenched out, and saw the midwife holding it in bloodied hands. Afterwards, when clean linen had been spread over her, and the windows had been thrown open to get rid of the smell, Barnard stalked in on tiptoe. He was unshaven, his face was haggard; he looked like some melancholy thief creeping to her bedside.

"Julia, my poor wife, how you have suffered!"

She nodded. Tears ran down his cheeks. The midwife offered him the bundle that was the baby. He looked into it solemnly, his face contorted with emotion. The midwife said something about a fine child, and well worth waiting for.

Turning back to Julia, he said, "She has cost you so much—she must always be my dearest child."

"Quite right, sir. Very properly expressed," the midwife remarked.

Julia thought to herself, I'll hold him to that bargain. But nothing of the sort had been necessary. Five years later, ten years later, Mary was still unwaveringly and devotedly loved. Unlike Joseph, who caused so much anxiety because of his weak character, or Euphemia, who was undersized and too reserved to be amiable, or George and Susan, who were dead, or Samuel and Julius, who were growing noisy and petulant, or Ellen, who, humanly speaking, must be considered a cross, Mary remained without flaw. It was as if he had received a license with her, an unconditional permit to love one child, free of tax or charges against deterioration. And though Julia could not feel quite as Barnard did about the obligation to love some-

24

thing that had cost two nights and a day of extreme anguish, she was very grateful to Mary for remaining an unqualified pleasure to her papa.

So Julia thought, for she was unspeculative and hopeful of pleasure. If she saw a cake covered with sugar icing, she expected it to be sweet inside. Looking at Mary, she saw blue eyes, regular features, a well-made frame, a disposition ready to be loved—in short, a creditable little Miss Barnard. From that she went on to think of blue ribbons, flannel, mutton broth, music lessons, and the dangers of catching cold, growing too fast, or turning her toes in.

But when John Barnard looked at Mary he began to think of angels and of worms. Once a week at least, usually on Sunday evenings, he asked himself whether, if it were God's will to take her, he could give her up without rebellion or despair. The answer took one or other of two forms: if Mary were taken from him he must despair and die. If he saw Mary threatened by sin or contamination he would relinquish her gladly that she might be preserved from the wrath to come. But he could not be sure which answer came truly from his heart. He knew it should be the second, and he tried to exercise himself into making it the only answer. If anything should happen to Mary —consumption, gipsies, mad dogs, softening of the brain, scarlet fever—then the angels would take her, and the worms would devour her flesh; and it would be more than he could endure. But there was also the worm that dieth not, and Mary's soul, that soft, bright, flower-like thing, would be an irresistible target for the arrows of Satan. Rather than see her fall a prey to that worm, let her die, let her be taken from him! And then he would lash himself with the thought that his love might already have blinded him to serious faults in her character, that the devil might already have a foot in her, and that it is not enough to teach a child christian principles, one must also put them to the test. So he would put Mary's principles to the test —a sweetmeat left unguarded on his desk, a trinket, an inter-

25

rogation that might trip her in a lie. The traps never closed on her. She would ask for the sweetmeat in serene confidence that it would be given; and if he withheld it (a provocation to anger) she would turn her mind to something else. A coral necklace or a reference to her curls left her unmoved, except to be pleased at pleasing him, and she was open as the day. Since, for the time being, he really could not find much wrong with her, and since her health was excellent, he fell back on tormenting himself with imaginations of future contingencies. Suppose, for instance, that she fell in love, a young girl's tremulous first love, with a Mohammedan or a Roman Catholic? Suppose she developed a high soprano voice and wished to become an opera singer? Suppose—his thought jibbed, but he forced it on—suppose she were debauched? Lathered in sudden sweat, his imagination reared, and he was unseated. There are limits, even to parental solicitude.

Meanwhile he allowed no one to know that Mary was more to him than any other of his children.

"Anyone might suppose that she is his firstborn, and that he gave birth to her himself—out of his hat," commented Robina, who had come to Anchor House for the christening of her namesake. "Not that I wonder at it, for she is a sweet little witch. I see more than a look of Baby Logan in her."

"Baby Logan." Julia bestirred herself. "What became of her? I don't seem to have heard of her for a long time."

"Oh, it is a shocking story! She took to wearing a sort of mantilla and sat up all night writing poetry."

"I know. She sent me some—'Stanzas to E.,' and E. meant Euphemia. All about blights and whirlpools—more like Lord Byron than Baby. But that was long ago. What happened next?"

"My dear child, she became a Papist. Worse than that, she went into one of their convents and became a nun."

"A nun?" said Julia, not showing so much reprobation as Robina had expected. "A nun? Fancy that! But I suppose it's

26

a peaceful life. We saw nuns walking about in Paris, and they looked peaceful."

Baby Logan had become a nun, and Robina had been to Calcutta and wore a false front of hair much more golden than the ringlets that had drooped over the guitar. Barnard said that Robina had grown hard. Julia was glad when the visit was over. Whether or no Robina had grown hard, she herself had grown soft, and the sensation of Robina darting through her like a bodkin had been disturbing. Heaped on her sofa, she set herself to forget everything that Robina had said except the assurances that Mary looked the picture of health. Time went on. With Mary, and Madeira, and comfortable middle-aged servants, and the last miscarriage remaining the last, Julia began to think her lot, in its way, no worse than a nun's. The business was doing well, in spite of hard times, and there was plenty of money. She would have liked to spend it more freely and enjoy some of the solid ostentation and richly rowdy festivities that had prevailed at Aunt Maxwell's, but as Barnard was born a wet blanket she contented herself by adding touches of richness and rowdiness to the family acts of charity, pink sugar icing on the orphans' buns, and wine to the good gravy soup for lying-in women. She was monstrous to the eye, but no one looked at her except those who saw her so habitually that they looked at her without seeing more than the pattern on a new shawl. Except for Mary, her children were variously imperfect; but either they would improve or their imperfections would be rendered less glaring by a patina of time. Joseph in his first year at Cambridge seemed to have run through his epoch of misfortune. Barnard certainly expected it to be so, remarking that Cambridge had made a great difference to him, he had been much improved by the change from school to university.

4.

It was the autumn of 1832, John Barnard was no longer suspect for his advocacy of the Reform Bill, for the Reform Bill had been passed, and Wilberforce was almost through with teething, when the postman brought a letter from Joseph's tutor to Joseph's father. But he put it aside unread because at the same minute three new-made widows came to the door. A fishing boat had been wrecked, and they were following the Loseby custom of coming to Mr. Barnard. Occasions of this sort found John Barnard at his best; he had an aptitude for calamities, and while he listened and condoled he had already decided which of the widows was best fitted to be given a donkey and set up as a fish-hawker, while the other two could be helped to a livelihood by being supplied with materials for net-making. Yet when they had gone his mind misgave him, and it seemed to him that by administering this sort of comfort he was in some way denying his Saviour, the true comforter of the afflicted—a misgiving sharpened by knowing that it was precisely for this false comfort that they had come to him, and that it was all they thought him good for. "As though I were the town pump!" he exclaimed, irritated, and ashamed of his irritation. He thought he would calm himself by taking a turn in the garden.

It was not yet nine in the morning. The gale which had drowned the fishermen had purified the air and strewn the lawn with small red apples. The gulls floating in the blue sky were so high in air that they looked translucent, and Mary was walking up and down the gravel path with a book on her head. To the gate into the kitchen garden, overhung by the elder-bush's swag of purple berries and bronze leaves, and back to the arbour, and to the gate again, she passed and repassed. In order to balance the book she walked proudly, as though maturity had touched her like a stiffening of the first

28

frost which at any moment now would loosen the leaves and blacken the gaudy annuals. She wore a white dress, and her long white drawers reached her ankles. It was as though all the colours of the autumnal garden were in a conspiracy to enrich her whiteness with their scarlet and crimson and purple and gold, just as rich aunts might bestow their Indian shawls on a favourite niece, knowing that they themselves had only a little longer to wear them. Seeing her so white and dutiful, he naturally began to think of angels; and at the same time he knew that the comparison in his mind was with the converted Chinese, who also walk among violent colours wearing white smocks and long white drawers and the curious hats of their native land. But Mary's feet were naturally small, and only in England could one find such ringlets, glossy, resilient, living under the hand that caressed them. And the Chinese, however truly converted, were primarily heathen; the recollection of vice and idolatries must remain in them like grounds in the coffee-pot, whereas Mary, by the mercy of God, was born in a christian home of christian parents.

"My love!"

She came towards him.

"My love, you would please me by repeating the sixth of Doctor Watts's Divine Songs."

She began immediately:

> "Lord, I ascribe it to thy grace,
> And not to chance, as others do,
> That I was born of Christian race,
> And not a Heathen, or a Jew."

He listened, gently waving his hand to and fro with the singsong rhythm of her repetition. Her face was faultlessly serious, faultlessly serene, and yet, he knew, it is considerably harder to balance a book on one's head when one is standing still. "Amen," he said at the close of the hymn. "Thank you, my dear child." And he went indoors to read his letters. The letter from Joseph's tutor told him that Joseph had been sent down. Joseph had got into a fast set, and to win a wager of ten pounds he had climbed onto the roof of the college chapel, naked and carrying a stuffed owl, which he placed on a crocket. Such behaviour could not go unnoticed, but the university was prepared to take him back after a term's rustication, since it was a single misdemeanour and not borne out by his general conduct, which was inoffensive.

It was not for this that he had sent Joseph to Cambridge! John Barnard felt it a crowning injury that a place which had meant so much to him meant no more than bad friends and a stuffed owl to his eldest son. The day ended, but Joseph did not come. John Barnard sat up all night, and Julia woke from a fuddled sleep supposing that she had had another baby, for why else should the pillow beside her have no head on it? Next morning John Barnard set out for Cambridge. There he learned that on the previous morning Joseph had left by the stagecoach for Ipswich, saying nothing of any destination other than Loseby. His bedmaker said that he had taken some clothes with him, and a kettle-holder which the bedmaker believed to have been made by the young gentleman's sister. John Barnard went to Ipswich. The ostler at the coaching inn perfectly remembered a tall young gentleman with a stammer, and that he had a portmanteau and had gone into the inn to warm himself. But that was all.

Euphemia was the first person John Barnard met with on his return. The kettle-holder came into his mind, and he began to question her. He did not expect to learn much by this, but it was his duty to follow every clue. Euphemia, as usual, was sullen and reserved, and he tripped her almost at once.

"I gave it to him because I thought it might be useful."

"Then you must have known what was in his mind. Where would a kettle-holder be useful?"

"Almost anywhere, I suppose, if one wanted to make tea."

"Euphemia, do not prevaricate. You cannot put me off so easily. Where is your brother?"

30

"I don't know."

"You only injure him by this concealment. Euphemia, my dear child, I know you love your brother. Surely you wish to help him, to rescue him from misery, from destitution or profligacy?"

In a considering tone of voice she said, "Yes."

"Then tell me where you think he is."

"I do not know."

He sent her away at last and sat on in despair. He could not think what he had done to deserve that his son, his firstborn, should have no pity for him. At last he got up and went to Julia. The candlelight played on the flanks of the cut-glass decanter, and on the ruby glass from which Julia sipped her Madeira. Mary sat beside her, hemming a handkerchief. He sighed. In his absence everything went wrong, even his ewe-lamb.

"Surely Mary should be in bed by now."

She rose without a word and went to the door. He called her back; he could not bear her to think herself dismissed. He laid his face against her rose-scented hair and kissed her forehead. After she had gone out he talked to Julia, trying to soothe her anxieties about Joseph. The strain was telling on her, poor Julia, and she was very argumentative and confused.

Next day came a letter from Joseph, written from Tilbury:

> My dear Father, I have disgraced myself, and I cannot come home. I have decided to emigrate. By the time you get this, I shall be on the Ocean. I am in such a state that I scarcely know what I am doing, but I am sure of one thing, I have always been a trouble to you, and perhaps I shall do better in a new country. I will write to my Mother as soon as I am there. Ask her to forgive her unhappy son,
>
> Joseph.
>
> P.S. I will send money as I earn it to pay my Cambridge debts.

Even in the distress of knowing that Joseph had thus made bad worse and had no trust in the scope of a father's love, John Barnard was shocked at this cold-hearted preoccupation with debts. He had never thought that Joseph was mercenary. He found out what was owing and paid it. It amounted to twelve pounds five shillings, not a large sum.

He could not decide whether it was through callousness or incompetence that Joseph had said nothing of his destination. To have been able to say, He has gone to Canada, to America, to India, would have drawn some of the sting of making the news public. It did not occur to him to try to keep it hidden. As a Christian he could not conceal what God had seen fit to inflict on him, and as a man of honour he could not muffle up the family disgrace. Oddly enough, this unworldly candour made him respected by the majority of his neighbours, though, being the majority, they were all of the lower class. It was a slap in the face for him, they said, but at least he was man enough to own it. As the Barnard cavalcade passed up the aisle of the parish church, it was regarded from the free seats with kindness as well as curiosity. The rented pews looked on the stricken family with more circumspection, managing to convey condolence without seeming aware what there was to condole about.

The promised letter came. Joseph was not starving on a quayside in Boston, or cutting down trees in the forests of New Brunswick, or catching yellow fever on the Gold Coast or cholera in Bombay. He was on an estate in the West Indies, with a salary and a house of his own. The estate belonged to a college friend of his called Marmaduke Debenham. Marmaduke had come to him after the rustication, and had tried to dissuade him from his determination to emigrate. Failing to do so, he had given him a letter to the manager of the estate, and paid his passage out. Joseph had a post as clerk, rode about a great deal, found the climate agreeable, wished his sisters could see the flowers and the butterflies, and was sending off a case of guava jelly and some rum for the poor old women of Loseby. The Negroes on the estate, he added, were all Christians and did not seem unhappy.

This letter arrived while John Barnard was attending the county sessions in Norwich. He noticed a change in the atmosphere of his house as soon as he entered it. Euphemia was practising her scales, they rang through the house crisp as a carillon, and from the kitchen came a jovial smell of hot gingerbread. On the stairs, positively hurrying to meet him, was Julia. But it could not be anxiety over Mary, though when he left she had had a little snuffling cold, for Julia was smiling and waving a letter.

"A letter from Joseph. And such good news! I feel twenty years younger."

He read the letter in silence, folded it, and put it in his pocket.

"It is good news, isn't it? You do think it is good news?"

"I hope so. We have every reason to be thankful."

"Thankful? I am indeed. Such a very kind young man! I suppose he is an orphan."

"Thankful to Providence. Joseph seems pleased with his lot, and he is working, which is to the good. And we know where he is, which is an inexpressible relief. For the rest, we must accept it and swallow the mortification. For myself, I admit it, I am mortified. My pride rebels."

"But Joseph says that Mr. Debenham tried all that he could to persuade him to come home."

"If Joseph's own feelings for his family could not bring him home, I am not surprised that Mr. Debenham's persuasions failed. And whether or no Mr. Debenham acted rightly towards Joseph, he has not acted generously towards us. He should not have left us in ignorance."

"Perhaps," she suggested, "Mr. Debenham did not like to publish a good action."

"Pooh! However, I will write to him."

33

"And to Joseph?"

"To Joseph. And to Mr. Debenham. How is Mary's cold?"

"No worse. But I'm afraid the boys have caught it. I am not letting them go out for their walk. The sun shines, but this wind is treacherous."

The sun continued to shine, and the east wind, a light, slight east wind, blew sneeringly round the house where Mary, Samuel, and Julius had developed measles. In the garden the hyacinths bloomed, the pyrus japonica blossomed, the gardener sowed peas and set little twigs to protect the first sprouts of the broad beans. On Tup Hill the masons began work on the new terrace. John Barnard owned land on this outskirt of the town and was building on it. He would have preferred to keep the ground to its old purpose of grazing the family cows, but there was distress and hunger in the neighbourhood, and the new terrace would give employment. The ground was levelled, the foundations dug, the wagons brought timber and loads of smart pale brick. Every day he went out to see what progress had been made, and came back with only the slightest notion of what he had seen. His foreboding was right: Mary was about to be made one with worms and angels. Giving up hope for her, he gave up hope for the two boys also. The Lord was smiting him in what a family man holds dearest. Joseph had cut himself off, and now measles would carry away Mary and the twins.

Before his dazzled, disbelieving eyes, Mary recovered. But while she was still in the stage of slops and blankets she was hurried away to finish her convalescence under the care of Madame Bon, who kept a small girls' school in Loseby; home was no place for her, for Samuel's measles had set up abscesses in his ears, and his screams of anguish rang through the house every time the hot fomentations were renewed. Bleeding, cupping, leeches, strong purges, a lowering diet, everything that Dr. Kitter could suggest was tried. Matter poured from Samuel's ears, he became deaf and stupefied. A second rash broke out

34

and he died. Before the coffin was nailed down, Mary was brought home to look her last on him. If it had not been for God's mercy, her father said, she too might have been lying in a coffin and about to be put into the ground to become the prey of worms and corruption. She nodded in agreement. She knew all about it. Madame Bon had been preparing her mind by reading aloud from a book called *Deathbeds of Eminent Christians*. This was her first corpse. Now she would be put into a black dress, and it would have to be almost a young lady's one, for she had grown much taller during her illness. But poor Samuel seemed to have grown smaller. There were several questions she would have liked to ask, whether the little pillow would also go into the grave, if he had had a death rattle, and if he had seen the heavens open before he died. But she did not speak, inhibited by her father's melancholy, devouring eyes and the stillness of the room and the presence of a bluebottle, which she instinctively felt should not be there. Julius too had been near death, they told her. She would ask him if he had seen the heavens open, and what death felt like when it was so near.

Julius seemed unwilling to tell her anything. He had seen nasty things, he said—Chinamen who put out their tongues, and knives not held by anybody, cutting slices of cake, and the Furies, the ones in the schoolroom pictures. She had not been ill enough to see things like that, he added, looking at her with listless malice. Besides, she was only a girl; she would never learn Latin or Greek, she could not understand the Furies. Julius was now alone with the Furies every evening, preparing his work for the morrow. He had forgotten a great deal during his illness and had got out of the way of applying his whole mind to the task before him. This became a matter for grief, and then for censure, and then for ostracism. But beyond eating bread and water for dinner, with his face to the wall while the rest of the family ate as usual, ostracism did not seem to make much difference to Julius, for he had grown

35

solitary, living in a world of his own where even the summer sun could not touch him. He was always cold, and his fingers went blue for no reason at all. In spite of the ostracism, Euphemia used to rub his legs after he was in bed, alleging that she was going upstairs to look over the lessons she would give at the next Sunday school. Everyone in the house except Papa and Mamma knew why Euphemia went upstairs, but it was Julius who told on her, saying that the bloodied handkerchief found under his bed had been dropped by Euphemia.

Self-examination had shown John Barnard that he was prejudiced against his eldest daughter (he was, in fact, rather afraid of her, though self-examination had not revealed this). Euphemia was convicted of disobedience, deceit, and something approaching a breach of the Third Commandment, for if invoking the Sunday school was not actually taking the name of the Lord in vain, it went near to it. But he wanted to be scrupulously fair to the girl, and to give her every advantage in the struggle, so the interrogation took place in Julia's dressing room. The presence of a mother is softening, and he did most anxiously hope that Euphemia might be softened, that her heart might be touched and forgiveness made easy.

Euphemia was in a state to hate everyone, most of all Julius, who had betrayed her. With the ease of hate she admitted that she had disobeyed, deceived, and taken the name of the Sunday school in vain. She produced her diary, a record of matters of fact expressed in contractions—"pr'd," for instance, for prayed, and "d'd" for darned—and established by entries of "r'bd J." how long she had been in fault.

"I'm sure Effie meant to be kind," said Julia. "She knows herself how one's legs can ache. And one's back. Don't you, Effie?"

This was tossed aside by John Barnard, who said that there was no kindness in teaching Julius to deceive, and that if Euphemia had felt true kindness she would have thought of that instead of her own pleasure and self-importance. Euphemia,

36

who had particular reason just then to know how one's legs and back can ache, broke off the interview by fainting away. Julia had meant to ask about Julius's nose (he had been forced to admit that the handkerchief was his, and said it was nosebleeding), but Euphemia's faint was more interesting to her, so the bloody handkerchief was overlooked until Julius, trying to suppress a cough during family prayers, had a hæmorrhage. He had been spitting blood for some time, but the thought of his brother's death and all the gaunt to-do of burial had frightened him so much that he was afraid to speak of it. It seemed to him that if nothing were said, less would be real.

Every window in the house was immediately closed, everything done that could be done to prolong his life and allay the fear of death that obsessed him. Once again John Barnard was shown that he did not possess his children's confidence. In helpless bewilderment he watched the child awaiting the oncome of death like some wretched criminal in the condemned cell. Canon Blunt was brought to assure Julius of the saving mercies of his Redeemer. Old Mr. Thurtle, renowned in Loseby for his efficacy at troubled deathbeds, came repeatedly, smelling of tar and liquorice, and wrestled in prayer. Hymns were sung, there was talk of lambs and harps and good shepherds. He was given a canary. The canary died, easily as a flower sheds its petals, and in October Julius died too. A few days before his death he suddenly remembered the world he was leaving and asked if the chestnuts had fallen, and if he could have one. His father went out into the glittering garden and picked up chestnuts where he had picked them up as a boy. Julius stroked them, polished them on the sheet, gazed at their bright mottle and the milky white of their undersides. The incredible thought that he might yet recover trembled like a fleshed arrow in John Barnard's mind. Julius looked up from the chestnuts and said, "Papa! Your hair is grey," in a tone of interested surprise.

After this second funeral, John Barnard lost his brief popularity in Loseby and was seen as a sinister or a ridiculous figure. From the quay, from the taverns, from the narrow streets, an east-wind criticism blew on him. "Mr. Barnard don't fare to keep his boys." It was remembered how he had busy-bodied through the town during the cholera scare of the previous year, talking about limewash and not emptying close-stools into the street, and telling people that cholera would carry off their children if they did not alter their ways. They had not altered their ways, the cholera did not come, they kept as many of their children as any reasonable person could expect to, whereas he had two sons dead in a twelvemonth, while the other one, for all that talk about sugar and slavery, was whipping the blacks on an island in the West Indies. Someone at this time nicknamed him The Grand Turk. The name stuck, and his new terrace was referred to as Constantinople. A man sensitive to public opinion, he remained unaware that Loseby had turned against him. He was too unhappy to notice it.

He dared not take comfort in Mary, and Julia would not even grant him the comfort of having to be a comfort to her. She refused to speak of the dead boys, and spent her time in reading novels or talking about Joseph, wondering how he was and what he was doing and when another letter would come from him. Unfinished letters to Joseph were always lying on her sofa-table. Joseph's guava jelly and Joseph's rum (which, as rum-and-milk, agreed with her better than Madeira) were the only foods that could tempt her appetite. Euphemia was now responsible for most of the household management, and life at Anchor House became noticeably bonier. Julia had kept her Scotch outlook on good fires and good meals, but Euphemia was her father's child, indifferent to fleshpots. To eat boiled cod with no accompaniment but boiled potatoes, to return to cold rooms and the smell of snuffed-out candles, was positively a solace to John Barnard—though he knew well enough that Euphemia did not intend it as such. There were times when he felt that Euphemia's coldness cut him to the heart. In fact, it was a salve to his conscience. Relying on her inability to become lovable, confident that she would never be in a position to break his heart by dying or perplex him by growing unaccountable, as Julia had done, he even began to admire her good qualities: her prudence, her even temper, her sense of justice—though this was too mathematical to be quite congenial to him. As for Mary, his vow that if she lived through the measles he would never again encourage her wilfulness (she had been quite remarkably wilful about physic) by making a pet of her still held, and was darkly reinforced by a fancy that he had in some way bargained for her survival at the expense of Samuel and Julius. Though his house now held four children instead of seven, there were just as many misunderstandings, reasons for anxiety, causes for regret. Ellen referred too often to the fact that she could sit on her plaits, and showed a daintiness at meals that was not in keeping with a house which God has chastened. Wilberforce, now of an age to begin schooling downstairs, was still in the nursery, and seemed impossible to dislodge. He was a puny, uncommunicative child with such a talent for rashes and bilious attacks that it was hard not to suspect connivance between him and Nurse Darwell. It was some time before Euphemia felt herself strong enough to suggest that she might end her own attendance at Madame Bon's day school and teach Wilberforce instead. Having got so far, she went farther and levered her father out of the morning room and back into his study, which she considered to be the best place for him.

By the time all this was accomplished, Euphemia was nineteen.

"When I was in my nineteenth year I was married," Julia remarked. Euphemia knew that this was not true. Mamma, in fact, had not married until she was twenty, for Joseph was born on her twenty-first birthday, a fact noted on the flyleaf of the family Bible. But that Mamma should tell fibs about it showed how important it was to be punctual in finding a husband. Euphemia had no idea how to set about it. No marriageable young men came to the house, and Uncle Daniel's invitation to Cheltenham had been quashed because Euphemia was needed at home. Sometimes she asked herself if she had not made a false step by becoming so necessary to Papa. If she had remained useless as well as disliked, he might have taken a little trouble to get her off his hands. False or no, the step had been taken, and usefulness had brought her one real gain. On the grounds of saving Mamma trouble she had written to thank Joseph for one of his consignments; till then, she had only been permitted to write for his birthday and at Christmas. The permission having been granted, she extended it and wrote often. He was the one person in the world she had ever loved and been at ease with.

5.

A white shawl collar and white undersleeves had tempered her mourning black, and it was the spring of 1835, and Papa was at the office, and Wilberforce was repeating the capital cities of Europe, when the door of the morning room opened and Hester, the parlourmaid, said in a voice more than usually hushed, "Miss Euphemia, can you see a gentleman?"

Before she could answer the door had closed, and the gentleman was inside. Her first impression was "Whipper-snapper." Wilberforce's first impression was just the opposite. The gentleman was leading a bulldog, and Wilberforce flung himself into Euphemia's petticoats so violently that he almost knocked her over.

"Steady, Wilberforce," said the gentleman, and introduced himself as Marmaduke Debenham, adding, "I thought you would like to hear about Joe. I've just come back from Trinidad."

"Oh!"

So this was the girl who had written those letters. "She's no
40

beauty. But she's game, you know." Reared in paths of strictest truth, that was as much as poor Joe could say of the sister for whom he pined like a spaniel. And an unbeautiful gameness had shown itself in the letters, written without the smallest grace of style, in short, tight sentences that imprisoned a character or a situation with bricklike firmness and exactness. Reading them, with the shadow of the acacia flitting over the perfectly filled pages, and the random sweet cries of the house Negroes breaking into the silence like juice gushing from a ripe fruit, Marmaduke Debenham had thought that Joe must indeed love his Euphemia a great deal to find comfort in these gaunt home truths of discomforts and calamities. It was only on the voyage home that he found himself nursing a resolve to see the writer. And here she was, with the red hands of youth, and a high white forehead already lined, and rusty Scotch hair fastened up in a Grecian knot. Her feverish attention, so savagely controlled, almost inhibited him from talking. Every piece of information about Joe was received with a little "Oh!" that came out of her like a strangled cough. He wished with all his heart he had not come, brandishing his freedom and his travels and his bulldog. It was as though he had unearthed some pale underground animal and flashed a light before its eyes. A clock in the house struck. Her face did not alter its expression, but her hands stiffened where they lay folded in her lap. He wondered if he could tell her that he had made sure that Mr. Barnard would be detained beyond his usual hour of return from the office, but decided against it.

The door opened. He saw that she did not flinch. Like a prisoner, she knew every sound of the jail. A nurse looked in, saying that it was time for Master Wilberforce to have his hair washed. Her manner reeked of an old servant's bawding, and before Euphemia could stop her she had taken the boy away. The amused excitement he had felt at the prospect of stealing an interview with Mr. Barnard's daughter in Mr. Barnard's house now seemed to him merely brutal and vulgar. Hearing

41

himself say for the third time that Joe had learned to play the flute, he became silent.

"Mr. Debenham, I know my mamma would like to thank you for all you have done for Joseph. If she—if you—"

He thought she was opening a retreat for him and leaped up. "If Mrs. Barnard could spare a few minutes, I should be honoured. But I know she is an invalid. Perhaps it would be better if I came some other time."

"Oh, no! That wouldn't be possible."

Why have I no presence of mind? Why don't I get him out of the house while I can? Why shouldn't Mamma see him? What will she be looking like? Why should I mind that? Her head ringing with questions, Euphemia led the way, and he followed her, and the bulldog followed him, its mailed tread ringing through the silent house.

"Miss Barnard, what shall I do with this animal?"

"Mamma would like to see it. She had a dog of her own once."

This was the completing touch to the portrait of Mr. Barnard as family ogre.

For all his independence and affability with the world, Marmaduke Debenham was still young enough to expect an invalid lady to be pale and thin. The enormous red-faced matron, smelling of rum and lavender water, with a rumpled cap and a slipping shawl, took him aback. He did not take Julia aback. To see a man who was neither a husband, a doctor, nor a clergyman roused her with a galvanic delight. He was Joseph's friend, he brought news of Joseph, he had a charming bulldog. In a flash she was at home in the situation, pressing cake alternately on Mr. Debenham and the dear animal. To Euphemia she seemed like a new being. This was near the truth. After so many years of existing on the confused remnants of the young woman who had married John Barnard, Julia in a couple of minutes achieved a glorious climacteric and was an old woman enjoying herself. She laughed and asked questions and told stories of Joseph's babyhood—that gay period when it was still wonderful and amusing to have a child of one's own. Indulging a young man's natural affinity for an old woman, Marmaduke Debenham remembered only just in time that Mr. Barnard might be back at any moment.

"Good-bye, then, and thank you. You have made us both very happy." She held out her puffy, trembling hand, and he realized that she was a drinker.

Euphemia conducted him downstairs and let him out. There was the wall, and above it the blue April sky and the clouds sailing. Blinking in the light, she looked more than ever like something he should not have dug up. "Forgive me for coming," he said.

"Hurry!" she answered and turned back into the house.

It was the first unconstrained word she had spoken to him. There was such pungency and freedom from nonsense in it that in a flash he made up his mind that it should not be the last.

Five minutes later John Barnard returned and went as usual to Julia's dressing room. She was lying with her eyes shut.

"How are you, my dear? I hope your head does not ache. You look rather feverish."

"I am a little tired, Barnard. That is all."

He would have liked to tell her about the man who had intercepted him, a groom dismissed from service because he had refused to attend his master to a cockfight on a Sunday —a shocking story, though much to the groom's credit. But he saw that she was not in a mood for conversation, so he went downstairs and told Euphemia instead.

Mother and daughter both hoped that their visitor would pass unrecorded. The only person who might blab was Wilberforce, and Nurse Darwell had stopped his mouth by her usual threat—that if he was naughty she would be sent away and Mr.

Moore would come for him. But at breakfast next morning Hester, bringing in the hot rolls, brought also a note for Mr. Barnard.

"Hester. Who brought this note?"

"A man, sir. I don't know who. In livery, sir. I can't say whose."

Julia began to fan herself, a preliminary to feeling too unwell to eat breakfast.

"He is not to come here again."

"No, sir."

"If he does, you are to shut the door in his face. And bar it. Do you understand?"

"Yes, sir. Of course, sir." She picked up a plate and hurried from the room. Breakfast continued in silence until the wretched Ellen choked, was rebuked for gluttony, and told to quit the table.

"Of all things I value frankness and candour," said John Barnard. "I shall not try to hide from you that I have reason to be angered."

Julia's hand went towards the butter dish and was withdrawn. This was no time to butter hot rolls.

"That note, furtively delivered by a groom, is from Mr. Debenham. He tells me that he has recently come back from the West Indies and is in this neighbourhood. He has the impertinence to ask if he may visit me."

"Perhaps he may have something to tell you about Joseph," said Julia, after thinking it over. Mary leaned towards Euphemia and whispered that she wondered if Joseph were dead.

"I shall not answer the note. If it were not for him, where would Joseph be now?"

This sounded almost as though John Barnard were making a belated acknowledgment that if Marmaduke Debenham had not intervened Joseph would not now be holding a respectable well-paid post and sending home consignments of delicious West-Indian produce. But even Mary knew better than that.

44

"Where would he be now, I say? At this table. Mary, hand your mother the butter dish. If Mr. Debenham thinks I feel no proper resentment, he is mistaken. He has robbed me of my eldest son and hardened his heart against us; humanly speaking, he has imperilled Joseph's salvation. And then he proposes to call on me. It is intolerable! But I shall not answer his note. I would rather be dumb in the face of the oppressor. If I were not a man of peace, I would meet him and thrash him."

He sat at the head of the depopulated table, biting his lip, turning his head from side to side like some perplexed, stricken animal. The storm was over, and no one the worse for it. Julia had buttered her roll, Euphemia was pouring the rest of the tea into the slop-bowl so that the tea leaves could be dried and given to the poor. Only Mary observed her father. The look she bent on him was grave and composed. She was thinking that he was unhappy. Papa was unhappy, as a day is rainy; it was a thing to accept but not to reason over. For John Barnard's children were almost without compassion. Talk about God's will, dispensations, sorrows sent as trials of faith or moderate expressions of justly merited disapproval, and quite sincere attempts on John Barnard's part to act up to this sort of talk, had smothered it. So while she was aware that Papa was unhappy, it did not occur to Mary that the deaths of two sons and the desertion of another was anything special for Papa to be unhappy about.

He looked up and saw her eyes dwelling on him, clear and steady in her calm oval face, and thought, She grieves for me. Alone of my children, she understands and feels for me. She continued to look at him without a change of expression. She was waiting to see what he would do next. He felt as though an angel were looking at him, and, having admitted the angel into his mind, admitted the worm after it.

"Today is Friday. Are you going to the churchyard with your sister, Mary?"

She smiled with pleasure. "Oh, yes, Papa."

45

On Friday afternoons Euphemia, taking a sponge and a flannel and a small pair of shears in a basket, went to the churchyard to trim the family enclosure and wash the marble gravestone, and when the weather was fine one or both of her sisters went with her.

Old Mr. Barnard had insisted on his rights, and his coffin lay in the family vault under the nave. At the time when he was so nearly a democrat, John Barnard had turned against the vault as insanitary, and bought a plot in the graveyard and had a neat ironwork border fixed round it. When the first sod was turned for George, he bought a gravestone, a white marble obelisk, and the record of Barnard burials began:

BELOW

lie the mortal remains
of George Molesworth Barnard
Son of John and Julia Barnard
Born Feb. 2, 1818. Died Jan. 12, 1826
Also of Susan Amelia Barnard
Born June 8, 1819. Died Jan. 19, 1826
Also of Robina Caroline Barnard
Born Dec. 31, 1827. Died Feb. 29, 1828
Also of Samuel Barnard
Born Nov. 17, 1822. Died March 30, 1833
Also of Julius Daniel Barnard
Born Nov. 17, 1822. Died Oct. 17, 1833

The obelisk was arrestingly large and white. It caught Marmaduke Debenham's eye as he went to church for the morning service, and he paused to read it. He was a regular churchgoer —in his own parish he read the lessons—and he would have gone to church in any case, but this Sunday he had a further reason. Two days had passed since his note had been delivered, and he felt pretty sure there would be no answer. The slight did not trouble him, but he wondered if his visit had been disclosed, and if Euphemia Barnard were suffering for it. At three that morning he had begun to think it quite likely that the family ogre was keeping her shut up on bread and water, and though this seemed rather exaggerated by daylight, he was relieved when he saw her walking up the aisle, looking none the worse except for an unbecoming bonnet. Mr. Barnard, Mrs. Barnard, Euphemia, the pretty one called Mary, the disfigured one who was Ellen, his young friend Wilberforce—they walked by and disappeared behind the walls of their pew. He blew a little dust off his hat and turned his attention to his Maker. Later the attention wandered. A recognition by Wilberforce would be very tiresome, so he must make an unobtrusive departure—and yet he would very much like to catch Euphemia's eye, if only to make perfectly sure that she was none the worse. He contrived to be delayed in the porch behind two doctrinal ladies discussing the sermon. Out came Mr. and Mrs. Barnard, and one of the doctrinal ladies began talking to them. Euphemia was halted at his elbow, he discovered by a little snuff that she smelled like a well-scrubbed deal table. There are no sibilants in the name Euphemia, and it was "Euphemia" that he said. The bonnet quivered; the Barnard group walked on. Detaching herself from the group with a gesture of injured tidiness. Euphemia bent down at the foot of the obelisk and removed a snail. Rising, she very deliberately caught his eye and gave a small, stern nod, then took her place again behind her parents. A stranger to Loseby, Marmaduke began to wander round the graveyard, reading epitaphs. By the time he had given his serious attention to a dozen or so, the last churchgoer was out of sight, and no one, he hoped, saw him stoop down and tweak out a screw of paper that had been pressed into a tuft of grass at the foot of the Barnard stone.

> Please do not write to my papa again. It annoyed him, and he will not answer you. I am sorry for this. Thank you for your kindness to Joseph.

Early on Monday morning he deposited his reply. It was larger than her note, as he had more to say, but the tuft of grass had grown some twenty-four hours' higher and contained it. He visited the Loseby tailor, was measured for a pair of breeches, and arranged to come for a fitting later in the week. Then he paid his bill at the Half Moon and drove away with the bulldog beside him and the groom behind him. As Loseby sank into its undistinguished landscape he wondered if he had committed himself to more than his feelings warranted. Friendship for Joe and dislike of Joe's father were approved novel-writers' motives for asking Joe's sister to elope with him, and it would be an act of mercy to get anyone out of that frightful house. But he was not a hero or a philanthropist, merely an English landowner, lucky enough to have come early into his inheritance, who meant to go in for modern farming but would keep the old rookery, who had enjoyed what he had seen of the world but intended to settle down with a wife and children under his Suffolk elms. He was by no means sure whether these qualifications were of a calibre to match the writer of those formidable letters to Trinidad. If rescuing one of Mr. Barnard's children were the essential, perhaps it would be better to abscond with Wilberforce. The obelisk rose before his mind's eye; in any rescue he would only be abetting a mightier hand —a bony one that had already removed five of Mr. Barnard's children from a father's care.

When he next visited the obelisk his note had gone, but there was no reply to it, and the space below Julius seemed yawning for another of John and Julia Barnard's bereavements. While he was at the tailor's the church bell sounded a single note, and another at a knell's interval. He broke off from an adverse comment on a wrinkle above the left knee to ask who was dead. Chalking arabesques on the breeches, Mr. Hodds gave a succinct account of the dropsical complications which had carried off old Mrs. Coulton, and later told Mrs. Hodds

48

that Mr. Marmaduke was a very fidgety customer, but what else could you expect from a gentleman his size, no larger than a lady, and legs like an oyster-catcher's?

Manners obliged Marmaduke to listen to his own parson that Sunday, but on Monday he was in Loseby for a further fitting. His second note, imploring an answer to his first note, and adding some second-thought suggestions to it, had been taken and replaced by another small screw of paper.

> It does not do for me to receive letters by the post, but I could send one. Pray oblige me by leaving your address.

At the second fitting the breeches were improved out of all recognition. He was wearing them on the morning when Euphemia's letter came to Rougham Hall.

> Dear Mr. Debenham:
> I have considered your letters very carefully and very gratefully. I am sorry that I cannot do as you wish. My papa would be angry, and his anger would fall on my mamma and my sisters. This would impair my peace of mind. If I had only myself to consider, I daresay I would not hesitate to elope with you. I am sure your intentions are honourable, and that you are right in supposing I should lead a happier life with you than I lead at home. But it will not do.

She was certainly a cool young lady. His intentions were honourable and had not boggled at a father in trade and a mother in liquor. Thinking that they merited, if not an acceptance, at least a more impetuous refusal, he read on.

> If you could get my papa's consent, I would feel differently. But he cannot overlook your kindness to Joseph, without which he supposes Joseph would not have got away. I can think of nothing that would shake his prejudice against you, unless you should happen to save Mary's

49

life. But how can this be brought about? Dangers do not come our way. Wilberforce was even alarmed by your bulldog. E.B.

Euphemia wrote the exact truth. She had thought over Marmaduke Debenham's proposal carefully and gratefully, considering it from every aspect but one. That aspect was its romanticalness. She was neither flattered nor surprised that a young man should offer marriage after less than an hour's acquaintance. Such abrupt pieces of behaviour were in keeping with the denouements of the only fiction she had been allowed to read. A little girl told a lie and an hour later was taken with a fever. A schoolboy played truant, and immediately a mad bull jumped over the hedge. Mr. Debenham's offer of marriage, though more insinuating than a bull or a typhus, was of the same kidney, and differed only in that it left her an option to accept or refuse. Perhaps she did not quite believe in it, as she did not quite believe in the bulls and the fevers. She had believed in it enough to throw out her indication as to how Mr. Debenham, if really determined to get her, might usefully proceed; but either he did not see hints very readily or he was not really determined. When no more notes appeared at the obelisk her residual sensation was one of relief. Hester's ogles lost confidence and were discontinued. Everything went on as usual. The midsummer sun brought out the sunblinds, stewed gooseberries disagreed with Ellen. At midsummer too Number 5 Prospect Terrace was rented by a new tenant—a most interesting character, said Madame Bon, who had produced him.

6.

The new tenant was Mr. Simon Kettle, the proprietor of a religious publishing house in Hull, who for reasons of health wished to detach himself from the drudgery of bookkeeping and proofreading (he had a son who would remain and deal with all that), in order, as he wrote, to give the whole of his powers to promoting the supply of wholesome reading at low prices on a well-drained soil. Mr. Kettle was already known to the Barnards by his wares: the tracts that were sent out to Joseph for distribution, the Moral Tales, Scenes from the Scriptures, and Conversations on the Catechism that were given to the prize scholars at the Sunday school, the Commentaries on Daniel, Expositions of St. Paul, and biographies of spiritual celebrities that accumulated on the Anchor House bookshelves. They were mostly on lower shelves, and to get there, even, they had to be rebound. Mr. Kettle's guiding principle of cheapness led to shaky backs and mean bindings. It led, too, to very small print in double columns on sallow paper. Much of the stitching was done by pauper children, who also coloured the illustrations to the Moral Tales. They were learning habits of industry and forwarding the Lord's work by working unpaid, but many of them were too young to be neat, and by the end of a day they lost interest and painted blue maws on crocodiles and rosy faces on Negroes singing hymns under the lash.

Such errors gave particular pleasure to Wilberforce, who dwelt on them in silent joy. Wilberforce's father was insensible to the beauties of bad workmanship, and if Mr. Kettle's books had been all he knew of Mr. Kettle he would have thought twice before accepting him as a tenant. But Madame Bon's recommendations had been exceedingly cordial, and she was a woman whose judgment he relied on.

Madame Bon and her husband were natives of Jersey and were called Mr. and Mrs. Bone in plain English when they came to Loseby to start a fish-curing business. The method was a secret process, invented by Mr. Bon. It was not a very good one, and Bone's would not have stolen the fish-curing trade from Barnard's, even if Mr. Bon had not died a couple of years after their arrival, leaving his widow with a quantity of debts, some equipment, and the trade secret. She offered the equipment and the secret to John Barnard, and he bought them, mainly because he knew that no one else would; then, because he did not feel that his obligation to help a widow and a stranger was discharged by that, and since she wished to remain in Loseby for the irreproachable reason that her husband was buried there, he settled her in lodgings, where she supported herself by mending lace and giving piano lessons. Later she inherited some money, bought a house, and set up as Madame Bon with a day school for young ladies. Teaching suited her better than needlework, making a good impression suited her best of all. By a dexterous balance of French-like-a-native and sound Protestantism, she satisfied the ambitions and scruples of parents in the neighbourhood, some of whom, having more zealotry than exact historical information, supposed that their excellent Madame Bon had been driven from France under the Revocation of the Edict of Nantes. It was during her lace-mending period that she submitted a translation of a book about the Camisards to Mr. Kettle. He paid her three guineas for it and commissioned other translations on the same terms. A correspondence developed between them, in the course of which Madame Bon's sick headaches and Mr. Kettle's difficulty in breathing came to supplant the sufferings of the French Protestants. Learning that her publisher was thinking of removing from Hull to some simple cot not too far from a living Evangelical pulpit, she saw how this could be applied to the vacancy in Mr. Barnard's terrace.

Mr. Kettle was a widower. He brought a sister-in-law, a Miss Mutley, with him to keep house. And when John Barnard paid his first call, Euphemia went too, to do the female part towards Miss Mutley.

For someone whose bodily frame required the seclusion of a cot, Mr. Kettle looked pretty vigorous. He was stockily built, with thick white hair that grew in tufts, and tufty white eyebrows. His forehead had not a line on it; low and receding, it resembled a pie-dish. His chin had a dimple in it, his lips were pursed. His neckcloth was fastened with a mourning brooch, his clothes were spruce, his waistcoat even skittish. Glancing from him to his visitor, Euphemia noticed that her father looked careworn and rather shabby. Presumably Mr. Kettle's excellent state of repair was due to the sister-in-law.

Speaking with a strong Yorkshire accent, Miss Mutley began to probe Euphemia about Madame Bon: was she not a wonderful lady? So well-educated too—a quite remarkable mind, so Mr. Kettle said, almost masculine in its grasp of business. It was a pity that she should have these headaches, but they always come if a female is so very intellectual. Miss Mutley expressed a warm desire to see more of Madame Bon, and Euphemia got an impression that she would be glad to hear that Madame Bon was at the bottom of the sea. But their conversation remained fragmentary, for the sister-in-law's voice was low and growling, and Mr. Kettle talked incessantly in a voice that was mellifluous but loud. He talked about his business, his aims, his achievements, and his authors. One author after another tripped from his tongue, and all of them were eminent, and all of them had at different times expressed their obligation towards him. Trying to listen to the sister-in-law, who had now got to tight lacing, Euphemia heard her father interpose a Cambridge celebrity of his own.

"Yes, yes, indeed!" Mr. Kettle exclaimed. "A most abounding man, and frequently in Hull. So kind to both my dear wives!"

He waved a hand towards the two miniatures above the chimneypiece. They seemed to be by the same artist and were equally bad; but a semblance of real life glimmered feebly from the wife with chestnut hair and a melancholy pout. "My sister is on the right," said the sister-in-law.

Euphemia replied, "What an interesting face," and continued to look at the miniature on the left.

As they walked home John Barnard said, "I do not like him."

"Neither do I," said Euphemia, pleased to find herself able for once to agree unequivocally with her father.

"Perhaps you are too young to form a decision on first sight, Euphemia. In any case you are too young to express it."

The Barnards found themselves seeing a great deal of Mr. Kettle during the summer. Informal meetings, he said, spontaneous exchanges of soul, unforced gatherings together were more in his line than the world's cold civilities. It was impossible to meet him, or even to catch sight of him choosing a turbot, without a spontaneous exchange of soul ensuing, and he was not the sort of man who can be good-byed on a doorstep; he would follow one in, talk standing, talk himself towards a sofa and sit down on it, or, if the weather were suitable, talk himself out into the garden. "Come, my young friends," he would say to Ellen and Wilberforce, "shall we enjoy the fruits of the earth? Shall we feast on strawberries?" Fluting like a blackbird, he ate the ripest, talking all the while of simple pleasures and the happy state of childhood, while Wilberforce, who was not allowed to eat strawberries, looked on sardonically. He showed great affection for Mary and gave her several pocketbooks. If heaven had blessed him with a daughter (he had two sons, one by each dear wife) he would have wished her to be just such another sweet girl, and with just such a schoolmistress as his esteemed Madame Bon. As for the betterment of Loseby, he was all for it, giving fervent goodwill and very moderate subscriptions to the existing good works, and pressing for several new ones, in particular, a Temperance Association. A band, even a small band, totally abstaining from all alcoholic liquor, what might it not bring about? He had seen it do marvels in Hull. They that go down to the sea in ships, that do business in great waters, see the works of the Lord. How true that was! Unfortunately when they were on dry land again they partook too freely of strong drink. Mr. Kettle had counted the taverns and gin shops in Loseby, and the total appalled him. John

Barnard deplored the amount of drinking in Loseby and had more knowledge of its results, but in common honesty he could not promote that small band of total abstainers while poor Julia's health still required rum and Madeira. There was nothing for it but to admit himself humbled under the hand of Providence, to trample on the pride of his lower man, and to keep up his credit in his own eyes by seeing that parcels of garden stuff for Madame Bon should be more choice and lavish than before. To make sure of this he had the gardener pick the fruit early in the morning before Mr. Kettle could get at it. How was he to know that Madame Bon selected the best of his best for Mr. Kettle? Julia said she would; but Julia had always been prejudiced against that excellent woman.

It shamed him to find that only two years after the loss of Samuel and Julius the petty exasperations of a Mr. Kettle should have such power over him. He sat in his study, one September evening with his diary before him. *It is as though they had died in vain.* The sense of what he had just written blazed out on him. His handwriting staggered, and tears ran down his cheeks as he wrote vehemently on.

> Wretched repinings, impiety of grief! Do I forget my Redeemer, who died for me? Will it be said that He died for me in vain?—that I am more attentive to my own trivial and well-deserved mortifications than to the death on the Cross? My miserable shortcomings!—every day makes me more aware of them.

He paused. Was that strictly true? Every day, at any rate, he felt more discouraged and more solitary. He closed the book and locked it away. In half an hour it would be time for family prayers. The sultry day was closing in rain, and a thunderstorm was going out to sea. He went automatically to sit by the empty grate, staring at the streaked windows and the wall beyond them. In the drawing room Euphemia had been playing the piano, a heartless rattle of scales and trills. Now she struck a chord, and Mary began to sing.

55

"An–gels!" Her voice wavered on the long holding-note. With her next breath it poised on the octave above, as a candle flame steadies and burns clear.

"Angels ever bright and fair,
Take, oh, take me,
Take, oh, take me to your care!"

John Barnard was not musical, but he knew what was Handel. Swaying, sighing, reiterating its "take me," the Air from *Theodora* garlanded the silent house. So pure, so virginal, and suiting Mary's voice so well, it bewitched him from himself. One of Handel's sacred songs—it did not occur to him, any more than it could to Mary, how amorously the melody sighed and pleaded. But the plea had its way with him. The love for Mary which he had for so long cautiously locked up came back and took possession of him, more powerful and pervading than before.

The rain fell all night, and on the next day, which was a Friday, Euphemia put the shears, the sponge, and the flannel into her basket, thinking with pleasure that it would take quite half an hour to clean the obelisk. The hope of half an hour to herself was frustrated, for Mary said she would come too, and so did Ellen.

Mary made a movement of dissent. "Why don't you go and sit with Mamma?" she asked.

"Why don't *you?*" Ellen replied.

Mary could think of no effective answer, and Euphemia told Ellen to fetch her tippet. "And your plain bonnet," she cried after her. Mary did not like to be seen out with Ellen, and the plain bonnet, whose brim was deep, meant that there was less of Ellen's port-wine stain for Mary to be seen out with. Loseby people had no interest in the birthmark. But in August Loseby had visitors who came for sea air and boating. Their smart clothes and spyglasses and free and easy deportment made them deeply interesting to Ellen, who gaped. Some of them stared at her and then looked quickly away. Others stared at Mary and continued to stare. Euphemia was thankful when the churchyard gate clicked to behind her, and glad to see that there was at least half an hour's tranquil cleaning to be done on the obelisk.

There was rather more than that. The springtime's tuft had been subdued by clipping, but now a stone lay where the tuft had been, and under the stone was a rain-sodden wad of paper.

"I've dropped my little sponge," she said. "It must have fallen out when I opened the gate. Will you go and look for it, Mary?"

The omission worked. Ellen ran after her sister, sure that she would be the first to find the sponge.

Euphemia was taken aback to find herself so much perturbed. Her hands shook with temper, and when she tried to unfold the wad of paper she tore it. The writing was blurred and almost illegible. "Don't be ala—" The word seemed to be "alarmed." Why should she be alarmed? She had no intention of letting Mr. Debenham alarm her, she was done with all that. She crumpled the note and thrust it into her bosom, where the little sponge already reposed. Her half-hour's holiday was now quite spoiled. The flies teased her, so did Ellen, fidgeting after the sponge, so did Mary, sitting gracefully on an adjacent tomb and as usual doing nothing to make herself useful. The note that was too wet to be read had spoiled everything. Having given up all interest in Mr. Debenham, she was not interested in reading it, but it remained annoying that, having crumpled it up so hastily, it would now be quite unreadable, even the word that might be "alarmed." Suppose it were so, and applied to some news about Joseph—that he was marrying a black, for instance? It would be just like that ineffective Mr. Debenham to tell her so in a letter she couldn't read.

Cross and preoccupied, she began the walk home, and there seemed to be twice as many visitors about with nothing to do but stare under bonnets. Old Mrs. Allen, one of Papa's pen-

sioners, came waddling across Church Street to express her
pensioner's hopes that all the dear family were well.

"And how is your leg, Mrs. Allen?"

Mrs. Allen's face, which had assumed the proper expression
for her reply, was suddenly contorted with terror.

"It's after Miss Mary! It's mad!"

Euphemia turned just in time to see a bulldog rush at Mary
and set its teeth in her gown. Growling and slavering, and
worrying at the white muslin, it bore every mark of savagery,
and Marmaduke Debenham would have enjoyed an unflawed
triumph if a slender young man had not rushed to Mary's help
at the same moment he began to do so himself—and with the
advantage of spontaneity and longer legs. It was no time to
shilly-shally. The slender young man was thrown off his balance by a kick, he staggered, and his hat fell off. Marmaduke
was seen to be holding the dog by the scruff of its neck and
saying commandingly, "Down, you brute! Let go, sir!" The dog
let go of the muslin but continued to growl and struggle in
Marmaduke's grip. "Who owns this brute?" he called out in a
peremptory voice, and a man with bowed legs and a fancy
waistcoat hurried up and said that he did.

"Then take it away and shoot it."

If anyone had been composed enough to look at the bulldog
he might have seen its look of expectation change to wistful
bewilderment as it was led away without a word of praise or a
single sweet biscuit. But at this juncture Ellen fell into hysterics. Screaming and sobbing, she drew attention to herself so
thoroughly that people at the back of the crowd believed that
she had been bitten and was already going mad. Supporting
Mary, keeping a tight grasp of Ellen, fending off offers of smelling salts, red-hot pokers for cauterizing, sal volatile from the
chemist's, parlours to sit down in, and the doctor to be fetched,
Euphemia addressed Marmaduke in an undertone bleak with
fury and said, "For heaven's sake, get us out of this!"

By assuring everyone in the crowd that they were most helpful and that their help was no longer needed, and particularly thanking an immensely muscular man in a jersey who came after them with Euphemia's basket, Marmaduke got them out of it and into a side street. By this time Euphemia had recovered herself enough to say, as one must to a stranger, "It's the first turning on the left."

They were approaching Anchor House when they heard its iron gates clatter and saw John Barnard run out. The news had travelled fast. He had heard that Mary had been set on by a mad dog and rescued by two gentlemen.

"Mary! Merciful God, what is this? What has happened?"

He saw her looking pale and startled, with a torn gown, and her paleness seemed to him deadly, and he thought the slobbered tatters were red with blood.

"Mary! My love!"

He clasped her in his arms. Raising their voices above Ellen's renewed howls, Euphemia and Marmaduke assured him that Mary was unharmed and that the dog had been pulled away before it did more than tear her flounce. Marmaduke added that from what he could see of the dog he did not think it was a mad one. They talked in vain. It was not till Mary spoke that John Barnard understood what was being told him, and it was not till she explained how the gentleman had dragged the dog away that he saw Marmaduke as something more than a person who happened to be propping Ellen.

"It was you? It was *you* who saved her?"

His voice was incredulous with relief, and it seemed to Euphemia that in the next breath he would add, "A man of *your* size?" She said hastily that Mary must go in and lie down. His attention swept back to Mary, and Marmaduke had to perform several attempts at a modest withdrawal before he could get himself begged to come in.

When the sisters had gone upstairs John Barnard began to recover himself and to be more in keeping with Marmaduke's dislike of him. He apologized for his display of feeling, he spoke of the criminal levity of those who allow bulldogs to run at large. But he could not keep up a conversation. The thought that Mary had been in danger came back and back like a weaver's shuttle. He could not believe that she was safe, he could not endure to think she had been imperilled. Opposite him sat the being who had saved her, a young man who had sprung from nowhere, like an angel, and now sat in his study, smiling with even teeth. He did not even know his name. He had not even offered him a glass of wine.

Rousing himself, he again apologized for being so inattentive.

"Not at all. These things are always worse to hear about than to take part in. If you had been there, you would not have found it so alarming."

John Barnard shuddered. The shuttle returned and dealt him another blow. If he had been there, and had failed . . . "I do not know how to thank you as I should. I cannot find words to express my feelings, my obligation. She is my dearest child. And if you had not acted so promptly, if you had not shown such coolness and resolution, if you had not caught hold of the animal in time—"

He broke off. There was an ambiguity in the young man's expression that he could not understand. In a stiffer tone he went on, "You must forgive me if I seem to rant. I am still bewildered. The circumstances are unusual. You have saved my daughter's life, and I don't even know your name."

"My name is Marmaduke Debenham."

Euphemia, coming in with a message that Mamma wished to see the gentleman who had saved Mary, heard her father say, "I am glad to make your acquaintance, Mr. Debenham."

How crestfallen he looks, she thought, surveying him without mercy. She delivered her message and hurried off to inform Julia that Mr. Debenham, having saved Mary from a bulldog, had now gone further and introduced himself to Papa.

"Goodness me! Well, I'm sure I hope it will turn out comfortably. Euphemia! Isn't it strange? Mr. Debenham has a bulldog himself."

"Well, Mamma, that's no reason why someone else shouldn't have a bulldog too. Quantities of gentlemen keep bulldogs."

"I suppose they do. But it is an odd coincidence."

"And this wasn't a gentleman. He was quite a common person."

"No doubt that accounts for it. Mr. Debenham's bulldog was a sweet thing. I'm sure it wouldn't have hurt a fly."

"I daresay not. Will you not wear your new shawl?"

Arranged on Julia, the shawl showed to great advantage. Euphemia secluded herself as much as possible behind that crimson bulk. She felt a sudden disposition to be glad of a mother to hide behind. Marmaduke stayed to supper, on Julia's invitation, and left soon after. He had hoped for a chance to explain to Euphemia the reasons for his apparent sloth in rescuing Mary: first, his own denseness, for he had reread her letter many times before he grasped what was required of him, and then what a job it was to get Bouncer to throw enough soul into attacking a stable boy dressed up in petticoats, and finally the need to make quite sure that Bouncer was safe for a lady, which could not be done till his sister Leonora came home from her London season. But between Julia's affability and Mr. Barnard's formality, and the obligation of doing the civil to those tiresome girls, and Euphemia's being so cool and collected, there was no possibility of a private word. Euphemia was so damnably cool that he even wondered if she was angry with him; and he went away feeling that he had taken a great deal of trouble and pleased no one.

PART TWO

1.

When he saw that there would be no need for his help, the young man with chestnut hair picked up his hat and walked down to the harbour. His temper required something allaying, and if he continued in his original direction, which was towards Prospect Terrace, only further exasperation awaited it: that canvas of pallid, smirking angels with limbs like link sausages, erroneously supposed to be a Sir Joshua and a bargain; poor Mutty, with her winking eyelid, patting a chair for him; and his father, rolling on the sofa with a manuscript, and saying, "Well, Thomas, so you've strolled yourself into an appetite. I wish I could say I had been as pleasingly entertained. Here is another book I cannot publish. The title is well enough— *Rosa, or the Poisoned Cup*. But some of the descriptions are rather too warm."

No one would have sprung forward to pull his father away from a young lady. Simon Kettle was renowned for his understanding of young persons and his solicitude for their welfare. England was his orphanage, he was the humble servant of little masters and misses, and the remainder of the orphanage put their eyes out in his workshops. But the bulldog was the wholesomer animal of the two. There was more generosity in its meat-eating, and its slobber could be washed off.

Mr. Kettle's younger son had refused to go into the family business, but its reputation still encompassed him. After several attempts to make him a clerk, his father had established him as a junior master at an Academy for Young Gentlemen at Clapton. To be the son of Mr. Kettle, the headmaster said, was recommendation enough; the son of such a father could not fail to be an ornament to his establishment. (Indeed, he used the name of Kettle very freely when talking to the parents of prospective boarders.) The air was bracing (if one walked on Clapton Hill when the wind was in the east, the ozone was remarkably perceptible), the position was genteel, though the pay was small the board was ample, and there were holidays three times a year. Dr. Price did not mention that his junior masters were expected to take turns as caretakers during the holidays, so that a week was all they could call their own.

This was the week that Thomas had intended to spend on a walking tour in Wales, and instead he was at Loseby.

A fisherman had just tossed some stale bait into the water, the gulls dived squabbling for it, and farther along the quay a boat was rocking up and down and men were loading her with fishing gear. Mutty's lamentations rang in his head. "Oh, my dear boy, I know what will happen. Only last week he was advising her about a mortgage. And she's so artful! A Frenchwoman, you know, and a widow. He calls her Sophie already, when they are by themselves. Whatever will become of me? For I haven't a penny laid by, he's never given me more than my keep."

There had been similar trepidations in the past. There had been Miss Juggler, whose *Tales from the Sickroom* were of an awful interest. There had been Mrs. Budlake, whose tract, *Poverty the Best Sauce,* always commanded a large sale before Christmas. There had been Mrs. P. P. Cartwright, author of *The Stony Path* and temporarily considered quite equal to

Bunyan. There was always a talent being encouraged and a hand being squeezed. And Mutty, permanent dupe among Mr. Kettle's transient dupes, was always expecting to be ousted by one of them.

"I feel it so much more than in Hull. In Hull I had several friends, and there was always Mrs. Cutler's little back room. But here I don't know a living soul, and the servants are so bold, they are like savages."

It was the complaints of loneliness in Mutty's letters rather than her fears of the lady called Sophie in private that had brought him to Loseby. Sister to the first Mrs. Kettle, housekeeper during his father's first widowerhood and dismissed at his second marriage, Mutty had been called back to nurse the motherless little boy. Silly and kind, her silliness had not irked him—or perhaps she was not so silly then. Her songs of The Derby Ram, and The Lady Turned Highwayman, her stories of ghosts and murders and elopements, had kept him alive under the oppression of his father's publications. Throughout his mistrustful childhood Mutty had been the only thing that was reliably safe and reliably entertaining. The very bows on her shoes were interesting, they came off so often; and her Sunday cap was as good as the Punch-and-Judy show. Even then he was a little condescending; in his boyhood he might have become contemptuous if disliking his father and loathing his half-brother had not been more congenial than despising their drudge and butt. So it became a point of honour to maintain a sense of responsibility for the old woman who had been kind to him and was such a simpleton and said so truly, as well as so frequently, that he was the only person in the world who took her part. The fact that she was the only person in the world whose part he could take was less apparent to Thomas; disillusioned about human nature, he reserved his enthusiasms for the dead and the picturesque. Nevertheless, he had given up Snowdon and Cader Idris to come to Loseby, meaning to comfort Mutty's loneliness and laugh her out of her fears about the person called Sophie. But since his arrival two days earlier the sense of responsibility had become uncomfortably tight-fitting. He suspected that this time Mutty was right.

He discounted the fact that Madame Bon came to the house with little gifts and remained to listen to Mr. Kettle as though she were in church. Others had brought gifts (larger than hers) and had worn those looks of rapt attention. But there was something special about the way Madame Bon gave her pears in leaf-trimmed baskets, her cucumbers, her napkined spice-bread. The other offerings had been propitiatory; hers were proprietary: it was as though she had Mr. Kettle in a coop and were fattening him. If Mutty were right and Madame Bon became the third Mrs. Kettle, Mutty would be sent packing. Where would she go, and what would become of her?

It was ominous that she did not refer to their old understanding, dating from his childhood, that when he was a man Mutty should come and live with him and lock up his tea-caddy and lose the key. He had been dreading that she would refer to it; that she did not involved him in pity as well as dread. What was he to do? If he left off boarding at the Academy and could persuade Dr. Price to pay him an equivalently higher salary, or if he found some hand-to-mouth establishment that would employ him as a daily teacher, no doubt there would be some cheap lodging where he could set up house with Mutty. But that would mean pinching and scraping and self-denial; and it would mean Mutty. Instead of going to the play, he would spend his evenings with Mutty. Mutty's conversation would spray on him while he read *The Duchess of Malfi,* and in her shortsightedness she would drop salted butter on its pages.

Turning again in his walking to and fro, he saw that the western sky was drained of its sunset, only a rusty tint remaining on the clouds that had burned so long and so brilliantly. Lighted windows peered out, and the smell of the town came

65

greasily puffing towards him. Six months ago he had not even heard of Loseby. Now it was the place where he must be his father's son. When those people who had seen him tripped up and hatless had finished guffawing over him, they would turn to the grateful subject of his father's third marriage, and the pretty girl would titter over it with the plain one. The silhouette of Prospect Terrace with its reiteration of little triangular pediments looked like a paper coronet, snipped out with scissors and plastered on the ramshackle town. Under the central spike of the paper coronet sat his father, cuddling the thought of a new wife. A man over fifty, heavy with tallow, who snored like a trombone—it was disgusting, and such things should be forbidden by law. Law forbade a simultaneous polygamy; to marry three times over, thought Thomas, working himself up, was no less lustful and more lecherous, as though one were a dog that buries a chewed bone and digs it up for another and another mumble.

He turned about and saw the solemn dusk of the eastern sky, the unshining sea, the riding lamp that had been lit on the fishing boat. A man standing in the boat called to him, "Will you come for a sail, bor?"

"Where to?" he asked, looking down on the neat clutter of the vessel.

"Down to Rigby Head and back by sunrise. Do you come, I'll lend you a slop to keep your clothes clean."

A night at sea, among strangers, the cool air blowing between himself and his thoughts. . . . He did not hesitate, and jumped into the boat. Standing on that swaying platform, he saw the outline of Loseby seeming to rise and fall, and remembered that Mutty would suppose him dead if he failed to be back for supper. He asked if there was anyone who would take a message for him.

The man shouted, "Crusoe!" and a boy ran up. "He's my niece's brother-in-law," said the man, as though that clinched

66

every recommendation. "He'll take your message, whether to Satan or anyone else."

Giving the message, Thomas thought, Now they'll know whose son I am. The boy pocketed a shilling and went off, hallooing to some friends farther along the quay.

The boat seemed ready to sail, yet they delayed for another half-hour before setting out. The crew was busy with one thing and another, and after Thomas had been given the slop no one spoke to him. He sat where he had been put, feeling the gait of the water through the boat and watching the topmost sky darken, and the clouds assuming a look of solidity. When the boat cast off he was not aware of it until he saw the nose of the quay seeming to turn away. The men talked among themselves, the bilge smacked to and fro, and the boat kept up a soliloquy of grunts and creaks. As they drew away from shore he relaxed inside his enormous garment and breathed more deeply, staring overhead and speculating which were the constellations that showed piecemeal between the clouds. The sea was calm and the wind so light that it barely filled the sail. Of all the things held in that globe of night sky, only the stars traversing the gaps between the clouds seemed to move and have purpose. The oars were got out, and presently the skipper ordered the sail down and steered the boat into a current, where it drifted on. Looking towards the seaward horizon, Thomas saw sparks of rose-topaz that burned on the water—the lights of other boats.

Watching them, he began to drowse and was hardly aware when the anchor went down and the lines went out, except that someone moved his legs aside in order to get at something. He murmured his good wishes and was asleep again before he understood the reply. Sleeping, he was still conscious that he was in an open boat at sea; his sleep did not differ from a suspended waking, until small shreds of mist, gliding upright over the sea's face, slowly gathered round the boat, approaching it from all sides; and as they approached they whispered among themselves. The noise went on as he wakened, but was louder and harsher, and was the shuffle of live fish in the boat. Their smell, raw and immediate, almost choked him, it was as if he were smelling the guts of the sea. It was horrible to waken into this rustle of fish writhing as they choked to death on air, and he felt a childish impulse to say that he must be set on shore immediately. Coming more to himself, he sat up and commented on the amount of the catch. It must be a good one, surely? One of the men answered with talk of a very large skate. The creature was held up for him to admire, its wings slowly twirling in the death agony.

Enlivened by the success of their fishing, the men were talking among themselves and laughing at repartees he could not understand. Their jokes and stories revolved round someone they called Old Turk. The night had lost its poetry but retained its immensity and endlessness.

"Fish have gone off," said the skipper. "So we'll have our bite. Where's that pie?"

He pulled a flask from under his slop, rubbed it with a handkerchief, and offered it to Thomas. It was rum. As Thomas swallowed, he realized how cold and hungry he was. With the first mouthful of pie, heavy as loam and powerfully flavoured with thyme and marjoram, the whole force of the summered earth seemed to leap into his mouth. His appetite pleased them, they asked him if he was enjoying himself and if he had gone out fishing before; and because he was both pleased and ignorant they took pains to tell him everything he should know about the longshore fishing: what weather to choose, what influence of the moon, what bait, and when he might hope to find sea trout among the ordinary catch.

Feeling that he must ask some question for himself, he said, "Who's Old Turk?"

"Who's Old Turk? Well, rightly he's called Grand Turk. Mr. Barnard, that's to say. This here's his boat—one of a couple he had built a few years back to make up for them we lost in the May blizzard. That were a day, that were! You wouldn't fare to think it was the same sea that we're on now. So Mr. Barnard, he have a couple of new boats built, and keep a master's share in them. Bound to do something of that sort."

"She's a good enough boat, though. The *Mary Lucinda,* that's her name. She's the one you got out of trouble, like, so I heard. Or was it t'other one?"

It seemed to Thomas the second speaker was implying that he had assisted one or the other of Mr. Barnard's boats. Puzzled, he looked at the men more closely and noticed that he could see the red of their hands and the yellow of their oil-skins, so that it must be near dawn.

"Mary Lucinda Barnard, that's his second daughter. T'other is the *Euphemia,* but she don't sail so sweet. Them dogs oughtn't be let run. Dangerous as vipers."

The man who had been watching the water now cried out that the fish were round them again. The wind had freshened and blew offshore, carrying a smell of smoke and wheat, as though from some distant baker's oven. The second catch did not come to much, and the boat turned back for Loseby. Busied with stowing away gear, looking over the catch, throwing the damaged fish back into the water, and casting up the value of the night's work, the crew had no more time to talk about Mary Lucinda and the bulldog. Thomas sat yawning, waiting for the sun to rise and bring some warmth with it, looking forward to being landed and able to walk the cramp out of his legs, and at the same time wishing he could sail on forever, or land on some shore where no poor Mutty awaited him.

2.

Because he had tipped them generously and was well mannered, the crew of the *Mary Lucinda* watched Shoulder of Mutton's son run up the harbour steps with eyes very different from those with which they saw Shoulder of Mutton. He was a handsome young fellow, thought he could do with fattening; and though he was dressed like a lady's maid there was no nonsense about him, for he carried off the two pair of soles as though he had been born to it. When Crusoe arrived to lend a hand with his sister-in-law's uncle's boat he added his voice to the chorus of approval. A shilling for running a ten-minute errand was good pay by Loseby notions. The errand had been run. Unfortunately the shilling had been spent first, at the Blue Fish Inn, where Crusoe invited a couple of friends to drink young Shoulder's health. When he knocked on the door of Number 5 Prospect Terrace, he knocked in vain. Mr. Kettle had locked up at half-past nine, his usual hour, and Mutty slept in a back room. Crusoe, who had been one of Euphemia's best Sunday scholars, chalked by starlight a perverse sentiment on the gatepost, and went away.

The door was still locked when Thomas got back. Mutty opened it. Her face was blotched with weeping, and her first words were, "Young men will be young men, I know, but why ever did you do it in Loseby? And just look at your boots!"

He looked. They were covered with fish scales. Supposing that his message had been delivered, he said, "Where else should I do it but in Loseby? I'm starving, Mutty. Don't fuss, but have these cooked for breakfast."

"Breakfast?"

Mr. Kettle had come to the door in his dressing gown. But the tone in which he said "Breakfast?" was without the playful chirrup that usually hailed a meal. "Breakfast, Thomas? Is

70

there nothing to be gone into but fish for breakfast? Charlotte! Take those fish into the back garden and bury them. I will not feed on the pledges of profligacy. Thomas! Since you have come home at last, come indoors."

Thomas started at a disadvantage, for he had lost his temper even before he understood that his father was convinced that he had spent the night with a prostitute. It was an accusation which he resented, and which embarrassed him; for he was timid as well as fastidious and had only visited brothels with the moral support of friends. With modesty and fastidiousness both up in arms, he could find nothing better to say than "Where do you suppose I have been?"

"Suppose? There is no call for supposition. I know it, and only too well."

"It must be delightful to be so easily convinced."

"You disgust me," said Mr. Kettle, enabled by righteousness to know exactly where to wound his son. "Pah! Faugh!"

"I smell of fish because I have spent the night in a fishing boat. And do you really think that if I had spent the night with a woman I should come here with scales all over my boots?"

"Certainly," replied Mr. Kettle, more realist than his son.

"And why shouldn't I? I'm not ripe enough to commend myself to widows."

"So you admit it," his father said.

Thomas might have left it there. But he saw Mutty looking at him with a dreadful palpitating coyness; and thinking of the evenings they might have to spend together and how that look would reappear if he tried to snatch an evening by himself, he went back into the fray. An hour later Mr. Kettle was still convinced that Thomas had been with a harlot, and Thomas had developed the conviction that his whole future self-respect depended on proving his father to be wrong. Towards the end of their discussion his self-righteousness (he was not his father's son for nothing) compelled him to feel ill-used as well as annoyed. Since his word went for nothing, and the fish

71

scales were evidence against him, and the freshness of the fish only showed the venality of a character that could accept fish under such circumstances, he would call in witnesses to clear his reputation.

"There were four men in the boat. They were Loseby men. And they will tell you that I was with them all night."

"I daresay they will, my boy."

Mr. Kettle spoke with something like geniality. He wanted his breakfast and was ready to be reconciled. Even apart from breakfast, he was ready to be reconciled. Having established Thomas as a prodigal son, he was prepared to play the part of forgiving father, and indeed to find him a more congenial companion, if he would only come down off his high horse. But at this juncture Thomas walked out of the house.

When Dawson said that there was a young gentleman waiting in the study, John Barnard made no comment. But the way in which he threw down his large, starched table-napkin augured ill for any young gentleman coming so soon after Marmaduke Debenham.

"I wonder if *he* has got a dog," said Wilberforce.

Euphemia said, "Come, Wilberforce," and rose with dignity.

The high-minded bad temper that swept Thomas away from Prospect Terrace began to flag as he neared Anchor House; he even suspected that he was making a fool of himself. As a result, John Barnard found himself awaited by a young man whose manner was icily stately, and whose sentences forbade interruption (Thomas had fallen back on his Academy methods and addressed Mr. Barnard as though he were a class of twelve-year-old boys). Nothing could have turned out better. John Barnard passed from curiosity to approbation, from approbation to sympathy. The young man was dignified, handsome, and injured—and the injury had come from Simon Kettle. With his own language rising to the challenge, he announced that Thomas could be assured of every assistance in the honourable determination to clear

72

his good name, and that he would immediately accompany him to the dwelling of the skipper of the *Mary Lucinda*. As though aware of what the occasion demanded, both men remained standing during this interview. Both of them were tall and by nature took noble attitudes, and their demeanour tallied with the lofty room and the Flaxman illustrations on the walls. As they went out together the Flaxman deities might well have materialized on the ceiling to wave them forward. However, it was Euphemia, who just then happened to be fetching Wilberforce a clean handkerchief, who saw them leaving the house and recognized the young man about whom Mary was beginning to be so tiresome, alleging that he had saved her quite as much as that little Mr. Debenham.

The *Mary Lucinda*'s skipper was asleep. His wife stood in the doorway with her arms akimbo, saying that whatever it might be, Mobbs must have his sleep out, and that if Mr. Barnard had spent the night in a fishing boat, Mrs. Barnard would say the same. Thomas with his whole being envied Mr. Mobbs, who was asleep, and Mr. Barnard, who was shaved. Breakfast too would have been welcome. Mr. Barnard, after explaining that he had an office to go to, hoped with such gravity that Thomas would give him the pleasure of his company until Mobbs could be fetched that there was nothing for it but to accept. Coffee and sandwiches were sent out for, and after a short interval of opening letters and questioning a clerk, the forenoon went by in showing Thomas round the warehouses and explaining the niceties of trade with the Baltic. Beyond supposing that trade with the Baltic was less disgraceful than trading in religious literature, Thomas was not interested; but his lack of interest, dressed in polite assents and a *nil admirari* stateliness about figures, John Barnard chose to interpret as showing a mind above vulgar astonishment. Mr. Kettle's injured son could scarcely have done anything that John Barnard would not have approved of just then.

At midday they went back to Mr. Mobbs's house and found him dressed and defensive. When the circumstances were explained to him, he became almost as partisan as John Barnard and set out with a warm determination to blow Shoulder of Mutton to blazes. His zeal was increased by the delicious smell of grilled soles preparing for Mr. Kettle's light luncheon. "Perhaps it would be better that I should introduce Mobbs," John Barnard said, and Thomas replied, "Pray do so." The regale of seeing his honour cleared and his father confounded was now at hand, but he had lost all appetite for it. He cursed himself for starting this rumbling landslide of Mobbses and Barnards. But his lack of interest appeared as conscious rectitude. Re-entering his father's house with every wish to be elsewhere, he cut a far more impressive figure than when, in genuine indignation, he had left it.

To John Barnard's astonishment, Mr. Kettle showed fight. Offering sarcastic thanks for Mr. Barnard's interest in his affairs, he implied that he might just as well have kept out of them. This was not the sort of thing John Barnard was accustomed to. Angered, and further thrown off his balance by the inconsistency of having such disinterested motives and feeling such violent personal animosity, he let himself be led away into argument. If it had not been for the presence of Mr. Mobbs, Mr. Kettle might well have won this engagement, for he was not an intimidatable man, and he had much more experience of slanging matches than his opponent. But Mobbs's silent attention impeded him. Mobbs was a man of the lower classes. So, by origin, was he. Instinct warned him that he would not be able to quarrel like a gentleman, and that Mobbs would not fail to notice this and report it. He gave way. His thanks modulated out of sarcasm and became heartfelt. He apologized for anything he might have said in the heat of the moment, explaining that his fatherly anxiety must be held accountable. "We fathers," he said, and John Barnard was compelled to swallow it. Finally he called Thomas his dear, dear boy and said it had been anguish to doubt his word, even for an instant.

Mr. Mobbs went home cheated of his expectations. It had been a poor show, scarcely worth coming out for, except for the novelty of hearing himself described by Old Turk as a man of the strictest veracity. John Barnard too had reason to feel that the interview had not been all he had intended it to be. But his thoughts were soon elsewhere, dwelling on that handsome, that remarkably handsome young man who had somehow or other escaped from Mr. Kettle's loins. He had invited him to dine.

A family dinner, he explained; and if it had been left to Euphemia's providing it would have been a poor exchange for the stalled ox at Number 5; but hearing that yet another young man was in the offing Julia sent for the cook, said that oyster sauce was imperative, that cold mutton, even hashed, would not do to accompany lamb cutlets, and that she herself would pronounce on the flavouring of the trifle. She would have preferred to be feeding her dear, delightful Mr. Debenham; but any stranger was better than nothing, and this one must be something quite exceptional for Barnard to be so pleased with him. Only very lightly fuddled, and wearing her best turban, Julia sat in her drawing room like a child at a party, with her eyes beadily fastened on the door which would presently open and let in the conjurer. Barnard in such good humour, too! If only nothing went wrong!

The door opened, a young man, flashily good-looking, was shown in, and immediately things began to go wrong. Euphemia's "How d'you do" was so glum that Barnard frowned. Rising in her turn, Mary began to blush. The colour suffused her neck, dived under her tucker; through her stockings her very ankles could be seen blushing. "How—how d'you do?" she said, breathless.

"And my daughter Ellen," Julia proceeded. At the same moment Mary was saying in an urgent whisper, "Papa!"

75

"Yes, my love?"

"Papa! *This* is the gentleman who first came after the bull-dog."

John Barnard turned on Euphemia. "Then, pray, why was I given to understand—"

Julia resigned herself. Her husband had many failings, and conscience had petrified most of them into faults, but unfortunately worldliness was not among them. There was no guest he would not have kept dangling, no dinner that he would not have let burn, if a moral fox broke covert. Mary had obviously spoken the truth, so Euphemia had been deceiving him. This must be looked into.

"Papa! Please let me explain!"

"I do not require explanations, Euphemia. All I wish for is the truth. Mary, do not interrupt. Ellen! Be quiet and don't posture. Now, Euphemia. Do not go into any explanations. Tell me plainly who saved Mary when the dog attacked her."

"Mr. Debenham, Papa. It was he who pulled the dog away."

"But Mr. Kettle was there first, Papa. He caught hold of the dog before Mr. Debenham did."

"Then why was I not told of this before?"

My own father before breakfast, thought Thomas, and now the Misses Barnard's father. Am I never to sit down to a meal without scrambling to it over a father? Raising his voice above Euphemia's, he said, "Your daughters were too kind, sir, to report the ignominious truth. As I was trying to catch hold of the brute, I slipped. I lost my balance, and my hat fell off, and the pleasure of hauling the dog away was lost to me, all through my own clumsiness. I am much obliged to Miss Barnard for sparing my blushes."

Speech and manner were so artificial that they fell silent as hens under a hawk. During dinner Thomas sulked genteelly, and as soon as he decently could he went away.

He went away, and except for a letter of thanks to Mr. Barnard, written from Clapton some days later, nothing more was heard of him. The letter was correct almost to the point of being an insult. Every kindness he had received—the family dinner, Mr. Barnard's assistance, Mr. Barnard's company during the two calls at Mr. Mobbs's cottage and the interview at Number 5, even the coffee and sandwiches that had been sent out for—was separately acknowledged and thanked for, as if it were being crossed off on a ledger.

If his gentility had not taken fright at the fracas before dinner, Thomas would have phrased his letter differently. Though Mr. Barnard was so pompous and looked so portentously gloomy stalking among his bevy of shawls, scarves, and petticoats (remembering the name used in the boat, Grand Turk, Thomas supposed this was the reason for it), he had been kind, unusually kind. Thomas at twenty-three was old enough to know that there are not many middle-aged men who will take a stranger at no more than his word and give a whole morning to righting that stranger's wrong. And the second daughter was even prettier than he had thought her at first sight. After dinner there had been a stroll in the garden, where the high wall imprisoned the warmth and scent of late summer. She had stood under an apple tree, tilting the apples within her reach to see if they were ripe enough for picking, and in her white dress and her pink scarf she looked as though the apple tree in its bloom had come back as a ghost to visit the apple tree in its maturity. Mary Lucinda was her name; the boat had been named after her. Between the one Mary Lucinda and the other, he was indebted to Mr. Barnard for what pleasure he had found in the visit to Loseby. But the fracas had spoiled it. He had a fixed distaste for brawling—it was something his father enjoyed and spoke of as "a good set-to," and Thomas had deliberately set himself to be different, to be the gentleman his father wasn't. Because the edifice was precarious, he dreaded coming into contact with anything that might shake it. A hectoring voice might provoke a similar voice from himself, a piece of bullying might call up an answering

77

Simon Kettle from his own foundations. So he wrote his letter coldly, telling himself that when he had said his thanks there would be no more to say.

He went back to Dr. Price's academy. It was a very refined establishment, with pupils drawn from the class whose gentility was careful, idealistic, and precarious as his own. He found himself glad to be back there, more glad than he had ever felt before, thankful for refinement and regularity and for having a great deal to do that could be done with the minimum of interest. And he tried not to think about the marriage to Madame Bon, and Mutty cast on his hands. The autumn waned; the landscape of elms and suburban villas foundered in the evening mists and reappeared every morning, later and more discoloured, and the clay soil grew colder underfoot, and the smell of London asserted itself on the damper air. The wind had to be due east, and strong at that, before the remarkably perceptible ozone was noticeable, even when you snuffed for it, as he sometimes did. Out yonder, far away, was the sea where he had sailed in the *Mary Lucinda*. A night in an open boat, a night at sea; that was an experience that no one else at the Academy had had, and marked him out as someone unusual, and who could not be said to have lived for nothing.

A letter from Marmaduke Debenham expressed more thanks for a slighter degree of hospitality, and invited Mr. Barnard to come and shoot partridges. John Barnard replied, saying that he did not shoot. After a decent interval there came three brace of pheasants, and after these some woodcocks, addressed to Master W. Barnard. Between the pheasants and the woodcocks Mrs. Debenham invited Miss Barnard and Miss Mary Barnard to spend a few days with her and her daughter Leonora, and go with them to the oratorio at Ipswich, regretting that the oratorio fell on a date when her son would be absent. Mrs. Debenham's son had thought this an immensely clever stroke. But it did not penetrate the defences, and Julia was told to decline with regrets. Her regrets were sincere, and she

78

spoke of them to Euphemia, adding that from the moment Barnard brought in young Mr. Kettle she had known how it would be. "If Mr. Debenham had sent begging letters instead of game, and had been an usher instead of a gentleman, your father would think him perfection." It was true enough that John Barnard, like many men of high principles, had a good deal of moral coquetry and, of the two young men, would prefer Thomas because Marmaduke was wealthy and a landowner—though he inconsistently omitted to think ill of Thomas because Marmaduke was undersized and ugly. But the real watershed of his favour ran elsewhere. Thomas was under an obligation to him, though not a large one. To Marmaduke, who had established Joseph in such very comfortable circumstances, he himself was under an obligation, none the less real because he chose to call it an injury; and though Marmaduke's claim to have rescued Mary from a bulldog seemed to be admitted on all sides, John Barnard felt that he had somehow done it under false pretences; at any rate, he had not done it in a right spirit. He could not go so far as to poohpooh the bulldog, but he could wish that Julia would leave off talking about it.

3.

In the third week of December, Madame Bon's pupils began their holiday and their parents expected Madame Bon's bills. Now, with the bills, came a circular, in which Madame Bon, in her smoothest copperplate, informed her patrons that she was closing the school, and in a fresh paragraph begged the honour of their presence on the occasion of her marriage to Mr. Simon Kettle, to be solemnized in the parish church on January 4, 1836.

"Well, Barnard," said Julia, having read the circular aloud. "Isn't this vexatious? I wonder what we should do."

"We can do nothing."

"I suppose we could find a governess for Ellen. Mary is old enough to finish, but Ellen can't be left to run wild."

"You must write and say we will not attend the wedding."

"Not attend the wedding? That would look very odd. Such an old friend, and your protegee—it would be a great slight. And though it is foolish to marry at her age—"

"It would be as bad if she were a girl of eighteen. She will be Kettle's third wife. There is nothing for it but disapprobation."

"Such a disagreeable man too," said Julia. "I disliked him from the beginning. He made my head ache."

Julia could never grasp a matter of principle. Evading the plain moral duty to discountenance all third marriages, she continued to assert that Madame Bon was an old friend and Mr. Kettle an old hypocrite, and to invent and then discard various time-serving pretexts for refusing the invitation. She was the more slippery because Daniel and Robina were visiting Anchor House and threw themselves into the discussion with all the animation and wrongheadedness of people who knew nothing about it. Almost a week had gone by, and Madame Bon's invitation was still unrefused. Julia, Daniel, and Robina were using this as a reason why an acceptance was now the only course, when another invitation had to be met.

"It is from Mrs. Debenham, Barnard. She asks us, all of us, to spend the New Year at Rougham."

Before he could reply, Robina was giving her opinion. "There you are! Just what you needed! A perfect reason for not going to that wedding. And you can easily hit on a little something to account for not having answered before. I call it providential."

Refraining from comment on Robina's outlook on Divine Providence, John Barnard said, "I should not like to attend a Watch Night service in a strange church."

No one answered this.

"We have made it a rule to begin the New Year at home."

No one answered this either. He looked round on them, seeking for something that might guide or encourage him. They sat with their eyes averted and maintained an air of being quite uninterested, all except Mary, who glanced up, vaguely smiling and fingering her coral necklace. She was Madame Bon's pupil; however bitterly he might regret it, he could not undo it; and as such, poor innocent child, she might justly expect to attend this unholy marriage feast, in fact, she had already said something about a sash. He said in desperation, "I cannot understand why these Debenhams are so persistent in their invitations. I think you had best accept this one. That will be the only way to put an end to it."

The Watch Night service at Rougham All Saints' was a mediocre affair; it had none of the unction and heartwarming terrors of a Watch Night at St. Andrew's. But in the grounds of Rougham Hall there was an ornamental lake, and the ice on it was thick enough to bear. John Barnard had not skated since he was at Cambridge, and it was an exercise he delighted in. He skated daily in a solemn, solitary joy. To the Debenhams he seemed no more than a middle-aged gentleman who was easily pleased in an easy, unambitious way, for he did not even cut figures. To his wife and children he appeared as a new man, harmless and aloof, as though death had translated him. "I believe I could grow quite attached to your father," Marmaduke said to Euphemia; for, by the nature of skating, when he was not supporting one sister he was supporting another. Euphemia said no more than "Indeed," for at that moment John Barnard came swooping towards them, and she did not wish Marmaduke's face to evince too much interest in her conversation. But John Barnard swept by unheeding, with his arms folded across his chest and his gaze fixed on the araucaria that grew at one end of the lake—a fine specimen, and the first to be planted in Suffolk. He approached it, he passed it, and with an energetic stroke of his right foot he set off away

81

from it on a fresh journey towards it. He did not even use it to count by now. It recurred like a Sabbath. With every circle of the lake he travelled a stage deeper into a region that was partly the kingdom of heaven and partly Cambridge. Not since Cambridge had he felt so inoffensive. Not till the kingdom of heaven could he feel so detached. In heaven it would be possible to see one's wife, and the children whose passport thither had been the dearest concern of one's life, with the calmness of mind that belongs to the place where there is no marrying or giving in marriage. One would see them and sweep by them. And there would be no speech or language, any more than there is among the heavenly bodies, but a voice would be heard among them, a solemn jubilee, as of wings, or as of the ice resounding underfoot. As for the train of events which had sent him skating round and round the lake whose araucaria had become so pleasingly familiar, a strange feeling of justification had smoothed away the doubts which troubled his arrival. A variety of motives (it seemed), hastily jumbled together, had conveyed him hither: to gratify a family majority, to show Daniel that he too had creditable acquaintances, to be equipped with a civil yet not servile or untruthful reason for non-attendance at that wedding; these were the motives which had seemed to impel him, and all of them were shabby ones. But now, turning once again towards the araucaria's furry gesture of welcome, he could only feel that he had been led. Blameless with exercise and open air, he could not attribute his well-being to any human agency, least of all his own.

In the evenings he talked to Mrs. Debenham about her cottage poor. At times she flattered him, which he did not like. But her household kept early hours, and she had been a widow for twenty years, and there was nothing about her to show that she had been a West Indian heiress. When the morning of departure came he was astonished that it should have come so quickly. The trunks were packed, the carriage was drawn up at the door and foot-warmers had been put in it, when Ellen, in the negligence of despair, tripped over a mat, fell against a bureau, and made her nose bleed. Mrs. Debenham and Leonora went out to help Julia with cold keys and towels; Wilberforce took advantage of this delay to demand another last appearance of the monkey that danced on the musical box. His host was winding up the animal when there was a cry from Mary. She had risen and was pointing towards the window. Pressed to the outside of the window was a large bulldog, who wagged his tail and licked the glass.

Marmaduke turned round from the monkey.

"Go away, Bouncer! You know you're not allowed indoors."

Bouncer pawed the window and wagged his tail. Mary clung to Euphemia, and Euphemia said, "I expect it's Mr. Debenham's dog, Mary. Look how friendly he is."

"Of course it's Mr. Debenham's dog," said Wilberforce.

"Yes, I've had him for years," said Marmaduke. "He's a silly old fellow and wouldn't hurt a fly. But I ordered that he should be kept shut up while you were here, in case Miss Mary should be reminded of that brute who tore her gown. He was a dark brindle too."

Mary was reassured and agreed that it was only in colour that Bouncer resembled the other bulldog. She went up to the window and commented on Bouncer's good-natured expression and smart collar. Even John Barnard looked at Bouncer with something like tolerance. Mary's preserver had kept a bulldog for years. As he was accustomed to the breed, the valour of his exploit was not so very remarkable. Though this did not diminish an obligation, it made it easier to bear. Ellen was brought back, the Barnards got into their carriage and drove off. At a turn of the avenue the lake came into sight. The ice shone like pewter, but no one was skating there.

At Loseby a rising northeasterly gale was throwing wet snow on the frozen ground, and the waves were grinding the shingle. Moisture clouded the looking glass in the hall. It reflected the returning household dimly and, as it were, unwillingly. Only Mary exclaimed, "How glad I am to be home!"

John Barnard longed to believe it. But could it be possible? None of the others showed a trace of gladness. The words had seemed to come spontaneously. But why had they been uttered at all? Why should she express gladness, when it was to be taken for granted that she would prefer her home to any other place? It would have been more natural if she had asked about her doves, or inquired if Hester had thrown off her cold (it was plain that she hadn't). Mary had always been faultlessly candid. If she had lost that grace, it was his undoing.

What else might she not have lost?

For as his house confronted him, a dark bulk behind scurrying snowflakes, and with no more lights in its windows than were strictly necessary, he realized with anger and remorse how weak he had been to leave it. If the return struck even him as gaunt, what effect might it not have on his children's sensibilities? He should have played the man and refused both invitations. Of the two, the invitation to the wedding now seemed the lesser evil. Acceptance would have been humiliating, but it would not have broken the solemn continuity of Old Year's Nights at home, and Mary would have been less endangered by the sight of Mr. Kettle taking a third wife (for they need not have gone on to the wedding breakfast) than by Marmaduke Debenham with no wife at all. Skating on that enchanted lake, living in too warm rooms and eating too lavish meals, he had seen only a host taking pains to please a girl on her first sally from the schoolroom. The mother, the sister, the servants, the gamekeeper's son who fastened on the skates —everyone had been charmed with Mary, and he had seen no more in it than a natural similarity between their judgment and his own. How could he have been so blind? The more he thought of it, the harder it became to believe that Mary's pleasure in being at home was unfeigned.

Saying that he must deal with the letters which had accumulated during his absence, he refused to take supper and went into his study.

Among them was a letter from Daniel, urging again what had been urged during the stay at Anchor House: that the firm should set up an agency in London. Old Mr. Barnard's will had bequeathed a third-share in the business to his younger son, and Daniel's first thought had been to get his share realized and paid over. When the improvidence of this was pointed out by both executors, Daniel, being in a hurry, consented to take half of his third-share in cash, with a promise of the remainder in five years' time. In five years' time the business was doing much better, and Robina was managing Daniel's affairs. She had no hesitation in preferring the interest on Daniel's one-sixth to the proceeds of a sale; in fact, she made a spirited try at reversing the earlier bargain and failed to do so only because she could not bring herself to offer more than the original sum, alleging that the subsequent appreciation of value was wiped out by the amount of interest that would have been paid on the capital if the capital had not been paid over. Daniel's one-sixth was a minor part of his income, for Robina had come into a substantial inheritance, but this did not prevent Robina from keeping a sharp eye on it. She brought her knitting into the study where the brothers were discussing the pros and cons of a London agent.

"I'm sure you can afford to. You do nothing but make a profit every year," had been Daniel's line of argument. "He can't afford not to," said Robina. "It's nothing but trading in a napkin, trying to keep all the business in Loseby. Buyers haven't time to come to Loseby nowadays, especially buyers from these new foreign markets. They'll do their business in London, where they can frisk about and see the sights."

John Barnard explained that in fact few buyers came to Loseby. They dealt by letter, and on recommendation from other buyers. The business was doing well, and he had just made a most satisfactory deal in horsehair, which he imported from Riga and would sell to a manufactory near Colchester with a twenty-per-cent profit. But as he spoke he remembered that the manufactory near Colchester had been negotiating with a London importer before he bore off the contract, and that he had recently missed selling a cargo of linseed because a buyer's agent had failed to get a seat on the Loseby coach. Perhaps Robina was right. She was often shrewd, especially about a long-term policy; an immediate profit excited her greed and made her as stupid as any other woman. He said that he would think it over. But now Daniel's letter referred to the agent as a decision already taken, and added that Robina had a second cousin who would be very willing to leave East Fife. It was strange to remember that when Daniel had entered the house with a young woman on each arm, John Barnard's wavering sensibilities had gone out towards the slender fair-haired one, because she looked the more feminine and poetical of the two.

The door opened, and Mary came in to say good night.

"Are you still glad to be home, Mary?"

"Oh, yes. Yes, I am." A shadow had fallen between the two assents.

"But are you less glad than you were three hours ago?"

"Poor Papa, what a quantity of writing you have here! So much to do, and no one to help you—though Euphemia says Wilberforce is clever at his sums already."

"I should have had helpers if your brothers had been spared."

"Yes. Or if Joseph came back."

Then Debenham had been poisoning her mind. "Who has been talking about Joseph?"

"Aunt Robina."

If Debenham had not come between him and Mary, Robina had, and others would. She was growing up. Soon she would be a woman; she would marry and have children; and then, one strange day, she would outlive him. It was death he used to be afraid of, the death that might snatch her out of his arms. He must learn to be afraid of life, which more insidiously would bear her away from him. After she had gone out he sat with his head between his hands, listening to the gale rumbling in the chimney. Rousing himself at last, he was astonished to see the candle flames burning so steadily in the shuttered room.

Aunt Robina had undertaken to find a resident governess for Ellen, since, with the poor child's blemished face, one really could not send her to a boarding school. Ellen was aware of this project, but it was of no interest to her, since she would so soon be dead. She was dying of a broken heart, though no one knew it. Standing behind a laurustinus in order to hitch up her petticoat, she had heard Mr. Debenham call Euphemia his darling, his darling Goody Jog-Trot. Euphemia had only laughed, for she had no heart. Ellen had ascertained this in conversation.

"Euphemia, do you think Mr. Debenham has a weak chest? He looks very delicate."

"Nonsense! He's undersized, but I expect he's as tough as a rat."

A rat! She could compare that fragile, dauntless hero with a rat. Mary would have been less unworthy of his love. Mary at least said that he was gentleman-like. But soon the heart which truly beat for him would be lying in a grave. She could not go on smothering such extremely violent feelings much longer. The governess would come too late; or perhaps she would come just in time to bend over the pallid form and stroke the fevered brow and catch the last gasping message. "Tell Marmaduke not to grieve for me. Tell him that I shall watch over him from heaven. And oh! tell him to beware of false friends."

In the short time that was left to her on earth Ellen took every opportunity to spurn Euphemia. Spurning took the shape of making faces, shuddering if Euphemia approached, being deaf if Euphemia spoke to her, and vomiting up the cod-liver oil which it was Euphemia's duty to administer. Euphemia would not have been the daughter of a united, godfearing family if she had not known that the surest way of putting Ellen out of action was to laugh at her. Six months before, she would have done it. But love had weakened her with scruples and superstitions. The purpled countenance haughtily glaring at her was no longer quite ludicrous or wholly repulsive; it was the visage of a female being who could never hope to be pleasing in a man's sight. Though Ellen was striking sparks in a powder magazine—for Papa was moody, and Wilberforce persisted in drawing dogs—Euphemia took no action, relying on the family convention of "not before Papa." So she had only herself to blame when Ellen, knowing as well as she did that Papa was just then in the newly installed water closet with the morning paper, followed her down the passage, clattering a pair of scissors against a buttonhook to imitate the jingle of household keys, and crying out, "Goody Jog-Trot! Goody Jog-Trot!"

She seized Ellen's arm and nodded towards the door. "Ellen! That will do."

"Goody Jog-Trot," the child screamed. "Mr. Debenham's Goody Jog-Trot. That's what you are. It's not Mary. It's you!"

Euphemia heard the newspaper thrown down. He can't come out now, she thought. He can't.

He did not. Silenced by Euphemia's look of despair, Ellen slid away, and Euphemia went on to the storeroom.

The storeroom was in the basement, a boxlike apartment constructed in the centre of the house and ventilated through two iron gratings. Shelves and bins covered the walls, and in the middle of the room was a solid table with weights and scales, an inkstand, and a household ledger on it. The cook was waiting for her by the door, with the tray and the candlestick. They went in together. "We shall soon need more vinegar, miss," the cook said. She made a note to order more vinegar and began to weigh out the oatmeal for the morrow's porridge. If I were to marry, she thought, I should still be doing this sort of thing. There is really no escape. A sense of intolerable boredom and apathy descended on her. She felt that she had no heart to begin scheming all over again, and that she would rather lock herself in here, with the four walls close round her, and the outer walls of the house corroborating them, and the outside wall beyond that. If I could stay here, and just enough of me be weighed out for one day at a time! The wish was ridiculous, quite nonsensical. She closed the ledger, and as she did so she heard the front door closing. John Barnard had gone out to his office ten minutes before his usual hour.

He had gone out because he could not stay. What he had overheard was shocking, and anything like eavesdropping was repugnant to him, and he had every reason to be annoyed. And yet he was not. It was Euphemia. It was not Mary. Do as he would, he could not control a disorderly rush of thankfulness that it was not Mary. Relief and then elation overcame all the feelings he was trying to feel, and it was to keep this joy to himself that he ran away. It was not Mary. He was not, after all, to be punished for his weakness in going to Rougham Hall, his luxurious isolation as he skated round the lake, a truant from fatherhood. It was not Mary. Presently he would recover a sense of proportion again and see the faultiness of Euphemia as well as the blamelessness of Mary. Ellen, morbidly entertaining notions unsuitable to her age, must go to a boarding school; and of course there must be no more intercourse with Debenhams. As for Euphemia—wretched girl, who could call forth such low endearments as "Goody"—perhaps it would be best to leave her to the uneasiness of her own conscience. Goody, indeed! Thank God it was impossible to imagine such a term being addressed to Mary.

4.

If on that morning Marmaduke Debenham had come to Loseby and asked for Euphemia, he might very well have got her, since she wasn't Mary. Instead a brief letter from Euphemia told him that everything planned between them at Rougham must be postponed.

At this period Julia was not so dependent on drink that she could not do without it if some other diversion was provided. Robina's company had brisked up her spirits, and the visit to the Debenhams had revived her self-respect. She began the New Year with two good resolutions: to put on stays every morning, and to pursue a social life. "This year I will endeavour to do myself justice," was how she abridged these resolutions in her diary, and at Rougham Hall, wearing her best clothes, exerting her best manners, seeing Mary admired and Euphemia treated with consideration, the endeavour did not seem beyond her power. Darwell's greeting of "Madam looks quite fagged out. But she'll feel more like herself when she's on her sofa. I've got the dressing gown and slippers nicely warming at the fire," was discouraging, but Julia had not been the mistress of devoted old family servants for so long without knowing that discouragement and disparagement are the perquisites of devoted service. It was more discouraging to see how instantaneously the warmth of his own fireside chilled her husband; in a matter of hours he was as morosely full of scruples as if he had never skated in his life. But the entry in the diary remained, and she meant to abide by it. She sent for the staymaker, bought new gloves, and threw away the heeltaps of pomade and bandoline which were part of the dull landscape of her dressing table. She gave up rum and drank only a civil quantity of Madeira. Next came the pursuit of a social life, which at that time of year meant dinner parties—she dared not just then hazard a return hospitality to the Debenhams. Dinner parties were being given—through Darwell she heard reports of several fine specimens—but Mr. and Mrs. Barnard remained uninvited. Julia had to face the fact that during the last few years Mr. and Mrs. Barnard had fallen out of the dinner-party rota, and that she had only herself to thank for it. She determined to re-enter the lists by a dinner party at Anchor House with two soups, turbot, a saddle of mutton, game, chicken patties, charlotte russe, and the Kettles. The decencies demanded all these, but especially the Kettles. It is the due of every newly married couple to be entertained, and if Sophie had been Simon Kettle's tenth wife it would still be her right to go in to table on Barnard's arm as the chief lady of the evening.

I must manage it by Mary, thought Julia, foreseeing trouble over this item. I shall say that if Mary does not make her first appearance at this dinner party there will be nothing for it but to exhibit her at an Assembly ball. The stratagem was not applied, for Barnard had no sooner expressed pained astonishment, asking if he had not already made his disapproval of the Kettles clear by refusing to attend their marriage, than Julia lost her temper and retorted that it was a pity he had not had the courage of his opinions instead of skulking behind the pretext of an engagement to the Debenhams. This sally was as unforeseen by her as by him. Stays and abstinence accounted for it, and spurred her on while she called him a Jesuitical Laodicean, a Mr. Facing-Both-Ways, and a prig, and finally grew so red in the face and so short of breath that he supposed she was going to have a fit and begged her to lie down and let him put lavender water on her forehead. The lavender water went into her eye, she writhed with pain and shouted him out of the room. There had been quarrels with Julia in the past, but never such a quarrel as this; and that night when, rising from his knees at the bedside, he tried to forgive her and be reconciled, she turned her vast back on him. She was feeling the worse for her victory and knew how easy it would be for even the mildest reconciliation to seduce her from the stern career of doing herself justice.

He said no more. He was particularly anxious not to think ill of Julia. Indeed he preferred not to think of her at all. For a long time he had accepted the thought that her health was poor and her nerves precarious; later he had come to accept the thought that she had never loved him as he would wish to be loved; later still, that even as a mother she was neglectful and only fitfully affectionate. At the extreme limit of thinking ill of Julia he achieved a rapid admission that she was lazy, selfish, and worldly, and that if she would get onto her feet and see to the housekeeping as other women did, her health might be the better for it and her appearance less immodestly profuse; but that was as far as he would go. Was she not the wife of his bosom and Mary's mother? It was better, and more like a Christian, to stop here and reflect on his own failings. It was also much easier. By force of habit his mind turned to his own failings as an old horse turns into its stable. They were not all he had to reflect on. He was no longer so sure that it was not Mary, for of the two sisters it was almost inconceivable that a wealthy libertine such as Debenham would prefer Euphemia, and "Goody Jog-Trot" was just how a libertine would address a prospective sister-in-law. Meanwhile there was the matter of a boarding school for Ellen, and Daniel had written another letter about a London agent.

So Julia remained no more than a regretful subject for not thinking about until the day of the dinner party, when an awakening of conscience took him down into the wine cellar. As a rule Euphemia kept the wine-cellar key, fetching out bottles as they were needed; and earlier that day, on his instructions, she had brought up two bottles of the second-best port. Having given these instructions, he began to question them; the disapprobation he felt for a man making a third marriage was too grave to be embodied in chicaneries about wine. Just before the guests arrived he mastered his lower nature and

92

went to get the best port. He had not been in the cellar for over a twelvemonth, and his first impressions were so pleasurable, since they were impressions of composure and seclusion, that he wished he had come sooner and could stay longer, steeping his mind in underground calm before the dinner party. Slanting the candle, he looked round. It all seemed to be in excellent order, Euphemia kept it very nicely. Cobwebs were where they should be, but not elsewhere, and the emptied bottles lay hindpart before, so that one could tell at a glance which bins needed replenishing. The candlelight moved on and showed him a ranked assembly of bottle rumps, and another beyond it, and beyond that another. The emptied bottles had held either Madeira or rum. Julia drank Madeira for the sake of her health. Daniel had twice brewed rum punch, but he could not have needed over two dozen bottles to do it with. The candlelight lunged forward, and a trickle of hot grease fell on his hand and hardened there, but the pain seemed to be taking place in the flesh of some other man, a man who had gone down into his wine cellar with no more serious thought in mind than a scruple about best and second-best port, no purpose beyond a trivial adjustment of self-esteem, and who, on entering, had received impressions of composure and seclusion. As well enter a den of wild beasts thinking so! *Wine is a mocker, strong drink is raging.* . . . So Solomon testified, though John Barnard himself had never found it so; but because he was immune to that temptation, he was not justified in putting it in the way of others. The Madeira might be medicinal, but rum, rum in such quantities! . . . Joseph's regular consignments now seemed direct interventions of Satan, mocking rejoinders to the tracts and baby clothes sent out so regularly to the labourers on the sugar-cane plantations. He should never have allowed Joseph's rum to enter the house. Better still, he should have closed the cellar when he became a family man. If he had done so he might by now have set up the Temperance Union which was so badly needed in Loseby and which Kettle would never be able to bring about—for a Temperance Union sponsored by the husband of three wives could be nothing but a mockery, and God would not prosper it. God had not prospered Anchor House with a wine cellar in its foundations. Could it be that Ellen's port-wine stain was an indication, a writing on the wall? With a groan he recalled the dinner party and quitted the wine cellar in a state of mind so clouded by portents and moral issues that the plain aspect of Julia's emptied bottles was already half obscured.

Entering the drawing room, he avoided looking at Julia. Mrs. Kettle, as he must now call her, was dressed in a pearl-grey silk so extremely light in tint that it might for all practical purposes be considered white. Poor woman, she thought of herself as a bride! Mr. Kettle was complimenting Canon Blunt on a sermon and saying how cheaply it might be printed in Hull. Canon Blunt was that creditable thing, a widower, and his son, who was also his curate, was making small talk to Euphemia about confirmation candidates. The remaining guests, two couples from Prospect Terrace, were shown in, and John Barnard led the lady of the evening into the dining room.

He could not be quite sure, for it was beneath his dignity to examine into such things, but he suspected that the lady of the evening was having the impertinence to patronize him.

"I suppose these fine pheasants come from Mr. Debenham's preserves? One always knows a Suffolk pheasant."

"They came from the poulterer, ma'am. More than that I cannot say."

He turned to the lady on his other side and discussed the prospect of a Queen of England till the end of dessert. The only tolerable part of a dinner party was after the ladies had gone out, but now that interval of repose began with Mr. Kettle refusing port, and young Blunt also refusing. Cold airs from the cellar rose into the dining room. Might not Julia be as comfortable with peppermint tea? Kettle was prating about the peacefulness of what he was pleased to call "our little

Loseby." Comparing his lot with the violet's, " 'Sheltered from the blight, Ambition,' " he quoted, " 'See me in my low condition, Laughing on the tufted bank.' " Daniel and Robina had implied much the same thing, and the matter of the agent in London was still unattacked. It was intolerable, and in the middle of a disquisition on the number of improving lectures in Hull, John Barnard got up to join the ladies.

One of the Prospect Terrace ladies was performing on the piano. He coughed to enforce silence, for anything was better than conversation, and sat down beside the other lady from the Terrace. When the performance was at an end he showed her pictures in an album. They were informing each other that they had never seen Mount Vesuvius when an unusual note of acerbity in Julia's voice caught his attention. He supposed for a moment she was speaking to him. "Then we shall not see Miss Mutley again?"

"She may pay us a visit from time to time," said Mr. Kettle, "but she is no longer an inmate. Her place"—he bowed towards his wife—"has been filled."

"Where is she going to live?"

"That is still undetermined. No doubt she will set up her little tent somewhere or other. Retirement is sweet. No one knows that better than I."

Julia said firmly, if mendaciously, "I shall miss her a great deal. I am sorry she has gone."

"I suppose she has some means of her own," said Canon Blunt.

"As to that, she has never taken me into her confidence. Single ladies of her age prefer to keep such matters to themselves, I believe." Mr. Kettle admitted ignorance in such a reassuring tone of voice that the lady who had not seen Vesuvius exclaimed that Miss Mutley was a fortunate woman.

John Barnard said dryly, "I am glad to learn she was so prudent."

"Prudent?" exclaimed Sophie Kettle. "Prudent? Quite the

95

contrary, I assure you. She has put by nothing. Nothing! I cannot understand such bad management. To live all these years at Mr. Kettle's expense, and to have nothing put by—I think it quite shocking."

The ant denounced the grasshopper in a voice quivering with wifely loyalty, for in the last few weeks Sophie Kettle had learned what a trial his sister-in-law's thriftlessness had been to her Simon. But the effect was displeasing. Simon felt the displeasure and said allayingly, "Come, come, do not be too severe! We cannot all be such excellent economists as you, my dear. Magdalen might have saved rather more, I daresay. But she will do. You need feel no anxiety on her account, I assure you."

"Where is Miss Mutley now?" asked Julia, whose mind had turned to parcels of groceries.

"With Thomas, with Thomas. I cannot say—I would not care to say—how long she will remain with him. She has been a second mother to him. It would be a delightful arrangement. I wish it may last."

He sighed, rearranged his handkerchief, and looked at his wife. She rose. The other Terrace-dwellers also rose. They were going to walk back together. Though the distance was less than a quarter of a mile, and the night dry and windless, Mrs. Kettle's "We shall enjoy it. We are all walkers, you know. It is nothing to us to go on foot," conveyed that since returning from Rougham Hall the Barnards had done nothing but loll in barouches.

As the door closed behind them John Barnard exclaimed, "Disgraceful!" and Julia, "Atrocious!"

"Horrid old hypocrite!" Mary spoke with vigour.

"You did not get that address, Mamma," said Euphemia.

Crawley Blunt said nothing. He was engaged in looking at Mary. He had never before seen her display emotion, and though this was not the kind of emotion he had imagined her displaying it made her look ten times prettier. If she could look as animated while expressing more domesticated sentiments, he might be ready to overlook the scandal of her mamma and the dangers of a Scotch heredity.

Canon Blunt turned to his hostess and said, "You are always the same, Mrs. Barnard. Your first thought is practical kindness." For though she was too often the worse for liquor, he did not know what the parish would do without her, and he was glad to say something that did not involve him in a condemnation.

"My first thought was to box his ears," replied Julia.

"Perhaps it is not quite so bad as it sounds. Even if she has failed to make some provision for her old age, she must have other relations than her brother-in-law. Besides, she is still healthy and active. And trustworthy. Mr. Kettle would not have given her charge of his household unless he was satisfied of that. She may easily find some modest sphere with—ah— emoluments."

"Mr. Kettle's son has taken her in. He, at any rate, has a heart," said Mary, and if she had spoken so on any other subject her father would have thought her manner pert.

Euphemia interposed a distraction in case it should be needed. "He teaches in a boarding school, I believe, near London. Miss Mutley could be very useful there, I should think."

"Mr. Thomas Kettle has already put that out of the question, Miss Barnard. He has quitted Doctor Price's establishment. His father mentioned it to me last week. He mentioned it with concern. I gather that Mr. Thomas Kettle is quite a rolling stone."

Though Crawley Blunt spoke to Euphemia, his eyes remained on Mary, for it was she he wished to disillusion. Now he saw her get up and close the piano lid with a bang. In a voice made tranquil by fury, John Barnard said he did not believe a word of it. Canon Blunt took Crawley away before he poked up another wasps' nest. Crawley was a good son and a promising curate, but he had not learned how to walk circumspectly.

John Barnard had not told the Kettles to leave his house; Julia had not boxed Mr. Kettle's ears. The dinner party could not be counted as satisfactory, though during the night John Barnard drew some comfort from a decision not to renew the Kettles' lease, and Wilberforce slept in unwonted voluptuousness, glutted with chicken patties and cold oyster sauce and with a leg of pheasant under his pillow. Waking into a sense of danger, Euphemia remembered the events of overnight, prepared herself for a period of Papa being in a mood, and hoped, as Joseph used to do, that Mary was as good as ever.

But Mary had also gone into a mood. Never having gone into a mood before, she could not achieve the unremitting sombreness of her father's performances. Lacking the control which comes from practice, she occasionally rose to the surface for air. But in some respects she surpassed him; for instance, she almost left off eating, and her sex allowed her one advantage that Papa could not claim, for she could sing.

> Oh, breathe not his name! let it sleep in the shade,
> Where cold and unhonoured his relics are laid

rang through the house as though a sword were being sharpened for battle. She sang it a dozen times a day, always making the same mistakes in the accompaniment, till Julia threatened to lock the piano. But to Papa, Mary's music was soothing as David's harpings were to Saul; and when she refused boiled beef and left pudding on her plate there was not a breath of the customary "Do not trifle with your food; others are starving." His dearest and almost perfect child was now more endeared and nearer perfection. She felt as he did about the Kettles.

She felt as he did, but more laudably, since she was without guilt. She had not skulked behind a pretext of Debenhams.

She had not given way to the pomps and vanities of Rougham Hall, she had only moderately enjoyed skating, she had been glad to find herself at home again. And when Crawley Blunt had tried to blacken the character of that high-minded young Kettle she had banged down the piano lid, an act of energetic rectitude after the style of Jael driving the nail into Sisera's temples. How much better she behaved than I did, he thought. What strength of character she has beneath such apparent mildness. Without irreverence, one might say that Mary was of the stuff from which martyrs are made; whereas he, by his timeserving and weakness, had laid himself open not merely to having the Kettles to dine, but, far worse, to a perspective of disgraceful dinings; for they had already been impertinent enough to invite the Barnards to a return dinner.

> "And the tear that we shed, though in secret it rolls,
> Shall long keep his memory green in our souls."

"Thank you, my dear! That is very beautiful. Euphemia, do you not think that Mary has improved in her singing?"

"Yes, Papa."

"It seems to me that she sings with more power."

"I think so too."

His glance dwelt on her long enough to convey, Soulless clod!

If I were to behave about Marmaduke Debenham as Mary is behaving about Thomas Kettle, Euphemia thought, I wonder what Papa would do. But the speculation was idle; she could only behave about Marmaduke Debenham as though he did not exist.

Assuring herself that Mary's behaviour was silly and childish, Euphemia was in fact deeply perturbed by it. It was all very well to say that rather than behave like that she would die; the truth of it was she had no choice in the matter; such behaviour was impossible to her; and how was she to know that exactly such behaviour was not what Marmaduke Debenham

99

expected of her and would one day demand? He had asked her to elope with him; if he could expect that, he might expect anything. At the very least he would expect her to be self-possessed, level-headed, and tenacious, for as such, and in good faith, she had presented herself. But in that appalling moment when Ellen proclaimed her Mr. Debenham's Goody Jog-Trot, even those jog-trot merits had failed; love—she supposed it was love—made a craven of her. Incredulously she saw everything going on as usual, a view which included admitting that her father did not mind what happened to her so long as nothing happened to Mary. This should have encouraged her hopes, but by then she had written to Marmaduke, putting everything off. Miss Mutley was cast penniless on an impecunious nephew; Papa was delighted, since this proved the villainy of the Kettles; Mary caterwauled, and Papa thought her singing much improved. The hour was propitious, but she did not write again to Marmaduke. For suppose the sight of Mary's extreme silliness were to put it into his head to expect a similar display from her? Mary had always been in the right, and how was one to know that she was not in the right now, behaving just as she should, and as any man, and not only a father, would wish? It was cowardly and dishonourable not to summon Marmaduke, for she had promised him she would. It was also imprudent and wasteful not to make hay while the sun shone. She knew all this, but she did not write. And presently she had a sterner reason to default on her promise.

In March, Papa set out for London. Mamma called her into the dressing room, thrust something under a cushion, and asked if this would not be a good time to invite the Debenhams. The worst possible time, Euphemia said, for the chimneysweep was coming and the cook had been promised a holiday. In the midst of these rational disagreements she burst into vehement weeping and declared that if the Debenhams were invited she would not stay in the house.

Julia looked at her with fury. "I never thought *you* would

remind me of your papa," she said. "But have it as you please. He who will to Cupar, maun to Cupar."

The taunt about resembling Papa scarcely grazed Euphemia's consciousness. It was not, after all, a concatenation of Papa and Marmaduke she dreaded. In the moment before she burst into tears she had uncovered a deeper dread: the concatenation of Marmaduke and poor Mamma.

Euphemia knew all about drunkenness, both in the abstract and in real life. In the abstract it poisoned homes, struck down little children with an oath, pawned its bedding, and fell senseless into the gutter. In real life it walked unsteadily, talked incoherently, vomited sometimes, and was usually to be met on the day after looking pretty much as usual. She also knew that drunkenness was far worse in a woman than in a man, though no one had explained to her why. As Julia's variety of drinking resembled neither the drunkenness of tracts nor the drunkenness of real life, it had never occurred to Euphemia that her mamma might be the worse for drink. At times Mamma was poorly (the servants referred to it as "queer," "one of Mrs. Barnard's queer days"), and at such times she grew hazy, spoke with difficulty, could not tolerate a strong light or being asked questions, and lay on her sofa in a dressing gown, breathing noisily. At such times she only cared to drink tea. At other times she drank Madeira or rum to keep her strength up. If it had not been for the interval during which Julia was trying to do herself justice, Euphemia might have gone on for a long time before putting two and two together. But recently Mamma had taken to being poorly again, and poorly in a new way, combative instead of comatose, suspicious and exacting instead of vaguely grateful for attentions. For Julia, gone back to her bottle, was drinking differently—not more, but harder; not complacently, but harshly and secretly. It was the secret that caught Euphemia's eyes and wrenched them open.

PART THREE

1.

John Barnard was going to London to look into the matter of a London agent. But there was another reason for his going, and this took him to Clapton on the morning of his first day in town. It was a raw, foggy morning. A brassy light shone harshly on the straggling suburbs, where new terraces elbowed clapboarded cottages. In the nursery gardens women wrapped in sacking were slashing off cabbage heads and bundling them into nets, their faces pale with cold and their hands purple. After the scolding, upstanding Loseby women they seemed like a race of unachieved beings, half human, half larval. Beyond Hackney the road descended into the valley of the Lea. The fog thickened, the cold clamped down, and women, even more larval and shapeless, were wading in the half-frozen watercress beds. But in Dr. Price's study, where John Barnard was asked to wait, there was a brisk fire burning, and the plaster busts on top of the bookcases were so clean that one might suppose they had been washed that same morning.

Dr. Price entered the room with that bland avidity with which schoolmasters greet strangers who come on wheels. He

102

apologized for the delay. He had been taking his senior class through an eclogue. When the visitor explained his reason for coming, the eclogue expression faded.

"Mr. Kettle left my establishment two months ago. I thought it better not to inquire into his reasons. If they had been good ones, no doubt he would have mentioned them. I did not trouble him for his address, either. I suppose his father is aware of it—Mr. Kettle the publisher; I daresay you know him. We make considerable use of his Juvenile Library in our junior classes, and in the sickroom. One could not call his publications scholarly, but they are edifying and pure."

"I am scarcely acquainted with Mr. Kettle, senior. I think highly of his son."

"Do you indeed? I am sorry that I cannot tell you his whereabouts. Very sorry indeed, yes."

Dr. Price's tones took on a waspish Welsh howl as he voiced his unavailing regret. He was preparing to consult his watch when John Barnard forestalled him by taking up his hat.

Halfway down the drive a garden boy was raking the gravel, and on an impulse John Barnard stopped the chaise and leaned out to inquire if he knew where Mr. Kettle had gone. The boy shook his head and went on raking. The drive was a short one, and at the end of it was a very small lodge whence a woman in a pinafore came out to open the gate. John Barnard repeated his question. She appeared not to hear it, or not to comprehend it. It struck him that a shilling might improve her hearing, but it only improved it to the extent that she believed Mr. Kettle might have gone to London.

The chaise had turned into the road when the garden boy scrambled through the hedge. He was breathless and waved something in his hand. "Here! But don't say I had it. And please to tell the young gentleman that Mother hopes he got the horehound tea and it did his cough good." He thrust in a screw of paper and ran back through the hedge.

Drury Lane had regrettable associations, and a coffee house was not too good, but Dr. Price had left no room for doubt in John Barnard's mind, and no address, from Rosherville Gardens to Lambeth Palace, could have shaken his resolve to seek out Thomas Kettle. Homerton's Coffee House proved to be shabby but cosy. The proprietor fumbled through a quantity of addresses and found that Mr. Kettle could be inquired for at Lawley and Denton, scholastic agents, Ave Mary Lane. At Lawley and Denton, John Barnard was told that Mr. Kettle could be found at 23 Jewell's Buildings, off the City Road. Twenty-three Jewell's Buildings housed a missionary society which had employed Mr. Kettle to copy circulars but did so no longer. His address had been kept in case there should be further need of him. It was near Smithfield, the house was a cooked-meats shop, and the woman who kept it had no recollection of a young man called Kettle. She did, however, remember a Miss Mutley, who had rented two rooms on her third floor. Miss Mutley had gone elsewhere, leaving an address in case any letters should come for her, but no letters had come. This last address took John Barnard across the river and through streets where dray horses slipped on greasy cobbles, to a cul-de-sac called Maund's Rents. As he knocked on the door he became aware that from other doorways, and from windows and from behind barrows and round corners, he was being closely examined by a number of seemingly uninterested people. Raising his eyes, he saw above the nearby roofs and chimneys a sombre mountain-top which was the dome of St. Paul's.

He knocked several times. When the door opened, it was Mutty who opened it. She looked at him without recognition and said in a feebly irritated voice, "Oh, I thought you were Leadbitter's."

"I am Mr. Barnard from Loseby."

She broke into a flood of tears.

104

She led him into a narrow entry, so dark that when she closed the door he could only just see her pale full-moon face, wagging on a rhythm of sobs. From below their feet, as from the pit of hell, came a level voice, reiterating, "Kindly reply to me, the Chief Elephant."

"He's been going on like that all day, my poor Tom. I don't know what he thinks he is. He's raving, you know."

"But why is he down there, in a cellar?"

"Cellar, Mr. Barnard? We haven't come to that! It's a half-basement. Will you come down and see him? It's a shocking sight."

She opened a door, and he could dimly see a descending flight of stairs. The voice spoke again and was recognizably Thomas's, haughty and detached.

"Kindly reply to me, the Chief Elephant."

Halfway down the stairs she turned on him, barring the way, and said sharply, "You haven't come from Simon, have you?"

"No."

"Because I'd die before I had to do with him or anyone sent by him, after the way I've been served. I've got my pride, if I've got nothing else."

Dandling her grudge, she showed him into the wretched room as though it were a throne room, and the bits of washing dangling on a line stretched across it, banners and trophies. Thomas was huddled on the bed, sitting with his knees drawn up and his arms clasping his shins. When John Barnard tried to pull the blanket over him he struck out violently, but there was no change in his voice as he repeated, "Kindly reply to me, the Chief Elephant."

"Oh, Mr. Barnard, what a mercy I opened the door to you! I'd be ashamed for you to have seen the other people in this house—the lowest of the low. And very likely I wouldn't have if I hadn't been expecting the boy with the medicine. I took the bottle to be refilled this morning, and the chemist said his boy would step round with it, knowing my difficulties. I must say,

105

London people are very obliging, though I daresay it's only skin-deep. Not that it seems to do him any good. But I never expected to see you, Mr. Barnard, though I'm sure I'm very glad to. I suppose you know all about it—what happened at the Terrace. I never thought I'd be turned away, with not so much as a thank-you-kindly, after all those years and nursing Thomas through I don't know how many illnesses. And here I am, nursing him again," she added with a sigh.

If John Barnard had not been a parental employer and accustomed to the self-righteousness of the poor in their affliction, he would have felt only scorn for Mutty. But he heard the sigh as well as the silliness. Polishing her injury and rancour as though they were the only remnants of respectability that had not gone to the pawnshop, she had continued to nurse and clean and cook and wash, and even brush her hair and have on clean stockings, and if she looked without horror and even without interest at the sick man, it was because for days on end she had seen nothing else. Her devotion was a true devotion. It was also true that rather than sacrifice her vaunt of injury and write to his father for help, she would have let the young man die; but this, since he had come to take a father's place, did not affect John Barnard's commendations, and when he hurried away to find a doctor and a nurse he left her under the impression that it was entirely to her credit that the patient she had nursed so devotedly was to be taken out of her hands as soon as possible.

"I suppose he's a copying clerk, this friend of yours," said Dr. McBride, looking at Thomas's right hand (he had diagnosed the new Russian influenza, adding without mercy that it had been aggravated by total mismanagement). "Poor fellow, I'd think more of his chances if he had a dozen calluses, instead of this single one."

"I'm sure no one could work harder than Thomas!" exclaimed Mutty.

"Exactly, madam. You take the words out of my mouth. If

he'd come off a boat and spent a week ashore getting drunk and watching cockfights, he'd be in better trim for this sort of thing. I don't say he won't get through it. I daresay he will. But he'll be so hipped for months afterwards that he'll wish with all his heart he hadn't."

Somewhat against his own consent, John Barnard formed a high opinion of Dr. McBride, even when he said in the privacy of the doorway, "Don't be taken aback by the nurse I'm sending. She's no better than she should be, but to my mind a loose woman who keeps off the bottle is the best nurse for a young man. She knows the ropes, d'you see, and respectable women don't. Call her Mrs. Larker, and keep the old cat away from her. I'll send you a sedative for *her,* knock her out for a couple of days."

Nursed by Bell Larker, and protected by John Barnard, who took Mutty to see the Tower of London, the West India Docks, the new cemetery at Kensal Green, and Wesley's Tabernacle, Thomas recovered. Staring alternately at an immeasurably remote ceiling (he had been moved into better lodgings) and at Bell Larker's mermaid countenance, he knew for a brief time complete happiness; for everything familiar had disappeared, and what replaced it was no responsibility of his. A headache boomed on inside his skull like sea waves booming in a cavern; but it was not his headache, and his head rested on a cool pillow, and the oval face bent over him, and the sea-green eyes gazed at him as though he were a newly opened flower. The bed still rose and fell, but the storm was over, and this time there were no fish in the boat, and instead of Mr. Mobbs calling his attention to the dying skate, a soft voice said, "There you are, now, my darling boy," in the tender brogue that Bell kept for best occasions. Later, when he knew himself again, and his remembered circumstances closed in on him, and he was well enough for Bell to go away, he despaired. She cast her arms about him and held him to her bosom, rocking him in a condoling embrace and murmuring, "I'd go through

107

the world with you, I would. It's a shame to part us, and that it is," while her tearless eyes glanced about the room for any belongings she might have overlooked.

She went away, the only person in the world who had ever loved him, and he was left to the intolerable mercies of Mutty and Mr. Barnard.

People do not return from the gate of death with much sense of obligation. Mutty's devotion, Mutty's thankfulness over his recovery, irked him like the itch. Three and four times a day he would provoke her (she did not need much provocation) into describing all she had felt and all she had done during his illness, because at the close she was certain to say, "But I wouldn't give in, my dear, not even at the worst. I never let myself think you would die. For what would have become of me then?" Recertified of her artless baseness, he would thank her for all she had done. As it was not so easy to discover a vile motive for Mr. Barnard's share in his recovery, he was reduced to taking it for granted: Mr. Barnard had somehow got to Maund's Rents; having got there, he became very assiduous and obliging and paid for everything. Once he mentioned that he was in London on a matter of business. It did not seem very pressing, and he had an air of containing a private satisfaction. Perhaps he kept a woman, a St. John's Wood songstress, and came to mate in spring. His hat would remain as black wherever he took it, an atrabilious hat.

After all, Mutty had not sold Thomas's books, though through a slit in his delirium he had seen her making a parcel of them. They had been brought to the new lodging in a pillowslip, forgotten during the joy of his recovery, remembered as a last talisman against his ill humour after Bell's departure. He could not read without a headache, but he could wander from page to page and shelter himself as in some old enchanted forest. And when Mr. Barnard came—for he still came daily with fruit or wine, or turtle soup from the pastry-

108

cook's, or amusing anecdotes of perfect propriety—his invalid was usually behind a folio, looking as uncomfortable as people do who read in bed.

"You will tire your eyes with such bad print. Pray let me read aloud to you. Where shall I begin?"

With languid malice Thomas gave over *The Anatomy of Melancholy.*

> *"Another thinks he is a nightingale, and therefore sings all night long; another, he is all glass, a pitcher, and will therefore let nobody come near him, and such a one Laurentius gives out, upon his credit, that he knew in France. Christopherus à Vega, cap. 3, lib. 14, Schenkius, and Marcellus Donatus, 1.2, cap. 1, have many such examples, and one amongst the rest of a Baker in Ferrara, that thought he was composed of butter, and durst not sit in the sun, or come near a fire, for fear of being melted; of another, that thought he was a case of leather, stuffed with wind."*

It would have been hard to find a voice better tuned to Burton than Mr. Barnard's—sombrely didactic, earnest, and unamused. Thomas's "Thank you" was for once spontaneous and without reservations, and he said to himself that on the morrow's visit (he was sure of their daily recurrence) he would get the Grand Turk to read again.

But on the morrow, having got Mutty out of the room, Mr. Barnard introduced a topic of his own—"a scheme which I have been considering for some little time."

It was the scheme which he had come to London to effect: that Thomas should become the London agent of Barnard and Son. He had found premises in Tooley Street that would do very well. There was a furnished second floor over an office where Thomas could live rent-free, and the rest of the house was used for storage by a firm of linen drapers. "I have been over it. It is a very tolerable house; I could find no trace of

109

damp in it. Living over your office, you would not need to go out in bad weather. London Bridge is always an entertaining spectacle."

He pressed his suit like a lover, and Thomas thought, I shall never get away from Mutty unless I drown her in the Thames.

"But sir, I know nothing of business, I should have no notion how to behave as an agent. If I try to drive a bargain, I always get the worst of it."

From anyone but Thomas, this sentence would have called out a lecture on commercial probity. "On the contrary. You have every qualification I could wish for, except knowledge of the subject. Naturally I have taken that into consideration, for I did not suppose that you are acquainted with the niceties of trading with the Baltic."

"I don't even know its elements."

"I daresay not. But I do not forget that morning last September when I had the pleasure of telling you something of the business. You showed an uncommon penetration, I remember. It struck me at the time."

Thomas remembered a sense of intolerable tedium, and enjoying the coffee and hot rolls.

"Commerce is not so difficult as people make out," said John Barnard. "Besides, as an agent you would not be called on to make any large decisions. Method and fair dealing should come easily to any educated man. You will soon master the rest."

Thomas shook his head. "I am sure I could not manage it."

John Barnard said, smiling a little, "In my opinion, a person who can teach the Latin grammar to a class of twenty boys can do anything."

"I found that easier than making five hundred copies of a letter about the Hottentots."

The bitter languor of the words halted John Barnard in the full flow of his benevolence. "God forbid you should come to that again! But I won't press you about my scheme. It is too early for anything to be thought of except your recovery."

"Here's Mutty," said Thomas, and was almost glad to be saying it. "I hope you won't speak of it to her."

"I shall not."

As if to flee temptation, he went away immediately.

But on the next day he began again, for during the night a further improvement to his plan had occurred to him, and he could not keep it to himself. To complete Thomas's recovery, he announced, a change of air must be taken. Sea air would be best, and the air at Loseby was exceptionally bracing. As Thomas was a good sailor, it would be least fatiguing for him to come as far as Yarmouth by boat.

"I doubt if my father would welcome me to Prospect Terrace, and I know I should dislike going there."

"Out of the question! I would not hear of it. You must come to Anchor House."

The recollection of the family scene before dinner came so livingly back to Thomas that he felt it buzz against his ears. He flinched.

"Would that displease you?"

"No, no! It is very kind of you to suggest it. But—"

"I make it a rule never to meddle in other people's affairs, or to listen to gossip," continued John Barnard, hurrying on to deliver his master-stroke of management, "but from things Miss Mutley has let fall, I cannot but be aware that she feels resentment—I could say a justifiable resentment, but I do not choose to pass judgment—against your father. So much so, I gather, that she might refuse to have anything to do with him."

"Yes, that is it. That's what I was going to say. Mutty is the obstacle. Nothing would induce her to go to Loseby; and I cannot ask her to."

"Why should you?"

Dealing the master stroke, John Barnard brought out his proposal that Basil Cook, his second clerk, should be sent to manage the preliminaries of setting up the office in Tooley Street; and that, as Basil was an elderly bachelor, Miss Mutley could be asked to keep house for him. "And while you are at Anchor House, when you feel equal to it, you can learn something of the business. I think that settles all our difficulties."

He looks as pleased as a child putting the last breathless card on a house of cards, thought Thomas; he almost has the tip of his tongue between his teeth. There was nothing for it but to give in. Rushing incautiously down the Mutty alley, he was caught without an exit, unless he were to fight his way out, and he had not the spirit for that. Meanwhile, there would be a respite from Mutty. He would get into a ship and sail away from her. Merely to exchange earth for water would sift him free from his cares, as the trip on the *Mary Lucinda* had done. As for the post of agent, time would get him out of it. He had only to prove unteachable, and Mr. Barnard would thankfully wash his hands of him.

"Well, Thomas, what do you think of it?"

"I scarcely know how to express my gratitude."

In fact, what he felt was a reckless relief. There was no gratitude about it. He had grown up emotionally paupered, and gratitude was not possible to him.

2.

When Mutty had been shown over the second floor of the house in Tooley Street and given twenty pounds to lay out in making it more comfortable, John Barnard returned to Loseby. He had been away for nearly a month, but as he had ended every letter by saying he hoped to be back shortly (he did not wish his family to feel slighted by the attentions to Thomas Kettle) his absence had not been commensurately enjoyed. Euphemia even wished he were at home; whether or no he knew that poor Mamma was given to drink, he was a man and a head of a household, and qualified to manage if Mamma should suddenly begin to behave like the drunkards in tracts or the drunkards in Loseby. Papa, too, with his forthright

112

outlook on disagreeable necessities, would not have left her to suffer agonies of face-ache before deciding that she must go to the dentist in Norwich—though one of Julia's reasons for delaying was that Papa would not like to hear that Euphemia had bad teeth, he would think that she had been neglectful of them or had eaten too many sweet things. Papa was to be spared this cause for grief, for the dentist told Euphemia that she had not a flawed tooth in her head; though he consented to pull one out, he assured her that it would make no difference, since her face-ache was neuralgia. During the homeward drive she listened to Darwell's gloomy jubilations—Darwell had said it was tic douloureux all along—and on entering the house she learned that Mr. Debenham and his sister had paid a morning visit.

"And I had let you go to that wretched dentist!" lamented Julia. "I could have beaten myself. My poor girl, who gets so little pleasure! It was my first thought when they walked in." Euphemia's first thought was whether Mamma's breath had then smelled as strongly of rum as it did now.

Most of Euphemia's life had been spent in calculation; she was stupid with pain and fatigue; even so, she realized that this was a disgraceful calculation. It can't go on, she thought; I can't spend the rest of my life wondering if Marmaduke noticed Mamma's breath. Julia, responding as she always did to her dear Mr. Debenham, was elated and benign. Patting Euphemia's cold hands, she mingled with anxiety that Euphemia should go comfortably off to bed a determination to recount how concerned Mr. Debenham had been about the face-ache, how kindly he had talked to Wilberforce, and how he had undertaken to convey parcels to Joseph—for he was making another visit to Trinidad in May. As if it were a face in a picture, Euphemia considered her mother's face—the remains of a rather noble nose, the long cheeks sagging from the high cheekbones, the full lower lip that slightly trembled. An intention of goodwill showed through it, as an intention of nourishment still shows through a spoiled harvest.

113

"He expects to be home before the autumn. And he spoke of a visit to Rougham then. He seemed quite confident it could be managed. I'm sure you would be the better for a little soup."

Poor Mamma, who must lose one of the few things she enjoyed! But Euphemia had made her decision. This tooth, at any rate, should come out. Some hours later she lit her bedroom candle and wrote a letter, saying briefly that she had changed her mind and must be freed from her promise.

There had always been a tincture of philanthropy in Marmaduke's love. Now he was even more convinced how essential it was to his happiness to marry Euphemia, if only to get her away from her father and take her to a London dentist. When John Barnard came home he found a letter from Marmaduke Debenham, formally requesting permission to offer marriage to his daughter. Before he knew what he was about, his hand crumpled up the letter and thrust it away. Shaking with rage, he compelled himself to sit quietly at his desk, and to open and read the other letters waiting for him—a letter from a co-trustee, a letter telling him of the death of an old pensioner, a letter soliciting his interest for a charity, a letter from a clergyman at Grimsby about a Loseby fisherman who had met with an accident there. He read, and perfectly understood what he was reading, and made notes of what the answers should be. All the while he was shaking with impatience to answer the letter from Marmaduke Debenham. Even so, he delayed to cut his quill pen to a finer point and to brush away a few grains of sand that had fallen from the pouncebox.

Dear Sir,

I have received your letter of April 10th.

The disparity in station between a merchant's daughter and a member of the landed gentry is such that I am unable to sanction your proposal.

I am, Sir,

your humble servant,

He signed his name and drew a deep breath, as though he had averted some imminent danger. Thank God she was untouched! When Julia mentioned the Debenhams' visit, artfully —he feared it was artfully—regretting that it had coincided with Euphemia's visit to the dentist, he had looked closely at Mary. She met his glance with perfect composure; there was no waver of colour, no blink of the candid blue eyes; indeed, if anything, she looked as if she had disliked the visit.

Calmly, or by comparison calmly, he could now take up the crumpled letter and read it through once more. Reading it through, he saw that the words ran: "your daughter Euphemia."

Euphemia! It was astonishing.

The mistake had been a natural one, a mistake that any man, not only Mary's father, might make. There was no slight to Euphemia in such a misapprehension. Euphemia herself— for, to do her justice, she was remarkably free from envy— would think it a very natural mistake. Yet a feeling molested him that it had been a reprehensible mistake, and that in some way he must atone for it. The mistake arose, as he now saw, from his own hasty temper. If he had exercised greater self-control and read the letter calmly through to its end, he would have seen that the name was Euphemia; his indignation would have broken out in its proper place, a sober and right-minded indignation. For of course he would have been just as indignant on Euphemia's behalf as on Mary's. He *was* as indignant, though the impetuosity could not be repeated, any more than one can call back the lightning flash for a second performance. Mary had come first to his mind; there was nothing shocking in that, even the patriarchs had preferences, and Jacob undoubtedly would have thought of Rachel before thinking of Leah. But Euphemia was also dear to him, he valued her much too highly to think of giving her over to Marmaduke Debenham. He need not even alter the letter of refusal; it named no name. Euphemia was equally the daughter of a mer-

115

chant, she had an equal claim to be preserved from the miserable fate of marrying out of her station, from relations-in-law who would sneer at her and a husband who would tire of her. He hoped her feelings had not been engaged. But even if her head had been a little turned, she was to be pitied rather than blamed. Having saved her from a lifetime of misery, he could feel nothing but tenderness for her now. Everything possible must be done to make her feel the blessings of home, and if the face-ache persisted he would take her to a different dentist.

The accessories to the change of air which was to do so much for Thomas Kettle were falling short of John Barnard's intentions. Simon and Sophie Kettle would not be smarting under a notice to quit Number 5 Prospect Terrace, for he had forgotten to give the notice by Lady Day, and Basil Cook flatly refused to be looked after by Miss Mutley. Basil was prepared to go to London and work in the Tooley Street office, but wild horses would not get him up onto the second floor. Mutty, meanwhile, had moved in and experienced a change of heart. Elated by Mr. Barnard's patronage of Thomas, delighted with her new quarters, she was wild to return to Loseby and triumph over Simon and Sophie. Not to tell Sophie about the carpet she had bought, the Dutch oven and the two large vases (it would be a long day before Sophie would get so much as a mat or a Staffordshire spaniel out of Simon) blighted her pleasure in them. The news that Mr. Cook intended to lodge with a niece in Peckham Rye was a lever put into her hand. She refused to be left solitary in that fearful place, Tooley Street, thinking night and day of the thieves who would break in after the vases. "I cannot leave her alone if she feels like this. I am now well enough to find employment, and I shall do so." So wrote Thomas, leaping at the pretext. Except as an escape from Mutty, he had never wished to visit Anchor House. There would be meetings with his father, or avoidances of them; there would be further exhibitions of Mr. Barnard in the bosom of his family; and there would be explanations of the Baltic trade, the smell of tallow, and systems of bookkeeping. It was too high a price to pay, even for escaping from Mutty. Thomas was in that state of hypochondria which Dr. McBride had forecast; he would rather endure the ills he had than experiment with new ones; besides, he had hopes of a walk-on part at the Surrey Theatre.

John Barnard folded up Thomas's letter. The blood mounted into his forehead; he looked at his watch. Seeing these danger signals, his family fell silent and devoted themselves to breakfasting as the most inoffensive thing they could do. Can they do nothing but stuff themselves? he thought—munching like cattle, their glances straying from toast racks to jelly pots, and not a syllable of rational talk among them. He would not speak of his disappointment; whether or no Thomas Kettle came would mean nothing to them except whether or no there would be an extra mouth at mealtimes. Mary was the only one who would share his disappointment, and at this moment Mary was exceeding with the marmalade.

"I do not know how much longer you all propose to guzzle. For myself, I have finished and have other things to think about."

He went off to his office, to its galling satisfactoriness; for it was the Lord's will that while his family life was full of crosses and vexations, the family business throve and mocked him with material prosperity. Now the Lord had mysteriously prepared another frustration for him, and all his hopes and plans for Thomas Kettle's welfare had gone awry. The young man's health was precarious, his constitution unsound; this miscarriage of the visit to Loseby might very well be the end of him. Mingled with thoughts of the young man's constitution came an unavoidable admission that the young man's heart was also faulty, that he lacked gratitude and even good manners; for the letter contained no more than a brief regret at not visiting, and no mention at all of the agency.

But among the business letters at the office was one in a very curly handwriting, marked *Urgent! Private!* and bearing every mark of having been sealed up in great haste by someone in a toss of emotion. It was from Mutty. She did not wish to alarm her dear kind Mr. Barnard, but she must tell him that Thomas's health was giving her the greatest anxiety, and now the dear unselfish boy actually proposed to stay in London rather than leave her alone on the second floor, which was, thanks to Mr. Barnard's generosity, so handsome and comfortable that it was indeed very strange of Mr. Cook to prefer his niece. But rather than this she would sacrifice her own feelings and come to Loseby, for Thomas's health was more to her than anything else in the world, while as for certain people in Prospect Terrace, she had nothing to be ashamed of and was prepared to meet them as calmly as they deserved, which was why she was taking the liberty to address Mr. Barnard at his office; she was sure he would understand her motives.

He was quite unable to understand why she should not write to him at Anchor House, but the gist of the letter was clear. The Lord had taken away with one hand and restored with the other. Beneath these seeming vacillations, the Lord's purpose was plain enough. The Lord had seen that John Barnard's wish to have Thomas at Anchor House contained an element of self-seeking; so, though the wish was to be granted, a little chastening had been thrown in. Thomas was coming to Loseby, and Mutty would come too. Julia would not be pleased. No earthly satisfaction can be perfect. When he went home he would tell Julia that Mutty was to be included in the visit, and, that done, he would renew his efforts to be particularly kind to Euphemia.

But a person suffering from neuralgia is an unrewarding subject for kindness. When he had said, "How have you been today, my dear?" and Euphemia had replied, "Just about the same, thank you," and Julia had amplified this into "I really don't know how she endured this afternoon. Any sudden noise goes through her head, and first there was a dogfight, and then Sally contrived to throw down all the dish-covers," there seemed little more to say, and the topic of Mutty was left in abeyance, since Julia's comments would undoubtedly fall into the category of sudden noises. It was hard to keep any cheerful conversation going during dinner. Julia was offended with a soup, Euphemia was speechless, he himself felt jaded and oppressed. Left alone with his wine, he was tempted not to go into the drawing room at all. But presently he heard Mary singing. Where there is music, pleasure reigns, and conversation need not be kept up. He finished his glass and joined them.

Euphemia was not there. She had gone to bed. "And I don't wonder," remarked Julia, in whom the soup still rankled. "Mary almost gives me a headache too when she sings with so much expression. I'm afraid there's nothing for it but another dentist. I believe there is an excellent man in King's Lynn."

"Perhaps a change of air—" he began, and was interrupted by Mary.

"Yes! Papa is right. Dear, dear Papa, you are so kind. Please let poor Euphemia go away for a change of air. She suffers so much, you know."

"With young Mr. Kettle coming, I do not see how I can spare her."

Julia addressed her husband, but Mary answered. "Mamma, I'm sure you can spare her. She's in such pain, she's really very little use to you. And there's nothing she does that I cannot do just as well."

Julia did not choose to say that Mary could not chaperon Mary, so she was silent. Because it was a pleasure to be persuaded, John Barnard hummed and hawed, but his heart had already yielded. It refreshed his heart to see Mary's sisterly concern. Not only was she ready to undertake all Euphemia's duties, she was the first to suggest where the change of air should be had. There could not be a more decisive change of air than to move inland from the coast, and Norwich was so nicely within reach that the journey could not possibly be tiring. The next morning Euphemia learned that everything was agreed on; she was to try a change of air, and Papa had already written to the Miss Binghams. The Miss Binghams were devoted to John Barnard, who, as their father's executor, had disentangled them from acting as unpaid servants to a bullying and fertile sister-in-law and settled them in a small house consolingly near the Close. Euphemia went to them thankfully, knowing that she could be sure of kindness and a decent assignation. Pencilled on the title page of an arithmetic primer which Leonora Debenham had found so useful in the Rougham school that she was sending Euphemia a copy were the words: "He has sailed; but I must and will see you. Where? When?" And though the meeting would certainly be disagreeable, it must be gone through with.

Two days after the carriage had taken Euphemia to Norwich it took John Barnard to meet his guests. After a stand of declaring that Mutty could go if she wished, but that he would not go with her, Thomas lost interest in his firmness of purpose and gave in. They went by boat from Tilbury, and Mutty was sick all the way. Revived by sea air and his own company, Thomas reached Yarmouth in a state of expecting to enjoy himself whenever he could contrive to stow away on the *Mary Lucinda*. "I must call on that good fellow, Mobbs," he said to his host, and his host thought even better of him for being so unaffected and warmhearted. It was a fine May day. As they drove northward by the coast road, views of the sea were often before their eyes, and the sails of the windmills twirled easily on a light sea breeze. "Norfolk is not picturesque," said John Barnard, trying to hide his affection for his native county, "but considering how much of it is flat, it has a great deal of variety." He was as nearly happy as it was possible for him to be, and his happiness extended to feeling hungry and looking forward to the lobsters. "You will find us a small party; only Mary and

120

Wilberforce are at home." That, though it was not in his power to know it, was one reason for his cheerfulness. Euphemia's absence made him feel younger.

3.

When John Barnard built Prospect Terrace he did it to provide work in a time of distress; he had no particular view as to what tenants would live in his new houses, except that they should lead reputable lives, pay their rents, and not be Roman Catholics. Presumably they would be people of the locality—retired merchants from Norwich, and so forth; for who else would wish to settle in Loseby? But as it turned out, his terrace became a settlement of aliens. The bad times had shaken loose a number of people of gentility from the home counties, who emigrated to cheaper parts of England. Loseby had sea air, and in some way its tonic qualities had become superior to the sea air of Brighton or Hove. "Of course there is *no* society. But the air is so exceptionally pure . . ." "As for amenities, one might as well be in Kamchatka, but I am prepared to sacrifice anything to Edward's chest." Such sentences, written in the bow-windowed parlours, with perhaps a light reference to really fresh crabs at threepence each, went outwards from Prospect Terrace and attracted fresh immigrants—so much so that Prospect Terrace developed its own colony of improved cottages, and a second terrace of run-up houses with no prospect and larger bow windows was built by a speculative person from North Walsham.

Where there is no society, a society forms itself out of those who feel its absence. The people of the Terraces were on intimate terms with one another and united in looking down on the townspeople. The clique was so exclusive and genteel that Mr. Kettle, actually in trade and coming from Hull, had to work quite hard to establish himself on the true Terrace footing. It was not until Mutty had been got off the scene that his anecdotes became amusing, his knowledge of the world extensive, his heart benevolent, and Mrs. Kettle, who was so stained with Loseby that she had actually gained a livelihood there, could be seen with new eyes as a native of the Channel Islands, whose shawls were draped with the taste of a Parisian, though over a Protestant and British heart. "A perfectly matched couple. Quite a romance," Prospect Terrace said, watching Mr. and Mrs. Kettle planting double daisies with their own hands in the back garden of Number 5. The match statement was true. As the bit of glass and the foil backing it make up between them a tolerable representation of a gem, Sophie and Simon made up a very fair representation of a happy marriage. His sham benevolence had quite a convincing glow, seen through her desire to please; her prudence gave a respectable glazing to his meanness; and his total selfishness fortified her ambition to make a good show in the world.

The news that Thomas had arrived on a visit to the Barnards reached Number 5 with a pint of fresh-boiled shrimps ordered from Mr. Mobbs and brought up by the boy called Crusoe. Hearing Crusoe at the door, Sophie hurried out to defend the cook's virtue—for Milly was imported from inland and not accustomed to young villains like Crusoe.

"These shrimps do not look so good as yesterday's. Are you sure, boy, that they are the best of the catch? Mr. Kettle eats only the best shrimps."

"Do he? That's right, then. He's a-eating of them now at Barnard's. That's Thomas, I mean." Crusoe turned to Milly. "Young gentleman, this one's son. Handsome as a picture, he is. Live in hope, Milly. He only got to Loseby yesterday, so he may come up here yet to see his old daddy. Like a nice live cod, ma'am?"

"No! And take away the shrimps."

"No shrimps?" said Simon, coming down for breakfast five minutes later. "No shrimps, my pussy-cat?"

122

"I had to refuse them. Do you know Thomas is staying with the Barnards? Actually under their roof?"

"Who told you so?"

"The boy who brought the shrimps."

"Very awkward! Very vexatious! Thomas never considers how such behaviour must distress me. I wish you had not sent away the shrimps."

"Young Bullen was impertinent. Mr. Kettle, will it not look very bad that Thomas should come to Loseby and not to us? Will it not look to people as though he intended to insult me?"

"I cannot harbour resentment. After breakfast I will go out and welcome the boy. Are there any potted anchovies?"

Breakfast was still on the table when Mutty walked in.

Simon had so confidently expected Mutty to harbour resentment that her reappearance momentarily disconcerted him. But, realizing that she had come to triumph, he listened graciously to the large vases, Mr. Barnard's confidence, Miss Mary's pretty welcome, the finest warming pan she had ever set eyes on, Mr. Barnard's consideration of her feelings, hothouse grapes, a wonderful folding washstand, beef tea, and the lions in the Tower; for a triumphant Mutty allayed his worst alarms, she would not be a liability to him. Thomas also, it appeared, was chargeable to Mr. Barnard; though he had turned up again like a bad penny, he was in another man's pocket. "Thankful indeed!" he could exclaim with the accents of truth. "This is truly gratifying." He was keeping afloat by such comments when the torrent of Mutty's narrative swirled in a backward serpentine to Thomas at death's door, cats yowling like foghorns, all alone with the cockroaches, the damp running down the walls, no one to turn to, an elephant, and Mr. Barnard saying, "Scandalous!" After one more "Thankful indeed!" Simon wriggled uneasily during the remainder of her story, blazing with Mr. Barnard. It was an awkward thing to have happened, the more so since it found him unprepared, breakfast not finished, and with no premeditation on his part.

123

But he did not see the whole extent of his condemnation till he happened to look at Sophie. For selfishness, if perfectly pursued, leads, like any other vocation, to unworldliness. Simon had heard Mutty's story with only personal qualms. Sophie had heard it as it would resound in the ears of Terrace society, and was aghast.

He misread her taut lips and her eyes dwindled to pinpoints. He supposed that she too, being a woman, would take up the cudgels on a young man's behalf. And after Mutty had gone he said, placatingly, the worst possible thing. "It seems that Master Thomas has done pretty well for himself by his influenza."

"He's done very badly for *us!* He and your sister-in-law— how dared they let things come to such a pass without letting you know? It must have been deliberate malice."

"Oh, I hope not deliberate! Thomas has often wounded me, cut me to the heart by his coldness and neglect. But it is the carelessness of youth. One must make allowances."

It was only by a great effort of falsification that Sophie held back her fury from leaping on its proper quarry—her husband, whose gross mismanagement had provoked the calamity. Staring at the chair still dinted by Mutty, she said, "In your sister-in-law's case it can scarcely be the carelessness of youth, can it?"

He glanced towards the previous Mrs. Kettles, unhelpfully smirking on either side of the clock. Neither of those dear wives had been schoolmistresses or widows or ladies hardened by independence. Still, this Mrs. Kettle was also a wife, and part of a wife's function is to bear responsibility.

"I expect you are right, my dear. Mutty was always spiteful, no doubt she has been nursing resentment against you. I was afraid that something of this sort would come of it. Old maids don't like finding themselves supplanted, you know. I think I warned you at the time. But it will all blow over."

"Blow over? With Mutty and Thomas established at Anchor House, telling everyone how you left them to starve, how they would have gone to the workhouse if Mr. Barnard had not

124

taken pity on them? Blow over! They only arrived yesterday, but the boy who brought the shrimps knew all about it and spoke to me as I have never been spoken to in my life. We shall be left without a shred of reputation to cover us. We shall be hooted at in the streets."

"Oh dear no, I hope not. People don't take a quarrel between ladies quite so seriously as that, and Barnard cannot say very much. He is in a weak position; his wife drinks. Still, it is a pity, a sad pity! That unhappy business with the key of the tea caddy, that was where the mischief began. I foresaw it. I am not a cynic, but I foresaw it."

"Did you foresee that they would turn up again at Anchor House?"

"Something of the sort. Persecutions. Misrepresentations. I am accustomed to such. You must become so too. The wife of a man who lives according to his conscience must be prepared for slander and false witness. 'Here ye shall have tribulation,' you know."

"I did not marry in order to have tribulation," said Sophie menacingly.

"Hush, my dear! Those words are scriptural. Our blessed Saviour spoke them."

"Neither did I marry to be hushed at. And it's no use trying to lay the blame on me, Mr. Kettle. If you had consulted me at the time, instead of being in such a hurry to get rid of her, I could have warned you not to send Mutty off with no money at all. Quite a small sum would have been enough to stop her mouth, and, managed with economy, it would have been enough to keep Thomas out of that cellar where Mr. Barnard must needs go and find him. Besides, they'd have written fast enough if they'd thought they could get more. Anyone would suppose you had no knowledge of the world."

"I fear they would be right. Knowledge of the heart—I hope I have something of that. But I have never laid claim to knowledge of the world."

"And what do you intend to do now, pray? What does your knowledge of the heart dictate?"

"I shall visit Thomas this afternoon. He may bear resentment. I do not. Loseby shall see that I do not."

"Well, I do."

"And why shouldn't you, my love? What more natural than that a wife should bear resentment on her husband's behalf? Feel it—express it, if you wish. I shall not blame you."

She looked out of her fury as a drowning man might look at a rope thrown towards him.

"Yes, yes," continued Simon. "Express your resentment by all means. Better so, much better so. Be open, my dear, be perfectly open. You know that hypocrisy is odious to me. No one will think the worse of you if you show resentment on my behalf. On the contrary, they will approve. They will see you behaving like a good wife, while they see me behaving like an affectionate father."

Throughout this speech he had been patting the air as though smoothing something into shape; now, as though the process were complete, the invisible object patted into perfect symmetry, he laid his hand restfully on his thigh.

"I see," she said.

"I thought you would," he replied.

Mr. Kettle took his first step that same afternoon by going to call at Anchor House. But it was a fine afternoon and they had all gone out, Mr. Barnard and Thomas on horseback, the ladies and Wilberforce in the carriage.

"There, I could have told you so," exclaimed Mutty on hearing of her brother-in-law's call. "I knew he'd come fawning." And she tossed her head, and the feathers on her new bonnet appeared to be pawing the air.

Sophie spent the afternoon at home. The Terrace had seen her in the garden, intently wielding a small green watering pot. The weather continued fine, and during the next few days Sophie was embowered in horticulture, tying up creepers, sup-

126

porting pinks, and wearing a little apron with pockets. Sometimes Mr. Kettle was with her, sometimes she was alone.

It was one of the occasions when she was alone, busy as Eve, that Mrs. Lovell of Number 4 spoke in a neighbourly way across the dividing hedge. "Still busy, Mrs. Kettle? You seem to find your garden a great resource."

"I do," replied Eve in tones of candour. "And I do not care to go out just now. There are people I am very unwilling to meet."

"How deliciously your sweetbriar smells this evening," said Mrs. Lovell and went off to spread the news of Mrs. Kettle's high-minded sentiments.

Sophie was pleased to find that she, as the loyally indignant wife, was making better headway than Simon in his role of magnanimous father. Though he had twice got into Anchor House, the first time he found nothing but Julia—as uncomfortable a visit as though he had paid it to a she-bear moodily dozing away the hours before its next meal—and the second time he blundered into a party of Loseby's young persons, who were absorbed in an archery match. These circumstances made it impossible for him to forgive Thomas with any degree of being attended to. He snatched a few sandwiches and came away.

Canon Blunt, paying a call on Mrs. Kettle, whom he had not seen about lately, commented on the festivities at Anchor House. "Your stepson seems to have wrought quite a transformation there. Excursions, archery, rambles along the beach—and Mrs. Barnard everything that is hospitable. I hope it will not be too much for her—hospitality is always a strain for the lady of the house. I daresay you are not sorry to be spared that sort of thing. But perhaps your turn will come later?"

"I think not."

"Will they be staying long?"

"I have no idea."

This was regrettably true. Sophie and Simon were at a disadvantage in not knowing how much longer Thomas was to stay at Anchor House. If they timed their campaign for a fort-night and he stayed for a month, it would look as though their strategy had petered out. If, on the other hand, he left sooner than they expected, he would leave them with some of their best ammunition unexpended. Sophie—a woman, and the more socially sensitive animal—had engaged much more heart and soul in the campaign than Simon, who would not have minded very much if the whole Terrace clique were to ostracize him. His wishes were moderate: he wished to damage and discredit his son if it could be done without much trouble or any ex-pense. Loseby, except as containing the butcher, the fishmon-ger, the grocer, the dairyman, and the living pulpit, meant little to him. Loseby meant a great deal to Sophie. It had seen her rise in the world, and she did not want it to see her fall. It was now a fortnight since Thomas's arrival, and, reckoning up her gains, she could count nine reliable gossips to whom she had imparted her feelings. Suppose they had spread the news into as many bosoms apiece; that would be eighty-one persons; but in their gossip they would certainly overlap—the number of informed bosoms must be estimated at, say, forty. Not all of these would be convinced. Halve it once more—twenty con-vinced believers. On the analogy of the Cities of the Plain, that should be amply sufficient. But Loseby was not like those cities, and there was evidence that the convinced be-lievers were losing faith or losing interest. Mrs. Firth at Num-ber 7 had not invited her to see the completion of a beaded footstool, though it owed several forget-me-nots and a whole passion flower to her cooperation. As for the garden, it had been so intensively cared for that now only a locust could find occupation in it. She must have information as to the enemy's movements, and the best way to get it was from the heart of the enemy citadel, from Mutty, whom she would ask to spend an afternoon with her.

But Mutty wrote that on the afternoon in question she would be engaged. Mrs. Barnard was taking her in the carriage to

Norwich to fetch home Miss Euphemia. That such a reply had been written had cost Thomas a struggle.

After her first week at Anchor House, Mutty began to feel those pangs of resentment which are peculiar to people with base natures and pure hearts. Her heart told her that no one at Anchor House really wanted her there, and that the kindness and polite attention she received were paid to a standard of good manners and not her. Her base nature seethed with a desire to tell someone or other that it was useless for the Barnards to try and pull wool over her eyes, for she was not taken in by their soft speeches. Sophie's invitation had come like a godsend: a whole afternoon away from the constraint of Anchor House, a listener to whom she could recount her injuries—that ineffable affront of being made welcome where you are not wanted—and an opportunity to reclothe herself in self-respect as a person who suffers flattery and is not taken in by it. But Thomas forbade her to go. She had held out against his persuasions and against his reasons; it was not till he lost his temper and said nothing that she gave in. When his face grew white and his nose grew peaked the look of his illness came back, and she feared him.

So Mutty was driven to Norwich, and Thomas went out in the *Mary Lucinda*. If it had not been for the friends he had made among the fishermen, he could not have endured his stay at Anchor House, with Mutty flustering after him like a feather bed in a nightmare, and Mr. Barnard only one degree less pursuing than Mutty, and Mary Barnard only one degree less pursuing than her father. The girl was pretty, lively, and engaging. But she had been spoiled; she had no notion how to behave herself, and what had first touched him as artless goodwill now alarmed him as artless infatuation. It wounded his pride to be so straightforwardly and fearlessly pursued—as though he were no more dangerous than a kitten. As an admirer, Mary was not to be compared with Crusoe, whose blue eyes flowered in a sunburned face, whose husky voice expressed an abstract, unpossessive adoration, and that only at long reposeful intervals. Thank God for low life! thought Thomas, stepping into his seaborne island where Miss Mary Barnard was no more than a legend of blue paint on the bows.

If Mutty has gone with Julia, then Thomas will have been packed off somewhere, thought Sophie, tying up a bunch of lilies of the valley. It was as she hoped. Mary was alone, a drawing-room Cinderella, when Sophie was shown in. The lilies of the valley, affecting pretext for the visit, were coolly received.

"You should not have picked yours," said Miss. "We have plenty, you know. I am quite tired of gathering them."

It was obvious that Miss had pleasant anticipations of how to be impertinent to the former Madame Bon, who had been her schoolmistress. But conversation on equal terms with Mrs. Kettle, as between two charming women of the world, was a more beguiling novelty. There is a give-and-take in all traffic between deluder and deluded; a wistful woolliness invades the fox while it is teaching the lamb to grow a little bolder. Sophie Kettle laughed more genuinely than she had laughed for years as she drew out Mary's opinion of Crawley Blunt, that sullen suitor. She cast off the layers of Bon and Kettle and was Sophie Tizard again, skipping down the country dance of "The Triumph." Mary's observations on life delighted her, they were so fresh and original; and what could be dewier than her heresies?

"My dear child, I suppose I ought to scold you, but, quite between ourselves, I am inclined to agree with you," said she, learning that Mary had come to the conclusion that if Abraham were not in the Old Testament one might think him a rather horrid old man. To see Mr. Barnard's upper lip imprisoned between those plump pink cheeks and neighboured by a dimple was in itself an entertainment, and when, after a sufficient half-hour of lamblike sporting, she rose up to depart, she had enjoyed herself a great deal, as well as getting the information that as yet no date had been fixed for the end of Thomas's visit.

130

"And give my love to Euphemia. How glad you will be to have her company again! But be careful, Mary. Do not let her take away Mr. Kettle—your Mr. Kettle. Elder sisters have been known to do that kind of thing, you know."

For nothing is better calculated to make a young girl behave badly than jealousy of a sister who has no claims to good looks. If Miss could be urged on from philandering into fireworks, Mr. Barnard would soon see what sort of young man he had taken into his home. And that would be the end of Thomas at Anchor House.

Euphemia had spent a month in Norwich. Her hostesses could not do enough for their dear Mr. Barnard's daughter; their kindness and hospitality enveloped her in a downy dullness, like a cocoon. After a week her neuralgia went away, at the end of a fortnight she remembered her father's leave-taking present and bought herself new clothes. At the close of the visit she stepped into the carriage looking almost as peaceful as the nuns Julia had seen in Paris. Like them, Euphemia had made her renunciation. The meeting with Leonora had taken place. Leonora, who had arrived in a state of exalted loyalty, determined to secure a sister-in-law whom only Marmaduke could find desirable, went back knowing that Euphemia was unobtainable, and wholeheartedly regretting it.

As her own stay with the Miss Binghams had lasted a month, Euphemia could not in decency ask how much longer Thomas Kettle would remain at Anchor House. But it was impossible not to compare his lot with hers. She as a guest had been happy and easy; he plainly was neither. The Euphemia who had sheltered Joseph and rubbed Julius began to extend a watchful protectiveness over Thomas, as though he were another of John Barnard's children. She found occupations for him when he looked bored. She arranged exits for him when he looked frantic. She disentangled him from her father's attentions—though these were kinder than he deserved; for it was as though Thomas were another Mary and could do no

131

wrong. Mary had never seemed to find Papa's approval op-
pressive, but Mary had been inured to it from birth. Thomas
Kettle quite obviously wilted under it, and was in any case a
nervous and fretful creature, who put on grand airs because at
heart he was afraid.

Though Euphemia was sharpsighted, she wore blinkers; she
could see only one reason why Thomas Kettle should feel a
need for shelter—for what was there at Anchor House to be
feared except John Barnard? Thomas was glad enough of a
refuge from his host's searching approbation, but this was not
his main motive for running under Euphemia's petticoats. An
eldest Miss Barnard to whom he could rightfully devote his
attentions would get him out of his embarrassment with the
younger sister; and as soon as he had assured himself that the
eldest Miss Barnard was not going to proclaim an ownership
too, he flung himself headlong into the convention. Mutty,
who had made up her mind that Thomas was to marry one of
Mr. Barnard's daughters (for why else should there be all
this talk of learning the business, and all these hospitalities?)
could not imagine why Thomas was now so attentive to the
plain one. She could see that Mary was put out. If only to show
kind-heartedness and that she knew what was going on, Mutty
took to sympathizing with Mary in corners, patting her and
assuring her that it would all come right in the end. Presently
Mutty added the torment of hope to the torment of jealousy.
"You see, Miss Mary, I was right. Your sister has found out
that it was all no more than politeness. She was quite chilly
with him this morning when he wanted to look at her water
colours."

Euphemia, in fact, had found that Thomas was taking up
too much of her time. When he tried to hide among the water
colours she remarked that her father had gone to the office,
and that if Thomas was to learn the business this would be an
excellent morning to begin. Cross and ashamed, he did as she
bid. During the next three days he was an exemplary pupil.

132

John Barnard, overflowing with pleasure, talked on of the Baltic trade each evening, and at the day's end Thomas was too tired to do more than say good night to the ladies and go to bed. Euphemia sighed with relief and turned her attention to Wilberforce, who had advanced to having lessons with Mr. Moore. Lessons with Mr. Moore had been the beginning of the end with George and Julius and Samuel; now it seemed that Mr. Moore was the one whose health might be impaired, for every day he left the house looking like a man shot by an elf-bolt. This was a welcome change, and she wanted to know how it had come about. And then she woke one early morning and heard Mary crying.

At first she did not recognize the sound and fancied that Mary's doves had escaped from their cage and were preening and croo-croo-ing on the window sill. What a nuisance, she thought. Their droppings will stain the wall, and Papa will be vexed; I must get up and catch them. Still she lay between sleeping and waking, lulled by the gentle, throbbing monotony of their note. *Croo-croo! Croo-croo!* But it was not Mary's doves. It was Mary herself. The sisters slept in adjoining rooms, and from long habit the door between them stood open. When Euphemia crossed the threshold the sound of Mary's weeping was so harsh that it was inconceivable that she could have supposed it to be the doves. She bent down, seeing a rumpled nightcap, and an averted red face.

"Mary, my poor Mary, what is it? Are you ill? Are you unhappy?"

"Go away!"

"But why are you crying like this?"

"Oh, how I hate you!"

With a darting movement Mary raised her head and set her teeth in Euphemia's arm. Then she buried her face in the pillow, shuddered, and lay still.

Discovering that she was on the brink of being violently sick, Euphemia went back to her room and plunged her arm in the

133

water jug. Looking at the bite, she was astonished that it should be so small. The skin was broken here and there, and the toothmarks stood up in white ridges that slowly turned purple. After a while she went to the wardrobe and got out the dress she would be wearing that day at the Powles's party, for now she must replace its muslin sleeves by something less transparent. As she moved she heard Mary get up and bolt the door between them.

4.

The party at the Powles's was a yearly event, timed to fall in with the blossoming of a large Judas tree which was somehow connected with Lord Nelson. There, since it was an omnium gatherum, the Barnards would meet the Kettles—a meeting which John Barnard was looking forward to; for though he felt the greatest unwillingness to see them in his own house, and positively refused to set foot in theirs, there was nothing against encountering them on neutral ground and watching their discomfiture. Hah! They would be very awkwardly placed when he appeared with their son as one of the Anchor House contingent. After dinner (the party did not begin till half-past six, as the Judas tree looked its best at sunset) he shaved with particular care and tied his majestic neckcloth. Old Mr. Powles sat under the Judas tree in a wheelchair with one eye closed and a rug round his legs. He held out a quivering left hand to his guests, for he was paralysed in his right hand. Mr. Kettle stood beside him in the attitude of a revering intimate.

"H'm. Gan and Marsilius," said Thomas to no one in particular, since he did not suppose there would be anyone to take the allusion.

He was wrong. A mild, modest voice replied, "Good evening, Thomas. I am glad you love the Italian poets. Such a wonderful canto!" Turning, he looked into a pair of black eyes,

134

calm as jet, in a plump, ageing face, and recognized his step-mother. As a schoolmistress, she would have to know that sort of thing, and was woman of the world enough to skip over the insult to her husband by talking culture. Out of perversity he began an affable conversation with her, thinking vaguely that to do so would annoy his father. Out of devilry, for she had just had a violent quarrel with Simon, she sustained it. After showing each other round Pulci and the *Gerusalemme Libe-rata,* they came back to the present. Mrs. Kettle congratulated him on looking so much the better for Loseby air, and was glad to think of the gaiety his visit had evoked at Anchor House. "Just what I would wish for my sweet little singing bird." This was to lead on to an inquiring hope about the duration of the visit.

Thomas froze. "Which of the Miss Barnards is she?"

Mary, who had come up naturally as a daisy to greet Mrs. Kettle, heard this. The fibber! He knew well enough that Euphemia never sang. Since she could not scratch the fibber's eyes out, she walked off, light as spindrift in her muslin, and attached herself to Lettice and Patty Cowper, who were talking to Crawley Blunt. It did not take her long to supplant them. She can't have bitten me because of Crawley Blunt, thought Euphemia. Yet to judge from the tender delight with which Mary was hearing of Crawley's experiments with a cucumber frame, there could be no justification for a bite on any other person's account.

"Look at poor Crawley," said Julia in a low voice. "Mary's making a pretty fool of him." Others also were glancing at Mary and Crawley, but Julia did not seem distressed by it. Out of humour with Euphemia, who had chosen to put on those clumsy cambric undersleeves, she was glad to think that one of her daughters, at any rate, took after Miss Julia Smith.

The sun was near setting, the Judas tree attained a delirious intensity of colour, there was the customary interval for admira-tion, and negus and sandwiches were served. When the sun was down and the refreshments consumed, the town band would emerge from the shrubbery and the young people would dance on the lawn, performing the country dances of old Mr. Powles's youth. Having danced the first two sets with Crawley Blunt, Mary felt so sure of his return whenever she wanted him that as the band struck up for the fourth dance she did not even look about her. She heard him called on by young Mrs. Powles to partner Letty Cowper, she heard him say, "I should be delighted, but——" and at the same moment she heard her father say, "Why, Thomas, are you not dancing this set? Here's Mary. She will partner you."

Slowly, not raising her eyes, she took her place. It was a longways set, and they were at the bottom of it. If I must stand here, Thomas thought, at least I won't jiggle. He stood motionless, and opposite him Mary stood motionless too. At the close of the figure the topmost couple came hand in hand down the middle, and after their passage the two lines of dancers moved forward, touched hands, and fell back again. When for the third time Mary's fingers came lightly to his, he said, for the sake of saying something, "What is this tune called?"

" 'Never No More,' " she replied. Her voice, which had begun at its usual pitch, curved downward into a sob. At intervals touching hands, they moved up the set, and at each clasp her hands were colder, and stayed more negligently in his. She had changed with such childish abandon from pertness to dejection that it was as though she were dying before his eyes. "Never No More." The words became part of the tune, floating like a pattern of foam on the brassy wallowing of the town band. She was staring at the ground, and he could look at her as much as he pleased. He almost could not understand why he withheld himself from falling in love with this charming creature, so devoted and downcast. But she was John Barnard's daughter, so to love her must be to marry her, to marry her must be to consent to a perpetuity of trading with the Baltic and stomaching John Barnard's anxious, restless, portentous

136

goodwill—a goodwill alternately ludicrous and intimidating. That was why. And that was why she moped opposite him, so lost in self-pity that after the latest couple had gone down the set she forgot to come forward to meet him. It was strange that he had held out. She was pretty, and so very much in love with him, and carried so many advantages in her pocket (if he could but accept them as advantages), not least among them the prospect of being rich enough to pension off Mutty. Now they were the topmost couple but one of the set, and as for the last time they met to touch hands he bent and lightly kissed her cold fingers. If for no other purpose, it would at least remind her that it was now their turn to dance out the figure and caper hand in hand down the middle to the close of the dance.

" 'Never No More,' " he said as they walked across the lawn. "What an uncommonly silly name for a dance."

"Yes, very silly. But I am not positive that it is called that, after all."

"Then what is it called?"

"I haven't the slightest notion. But it's sure to be called something or other." She spoke with such solemnity that he was shaken out of the constraint of the dance and laughed so wholeheartedly that John Barnard turned to see who had been able to amuse Thomas, and saw Thomas walking with Mary and thought that Mary was becoming quite a wit. She seemed to have grown taller too—an effect of the dusk.

The dusk inspired her to another profound remark. "Now that it is beginning to grow dark the Judas tree seems to have black flowers—except that one knows they are pink."

"I prefer them black."

"What, don't you like pink? I am wearing a pink sash."

"It is beginning to look black now."

"How can you be so unkind? My poor sash! Don't you admire it? Mr. Blunt liked it very much."

137

"If we walk between these hazels it will look even blacker, and I shall like it even better."

If she had consented they would have walked down the nut alley and sighed and held hands, and emerged no unhappier than they had gone in. But as if the mention of Crawley Blunt had turned her head she began to flirt and protested that the alley had a bat in it; did he wish to see her with a bat in her hair as well as a black sash? Again he felt himself treated as though he were no more dangerous than a kitten. Pulling her into the alley, he gave her a violent, humbling kiss. When he drew away his lips, hers followed and remained pursed; and, looking down, he saw her eyelids closed and her face unrecognizable in its look of doting abstraction. Still holding her embraced, he knew that they were being looked at. His pride would not let him release her, and he did not want to kiss her again. He waited, and she reclined on his embrace, her bosom tranquilly rising and falling. Presently he heard a murmur of a retreating petticoat and the slow thump of large shoes, and turned his head sufficiently to see his stepmother guiding Crawley Blunt away.

"Oh-h!"

She had sighed. There was such an infinity of self-gratulation in the sigh that he winced and took his arm away from her waist.

"Oh!" This was a brisker exclamation.

"Won't you take my arm? I think they are serving lemonade." Leading her towards the group round the dumb-waiter, he commented on the appearance of the first stars, saying that they were in fact unimaginably large masses of burning vapour, and that considerations such as these made anything that happened on earth seem ridiculously insignificant.

Never No More! Combing and combing her hair, Mary thought what tragic words these were, and how at last she understood them. Perhaps the one romance of her life was already over, in any case the first kiss can never, never be repeated. It

138

was sad to think how young she was, how brief the rapture, and that henceforward she would be little better than a widow, or it might be truer to say a memorial urn. But she believed it was often so. There was Lucy Ashton—she went mad. There was Margaret, who walked with Faust in a garden, just as she had done with Thomas, except that Margaret had plaits—ringlets are prettier. There were all those heroines on the Continent, who after one kiss went into convents, and whom she read about when she went to the Cowpers' for the sewing circle. There was—no, there was no such example of lofty romance in the Bible; in the Bible people marry and have families, much as in modern England. There was Alexander Moir, who had loved Mamma so passionately that he stepped backward down a waterfall; if he had been drowned, surely Mamma could never have brought herself to marry Papa at the age of nineteen—oldish. These sequels were prosaic; she would never do such a thing. It would be uncalled for, for already she had lived and loved, like Thekla—another of them. She would practise that song tomorrow. This would make a great difference to her music, for one cannot really sing until one has known love. There would be plenty of time to practise, as she would not be going out to parties now. Everything would be different because everything was over. Her heart had awakened; her heart was broken. For surely Thomas had behaved very oddly—after one impassioned embrace, one burning kiss, to begin talking about the stars and handing lemonade. Surely it was very rude of him, and she had every reason to be offended.

Indignation and fear burst up from a lower level of her consciousness and scattered Lucy Ashton and Alexander Moir and "The Maiden's Lament." She was within an inch of knowing that she had been experimentally kissed by a young man who an instant later regretted it, and it was only by sublimating Thomas's retreat into the heartlessness of a Don Juan that she saved herself. Yes, he was heartless, a desperate heartless man

139

who had tossed her away like a withered flower. Vicious and savage, he would never know what he had lost. The stars indeed! How pale he had looked as he handed her that glass of lemonade. How savage he had been when she stood up for the first dance with Crawley Blunt; for though he had tried to conceal it by looking bored, she had not been deceived. Indignation and fear and tragedy and "The Maiden's Lament" vanished like smoke, and Mary Barnard was left with the absorbing, triumphant knowledge that at her first essay and only a month after her sixteenth birthday she had been kissed with passion by the young man she had fallen in love with.

She got into bed and blew out the candle. She could remember the kiss even better in the dark. She was asleep three minutes later.

Waking, she could not at first remember why everything was different, and why it was inevitable that she should wake with a start, with such a sense of hurry and heartbeating, in such a sweat, and so early, knowing and not knowing that something ineffable and irrevocable had taken place. A pink sash had turned black? The complete recollection burst open within her. Instead of pride, exaltation, sublime sorrow, she felt a blighting dissatisfaction.

Was that all?

Was that all, that papery recollection, perfectly lifeless and distinct? And what had become of that impression of something ineffable and irrevocable which had pervaded the first moment of waking? Now she could only remember Thomas saying, "Won't you take my arm?" and leading her out of the nut walk and towards the dumb-waiter. Why had she taken his arm and submitted to such falseness and allowed everything to fall so flat? It was over and could never be revived. In a couple of hours they would meet at breakfast. What could be done at breakfast? Her heart beat so intolerably that it tumbled her out of bed. As if she had been wakened by an alarm of fire, she threw

140

a shawl over herself and ran barefoot to Thomas's bedroom.

Thomas was not there. He had slept less well than she. Furious at being kept awake by a necessity to go over every particle of his blunder, to revise it and take it to pieces and put it together again, he had dressed and gone out. The wall prevented him from leaving Mr. Barnard's property, but he could walk in the garden, and later, when the servants were up and about, hide in the arbour. Mary sat down on his bed, arranging the shawl more modestly over her. He was not there; the moment was lost, and she could not possibly stay, for how could she bear it if he came in and found her? But she had not the strength to go back to her room just yet. She must wait for movement to come back into her limbs, and for the roaring noise in her ears to leave off. He was not here, and she was, looking at his brushes on the dressing table. It was strange to be in a man's room—though there was nothing unfamiliar, nothing that she could not account for from recollections of being allowed into her father's dressing room when she was a little girl. He had opened the window. The morning air blew in, and everything was so still that she could hear the sea. In another moment she must go. Saying this to herself, she lay down on the bed, clasping his pillow in her arms, and a minute later her bare feet wriggled under the cover of the blanket he had thrown back and she lay still. She was asleep in the same attitude a couple of hours later, when Thomas, routed out of the arbour by the conversation of the gardener, saw that his coat was covered with cobwebs and ran up to his room to brush them off before going in to breakfast. It was nearer breakfast time than he supposed, he smelled coffee preparing and heard people moving about. He hurried into his room, leaving the door half open. He had taken up the brush when he saw her, reflected in the mirror. She was still no more than something graceful and appalling that had got into his bed, when John Barnard came along the passage.

"Good morning, good morning. You are an early riser today.

I saw you in the—" Full of approval and affability, he entered and saw her.

Before he could speak, Thomas, signing to him to be quiet, had pushed him back and was gently closing the door behind them both. But it was too late. She had awaked and cried out, "Thomas!"

5.

John Barnard walked downstairs and into his study, and Thomas followed him and sat down to wait. He had no idea what to say, and John Barnard was incapable of speaking. They sat, not looking at each other, and beyond the study door the noises of the beginning of an ordinary day proceeded—the scraping of chairs, the clatter of dishes, Julia's slow, heavy tread crossing the hall, and Euphemia's voice calling, "Mary!"

Thomas looked at the cobwebs on his sleeve, which he had not had time to brush off. They might help to establish his alibi, and yet he felt that they put him at a disadvantage.

He began to hear the clock on the mantelpiece, and remembered the first time he had entered this room. Then, instead of cobwebs on his sleeve, he had fish scales on his boots; but it had not troubled him. Secure in his fury and rhodomontade, he had moved John Barnard to his purpose as easily as the wind twirls the grunting sails of a windmill.

"You believed me then," he said suddenly.

John Barnard gave no sign of having heard him, and the silence continued. After some time the door was opened and Euphemia looked in. "We are quite ready for prayers."

"I cannot read prayers this morning," her father replied. She made no comment and went away.

It is ridiculous to sit here being browbeaten by a clock and an old gentleman, Thomas thought. I am not in the wrong; I have nothing to be afraid of, though I cannot tell him that his

142

daughter has been pestering me ever since I came to the house. He saw me in the garden, and I scorn to remind him of it. There is nothing I can do, and nothing that I wish to say. I have nothing to fear. On the contrary, I shall leave the house, which is what I wish to do, and never see him or any of them again, which is of all things what I most desire. If he chooses he can sit here till doomsday. It is his affair. But there is no reason why I should keep him company. I shall leave him and have my breakfast.

So thinking, he remained seated. But he did not expect to stay much longer. Glancing at John Barnard, he saw that his expression had changed from an incredulous to a settled fury.

Again the door opened, and a servant's voice said, "Mr. Kettle to see you, sir."

"Send Mr. Kettle away."

It was too late; the door had already closed, and Simon Kettle was in the room. Thomas saw a chance to escape and got up, but his father cut off his retreat by standing in front of the door in a heroic attitude, puffing a little, as if he had been striving with Apollyon just outside. His hair was superlatively brushed, he smelled strongly of attar of roses, he was dressed with solemn spruceness. Sophie had seen to that; but it was his own idea, his tribute to the sweets of the occasion, to stick a tulip in his buttonhole. Delight in his mission had made him set out before breakfast and walk faster than usual. Though he had not expected to find Thomas with John Barnard, he welcomed this adjustment to his programme. Two birds would be hit with one stone, and each of them would suffer more acutely for the other's being a witness to his suffering.

"Good morning, Mr. Barnard. I shall not trouble you long. If I consulted my own feelings, it would be needless for you to tell your servant to send me away, for I should not have come. No! I do not look to be welcomed. It is some time since I have felt myself agreeable here. Some might be surprised—I daresay they are—that you should have entertained my son for so

143

long in so marked a manner, and not once invited Mrs. Kettle, or Me, inside your doors. But it doesn't surprise me. On the contrary. I expected it."

He tossed his head with a hoity-toity, and the smell of his hair oil was further diffused. Thomas, who had already withdrawn from the immediate neighbourhood of his father's bower of roses, affected to sneeze. He knew what was coming. But this was no fault of his either, for he could not be held responsible for having such a man for his father.

It was a slight mitigation to his feelings to see that John Barnard preserved his air of being totally inattentive. Nothing could wound Mr. Kettle more.

"If you had taken the trouble to consult me, if there had been the slightest acknowledgment that I am Thomas's parent, even in the smallest degree and merely as complying with the usual conventions of society (Thomas, I don't advise you to sneer), I should not have felt obliged to inflict my company on you. There would have been no painful reason to bring me where I know well I am not wanted. Then matters might have been very different. Some of us might have been spared. Others might have been preserved. One of us might have been cut short (Thomas, I say again, this is no time to sneer). For I would have warned you. Painful as it might have been, I would not have hesitated in my warning. But now it is too late."

And now, thought Thomas, who had turned his back, he is licking his lips and rolling it on his tongue for the last taste.

"Too late for anything but the truth!" exclaimed Mr. Kettle, rising on his toes and swaying heavily. "Mr. Barnard, my poor friend—for I will call you so—you have been taken in, sir! Deluded! Taken advantage of! No wonder that he cannot look me in the face. Thomas, my son Thomas—oh, that I should have to say it!—was seen last night behind a bush, forcing his embraces on a certain young lady. Mrs. Kettle saw him, and so did Mr. Crawley Blunt. They saw it through the bush plainly, and as if face to face. That is the young man you made so much of. That is the hypocrite you preferred to me. Deluding the poor young lady, corrupting her modesty, hugging and kissing her—and in public, too! Such a thing can't be kept quiet, you know. Everyone will talk of it, the more so since she's your daughter. There's not a hope she will keep her good name, poor little Miss—"

"This is intolerable!" Thomas shouted. Even in his fury, the thought of handling his father was too disgusting. He snatched a book from the table and threw it with all his force. It hit Mr. Kettle on the chin and dislodged the tulip.

"Thomas," said John Barnard. "Thomas, remember yourself." His voice was oddly mild. It sounded almost cordial.

"I cannot endure my father," Thomas replied, "but I am sorry to dirty your book. I will have it re-bound."

"Sit down, Thomas. Mr. Kettle has been addressing himself to me; you will kindly leave me to answer him."

He paused for a moment and took a deep breath. The face that he turned on Simon Kettle was pale and shone with a steely light.

"You will take back what you have said, sir, when you have been better informed. As you say, of late you have not been invited to this house, so ignorance must be your excuse. It is regrettable that Thomas and Mary should so far have forgotten themselves as to kiss behind a bush, but it is not criminal. I have given my consent to their marriage."

He stared down into the dark mirror of the tabletop and added, "Thomas, will you oblige me by showing your father out?"

When Thomas returned, John Barnard had risen and was tapping the barometer. Seeing Thomas pick up the book, he smiled faintly and said, "I think you are right, and we must have it re-bound. Your father has an unpleasant kind of eloquence. If you will wait here, I will send Mary to you."

PART FOUR

1.

An early riser, John Barnard was in the habit of reading, praying, and meditating for an hour or so in his dressing room before breakfast. On this particular morning he had been watching Thomas in the garden, pleased to observe that the young man was so well at home in Anchor House that he could go out for a stroll without waiting for his host's door to be unbarred by his host's servants. During the last few days Thomas had begun to show a proper interest in the business; now he was walking early in the garden on his own initiative. John Barnard turned away from the window to fall on his knees and thank God for these hopeful signs that Thomas was settling down. Later, hearing Thomas running upstairs, he had gone in by the open door to good-morning him—and there on the bed was Mary. The blow was incomprehensible, it had the abruptness and detachment of a sudden death. When Thomas signed to him to be quiet and pushed him out of the room, he had a momentary surge of gratitude at being sheltered and taken charge of. But she had waked and cried, "Thomas!"—and the sound of her voice ripped away his bewilderment and left him nothing but fury.

146

The evidence of his own eyes was turned topsy-turvy; for what had he seen but Mary's seducer, strolling off the fumes of a night's lust, so cold and unmanly in his satisfaction that he had not even troubled himself to convey her back to her own room? This was the young man he had befriended—an ingrate and a libertine. The ingrate and libertine followed him into the study and sat down like someone well at home there; but he could not connect the Thomas he knew with the Thomas he had discovered a few minutes earlier. His rage skirted round the man in the room in order to pursue another, a being of such villainy that he was almost an ideal creation, a phantom rather than a man. Trying to run down this Thomas in the past, and catch him out in some earlier wickedness that would substantiate the present, it was as if he sought to net a phantom in a raiment of flesh and blood; not till he had caught the phantom and clothed it would his enemy be real enough to match his fury and his sense of injury.

"You believed me then," said the voice in the room, and as positively as if he had been drenched in cold water he knew that he heard integrity in that real voice. The indifference with which he heard it compelled him to realize that Thomas's guilt or innocence was only a minor consideration. It was not against Thomas that his anger was kindled. It was against Mary.

The change that Thomas had seen on his face, a change from an incredulous to a settled fury, took place. As trustfully as he had loved her, he began to loathe her. She had done this to him. She was no sooner rid of her childhood than she had done this. In the expanded flowering of his love for her and his pride in her, she had taken herself to a man's bed. Whether or no she lay there still a virgin was a formal quibble, and he had no patience to consider it; the wound was in *his* belly. She had eviscerated him, clawing out his bowels of compassion as inattentively as the girls on the quayside, cleaning herrings, pull out the guts and throw them into a tub. But the herring is dead; no more torment lies in wait for it. He had been disembowelled of love and tenderness only for hatred and disgust to be rammed into the wound. He had not known that such hatred was possible. In some distant part of his character he was appalled to find such hatred having its way with him, flowing out of his accustomed paternity like lava flowing from a rended mountainside that has a village on it. But he felt no power to condemn it. He was abandoned to it as the damned are abandoned to hellfire—not the shrieking damned of christian art, but the damned in truth and by predestination, who fall into hell with a gloomy consenting. For many years he had thought that fiends were irrelevant to the state of the damned, and that their introduction into sacred art was childish and trivial. Simon Kettle came in as just such a superfluity. It was obvious why Kettle had come, and what he would say, after he had wallowed through the self-gratification of leading up to it; but he came too late, and it was as though he had brought the parlour bellows to the edge of the lake burning with fire and brimstone. "A certain young lady." Well, what of it? In a moment she would be named. And what of that? He knew it already; it could be endured.

He heard Thomas's exclamation. Raising his eyes, he saw the book whiz across the room, Simon Kettle's mouth slammed shut by its impact, and the tulip falling. The young man who had compromised his daughter had started up in her defence, while he, his daughter's father, had sat without a word. A compunction of what is called honour noosed him and dragged him out of the pit. Without the slightest sensation of relief he passed from fury into a dry, rarefied composure. It was not that Mary was any less dead to him, but the removal of the body was put into other hands.

By the end of the day, the day had assumed an appearance of being pretty much like any other day, except for being twice as long, and darkened by Julia's steadily thickening ill humour. Mutty pounced on this, assuring Julia repeatedly that the feelings of a mother when she finds herself about to lose a daughter

148

are bound to be very anxious and distressing, and that a mother who did not feel exactly as Mrs. Barnard was feeling could hardly be called a mother at all. Mutty also assured Euphemia that there is nothing like one wedding in a family to bring on another, and did not doubt that Wilberforce was already looking forward to a big slice of wedding cake. She was as innocently happy as a fairy tale, and John Barnard's was the only patience she did not exhaust.

Long as the day had been, he went to bed knowing that he would not be able to take off his armour yet.

Julia was sitting up in the bed, scratching her left wrist. He had forgotten the gesture. In the past it had been a danger signal; seeing it again, his heart staggered at the contrast between that rich, full-bosomed bedfellow and the creature of sexless bulk who clawed with gouty nails on a flabby skin. Less than twenty-four hours before, he had lost Mary. Twenty-four years ago he had had Julia, and how and when he had lost her he did not know.

"Unless you propose to stand there all night, playing at Hamlet's ghost—"

He got into bed beside her.

"Well?" she said.

"Well, my dear?"

"I hope you are satisfied with this day's work?"

"Aren't you? They love each other, and he is a young man of excellent character."

"I've no doubt he is. Such excellent character that he hasn't a spark of love for anyone but himself. But he'll marry her. After you spent heaven knows how long this morning persuading him to it, he'll marry her. Anyone would think he'd got her into trouble, he's so wonderfully ready to marry her."

"Julia, that is not like you."

"No? And how do you know what I'm like? I see I have been totally mistaken in you, for I would have gone down to my grave swearing that you loved Mary."

149

"You would have been right," he said, riveting his attention on the scrolled rim of the candlestick.

"If she had been ten years older and plain as a boot, it would still be a wretched match. What a day! The worst day in my life. Every time I looked at him, I thought, Now you're my son-in-law, and I shall never be quit of you and your old Mutty!"

"If that is what disturbs you, my dear, you are taking too black a view. I suppose they will be leaving for London before the end of the week."

"Leaving?"

"It would not be proper for him to stay in the same house as Mary now."

"So you'll rob the poor child of what little pleasure she'll ever get out of him?"

"I hope she will have some pleasure after marriage. If he proves the unsatisfactory husband you expect, she will have the pleasure of telling him so."

He retied the strings of his nightcap and blew out the candle. It seemed to Julia that as the culmination of an unpleasant day she was in bed with a strange man.

The strange man would have been familiar enough to those who met John Barnard in the way of business. Among them it was agreed that Barnard of Loseby was a shrewd dealer, a man you wouldn't often find at the wrong end of a bargain, a man who never spoke more or less than the truth and who, unless you kept a sharp lookout, would by mere discretion get the better of you.

The strange man who had got into Julia's bed appeared the next morning and seemed to be there to stay. Blasted, disillusioned, renouncing love, John Barnard began to treat his family much as he treated his business. Like the business, the family responded. By some magic, it became possible to speak one's mind and to entertain a reasonable hope of carrying a project to its conclusion. Wilberforce was able to digest carrots,

150

his hair began to grow, and when Ellen came home from the boarding school her nervousness stood out from the family contour to such an extent that her father found another school for her, as it was plain that she must have been bullied at the first one. In August, as a suitable interval had elapsed, Thomas was invited for another visit. He too was treated like the business and responded by finding it possible to be in love with Mary. It was settled that their marriage should take place in May of the next year, when Mary would have entered her eighteenth year. John Barnard then wrote to Joseph, saying that if he could be spared from his duties everyone would be glad to see him at the wedding. Magnanimity, which, in replacing love, made every act of renunciation as easy as lifting a dead leaf, carried him even over this. He supposed Julia would be pleased. When Julia chose to say that of course Joseph would not be able to come, would not wish to come, would be like a stranger if he did come, and that to see him would only reopen a wound that had taken five years to heal, he was disappointed. But it was a small disappointment compared to a disappointment he had already endured and surmounted. When life was newly on this business footing, when magnanimity was imperfectly established and hope could still get in through its sutures, he had waited in trembling for Mary to discover that he loved her no longer. Absorbed in severance from Thomas, she would not of course notice it immediately. She did not notice it at all.

After Thomas's second departure she pined so emphatically that Julia began to talk of hurrying forward the marriage. Instead, Basil Cook was called back from Tooley Street, where he had been shoehorning Thomas into the duties of an agent, to take charge of the Loseby office while John Barnard took Mary for a tour on the Continent. It was then that Mary began to suspect that her papa did not love her so much as formerly; he was taking Euphemia too.

It was strange to be in Paris again, and again with a young

woman on either arm. Now he drove in the Bois, observing that the horses were as shiny as ever, but that their riders wore such wasp-waisted coats that the pattern of the barrel of the man rising from the horse's barrel was lost, and with it the air of unity between the man and the mount. In the same way, a unity was gone from Paris itself: here it was respectable and there it was vulgar, and between the two something had been mislaid—the serene unrepentance, perhaps, which had perplexed and challenged him during that first visit. Whatever it had been, it was gone. He was glad to leave Paris and go on to Switzerland. They stayed at Geneva and then at Neuchâtel, and at Neuchâtel, he met a Swiss pastor who talked about the Moravian settlement of Herrnhut. The pastor could not tell him much that he had not read or been told of before, but to be hearing about Herrnhut from someone who had actually been there fired him with such a desire to see the place with his own eyes that he put off the return to Loseby. The preparations were immense. Euphemia and Mary had to be equipped with muffs and beaver jackets and fur-lined boots and bonnets for the winter journey, and for himself there must be a leather waistcoat. Up till the hour of their departure Monsieur Tuggli remembered more items: insect powder to be sprinkled in post-chaises, a case of tea, a bottle of hair oil—for the young ladies would not find hair oil at Herrnhut, and as a parting gift he thrust in a guide to the battlefield of Bautzen.

Except for castles on the Rhine, there was nothing Mary wished to see in Germany. The thought of Thomas, her only comfort, dwindled into unreality under the pressure of such leagues of ugly forest and uglier plains. Rain spattered against the chaise windows, and Papa prosed on about the Moravians, who were not a sect, and acknowledged bishops like any other Christians, but who slept in dormitories, married missionaries because they were bidden to, and distinguished themselves by zeal, method, and simple goodness; or, consulting his map, he would exclaim that they were now farther east than Malmo,

152

farther east than Berlin—facts which gave him an uncalled-for degree of pleasure.

They reached Herrnhut early in November. "Thank heaven we are here," said Mary to Euphemia. "We are here, so we can go back again! What a horrid little place," she added, looking down from the window of their bedroom in the Gasthof. "Do you suppose there are wolves?" No wolves appeared, but she could not evade the round of pious sightseeing, with nothing to see and so many incomprehensible lectures to hear; for apparently every Herrnhuter they met felt it a duty to answer Papa's questions with half-hour lectures, and in the intervals of lectures there was singing of hymns and prayer meetings. The lectures were addressed to Papa, but presently Mary noticed that it was Euphemia who attended to them and even provoked them. That showed Mary what it was to be without a Thomas, or hope of a Thomas. Euphemia would never have a house of her own, she was forced to take an interest in Moravian store-cupboards; lectures on doctrine, lectures on pickled cabbage—Euphemia could listen to anything. Perhaps she thought of marrying a Moravian. At last it was their last day; and, offered a choice between one more visit to the cemetery with Papa or a lesson in straw-plaiting with Euphemia, Mary, her wits quickened by desperation, found that there was so much she must put in her diary that she would stay quietly beside the bedroom stove.

John Barnard's last wish in Herrnhut had been granted, but he did not expect much to come of it as he walked up the hill to the cemetery alone. It was not that he had been disappointed in the place or in the people who lived there. Their German prolixity, the tinge of self-satisfaction with which they attributed every creditable doing to the Lord, had not obscured the solemn spectacle of a people living austerely and in unity, entirely purposed to serve God. It was in himself he was disappointed. The seed had fallen on a dry heart, foiled by his stiffness, his inability to forget that time was short and his

153

untrustful anxiety to make the most of it, his parental vanity which made it impossible for him not to be conscious that Euphemia's interest was only in details of administration and that Mary was not interested at all. But his sense of unworthiness fell off like Christian's burden as he passed in through the cemetery gates; for there is no man, however good, however bad, who is not worthy of death. A faint whining wind blew quietly from the east, stealthy and yet steady: so stealthy, so steady, that he was only aware of it by the rustle in the sheltering alleys. In dark geometrical order the hedges of clipped hornbeam closed in on the central group of altar tombs, where Count Zinzendorf, the founder, lay buried with his family around him. In such a family group there is no unrest, no dissension. He looked for a long while at the Zinzendorf tombs; but after all it was not these graves that he envied, but the stones which, among the uniformity of the dead, were distinguished by bearing neither name nor date, only a number—the number of a death as it was registered in the book of burials. To lie hidden under such a gravestone—that was what he would choose. But in England such a gravestone would be declamatory by its mere oddity. After all, he still had a wish, and one that was not likely to be granted; for to lie under such a stone he must die at Herrnhut, and die as one of the community. If he should live to be old and disencumbered of his duties as a husband and a father, perhaps indeed he might come here at the last and be buried under a nameless stone. The wind had strengthened since he entered, and the winter dusk was drifting out of the impartial winter sky. The hornbeams clattered as he walked down the clipped alley towards the gate. The aspect of the cemetery had changed, it had grown mournful and forbidding. As they drove away next morning the first snow was falling. The pale shuttered houses had a close-lipped appearance behind that flitting veil.

2.

As they re-entered Anchor House, Mary exclaimed on how glad she was to be at home and added, "The next time I come home I shall be a married woman." He did not question her truth as he had done when she was glad to come home from Rougham. For one thing, it was plain that she had not enjoyed the tour; Paris had been liked better than Geneva; Geneva had been faintly regretted from Neuchâtel; and at Herrnhut she had felt only distaste and boredom. For another, he need not now concern himself how Mary felt: he could love her no longer, and in a few months she would marry and go off to a home of her own. He had known that some such thoughts as these lay in wait for him on the threshold, but he put them by and noticed that there was a smell of roasting partridges. After dinner the presents could be unpacked, and meanwhile he could express a true pleasure in being reunited to English cooking and Mrs. Hewitt's bread sauce. A lesser demon also was lying in wait just inside the door. It had not been possible to give the Kettles notice at midsummer; to do so so soon after the tulip had been dislodged from Simon Kettle's buttonhole would have seemed vindictive. The notice to quit had been sent at the Michaelmas quarter, after his departure for Paris. But to quit Prospect Terrace was not to quit Loseby. Suppose they moved to another house in the town? How very awkward that might be. There they would squat, triumphing over him and telling everyone how they had been turned out and really found themselves more comfortable for it. This was a demon of short standing, for presently Julia told him that the Kettles, who till a week before had said nothing of their plans, had settled their accounts, distributed cards of departure, given a farewell supper party to a few Terrace friends, and gone away. They had gone to Walton on the Naze.

There remained two other problems of disposal which must be settled before Mary's marriage. A home must be found for Mutty, and an occupation for Thomas. Basil Cook reported that Thomas would never be fit to trade with the Baltic or with any other place in this mortal world. Old customers had written complaining of the inefficiency of Mr. Barnard's London agent, new customers, after one experience of him, had taken themselves elsewhere. The person who made no complaint was Thomas himself. "Too high and mighty," said Mr. Cook, "to mind if he makes a fool of himself or not." To satisfy himself that these complaints were well founded, John Barnard travelled to London and paid a surprise visit in Tooley Street. He had never seen an office so precisely, so almost elegantly neat, and whatever he asked for was instantly produced in a state of exemplary preservation. Thomas, too, the lady of the bower, was the picture of tranquil confidence and showed him a display cabinet which he had had made. It was certainly a very handsome piece of cabinet-making, and displayed such things as strips of hide and samples of linseed as advantageously as a reliquary. For a while John Barnard forgot Basil Cook and almost persuaded himself that by applying the methods of someone who edits a classical text Thomas had invented a new way of trading with the Baltic; but the decrease in the volume of trading was too plainly evident. Thomas would not do, and John Barnard had to tell him so.

"We will find something else—something more congenial."

Thomas shuddered. His quiet, unfrequented office had become pleasant to him, and he loved the neighbourhood of the river. Now he was to be haled off to something more congenial. The mere word was offensive. How should John Barnard be a judge of what was congenial and what not?

"I suppose I could find another post as a schoolmaster."

"No doubt. Holt, North Walsham, King's Lynn—there are several good old establishments in Norfolk. Did you like being a teacher?"

"Not particularly." Wild horses should not drag him towards one of those good old establishments within reach of his father-in-law.

"I suppose—it would make a difference to any scholastic career—I suppose you do not consider taking Holy Orders? It is not a thing to be lightly undertaken."

"No indeed! I could not consider it."

Looking round on the neatness and at the cabinet, John Barnard thought how well Thomas would do in something like a museum. Unfortunately he knew very little about museums, and what little he knew suggested that they did not pay a living wage. On the journey home he decided that Thomas would do very well in the firm of Powles, Powles, and Bellowes. Integrity rather than enterprise is what makes a solicitor. He called on Henry Powles the next day, but learned that the firm had no place in it for young Mr. Kettle.

Entangled in the question of Thomas was the question of Mutty; but the question of Mutty was worse. A little delay in finding the exact hole to drop Thomas into did not matter, but at all costs Mutty must be disposed of before the wedding; and though finding a hole for her was not complicated by exactitude, for woman is a fluid form of matter and can be poured into almost any shaped receptacle, Mutty was as ticklish to manage as a confectioner's boiling syrup. By February all attempts at decency had been thrown aside. John Barnard listened without protest when Julia said it was no wonder that Simon Kettle had married in order to be rid of her, and Euphemia added that it showed what a thick hide he had that he could endure her for so long. Retirement with a pension was useless, for she would only retire in order to come forth and pay long visits. Charitable institutions needing matrons needed them with qualifications. Her kinsfolk had emigrated to Canada, and she would not hear of another sea voyage after what she had endured coming to Yarmouth. It was mid-March, and they were at their wits' end, when the problem was solved through an invitation

157

to the wedding. The invitation—decorum dictated it—was to Hannah and Hartley, who had remained together after Selina's death. With the acceptance came the information that Hannah's dropsy had increased so much that she could no longer look after Hartley, and that Hartley, in buying comforts and delicacies for Hannah, had got so behind in paying the rent that they were threatened with being turned out of their lodgings. Hartley was a bird in the hand. He would consent to anything for the sake of some ready money and a change from Broadstairs (where the tradespeople were exhausted) to Dover. Mutty was harder to catch, but in the end the combined allurements of a gentleman, a dropsy, a salary, and Dover Castle (whose likeness she had on a mug) snared her, and she went off a week later to be a comfort to Hannah and a purse-keeper to Hartley.

"When Hannah dies, Hartley will marry her," said Joseph.

Joseph reached Loseby on the twentieth of April. A black northeaster was blowing, the shingle beach resounded under the force of the waves as though a vast iron chain were being dragged interminably along the shore, and everyone was saying that things would be better once it had snowed. Cowed by the cold (his height seemed to expose him to an undue amount of it), his knuckles blue and his teeth chattering, Joseph, on his entrance, looked much the same as the Joseph who had run away. By the evening he had thawed out, and a different Joseph appeared. To Euphemia it was as though Marmaduke were among them, wearing Joseph as a disguise: the cock of the head, the hand laid flat on the knees, the unindented voice, the way of commanding attention by speaking with an air of diffidence—all these were tricks learned from Marmaduke. What else had he learned from Marmaduke? She found that he knew nothing beyond the fact that Marmaduke had happened to be in Loseby about a pair of breeches when a dog of some sort frightened Mary, and that later the Barnard family had spent a few days at Rougham. Joseph had news of his own to tell her. At a ball in Port of Spain, a matron of many diamonds had introduced herself to him as Mrs. Tower, asking if he were not related to Euphemia Smith who had married a Maxwell of Phawhope; after a genealogical jaunt which finally established an intermarriage between a Tower and a Smith early in the eighteenth century, she came back to the present day and introducd him to her three daughters, Lizzie, Grizzie, and Annabel. They were considerable heiresses, and the moment Lizzie was settled Joseph would propose for Grizzie—it was a family where precedence was observed. Grizzie had an estate for her portion. He would settle there and have three daughters called Effie, Euphan, and Phemie.

"And I don't see why my place at Pepper Hill should not be filled by Thomas Kettle. My father cannot expect him to spend the rest of his days sorting oyster shells."

"He would not wish Mary to be so far away, I think."

"He's taking this marriage coolly enough. What's become of that devotion to Mary you used to write about? I see no particular sign of it. And what's happened to his temper? Surely he's much milder than he used to be?"

"You are not so much afraid of him."

"God forbid!"

Before the visit was out, Joseph was as much afraid of his father as ever he had been in his life.

The wedding had taken place, and Mary had come downstairs in her travelling bonnet—a married woman's bonnet with feathers waving—and had given her last embraces and got into the carriage with Thomas and been driven away—alone with her husband, for the convention of a female companion was old-fashioned and discarded. The guests dispersed, Hartley was dislodged from his reminiscences and carried off Mutty with suitable chivalries, and everything was over except the clearing away and the washing up. The noise of the wind resumed its ownership of the quieted house. It was a gathering, veering wind, whose gusts had muffled and then magnified and then muffled again the chimes of the wedding bells, and fluttered Mary and her bridesmaids into a flight of sea-mews across the churchyard. During the evening it steadied into a true Loseby east wind, and blew with that high-pitched sneering note that was familiar to them as the Old Hundredth. As they stood in the hall, taking their bedroom candlesticks, they heard a hailstorm strike against the window, and Joseph said, "What a day! I hope you will have better weather in January."

"Why in January?" said Julia, coming out of a yawn.

"For the christening."

"Joseph!" said his father. They started, hearing the crack of the whip again. "You would do better to leave such reckonings to servant maids." He walked into his study and shut the door.

They looked at one another in silence; after a minute or two Ellen began to cry. She cried in a noiseless, helpless way, and Julia looked at her with an expression of wearied and yet envious acquiescence.

"But what was wrong in that?" said Joseph. He turned to Euphemia for an answer, but she was looking at the floor and did not seem to hear him. Ellen pulled out her handkerchief and mopped her eyes. Her hands shook with cold, and the birthmark showed almost black in her paled face. She was only expressing what they all felt, so no one attempted to comfort her.

3.

It was after the second cockcrow, and the wind had blown itself out, when John Barnard came out of his study and wandered about the house. Euphemia woke up and saw the connecting door between her room and Mary's outlined in light, and heard his feet shuffling the dust-sheets that had been laid on the floor when Mary dressed for her wedding. Her thoughts went back to the morning when the croo-croo of doves turned

160

out to be Mary sobbing. That was the day of the Judas-tree party, and on the morning following, her bite had been really extremely painful and Papa had given his consent to Mary's marriage. From then on had flowed almost a year of rational calm. Now the Black Dog had leaped onto her father's shoulders again. Thinking how very unpleasant the morrow would be, and that she would need all her wits for it, she set herself to go to sleep for what remained of the night, and did not hear him when he went downstairs again about an hour later.

He was in despair—a useless despair, for it was too late. She was Mary Kettle now, called by the name of the man who had bedded her and whose children she would bear, and whose voice, saying, "Mary," would dull the ring of all former voices. Her maiden name was over, and her maiden self. Gay, blooming, smelling of youth and orange-flower water, she had embraced him in farewell, pressing her lips to his cheek. The lips were hot, they burned already with the kiss she would give Thomas when the last distracted wave of the hand had been dispensed and in the swaying carriage she could cast herself into his arms. She was married and gone; and now that it was too late he could not imagine what had possessed him to give her away so lightly—to give her away, good God! even before she had been asked for. What was that but prostitution? Man walks in his own darkness, and at the time it had seemed to him that he was doing right. It was Thomas she loved, and at the Judas-tree party she had been seen in his embrace. Her reputation would have been torn to shreds by the Kettles, and if Thomas had been dismissed her heart would have been broken. And Thomas had acted very properly when he sprang up in her defence and threw the book at his father. All these were good reasons—or seemed so at the time. A wintry relief had lightened on him when he spoke of their marriage as a thing already settled; even his conscience had approved.

Only his heart had stood away from the transaction and had remained cold and emptily shrivelling. The wealth of Mary's happiness, her violent, artless rapture, which had transfigured those summer days like a golden pollen hanging on the air and causing everyone to sneeze and exclaim with pleasure at such sweetness, had only impoverished him. It was the shock, he told himself, the shock of seeing her on Thomas's bed. Such a shock must leave one cold. And though he felt morally sure that Thomas had no hand in it, he had no notion how or why she had got there. It might be love, or it might be sleepwalking. He could have known for the asking, but he could no more frame such a question than he could take off his trousers in public. And so things had gone smoothly on; everything had gone as he decided it should go. And now, when it was too late, he knew that he had given her away—no, not even that; say, truly, disposed of her—because the agony of possessing her in hatred had seemed so intolerable, and also because he could not humble himself to being worsted by Simon Kettle. This last truth was revealed in the dining parlour, whither he had strayed back, sitting for a long time at the head of the table, which was still extended with extra leaves, as it had been for the wedding breakfast. Raising his head from his hands, he saw himself encompassed by a volley of golden spears; for the sun had risen, and light was coming through chinks in the shutters. So it was morning. He got up and unbarred the shutters, and the whole force of the eastern sky hit him in the face. Because of the wall he could not see the sun, but he saw the sky pulsating with light. Overhead were a few wisps of rosy cloud, like Cupids on a painted ceiling. They were all that remained of the storm. Possibly at this very moment she was waking in her marriage bed, a bed into which he had thrust her because he could not bear to keep her, and because he could not throttle Simon Kettle. In an agony of remorse he closed the shutters and turned back into his old self as though he had never been that cool, efficient father who had given a kind consent to his daughter's love-match.

With all the energy of being too late, he cancelled the godless interval of treating his family as a branch of the family business, and before long they were creeping and glancing and trembling just as before, except that now there was no Mary to be held up as a saving relic. After a week Joseph went off for his visit to Rougham Hall. His host gave him one look and recognized the Joseph who had sat among half-packed boxes saying he dare not go back to Anchor House. "Is your father still playing at Giant Despair?" he inquired.

"Worse than ever," was the answer. "Mary can thank her stars she's married and out of it, and I suppose Effie won't be long in following her."

"I shall not blame her," Marmaduke replied. The words were no sooner out of his mouth than he realized they were indiscreet, but Joseph, whose remark had been fathered by nothing beyond deploring Euphemia's lot and hoping that she would contrive to take a woman's way out of it, did not take them up. Certainly Marmaduke would not blame her; but for all that he would not inquire further. What he had felt for her was perhaps not so much love as fascination. It was fruitless, and he would turn his mind to marrying someone else. He lived in a world full of eligible daughters and he had no intention of being blighted because he could not get Mr. Barnard's. But though there is such a variety of vegetables, one would feel regret in knowing that never again could one eat cucumber; and it was so that he would always regret the loss of Euphemia.

From Rougham, Joseph went on to visit his Uncle Daniel. He had not many visitable friends in England, and he was at his wits' end how not to return to Loseby when Hannah providentially died and he could go to Dover to represent the family at her funeral. By means of this, less than a fortnight remained before he sailed, and part of that time was spent with Mary and Thomas in their cottage at Graveton Hall, where Thomas was employed in cataloguing Miss Caroline Basham's collection of shells.

It was an odd occupation for a young man—particularly for a young man with no knowledge of conchology; but Miss Basham was quite satisfied with the arrangemnt. A half-century earlier Caroline Basham had seen the *rocaille* grotto at Rambouillet and was fired to decorate a summerhouse in her father's park with shellworks of her own making. From the summerhouse she proceeded to the orangery, from the orangery to the private chapel. Her sisters married, her brother was killed in the hunting field, her parents died; she inherited Graveton and surpassed herself in a mausoleum. Shells were dispatched to her from the coasts and waterways of four continents, and generations of children on the estate kept her supplied with snail shells. In her seventh decade she decided to set her collection in order, house it, together with the appropriate books and plates she had acquired, in the orangery, and bequeath the whole to the county of Norfolk. She commissioned her solicitor, Mr. Powles, to find her a salaried assistant. This was in February, soon after John Barnard had tried to place Thomas in the firm of Powles, Powles, and Bellowes. Remembering that there had been commendations of the young man's handwriting, and something said about neatness and a well-arranged cabinet, and thinking that anyone who had been a schoolmaster would have Latin enough to compass the lingo of Miss Basham's hobby, Henry Powles recommended Thomas for the post.

Thomas was escorted by him to Graveton, inwardly commenting on whimsical old maids, and determined to have nothing to do with Miss Basham. Seeing her, he began to change his mind. It was apparent that she took to him, which is always persuasive; it was equally apparent—and to him this was more persuasive still—that she would not have cared a snap of her fingers if he had fallen dead at her feet. "Poor young fellow," she would have said. "Powles must get me another." Tousled by John Barnard's solicitude, Thomas saw servitude to Miss Basham extending before him like a bed whose sheets would

164

be immortally smooth. Yet he stayed on his guard till the shell-works caught him. He was standing in the orangery, where the February sunshine fell with a watery light on swags of mussel-shell foliage and clusters of pink shell roses, when he saw a petal detach itself and fall and splinter on the marble floor. Enchanted by this concord of artifice and decay, he felt his whole future happiness depending on a shellwork rose. At the same moment he heard Miss Basham say, "I can't have you keeping a dog. Nothing of that sort, you understand."

Did she know he would shortly be keeping a wife? Armouring himself against a disclosure that Miss Basham classed wives with dogs, he said, "Has Mr. Powles told you that I hope to marry Miss Mary Barnard in May?"

"Did he? I daresay he did. Well, Snipe Cottage is empty. I'll have some furniture put in, and you can live there." It was a pity, she thought, that he was so insufferably aware of the splendour of marrying a Miss Barnard. But his private life would be no affair of hers, and for the rest, his voice was agreeable, and he would do. A couple of days later he was installed.

Snipe Cottage had been a gamekeeper's cottage. It had stood empty for some years, it was damp, the smell of old wood-fires hung about it, and Miss Basham's loaned furniture sat in it like exiled Bourbons, magnificent, incommodious, and creaking. Every morning he walked across the park to his work in the orangery, sorting and classifying and unpacking: many of the cases from abroad had never been opened. Or he would mend another yard or so of the orangery garlands, until the cold was too much for his fingers. Miss Basham seldom appeared. Having made up her mind he would do, she left him to himself. The orangery was unheated, and he was offered neither food nor drink. He had every reason to feel aggrieved and insulted, and was paradisaically happy. Through March and April he lived alone in Snipe Cottage, coming back in the evening to cook his own supper and to read as he ate it, and falling asleep in a wide bed under a trophy of ostrich feathers —a life as rhythmical and obscure as though he were living it under the sea. When the time came for his marriage he was so well established in the pattern of his days that marriage did not disrupt it. The suppers were cooked by a servant girl from the village who could not grill as neatly as he did but who excelled him in pastry, and he made love in the wide bed. Before long he knew that matrimony was a more positive pleasure to Mary than to himself, but this did not fret him. Indeed, he was glad it should be so, since his private life was protected by Mary's pleasure in being married to him. Walking home from his solitary days, longer now that the summer daylight stretched out the time he could work in, he sometimes wondered what there would be to talk about during the evening. Their minds were dissimilar, and their lives had afforded them very little to relate; but somehow, with mice, ghosts, a cowslip wine that was never made, and stories about Graveton which Mary learned from the servant girl, there was always something to say, and fern-owls and nightingales filled up any pauses in the conversation.

It was from the servant girl that Mary learned that Miss Basham had taken to shellwork after being crossed in love, and that the plaster in which the shells were set was mixed with beer. Neither story was true, but Mary felt better for believing them; they rendered Miss Basham a slightly ridiculous figure, so that it was less wounding that she did not ask them to dinner. Strawberries, however, asparagus, guinea fowls, melons, and peaches came with Miss Basham's compliments to their own table; they were allotted a pew in the private chapel, where parson and clerk emerged like tritons from a bower of Queen Conchs and Spiny Oysters, and Mary in her Sunday bonnet was duly asked how she did, and if Snipe Cottage needed any repairs or improvements. Replied to, Miss Basham moved on and was heard addressing the same sort of conscientious landowning inquiries to Mrs. Ewart, the wife of the head gardener.

Seeing Thomas take this as a matter of course showed Mary that she had married beneath her. Nine times out of ten this revelation assured her that in marrying the handsome, the remarkable, the slender, devoted, and unappreciated son of Mr. Kettle the printer, Miss Mary Barnard had done something uniquely elevated and thrilling; on the tenth occasion she knew that she had condescended, and the sense of romantic daring was replaced by a sense of virtue. Thomas, dear Thomas, should never be reminded what she had forfeited by marrying him. Never, never would she breathe a word of reproach! She got into the way of keeping a little apron for these fits of priggishness, and Thomas got into the way of associating the apron with cooler evenings and more impassioned nights. Much as he loved her (and he was coming to love her pretty consistently) he continued to view her with a shepherd's or a mariner's eye. In his earliest childhood he had needed to learn watchfulness and calculation in order to protect himself from his father's bullying and his stepbrother's ill will; what he had seen of the world had not changed his mistrust of it. Now it was only variations of love and fondness that he had to be beforehand with, but the habit persisted and embellished him in Mary's esteem. Alone of the family at Anchor House, she had never gone in fear, growing up, as her father said, incapable of slyness or dissimulation—in fact, straightforwardly selfish and obtuse. Thomas's sensibility amazed her. She had never dreamed of such insight, such considerateness, such powers of foretelling what she felt and what she wanted; she had not imagined it possible to be loved like this. As for her father's love, immeasurably more adoring and solicitous than anything Thomas felt for her, it was not diminished in retrospect, because she did not look back to it.

From time to time Julia and Euphemia drove over to Graveton, emptied a hamper, and said that Papa sent Mary his kind love. "Papa does not approve of Sunday travelling," Mary explained. Thomas, who had foreboded that by marrying Mary he would marry the entire Barnard family, found that his self-respect demanded rather more consideration of his father-in-law's sensibilities than merely keeping holy the Sabbath day. But it was not till August that he told Miss Basham that Mary needed sea air, and that in her condition he could not gainsay her wish that he should go to Loseby with her.

"Oh, is she? Yes, of course. Stay as long as you like. I'll tell Dixon to see to that hole in the floor while you are away." Miss Basham was sitting in her dusky drawing room, heating glue over a small brazier and beating off a wasp with a fan. Leaving her engaged with the wasp, Thomas was beset with a superstitious recollection of the saying about letting well alone. An apoplexy might strike her down, a wasp-sting on the lip stifle her. Her death would snap the soap-bubble world he lived in, and she would die without giving a thought to these consequences. Though the wasp or the apoplexy would not be warded off by his remaining at Graveton, he felt that by going to Loseby he was invoking a calamity. Perhaps while he was away she would hire someone else; he would come back, and a supplanter would be tripping it over the new floorboards.

The wasp, the apoplexy, and the supplanter thronged into his mind ten days later, when a letter from Miss Basham came to Anchor House. It was only to say that she was going to Harrogate and would be obliged if he would bring back three dozen well-matched cuttlefish for renovations to the font, but he lied, saying that he was summoned; and leaving the collection and dispatch of the cuttlefish to Crusoe, who asked no better than to be of service to him, he returned to Graveton the next day. Julia congratulated him disagreeably on being so dutiful and was glad that Miss Basham did not also expect Mary to be at her beck and call. For Mary had settled back into her old place as the centrepiece of the Barnard family, only now, being married and with child, she made more demands and was of more consequence. The park smoked with bonfires of summer refuse before she rejoined him; the salt air

168

seeming to have travelled back with her, for her hair smelled like a mermaid's, and after she had fallen asleep he lay for a long time holding a tress to his nose and reviving in himself the recollection of the night in the *Mary Lucinda.*

It was September, two years almost to the day since that evening when he had walked on the quay and sent that miscarrying message that he would spend the night in a fishing boat. What he had set foot in, that solid yet sidling floor, was anonymous, a boat only. It was not till the early morning that the conversation had told him that he was sailing in the *Mary Lucinda,* and that she was named for the young woman to whose rescue he had run to no more purpose than to have his shin kicked and his hat dislodged. And now, through the one Mary Lucinda, he was lying in a bed with the other, and his child was in her womb, anonymous, a child only. In time it would become real. One morning it would be held out to him, naked and writhing as the skate had been, fresh from the womb as the skate had been fresh from the sea. And like the dying skate, the living child would come to be taken to market, and life would eat it. If he had not gone sailing in the *Mary Lucinda* none of the events of the last two years would have happened. But it was worth it! This dispassionate cry from his heart shocked him a little but did not surprise him. It was true: the sharp, intense reality of that night was so dear a possession that a happy marriage to a propitious young wife was not too much to pay for it.

The smell was evaporating from the tress of hair, and though, during the time of his visit at Anchor House he had made several trips in the *Mary Lucinda,* the reality had evaporated from them too. He had gone out in Mr. Barnard's boat and come back again, and that was all. The charm was lost. The boat did not carry him away from himself, there had been nothing but pleasure and bodily recreation and the knowledge that presently he would be put back on shore. Already, in fact, the payments for that night of two years ago had begun. "It was worth it," he repeated, this time speaking the words aloud. Listening to the late brood of house martins under the eaves of Snipe Cottage, he heard their chirping voices turn into the chirp of oars in the rowlocks, and began to dream that though in bed he was also in a boat, hearing the child in Mary's womb flapping and flustering like the catch on board the *Mary Lucinda.*

4.

About the same hour when Thomas was falling asleep, John Barnard had awakened with a start of remorse and had gone into his dressing room to examine his conscience and to pray. Mary's visit, so passionately and reverently (for a young woman in her first pregnancy must be an object of reverence to any right-thinking man) anticipated, had turned out to be little better than irksome. The object of reverence had yawned and moped and given a great deal of trouble to the servants. She was in blooming health, and the airs of languor and fretfulness that she put on like some new variety of blue ribbons did not disturb her mother or Euphemia; but whenever her father appeared she intensified them. It was as though she were carrying out some peculiar flirtation with him, compelling him to admit her bulk, her breathlessness, her ferocious whims of appetite, as a girl enforces attention to her lightness of foot and smallness of waist. Eventually he even looked forward to her departure, and witnessed it with a sombre calm. She was no sooner gone than he began to reproach himself. The sallies that had seemed to him so ill-timed, and indeed so unladylike, reappeared as appeals to his pity and understanding, appeals against which he had hardened his heart. She was unwell, she was frightened, she was not happy. She had turned to him for comfort, and he had not given it. He had let her go back alone to Thomas, who would neglect her. She would die. The issues of life and death are in the hands of God; for all that, he found himself consulting Julia. Was Julia satisfied that Mary's health was all that it should be, that her high colour was healthy, and not hectic, that it was usual for a young woman in her state to be so easily out of breath, and to eat salt beef with such voracity? Julia assured him that Mary was perfectly well, and no fonder of salt beef than she should be, but dashed away these consolations by stressing the triumph of Mary's constitution over her circumstances. Most young women, said Julia —who resented that her prize daughter should be married to a young man who catalogued shells and lived in a gamekeeper's cottage and was not invited to Miss Basham's dinner parties —most young women would be frightened out of their wits by expecting a baby in such a wretched out-of-the-way hovel as Snipe Cottage. "I shall be surprised if my own health does not suffer by it, when I go there for Mary's confinement," she said, staring at him vindictively, already prepared for his total indifference as to what she might suffer in the birth of a grandchild, after all she had suffered in the birth of his children. His indifference came up to her expectations, and she drew an acrid pleasure from it.

He was defeated and said no more. To grieve and be solitary, like the pelican on the housetops, was the lot appointed for him. But one day, late in November, he could endure it no longer and rode to Graveton. The decision had not been made till midday; when he reached the park gate the armorial stags trippant on the pillars were blunted by the oncoming dusk. The lodgekeeper came out and, hearing that he was come to visit Mrs. Kettle, told him to ride round to the other gate. The diversion along a muddy lane, companied by a high brick wall, seemed interminable, as long as the whole previous ride, and as though Mary must die in the interval between one set of gates and another. The second gateway was socially inferior; two or three cottages stood just within it; and, having been brooding on Mary's isolation within that cruel wall, he was suddenly furious to think of her living jostled by cottage neighbours. A man came forward and directed him to Snipe Cottage. It was about half a mile farther on if he rode, but if he would walk over the grass towards the light shining in Mrs. Kettle's window he would get there as soon on foot, and the horse could stand in the stables nearby.

"You've rode him hard," said the man, taking the horse from him. "If you've brought bad news, best keep it from Mrs. Kettle. She's breeding."

"I am her father," he replied; and it seemed to him that the conversation denounced his whole existence.

The light, a smudge of brilliance when he began walking towards it, diminished and was confined in a latticed window as he approached. Walking over the grass, he made no noise until their wicket creaked under his hand. He heard her speaking in the house. "Thomas! It's old Friday. Tell him we don't want any fish." He heard a door on the other side of the cottage open and close, and Thomas saying, "There's no one there," and Mary answering, "I could have sworn I heard someone. Never mind. Your throw." And then he heard the rattle of dice in a box and knew they were playing backgammon. Why should I disturb them? he thought. She is well and happy, and that is all I want to know. But the wicket which he had closed behind him would creak again, and she might think of thieves. He knocked, and Thomas came to the right door and let him in. To announce himself, and make it plain that his visit was harmless, he said at once, "I had some business to do in Fakenham, so I thought I would ride on and pay you a little visit."

"We are delighted to see you. Mary! It's your papa. Walk carefully, Mr. Barnard, there is a hole in the floor to your right."

A low table was drawn up before the fire; on it were the backgammon board, glasses and a decanter, and a dish with raw sausages. A Mary he had not seen for sixteen years sat in an armchair covered with red velvet. In this last stage of her

172

pregnancy, as though to companion the child within her, she had gone back to the looks of her babyhood—bland, dimpled, majestic, a splendid child for her age. "Papa," she announced, as though she were saying it for the first time.

"My darling!"

"We're just going to toast our sausages. We eat our supper before the fire and go to bed early." She spoke with an infantile complacency—from the centre of her world, as a baby does.

"Like two good children." The commendation—one of the few unpreconsidered commendations John Barnard had ever spoken—fell flat. At his elbow was Thomas, an alien child not of his nursery, offering him a glass of wine. Our low ways, and our sausages, Thomas was thinking. Presently we shall have a lecture on deportment. So he redoubled his civilities, making separate inquiries after the health of everyone at Anchor House, and extending an invitation to stay for supper with such dignity that only a dullard could have failed to refuse it.

"But do not let me interrupt you in yours."

"No, no! You do no such thing. As you see, we have not begun." Thomas indicated the raw sausages as though they were some unworthy haunch of venison. Mary put down the toasting fork and folded her hands on her belly. The glass of wine and the biscuits occupied a half-hour, during which time Thomas made conversation and Mary looked dreamily at the sausages. After that there was nothing for it but to go.

"When you come again I hope you will be able to stay longer," said Thomas.

"When you come again there will be a baby," said Mary, turning her smooth, warm brow to be kissed.

He rode home through a foggy moonlight. The air, as often at that time of year, had become mild with night—a seasonless clemency, as though it were a climate of moonlight. He rode on, lost in a dream, still seeing the lavish, untidy wood-fire on the wide hearth, and the low-ceilinged room, littered with books

173

and needlework as a cave would be littered with bones and flint implements and fox skins. It was a foreign domesticity, equally unlike the parlours of his own life and the front kitchens of the Loseby fishermen. No wonder there was no place for him in it. He had been given a cold reception and dismissed as soon as possible, and he was saddened and heavy with disappointment. Yet he was at peace. It seemed to him that the warfare of the last eighteen months was over, and that he could now renounce Mary without bitterness. She belonged to her husband and to her child. His part in her, for good or bad, was cancelled. He was astonished and thankful to find how painlessly he could renounce her. But in fact this was not so surprising. Startled by her return to the infant he had so especially vowed to love, he also had gone back in time and loved her as painlessly and entirely as he had done then.

Early in the new year Julia came back from the lying-in, reporting that the child was everything that a baby should be, and that Mary wished it to be called John. Julia did not mention that at birth the baby had looked exactly like Simon Kettle.

Both pairs of grandparents met at Graveton for the christening. Again Simon was wearing a buttonhole—this time a Christmas rose. Sophie carried a bunch of snowdrops. They looked all that was virtuous and prosperous, a demonstration of virtue rewarded, and talked about Loseby with tender inaccuracy, as though they had not been there since childhood. Sophie's condescension was particularly well contrived to gall. Gazing at the baby, she said, "How little I thought, when I was first a widow and mending Mrs. Barnard's bone lace, that this dear little fellow would be the outcome of it all! Cast your bread upon the waters . . . Mr. Barnard, I am sure you must agree with me that this is a case in point."

John Barnard could only bow, but Julia took up the challenge. "If we are reckoning up the preliminaries, pray do not let us forget the former Miss Mutley. If my husband had not

174

found her nursing Thomas in a cellar, I suppose Thomas would not have come to Anchor House to recover."

"Which makes it all the sadder that she cannot be here today. Her husband's health, I understand. Poor Magdalen! She seems destined to be nursing someone or other. I am spared such anxieties with Mr. Kettle. His health is remarkably good, although he works so hard. But I don't think *work* impairs any constitution." She glanced meaningly towards her stepson. But when talking to him, she was all that was amiable.

"Thomas is conceited enough," Simon remarked later that day. "What made you flatter him so about those fiddle-faddle shells, and living in that fool's paradise of a cottage? It's not a fit place for the child to grow up in."

"No indeed! But I thought a little flattery would not come amiss, now that for once in his life he has shown some steadiness." (She did not choose to state her real purpose, since it would be humiliating if nothing came of it.)

"I am surprised that Barnard permits it. If the child had been named after me I would insist on something more respectable."

"My dear, let them name it what they please. It is you it resembles."

Simon was mollified. His character was too base to maintain a steady ill will, and now, well fed and well groomed by a good wife, he was inclining to see no great harm in Thomas. His attempts at slander had oddly miscarried, and Thomas had thrown a book at him; but these things were in the past, he felt no particular rancour about them. The current Thomas was off his hands, married to a pretty wife and mysteriously in with the aristocratic Miss Basham. Was not the child christened in a font ornamented by her own hands, and did she not—though by proxy—stand sponsor to it? (He was unaware that Miss Basham stood godmother to all the children born on the estate.) He did not object to the proxy part of it at all. It was for a propitious reason. She was too old to come out on a cold day, and he hoped that her death would be followed by a handsome legacy. Though he felt obliged to rebuke Sophie for praising Snipe Cottage, in private he agreed with her. Snipe Cottage was ideally placed in relation to Graveton Hall. The grandson, too, was an ideal grandson, combining the tribute of a resemblance and the unction of an injury. Nothing could be more advantageous to his penchant for a bleeding heart than to have his first grandson (Sim got nothing but girls) named after its other grandfather. His heart had not bled for some time, it yearned for a phlebotomy. All in all, he was quite ready to be reconciled with Thomas and to do no more than reproach him with that unfilial "John." For a grandson named Simon he would have been prepared to make considerable alterations in his will. Later, perhaps, that could be implied—not harshly, but as a Christian and in the light of the Fifth Commandment, the first with promise.

Sophie was less placable. She had her own wrongs to avenge, as well as her husband's. A woman of exemplary patience, she proposed to begin in quite a small way: by aiding Thomas to differ with his wife and his wife's relations. Some harm might come of it. If not, she could begin again, with the model of Bruce's well-known spider before her. One glance at the Barnards had shown her that John Barnard's self-respect was chafed by his son-in-law's way of life, and that Julia intended to use the baby as a lever to get Mary away from gipsying in Snipe Cottage. Julia could be trusted to do all that was necessary to frighten a young mother; Sophie's part would be to stiffen a young father. A word in season . . . She hoped that she had spoken just such a word. By nature and destiny Thomas was shaped to be unfortunate, and it would be a queer thing if she could not do him an injury.

Sophie Kettle's trust was not misplaced. Julia had already begun to talk about convulsions, croup, winter bronchitis, summer dysentery, cramps, gripes, choking fits, and wasting, and of the dangers of damp cots and village nursemaids. Mary

176

had repeated these stories to Thomas; seeing his appalled face, she had laughed and plucked up her spirits. Thomas could not recover so easily. Responsibility frightened him, and, not having risked his life in the process of giving birth, he lacked the gamester's confidence that supported Mary. Though his stepmother's kind approvals made him feel braver, he had just enough sense to opine that his child might need more experienced handling than it would get from Mary and the local girl who had been hired as nursemaid. He asked Julia if Nurse Darwell could be transferred from Anchor House to Snipe Cottage.

He was told that Darwell could not be spared.

5.

This was Darwell's decision, Julia only reverberated it; but what Darwell put into her mouth, Julia had to speak. Before Joseph's visit Julia again resolved to do herself justice and forced herself into sobriety. In the past so much had been said of the benefits of Joseph's West Indian produce that consistency and good manners obliged her to drink a little rum while he was at home. She drowned it in milk, with every hope of giving it up when Joseph sailed. In the frightful period after the wedding, when Barnard's Black Dog returned, blacker than ever, and Mary was no longer available as a talisman, it was the milk that Julia gave up. Soon she was drinking heavily. No one noticed it, she told herself. "No one," in Julia's estimation, meant no member of the family—an ignorant class prejudice, as she was to learn. Wilberforce being in his tenth year, Darwell's days of power were ending. Darwell was convinced that if he was taken out of her management he would die. In the course of a dispute about a flannel waistcoat, she struck. If the waistcoat was not worn, she said, she would feel it her duty to tell Mr. Barnard that the child's mother was not fit to decide on such matters, and to tell him the reason. Julia, racked with a headache, accepted blackmail as just another incommodity in her wretched lot. As time went on, she grew reconciled to it, for Darwell was a devoted tyrant. Darwell could understand how Madam felt. She was addicted to headaches herself, she knew what it was to be a woman. She also knew a very respectable Mrs. Hitchcock, an old-clothes woman, who often wondered what Mrs. Barnard did with her shawls when she grew tired of them. Mrs. Hitchcock now speculated no longer. The shawls were sold, and came back in bottles, which was a great deal better than having to depend on Joseph's goodwill towards poor old women in Loseby.

But when the teething baby came out in a rash, scratched himself raw, and bellowed himself blue in the face, and Mary herself demanded Darwell, no combination of blackmail and devotion could withstand John Barnard's determination to send Darwell immediately. Grumbling, snapping, and counting bundles, she was packed off in the carriage, her servant's dignity outraged by the thought of having to belittle herself into a gamekeeper's cottage; not even the prospect of arriving as a ministering angel to Miss Mary and an avenging angel to the Graveton nursemaid could plaster the social wound. One glance at Snipe Cottage enabled her to diagnose that the baby was in such a precarious state that the only hope for his life was to take him to Loseby. While the horses baited at the Basham Arms, she dismissed the nursemaid, administered some healing slaps to the child, and combed Mary's hair, which Mary had burned in the candle flame while searching for guidance in a dreadful bible about the diseases of infancy. Alternately consoled and condoled with, terrified and set to rights, Mary was in too great a fluster of panic and relief to think more about Thomas than that when he came back from work the servant would tell him where she had gone. Darwell, better aware of the conventions of matrimony, did not choose to remind her of them. She had long been of the opinion that the young Mr.

Kettle was no better than the old one, a neglectful, miserly, penniless beast to keep a young lady in such an out-of-the-way pigsty, and she was delighted to think of the slight she had contrived for him.

Thomas had been as much agitated as Mary about the child, and suffered in addition from a sense of guilty inadequacy, for though he had more natural talent than she for soothing a cross baby, Mary had relieved her nerves by not allowing him to touch the child. Kept inactively sleepless and ravaged with morbid hungers and nervous indigestions, Thomas was in no state to feel one slight worse than another, and, returning to his emptied house, he noticed first not that it was empty but that it was quiet. The servant girl gave her message and stood staring at him, ready to take his part; but he was too spiritless to be interesting, so she went off to the village to spread the news.

It was not till some days later that John Barnard learned that Mary had come away without waiting for Thomas's permission. He wrote a letter of apology to his son-in-law, saying categorically that Mary had behaved badly. It was so painful to make such an admission that his pen halted, and his gaze roamed among the Flaxman illustrations for a hint what to say next. The Flaxman illustrations yielded nothing beyond a general high-mindedness, so, forced back on his own invention, he reminded Thomas that Mary was young and needed guidance, the more so as her maternal feelings, etc.—in short, that Mary would not have run off without asking leave if Thomas had taken more pains with her. He added that the child seemed well, and was Thomas's faithfully.

His writing paper was of the best quality. Thomas made some notes for a sonnet on the blank tail of the page and put the letter into his pocketbook. Since the boy was better and Mary only morally ailing, his father-in-law was welcome to pontificate. "I may not be a Barnard of a husband," he said to the cat, "but at least I know more about married life than he does. My wife is not afraid of me, and I will never be a bore or a tyrant to my children."

As this kind of husband, Thomas was living very serenely. Snipe Cottage had been set in order, the rooms aired, the smell of milk and excrement got rid of, the window panes polished, the books dusted. It was as calm as an empty shell. Not since the summer, when the baby did nothing more alarming than stuffing its mouth with rose petals, had he felt so capable of enjoying a quiet country life. His sensibilities sharpened. Ideas came agreeably into his mind, he wrote poetry every evening and did a little gardening. In the reply to Mr. Barnard he said that he hoped Mary would stay at Anchor House as long as she wanted to, and by the same post he wrote to the same effect to Mary, told her about his gardening, and enclosing a couple of sonnets. Neither letter was well received. Mary thought Thomas might find something more poetical to write about than squirrels, and her father was shocked by Thomas's willingness to do without Mary for as long as Mary pleased. The fact that he himself was so dotingly happy in her company, and had to whip himself morning and evening with the thought that he must be ready at any moment to part with the joy of his life, made it shocking that Thomas did not demand her return. It was not for this that he had renounced her. As so often, there could be no doubt what God wished: Mary must go back to Snipe Cottage and, for the sake of the child, Darwell must go with her.

Darwell had not the smallest intention of going to Snipe Cottage. The baby, snatched from death by her intervention and thriving in wholesome Loseby air, was discovered to be again in a most precarious state. He might seem a healthy child, but to her experienced eye he bore all the marks of the Barnard constitution, together with a tendency to rickets, inherited, no doubt, from his papa. Bursting into the study, she invoked the obelisk. George, Susan, Samuel, Julius, poor little Robina—did Mr. Barnard wish to bury his first grandchild among them?

Wilberforce, who should have been seen but not heard, looked up from the celestial globe. "But they all died here, and you were their nurse. Why should you say—"

On the lips of so young a child such logic was impious. Wilberforce was reminded that death is an awful subject. But Darwell's most precious arguments were kept for Julia in her dressing room: Madam's impaired constitution, which only Darwell understood; Madam's dependence on Mrs. Hitchcock, which Darwell would lay down her life rather than disclose, unless circumstances positively drove her to it. For the first time in his life John Barnard felt the whole force of an embattled servant (servants had been embattled before then, but Julia had been a wifely buckler to him). Mystified and irate, he gave way. There was still an alternative version of what God willed, not quite so painful as parting with Mary, but still wholesomely vexatious. He wrote another letter to Thomas, pressing him to give up a dwelling which was not fit for Mary and the child, and an occupation which was too trifling for a responsible family man. Thomas had better come to Loseby and apply himself to learning how to trade with the Baltic—more seriously this time, and under supervision. This was followed by a sermon on the estate of matrimony. Wives were the weaker vessels; nothing but harm could ensue if husbands failed to assume their proper authority. Mary was not faultless, she should not have left Snipe Cottage without asking Thomas if she might do so. But her upbringing had been so careful, her disposition was so docile, and the example of her mamma so plainly before her, that as a father and father-in-law he earnestly recommended Thomas to examine himself for shortcomings of his own. He did not doubt that such an examination would prove fruitful.

The implication that his main function as a husband was to be a moral lady's maid to Mr. Barnard's daughter threw Thomas into a fury. All Sophie Kettle's assurances about Snipe Cottage charged into his mind. He forgot that when he heard them they had been reassuring because he himself had been

181

in doubt. Now there was nothing wrong with Snipe Cottage, and nothing wrong with himself, except that he had for far too long put up with Mr. Barnard's interference. His first impulse was to borrow a horse from Miss Basham's stable and ride over to Loseby for a face-to-face quarrel with his father-in-law. But to appear on a borrowed horse was lacking in dignity. Mrs. Kettle's stepson, inhabiting that irreproachable dwelling place, Snipe Cottage, and earning his livelihood in an occupation so very much more skilled and interesting than mere trade, need not hurry to Loseby on a borrowed horse in order to state his case. He would write a letter; and he would not do so by return of post, either. The letter was written the next day, however. Mrs. Kettle's stepson did not choose to have another night's sleep ravaged by considerations of how to phrase a letter which was of no real consequence to him. The shorter, the cooler, the less like Mr. Barnard's, the better.

The letter, admirably short and cool, stated that Thomas saw no reason why he should leave Miss Basham's employment (the word "employment" gave him a stinging pleasure); if Mary wished to remain at Anchor House until Johnnie had finished cutting his teeth, and if her parents could keep her without inconvenience to themselves, Thomas would gladly fall in with her wish, confident that she and the child would come to no harm there. He did not comment on the example of a mamma who was so often tipsy. To do so would not have been the act of a gentleman.

The effect of this letter was all that Sophie could have desired. She still had a Loseby intelligencer in Mrs. Lovell of Prospect Terrace, and towards the end of March Mrs. Lovell wrote: "Your daughter-in-law and her babe are still at Anchor House, while Mr. Thomas remains at Graveton. It seems very strange, but no doubt there is some reason for it. He is never mentioned, and I do not care to inquire, as there is so much talk about it already that one feels a certain delicacy. Mr. Cowper died last week in acute suffering—dropsy, alas!—but his

182

frame of mind . . ." When the passage about Thomas at Graveton was read aloud to Simon he rubbed his hands and repeated coyly, "No doubt there is some reason for it," adding that Thomas knew which hole the rat would pop out of. For avarice can bear its flower: Simon was a skinflint over every penny of his own getting, but the vision of an unearned increment made a romantic of him. When Mrs. Lovell's handwriting appeared again a few days later, with the news of Miss Basham's sudden death, the thought of little Johnnie's legacy almost made little Johnnie into a little Simon. Why, the discreet Thomas himself might come into something—a codicil, you know. "Well done, thou good and faithful servant." And he dwelt warmly on the snub to those starched and purse-proud Barnards. The wax melted, the soaring wings fell off, when all that came from Snipe Cottage was a request, most crudely and unfilially phrased, that he should lend Thomas twenty pounds to tide him over the interval of finding another home and another employment. Under strong compulsion from Sophie, he overcame his wounded feelings sufficiently to send a five-pound note—which in fact Sophie supplied from her own pocket. She had not done this without misgiving. Henceforward Simon would be even more censorious about the household bills. She also had a misgiving that five pounds might not be enough to prevent Thomas from falling back into the arms of the Barnards, but she dared not disclose a larger margin of economies. Both misgivings were justified by the event.

The news of Miss Basham's death, heard with such elation at Walton on the Naze and then spluttering out like a damp squib, was taken in a more christian spirit at Anchor House, and acknowledged to be a judgment. Thomas had seen no reason why he should leave Miss Basham's employment; Miss Basham had been his pretext for idling like a bachelor at Snipe Cottage; and lo! Miss Basham was removed. It was as though the swine had enforced a return on the Prodigal Son by refusing to share any more husks with him. For details of the judgment, Anchor House had to rely on Mr. Powles, who, as Miss Basham's lawyer, had been present at the reading of the will. The will had been made ten years earlier, and though Miss Basham's draft of a codicil leaving the shell collection to the county of Norfolk was pinned to it, it was a draft only, and of no legal force. The heir, a cousin twice removed, was with his regiment at Gibraltar, but would travel home. It did not seem probable, said Mr. Powles, that he would be much interested in conchology.

A week or so later Mr. Powles reported the rightness of this forecast. Colonel Basham had a numerous family, and was a fervent Methodist. His first concern was to get rid of those godless fripperies in the private chapel; the second, to recoup himself for the inordinate extent of Miss Basham's legacies by a sale of books, furniture, and pictures. Mr. Powles added that Thomas seemed to be in a bad way—some sort of low fever. The executors had, as a grace, paid him another month's wages; but Basham Hall was closed, he had no occupation, and most of the furniture had been taken from Snipe Cottage to be included in the sale.

Seeing John Barnard's lips compressed, Mr. Powles turned to a more reliable subject. "I need not ask if Miss Mary— Mrs. Kettle, I should say—is well. I met her with the little boy this morning. I have never seen her look more blooming."

She had never looked more blooming. . . . John Barnard had all the trump cards, but conscience dashed them out of his hand. Thomas had refused to quit Miss Basham's employment, and Miss Basham was dead. Thomas had persisted in living at Snipe Cottage, and Snipe Cottage was being dismantled. Thomas had been insolent, contumacious, and frivolously self-confident, and his shellwork structure had fallen in ruins about him. Those were the trump cards. They could not be played because Thomas was at Graveton, solitary and sickly, while Mary was blooming at Loseby, so little her husband's wife, even with his child beside her, that Powles had spoken of her

184

as Miss Mary. It was nearly three weeks since Miss Basham's death; and during that time Mary had sometimes supposed that Thomas would soon come to Loseby, and at other times had complained that he did not, and at other times again had wondered if he would remember to pack up Johnnie's drum. And he had known in his soul that her behaviour was heartless, but to himself he had continued to call it wifely patience. All this was his doing, or rather his failure to do. He should have held out in his first intention, and sent Mary back to Snipe Cottage, and Darwell with her.

"Mary, I met Mr. Powles this morning."

"So did I. And Johnnie waved his hand to him so prettily."

"He gave me some rather grave news about Thomas. He thought Thomas looked very unwell."

With infinite relief, he saw her turn pale. "Oh! Oh dear! What shall I do? I could not possibly take Johnnie there, and how could I leave Johnnie? Besides, I should not know what to do. He said in his last letter that the furniture is being taken away. Perhaps Euphemia could go."

"I will go," her father said.

"Yes, that will be best. How kind of you, dear Papa! You are always so kind. And would it be too much trouble . . ." She began charging him with a list of her possessions—Johnnie's christening mug, the tea set, her wedding dress which was folded up in a linen sheet and tied with white ribbons.

"Thomas ill again?" said Julia. "What a wretched constitution! I'm sure I hope he has not passed it on to the child. Darwell thinks so. She does not like to see such heavy sleeps. If he really is ill, you must find some woman about the place to look after him. Euphemia is out of the question, for I cannot possibly get Wilberforce off to school single-handed. Surely you need not set off till tomorrow?"

An April dusk, cold and austere, had fallen before John Barnard reached Graveton. Silent and scentless, for the birds had finished their singing and the primroses had filled with dew, the air had a searching purity, and it abashed him. There was no place in this dispassionate evening for any human errand, even a good one. The man at the second lodge recognized him, but he had difficulty in recognizing the man. He was changed with the circumstances and looked timid and rootless. The great house resembled something in a stage backcloth, being so architecturally perfect and without any vestige of inhabitation.

"They say he's queer," the man said of Thomas, as though Snipe Cottage were in another parish. But a light was in the window, and the garden beds were neatly tilled and edged with primrose clumps. He knocked. There was no answer, and he went in. Emptied of so much of its furniture, the room looked large and garret-like. Thomas, who was sitting hunched up before a fire, turned round at his entrance. His face did not exhibit the smallest surprise; he might have seen John Barnard five minutes before. When he spoke, his manner was both sullen and easy, and his words acknowledged no interval of absence and umbrage between them.

"I've been polishing this shell—a Venus-ear—for Johnnie. I've stolen it, of course. As a matter of law and honour it should be thrown away with the rest of the collection. But Johnnie must have a present to remember Snipe Cottage by."

He shivered, his eyes were sunk in his head, he spoke in a loud, unadjusted voice as when he had raved of the Chief Elephant. The first thing to do was to give him a hot drink, and the next, to put him to bed.

"Have you any spirits in the house, Thomas?"

Thomas laughed in his face. "Not a vestige of either kind. The family ghosts went away with the furniture, and the washing-woman finished off the brandy. I'm sorry to disappoint you, sir. I hate to be inhospitable. If you will have the goodness to be seated, I'll run to the Arms and bring back a bottle, and then we can be merry together. I'm very much in the mood to be merry."

186

"I have a flask." He had to turn away while he searched in the pockets of his riding coat, for he knew his temper could not endure the savage amusement of Thomas's face. In silence he found his way to the kitchen, picked up a kettle, filled it, and came back and set it on the fire. While it boiled he went back to the kitchen and got a tumbler, a spoon, and a lump of sugar.

"An old hand, I see," remarked Thomas.

When the kettle had boiled John Barnard mixed a strong grog. "Thomas, you are not well. Drink this, and don't be foolish."

Thomas looked at him with the disdain that only youth has at its command.

"I nursed you before, you know," said John Barnard humbly.

"Yes. You did. And sometimes I wish you had not. But it's all too late now, isn't it? And you read to me out of old Burton. Well, here's long life to old Burton!"

While he drank, John Barnard looked at the fire, burning on the cushion of fine wood-ash. Among those ashes there might even be a powder from the fire of that other night, when Mary and Thomas had sat with the backgammon board between them, about to eat their supper and go early to bed. "Like good children," he had said. Now there was but one child, and that a sickly and cantankerous one. Thomas, who had eaten nothing all day, grew tipsy in a flash and began to fall asleep. There was only one bed left in the house, and that was a single bed which had been bought for the nursemaid. This too was his doing, thought John Barnard as he tucked Thomas up in it.

Daylight found him busy about the house. There was the hearth to clean, the fire to lay and kindle, breakfast to get for Thomas and for himself. The dishes of the day before were in the kitchen, unwashed, and while the kettle boiled he found a broom and began sweeping the floors. After setting out on these domestic labours in a spirit of stern humility, he presently began to enjoy himself. He had done nothing of this sort since he was a fag at Harrow. He waited impatiently for the fire to have enough heart to make toast at; at Harrow he had learned that toast made before a smoky fire does not please.

Thomas felt that he had lain for hours listening to his father-in-law scampering about with brooms and kettles. The smell of toast, the light clatter of crockery told him that he might expect breakfast brought up to him on a tray. He wished he were dead and that the earth lay on him instead of yet another obligation.

Three days later he was well enough to be moved to Loseby.

PART FIVE

1.

Wave after wave fell on the Loseby beach. At high tide they broke on the ridge of large pebbles, and the iron chain turned. At low tide they broke with a dulled sound on a stretch of white sand, where Johnnie was beginning to walk in leading-strings. It seemed that a cycle of longer interval would continue to cast up Johnnie's father on this inevitable shore.

"Thomas is back again, and I pity him with all my heart," wrote Euphemia to Joseph. As spring went on into summer she ceased to pity Thomas, though she saw that his state was as pitiable as ever. Pity is a sequestered emotion; it evaporates in a heart exposed to pinpricks, and the eldest Miss Barnard, so prim, so cold-bloodedly reserved, was the natural target for Loseby surmises: inquiries if Mr. Kettle would be spending the whole summer at Anchor House, charitable suppositions that he was not so strong as he looked, exclamations on how delighted Mary must be at this reunion. Terrace society in particular was charmed to see Mr. Barnard saddled with a son-in-law who did no work and frequented low company.

"Your brother-in-law seems to find endless occupation in

189

going out with the fishing boats. Quite an old salt! I suppose he has seafaring ancestry?"

"Not that I know of."

Thomas, brought away from Snipe Cottage like a cat in a hamper, said to himself that nothing remained but to go down fighting—in other words, to die as disobligingly as possible. When his vitality slunk back, vindictive and self-preserving, it told him to use the bed and board of Anchor House, the leisure and the restorative veal and Mary, familiar as a slipper and becoming as warm by wearing, just as he would use the conveniences of an inn; and for the rest, to find a pastime that revived his senses and a society that restored his self-esteem. They were not far to seek. He had only to go down to the quay to find an ever-virgin *Mary Lucinda* and friends who had become old friends. Mr. Mobbs was very ready to be a father to Grand Turk's son-in-law. Mrs. Mobbs baked cakes for him, Keziah Bilby boiled shrimps for him, her sons, Dandy, Christmas, and Cheesecake Bilby of the *Euphemia* competed with the crew of the *Mary Lucinda* for his company, and wherever he went Crusoe danced attendance on him like an affectionate bear. Grown in a twelvemonth from an oversized urchin to a young Goliath, Crusoe was now old enough to have his fits of melancholy, during which he put a great deal of grease on his hair, saw nothing but bad omens, and was certain sure that he would die drownded.

"Why don't you learn to swim?" said Thomas at last, though he knew that Loseby discountenanced learning to swim on the grounds that if you had to drown, you died easier without it. "Crusoe, why don't you learn to swim? I'll teach you."

For a moment Crusoe looked at him with the eyes of a drowning man who sees a rope thrown to him. But a refusal as passionate as the desire was in the look, and he answered primly, "No, thank you, Mr. Thomas."

It was a rebuff and stayed in Thomas's memory, obstinately unthawed—perhaps because it was the only rebuff he met

190

with in a career of increasing popularity. It was a season of unusually good catches, money was plentiful, so were festivities, and Thomas had the particular social grace of the shy person who unexpectedly finds himself at his ease. He went to dances at the Bluefish Inn, and to the bowling green and the skittle alley, and ate large suppers in small kitchens where he was entertained with horseplay and brilliant mimicry, and with stories about portents, wrecks, wagers, mermaids, donkeys, highwaymen, sea serpents, and mourning coaches driven by headless men. It was as though a new *Anatomy* were being poured into his ears, only with the Norfolk dialect replacing the Latin, and all the authorities cited by nicknames; and an hour later a boat would put off, and the impartial chill and austerity of the sea unenfoldingly enfold him. In this society too (he knew it well) he was useless and an alien. But it was a kinder society.

John Barnard saw all this, yet he did not disapprove. He had decided to believe that, by frequenting the fishermen's cottages and the Bluefish Inn, Thomas would insensibly develop a vocation for trading with the Baltic; at times he even congratulated himself on being so astute as to encourage these freaks. It had appalled him to discover how nearly he had wrecked Thomas's marriage by absorbing Thomas's wife and child into his household, and in the light of his own narrow escape from guiltiness, Thomas's faults were overlooked. While the rest of the household quailed at hearing Thomas's flippant replies to his father-in-law's recommendations, John Barnard heard them smiling, and thought they showed that Thomas was learning to have confidence in him. Never able to feel by halves, he had gone back to his old opinion: Thomas, now that he had wronged him, could again do no wrong.

The Judas tree in Mr. Powles's garden displayed its remarkable pink blossoms and presided over another garden party, Canon Blunt made a speech congratulating old Mr. Powles on his eighty-fifth birthday and himself died a week later—a

191

mere sixty-seven. A fine Loseby funeral followed, a viper was killed in Church Street, and there was talk of a flower show. Mary became interested in geraniums. A Danish cargo boat missed the entrance into the harbour and ran aground on a sandbank, an extraordinary sermon was preached by a *locum tenens,* and Johnnie wore out a pair of slippers. By then Thomas's satisfaction in the advantages of living at Anchor House as though it were his inn was worm-eaten by the knowledge that he could not call for his bill and go. Though he felt no shame about living in idleness, it irked his pride to be treated as unemployable. He brought himself to ask if he might not return to the office in Tooley Street. Pride made him speak in a sour and slighting tone, and John Barnard heard it as unwillingness and duty. "Time enough," he replied. "You would find London very unwholesome at this season of the year." He was thankful that he could put it by so kindly, without having to refer to a letter in his desk, a letter from the Daniel-and-Robina section of the business, saying categorically that, wherever Thomas might be put, he must not be put back into the agency. Once or twice he hinted that Thomas might settle in the Loseby office, but the hints were ignored. It seemed to Thomas that if he let his feet carry him for three days running to the office in Ship Street, they would carve such a rut as he would never be able to hoist himself out of. It would be Anchor House forever, and the Barnard family pew every Sunday, and year after year the Judas tree rosily reminding him of the dance tune "Never No More," which had piped his neck into the halter. He was not out of love with Mary, and if he could get her away and have her to himself he was ready to love her as much as he had done in Snipe Cottage; but it was not possible to love her at Anchor House, where love was approved and supervised by his father-in-law, and no more his affair than Darwell and Julia allowed his fatherhood of little Johnnie to be. There seemed nothing for it but to wait for the climate of Tooley Street to become less unwholesome. His pride would not let him ask about the agency again, but he supposed that by waiting it would become his; meanwhile he sometimes pricked his father-in-law's attention by reminders that trading with the Baltic was not the only profession open to him. On one such occasion he took out his pencil and ostentatiously marked something in the newspaper.

"What's that, Thomas?" asked Mary—for Thomas and Mary were new-fashioned and employed christian names.

"An advertisement for a tutor," he replied. "Shall I apply? Would you like to live in Wales?"

"I thought tutors had to be unmarried," said Mary—an untimely exhibition of what was called Mary's common sense.

Julia exclaimed, "Goodness, Thomas! You don't want to go and live in Wales." Thomas said nothing and looked a good deal. The fact that Thomas could do no wrong and must not be crossed in anything was so well established as a household law that she added, appeasing her husband quite as much as Thomas, "Though I'm sure they would be very glad to get you—those people in Wales. I was thinking only this morning how unfortunate it was that we sent Wilberforce off to school just before you came here. It would have been so much better for him to have had lessons from you."

Shuddering at what he had escaped—tutoring Wilberforce would have been even more domesticating than going to the office in Ship Street—Thomas said politely, "You are very kind." Julia bit her lip, and Euphemia supplied a new subject for conversation.

John Barnard said nothing, but he remembered what had been said, and when Ellen came home for the summer holidays accompanied by a bad report on her arithmetic, he asked Thomas to give her a daily lesson. His patience with Thomas had not run out, for conscience still pricked him; but conscience was now overhauling patience, and though the request acknowledged that Thomas's qualifications were far beyond Ellen's deserts, there was a rap in it.

"By all means. I shall be delighted. Do you wish me to cram Wilberforce too?"

"No, thank you. I have no reason to be dissatisfied with Wilberforce. He is not an idler."

Not since the return from Graveton had Thomas seen his father-in-law so nearly unseated from his benevolence. The sight was a welcome one. A little cloud, no bigger than a man's hand, was in the sky that had been so boringly and sublimely blue. The cloud would swell, the storm would break, and with all his heart he hoped the floods would wash him away from Loseby and into any sea but the Baltic. Meanwhile, he had to give Ellen lessons in arithmetic. The weather was close, and he could not rid himself of a conviction that the blemish on Ellen's face brought in bluebottles. Much as Thomas disliked Ellen, Ellen disliked Thomas infinitely more, and before long she was hating him with a virgin intensity. If he had been even a little kind to her—Ellen's fondest dream was to reward a momentary kindness by the devotion of a lifetime—she would have been a willing pupil. But finding her even more repulsive when she goggled and puffed at him, he wore his coldest manner as he hunted her through vulgar fractions, extorting from her every pennyworth of the bargain which he piqued himself on paying in full to the landlord of the Anchor House Inn. It was a miserable situation, and Wilberforce, surveying it with the pure eyes and perfect witness of someone who has been away from home, remarked to Euphemia that sooner or later, but probably sooner, there would be the devil to pay. Euphemia was of much the same opinion. She saw that Thomas was near the end of his tether, behaving as rudely as he could allow himself to, and every day allowing himself a little more. She saw that Ellen had brought back a displeasing variety of giggle as well as a bad arithmetic report, and was rapidly qualifying to be a quite startling sorrow to her papa if Thomas did not precede her. She saw that Mary, firm as a limpet in her old place as central child of the house, would not stir a finger to

194

help her husband, she saw that Darwell was now often unmistakably the worse for liquor. It had been more respectable when Mamma drank alone. She even discerned that her own character had worsened, for in the past she would not have seen what was wrong without trying to amend it. But the energies that should have flowed into a household of her own would not turn backward into the household of her birth. She was in her twenty-fifth year. She was past marrying and a long way from burying.

2.

Also Euphemia . . . Euphemia looked at the blank space below Julius, whose legs she had rubbed. For it was another Friday evening. She and Ellen had gone to the churchyard to clean the obelisk, and Mary had come with them, bringing Johnnie. Ellen was anxious to shine as an aunt. "Look, Johnnie! Here's a B. B for Barnard. Say B, Johnnie."

"Me, me, me!" said the child.

"And here's an A. A for Amelia. Say A, Johnnie."

Johnnie said, "Me," with willingness. So far it was his only word, and he enjoyed using it, but Ellen tired of the conversation and said to the world at large, "Do you know, I taught myself to read off this stone. That's really how I learned my letters."

"It's a pity you didn't teach yourself to sum at the same time," retorted Mary. "It would have saved Thomas wasting his time. He says you are the greatest dunce he has ever known."

"Except you, I daresay."

Luckily, at that moment Crawley Blunt came by and stopped to praise Johnnie as a fine child, and to gaze at Johnnie's mother as a lovely young woman. He even got so far as to say to Euphemia, "Quite a Raphael." On the way back other

195

people turned to look at Mary and Johnnie. To those who had never known Mr. Kettle, senior, Johnnie was a pretty child, and a touching and sanctifying embellishment to a bloomingly pretty mother.

"Everyone stopped to look at Johnnie," said Mary as she handed him over to Darwell. And then she smoothed her hair before her mirror, and thought of Crawley Blunt's comparison with a Raphael, and went downstairs to join Euphemia and Ellen in the drawing room. Euphemia was sewing, Ellen was doing nothing. Mary opened a book.

Presently Ellen said, "Mary! Did you see what I saw as we walked home?"

"No. What?"

"Never mind."

Mary did not mind. She put down the book and took up her embroidery.

Ellen began again. "I suppose you did not even learn to read, Mary? Or you would have seen what I saw."

"Well, what did you see? Don't make such marvel about it."

"Something that was written on a wall."

Her sisters told her with one voice that she knew very well that it was forbidden to read anything written on walls. Euphemia added that if she could not talk more sensibly she had better practise her scales. Ellen chose the chromatic scale, and presently Mary, complaining of the din, offered to take part in a duet and sat down at the keyboard beside her. Euphemia could have guessed the reason for this, but she preferred to keep her attention averted from the voices that presently rose and fell among the solemn bounds of a Handel overture.

"No, I won't. I tell you, I won't. You can go out and read it for yourself."

The performers played louder.

"What?" said Mary. "I didn't hear. *Who* goes with Dandy Bilby?"

"Are you at the end of the page? I am. Turn over! One,

196

two, three! One, two, three! 'Thomas Kettle goes with Dandy Bilby.' And you know what that means. *Loves*. That's what it means."

It can't be anything so very bad, thought Euphemia, hearing Mary's untrammelled laughter, and she opened her desk and began a letter to Joseph.

"How perfectly silly! So silly that you must have made it up. Why, they're both men. I see what it is, Ellen. You have been reading things on walls, which you know quite well you are forbidden to do. And all the time you haven't understood what they mean. You've given yourself away finely, miss. We're in two sharps now, I wish you'd remember."

"I do understand."

"But they're both men, you silly girl! Men can't love each other."

"Oh yes, they can. And I can tell you, but not now. At the Allegro."

The minuet was played without conversation, and towards its close only the bass part was sustained. Mary had noticed that Ellen was sweating and that her fingers withdrew from the keys with a slight squeak. The thought that her own fingers might fall on a key that was slimed by Ellen's touch unnerved her. She was unaccountably afraid; her heart quickened its beat, and the black double bar before the Allegro seemed to lean out of the page and menace her.

"One, two! One, two! Are you ready?"

Ellen's repeated quavers broke on her like the rattle of a hailstorm, and among them Ellen was saying, "Shall I tell you? Shall I tell you?"

"No! I don't want to hear it. It's all nonsense."

"Play louder! Keep on playing louder. You know what dogs do in the street when we aren't supposed to be watching them. They do it like that. Like dogs."

A scream rang out, reverberated by the piano strings. Mary was on her feet, struggling for breath, as though the scream had emptied her lungs forever. Then, with a look of reckless delight, she threw herself on the floor and screamed again and again. The rattling quavers of the Allegro slowed and broke off; while Mary screamed and Euphemia knelt beside her holding smelling salts to her nose, and the house began to resound with voices, doors opening, and footsteps hurrying, Ellen closed the piano lid and laid away the music book. Mary on the floor, implacably screaming, the baby upstairs beginning to scream too, everyone gathering, Papa coming in, tall and terrible as death—only now did Ellen guess what degree of peril she had unloosed. And she gave herself up for lost.

"Papa!" It was Mary's first articulate word, and, having spoken, she burst into tears.

"Hysterics, poor love," said Julia pretty calmly. Hysterics would delay supper, but there was neither danger nor culpability attached to them, and by the morrow things would be going on as usual. She took the smelling salts from Euphemia and revived herself with a sniff or two, and then ordered Ellen and the servants out of the room. Barnard was hanging over Mary in just the sort of agony one might expect, reiterating, "What is it, my child? What is it?"—as though he supposed he would get a coherent answer. But men always chose moments of this kind to ask questions, thought Julia.

Sure enough, a few moments later another question occurred to him. Looking round the room, at first vaguely and then sternly, he said, "Where is Thomas?"

"No! Oh, no, no, no, no, no!" Mary writhed herself out of her father's embrace. "I can't! I won't! Tell him to go away. Tell him to go and love Dandy Bilby!"

"She hasn't the least idea what she's saying," said Julia. But there was no answer. Euphemia had sunk her head in her hands, and John Barnard's face wore a look of fatal composure.

With supper, with tomorrow, with the peace and good name of endless tomorrows hanging on the event, Julia spoke again.

198

"Mary, be quiet! The servants will hear you. If you make any more noise we shall have everyone in Loseby knocking on our door to ask what has happened."

"Thomas Kettle loves Dandy Bilby! They can see it for themselves, for it's written up on the wall. Ellen saw it. Ask her. She'll tell you. It's on the wall. Thomas Kettle goes with Dandy Bilby."

Thomas, walking up from the quay, had seen the words. It seemed to him that shock had halted him before them, but in fact he continued to walk on, no faster and no slower than before. His immediate fury at the affront was overwhelmed by a no less furious discouragement. This was the upshot of his jaunts in fishing boats, of Keziah Bilby's shrimps and Mr. Mobbs's loud, stiff singing, and of the solace and flattery of thinking himself accepted among the company he had chosen. This was the upshot and the end of the only pleasure he had found in Loseby. His heart had warmed, poor serpent, on the hearthstone where these people sat in their magic circle of class and kindred. Knowing that his charm for them lay in his unkinship, he had chosen to fancy himself accepted as one of them—just so much accepted that Thomas Kettle was mocked with loving Dandy Bilby. As he entered Anchor House the words were splashed on him by Mary's voice, and Mary's voice, so loud, so vulgar, and jolted with sobs, matched itself exactly to the uneven, sprawling calligraphy on the wall. Wilberforce was sitting on the window seat of the half-landing. He had a book on his knees, he was intently reading; only a faint frown showed that he was finding it slightly harder than usual to keep himself unspotted from the world. Hearing Thomas's foot, he looked up. A momentary grin flickered over his sallow face; he jerked a thumb towards the drawing-room door and mouthed, "Better keep out." Thomas went in.

His instantaneous impression was of Mary's friendlessness. She was as friendless as a wild animal among its capturers. Her father's air of being nobly aghast was no falser than Julia's expression of outraged maternal common sense. Euphemia's back was primly turned.

"Mary!" he said, full of pity.

As he spoke, Julia turned on him. "There you are, Thomas! I hope you can make Mary behave more sensibly, for we can do nothing with her. The truth is, her father has always given way to her; she's nothing but a spoiled child."

If it had not been for the compassion in Thomas's voice, and the desolate envy of age, Julia would not have been so rough-handed.

"Mary," he repeated. But Julia's onslaught had tarnished his compassion, and Mary's friendlessness became only another aspect of being responsible for Mr. Barnard's daughter.

She fixed a long, groping glance on him. "You're one of those things in the Bible," she said intensely and broke into hysterical laughter.

"Come with me." John Barnard's hand was on his shoulder and it propelled him out of the room. The study door closed behind them, but they still heard her wild chuckling cries, her shrill whoops as she took breath. There was a heavy twilight in the room that seemed loth to be broken in on.

"Do you know the reason for this—this loathsome, this appalling accusation?"

"That I'm one of the things in the Bible? Yes. I saw it a few minutes ago. 'Thomas Kettle goes with Dandy Bilby.' A local custom, I believe."

He was astonished that John Barnard did not react with a speech about levity. He had not realized that during the course of the summer his host had become accustomed to pert and scornful replies.

"I do not wish to believe it—God forbid that I should believe it—" John Barnard broke off. Thomas said nothing.

"In honesty I must admit that in some measure you have yourself to blame. You have been indiscreet. You have frequented a society that you are not fitted for, and which is

200

unfit for you. But indiscretion can be atoned for. I do not—"
He broke off again, the solemn syllables like a clock running
down.

Galled by the reference to atonement, Thomas asked himself, How many more times must I defend my innocence in this
study?

"Well?" he said after a negligent pause.

John Barnard took hold of the marble mantelpiece to steady
himself. Its smooth cold surface felt like a rejection. "You
force me to it," he said. "You are perverse, you are bent on
compelling me to ask a question that disgraces us both.
Thomas, have you nothing to say?"

"I think not."

Rapidly considering, Thomas chose this as an answer. Waiting for his father-in-law to speak again, he glanced round on
the study with a dispassionate scrutiny and awaited the moment when he would let himself out of it. Come what might, he
was tired of defending his innocence. He saw a future of sur-
veillance, imputations, interrogations, and an ignominy of always happening to be innocent—by misfortune, by inadvert-
ence, by the consistent malice of circumstances. If he did not
frustrate it now, it would endure till his life's end.

"You wish me to conclude the worst? You cannot deny it?"

"I do not deny it."

"O my God!"

It was as though the chimney had spoken, uttering a hollow,
disembodied groan. Thomas was startled into fear. Mary, and
the child, and a roof over his head, and a path for his feet—
he could not believe that he had lost them all.

"Do you wish to see Mary?" asked John Barnard.

He was observing the strictest justice. It did not occur to him
that to suggest that a husband should see his wife was anything
but the strictest justice. It occurred to Thomas. "Would you like
to put a collar and chain on me first?"

John Barnard made no reply, and they went into the hall.

Mary had come out of her hysterics, the door of the drawing room was open, Darwell stood just within it, saying something about sal volatile. Julia, her voice forcedly smooth, replied that there was no need for it, Mrs. Kettle had—

She was interrupted. "Mamma! Never speak of me by that horrible name! I hate the very sound of it."

"Poor little Miss Mary!"

"I wish I'd never heard it. I hope I'll never hear it again. I don't want to be anything but Mary Barnard. Darwell understands; she has always called me Miss Mary. I think I will have some sal volatile."

Turning to take the glass from the tray, she saw her father and her husband in the door. "Papa! Papa! Send him away. I don't want to see him again. Ever!"

Thomas shrugged his shoulders and walked out of the house. He was halfway to the gate before John Barnard spoke, standing in the doorway of his house like a family ghost. "The Dutch boat is sailing for Ymuiden tonight. You had best go on her. I will send your belongings to the Half Moon, and money for your passage and your needs."

The flint anchor set in the brick façade reflected the light of the moonlit sky. Thomas, looking from the anchor to John Barnard, thought that his father-in-law's face was the stonier of the two. But though he spoke so calmly, he had to struggle for breath, panting, as though he had been in a wrestling match. As one sees the contours of a landscape through which one has travelled fall into an ordered and comprehensible pattern behind one, Thomas realized that from the moment of his marriage he and John Barnard had contested for Mary. John Barnard had won. He had got her back. He had outfought and outwitted and outlasted the younger combatant, while continuing to act like a man of honour and keeping strictly within the rules. It must be admitted that the better man had won. So Thomas walked on, and the gate clanged to behind him.

The noise of the gate seemed to have lodged in his spine, and every step he took on the cobbles jarred out another echo of it. Without knowing where he was going, he retraced his way to the wall in Church Street. Level with the chalking, he stopped and looked at it. It meant nothing to him. It had done its work, and now it meant nothing. Someone had written a lie on a blank surface, and he had let it become a truth, and there was no way back. People went along the street, but he paid them no attention. Like the chalking, they meant nothing. There was no way back, there was no particular way forward; for he would be damned if he would take the Dutch boat, and John Barnard's banknotes could rot at the Half Moon. So he might as well stay where he was, reading that Thomas Kettle went with Dandy Bilby—a wistful statement, for no such love had occurred to him. Thomas Kettle loved—who? No one, perhaps. If he were to rub out the second part of the inscription and substitute Mary Barnard, that would not be true either; and what proved it was that he was so little identified with his marriage that Mary came into his mind wearing, as she would wish, her maiden name. The best thing would be for Thomas Kettle to love Thomas Kettle, since no one else did. He had stood for a long while turning these thoughts over in his mind as one might turn over in one's pocket coins that wouldn't buy anything, before he saw that his name had been spelled Tomas.

On the parcel with the cuttlefish which Crusoe had sent to him at Snipe Cottage, the H had been omitted too. He had noticed it, for the cuttlefish arrived on a day when he had been reading *Don Quixote,* and the omission had pleased him, as though it admitted him into the circle of those who sat under the oak tree, hearing the eulogy of the Golden Age. How green a shade—and how green the ass beneath it! It was Crusoe, who seemed his friend, who had written those words with patient, scrawling malice. Almost running, he set off towards the Blue-fish Inn, where Crusoe was likely to be found at this hour;

and as he rounded the corner of Ship Street he saw him going down the steps to the quay. He called out, "Crusoe!"

The enormous young man stopped, neatly as a weasel, and then walked on as though he had heard nothing; but his pace slowed, and at the foot of the steps he stood and waited, turning his swarthy face to watch Thomas following him.

"Crusoe, why did you write that thing in Church Street?"

For once in his life Thomas could not put on his grand manner. It was Crusoe who spoke with the composure of someone sequestered in a private dignity. "Why should I, Mr. Thomas? What business would it be of mine?"

"Your intolerable horseplay, I suppose"—for he saw Crusoe's face beginning to work as though with laughter.

"No, 'twarn't that."

"Or else you were drunk."

" 'Twarn't that, neither."

"Oh. Well, I must take your word for it. You weren't playing the fool, and you weren't drunk. So there's only one other reason. You did it from malice and because you wanted to do me an injury. You've succeeded. That's all I need say. Good-bye to you, and damn you for an ill-conditioned oaf."

"Stop!" Crusoe's hand fell on his shoulder. Even through the cloth of his coat he could feel that it was hot and hard as a blacksmith's tongs.

"You've got to hear me out, Mr. Thomas. For there's something I've been meaning to say." He paused and stood for a minute, looking out to sea, as if his words must be dredged from the waves.

"Do you see that there moon? There won't be a night of my life when I see that there old moon but I'll think of you. For there's never been a handsomer, nor a stunninger, nor a more remarkable, nor a dearer than you, and never will be. Nor one I shall love as I love you, be he rich or poor, he or she. The first time I seed you, the *Mary Lucinda* she was a-going out, and you was aboard her, and you gave me a shilling to run

204

an errand to your dad. And I did too, but the old whelk was asleep and a-snoring, and I couldn't rouse him. Soon as I clapped eyes on you I took a liking to you, no more than a boy then. Now that I'm man grown, I love you. And I could go with plenty, and I go with some. But never as I'd go with you. I'd follow you round the world, if you'd have me. I'd give you the eyes out of my head, if you was to ask for them."

Thomas was silent, staring at the ground. When at last he spoke, it was to say ponderingly, "Then why the devil, my dear Crusoe, did you write up that I loved Dandy? I don't, you know."

"Course you don't. I know that as well as he do. Nor yet you don't love me. But I love you so strong, I was fair busting to tell it, and yet, try as I might, I couldn't get it out. There was no other way but to make you angry, so as you'd leave off feeling as a gentleman. I had to get it out somehow, d'you see? And now I have."

"I understand."

Rather to his own surprise, Thomas did understand. Crusoe's declaration sounded neither classical nor reprehensible. So rang the long harsh sighs of the waves embracing the shore, an elemental voice, alien and indisputable. For the first time in his life he felt himself loved. To be loved brings responsibility, and for the first time in his life Thomas considered the lot of someone besides himself.

"What will Dandy think of this?"

"Dandy, he won't mind. He'll know it's not true, but he'll be pleased enough, for all that."

"For a man to love a man is a crime in this country, Crusoe."

"Not in Loseby, Mr. Thomas, not in Loseby. Nor in any seagoing place, that I've a-heard of. It's the way we live, and always have been, whatever it may be inland. I can't say for inland. I never went there, and wouldn't want to particular. But in Loseby we go man with man and man with woman, and nobody think the worse. Why, they darsn't even preach

205

against it. Seen you sit in Grand Turk's pew, Mr. Thomas. You ever heard old Reverend preach against it?"

"No, I can't say that I have."

"No! Nor ever you will. Nor young Hodmedod either. They hunt out a queer old lot of sins to preach at, but not this one. They darsn't."

The tide was rising, and the Dutch boat rose on it, as a shadow rises up the wall when the sun lowers. Thomas said, "I shan't be hearing any more sermons from Grand Turk's pew. I've just been turned out of Anchor House."

"Because of what I wrote up? Do he pick on you for it, we'll put such a red jacket on his warehouses as they'll shine from Lynn to Lowestoft."

"No, it's nothing to do with that. But it seems that I've been eating the bread of idleness too long. So I am to take myself off in the Dutch boat, and he'll pay my passage, and so forth."

"Would you go back?"

"Never!"

"That's right, Mr. Thomas! You hoist sail and go off with a merry mind. It's nice to see the world. Aren't you taking no luggage, though?"

"It's waiting for me at the Half Moon. But Crusoe, I'm not so sure I'll go in the Dutch boat. I don't care to take his money."

"Now don't you go acting like a young woman! Take it and have some good of it. Do you don't take it, he'll give it to the missionaries. Have you had your supper?"

From the Bluefish Inn the news spread, and Thomas was seen off by the entire seagoing population of Loseby. The skipper of the Dutch boat, impressed by this tumultuous tribute to Mr. Barnard's popular and influential son-in-law, who would no doubt inherit the business, and judging that some very pressing mission accounted for his travelling in such a modest vessel, took pains to improve Thomas's accommodation, and put a clean pillowslip and a bottle of gin in the berth. The

206

young gentleman looked a coxcomb, but he was not proud. No proud gentleman would let himself be hugged by a fisherman, nor make such a good attempt to return the embrace. "These are your good friends," he remarked. Thomas assented. The interval of water was already extending, the view of land had shifted into being a view from the sea. His good friends were still on the quay, waving and hallooing. All of them but one watched the departing boat. Crusoe's face was tilted upward. He was looking at the moon. Now the interval of water was wide enough to show the fragmentary wreaths of sea mist lightly twirling. The boat was full of cries and creaks and thuds, taking up her soliloquy of seafaring.

3.

Before midday all Loseby knew that Thomas Kettle had been packed off, and that his last hours in the town had been spent at the Bluefish. Not since the last death in the family had Darwell felt so gloriously enlarged. Indeed, this was better than a death. There is an inherent flaw in even the best death-bed: over the climax of its drama, just when Darwell is at her grisliest and most essential, hangs that final curtain. The dead will not return; there is not another groan, last word, convulsion, death rattle to be got out of them. But Thomas might very well come back, and, considering his poverty, Darwell felt confident that he would.

"If there's one thing I pray on my bended knees, madam, it's that we never see his face again. It would be the death of poor little Miss Mary. Besides, what would the master feel? Oh, surely he'd not be such an unnatural blackguard as to come back? They say he was so drunk, madam, that he had to be carried on board. They say that half Loseby was at the Half Moon, getting his traps. Oh, the beast! It's a thousand pities the master ever took up with such a reprobate."

"Well, he's gone now," said Julia.

"Ah, but he might come back. It's frightful to think of. Suppose he did come back, what could be done? Poor Miss Mary, she's his wedded wife. She'd have to go with him—and the boy too. When I think of what's hanging over us, it chills my blood."

"You would have to go with them, Darwell."

This stopped Darwell's mouth, as Julia had intended it to do. To stop even one mouth, for even one quarter of an hour, was a solace to her feelings. She had longed to be rid of Thomas, but this riddance threatened to be worse than any presence. However badly Thomas had behaved—and she was under no misapprehensions, since Aunt Maxwell was not one to spoil a story by a fig leaf—Thomas had not behaved like a fool. John Barnard behaved like a fool.

Having got rid of Darwell, she sat down before her dressing table, and solaced herself by scratching. All this worry had brought on her nettle rash. "I wish I could get blind drunk at the Bluefish, and be carried on board a boat sailing for Holland!" she exclaimed to the blowzy old hag in the looking glass. The hag looked back at her with something uncommonly like jauntiness, for Julia was not far from enjoying what she deplored. The calamity was also a spree. Its consequences would be appalling: the family vessel lurching from reticence to mendacity, the truth always ready to whistle about their ears, Mary on her hands in an uneasy perpetuity of being neither one thing nor another, old Mr. Kettle liable to arrive in a fit of grandfatherly solicitude—young Mr. Kettle, for that matter, a possible arriver too; and, sure as death, Barnard presently taking it into his head to have visitings of conscience and remorse. Yet where is the spree without its consequences? Headaches follow drinking; indigestion and household bills follow festivities; and family life follows a wedding. After another good scratch, Julia got up with unusual alacrity and went off to see Mary.

208

Mary lay in a darkened room, pale with laudanum, and ice had been got from the fishmonger to put on her forehead. Darwell said that she would develop brain fever, and then there would be nothing for it but to cut her hair off. Overnight, knowing that the only thing that might turn away her father's wrath was an abject contrition, Ellen had prayed with desperation for a broken and a contrite heart. She then lay awake all night, feeling nothing more to the purpose than terror. In the morning not a word was said to her. All the talk was about Mary and how soon the ice would come from the fishmonger. It was not till the afternoon that she heard Darwell saying that Mary's hair would have to be cut off. The prayer was answered. Her heart broke open in an agony of repentance. She wept and howled, and immediately Euphemia was upon her.

"Mary's hair! Mary's hair! It will be cut off. And it's all my doing."

"If that were all the mischief you'd made, you could count yourself lucky. If you can't be quiet, go and cry in the arbour. Papa will be back at any moment now."

On his way home John Barnard was pelted with fish-heads. As a result, he entered Anchor House in a state approximating serenity. He had been persecuted for righteousness' sake. He learned that Mary was a little better and had asked for soup. Later, no doubt, she would ask for her child. She had a man-child, she had her own family. It was only Thomas she had lost; and when time had healed the anguish of her disillusionment she might be happy again, and the core of his happiness.

At the conclusion of evening prayers it became apparent that there was more to follow.

"Let us pray."

Once again they went down on their knees.

" 'When the wicked man turneth away from his wickedness that he hath committed, and doeth that which is lawful and right, he shall save his soul alive.' "

Wilberforce started rebelliously. This was no hour in which to set forth on the Order for Morning Prayer. But his father had turned on to another page in the prayerbook.

" 'O most mighty God and merciful Father, who has compassion upon all men, and hatest nothing that thou hast made; who wouldst not the death of a sinner, but rather that he should turn from his sin and be saved.' "

Now it's the Commination Service, thought Wilberforce.

" 'Thy property is always to have mercy; to thee only it appertaineth to forgive sins.' "

It was not the end of the prayer, but his father had paused. What would it be next—Forms of Prayer to be used at Sea, or something from the Thirty-Nine Articles?

" 'From all evil and mischief; from sin, from the crafts and assaults of the devil; from thy wrath and from everlasting damnation.' "

As it was plain that a reply was expected, his family responded with, "Good Lord, deliver us."

"Amen," said John Barnard and rose. "From this day the name of Thomas Kettle is not to be spoken in this house."

To Ellen it was as if an angel had spread its wings between her and the wrath to come; for Papa was a man of honour, he would never allow himself to speak a name forbidden to others. She stole reverently away and was sick.

As Mary had not heard the prohibition, she could not be blamed for disobeying it, and in any case she could not be stopped. The soup had been injudicious. By the next day she was refusing laudanum and demanding mutton chops. Julia reported that Mary was not so well, restless and wandering in her talk. Brandy was given instead of laudanum, Mary's condition became less alarming; but on the third day the facts had to be faced: Mary was in perfect health, refusing to stay in bed any longer, complaining that Thomas did not come to see her, and asserting that she never wanted to see him again.

"You must speak to her, Barnard. You are her father."

210

She had been moved into Julia's dressing room and lay on the sofa. Her hair hung over her shoulders, and she was combing it. She had never seemed to him so beautiful.

"Dear Papa, how glad I am to see you! My hair is in such tangles because of the ice. I don't ever want ice put to my head again."

"You were very ill, my child. You were in great danger. It is by the mercy of God that you have been spared to us."

"Yes, I know. It was all Thomas's doing. How could he behave so shockingly? He has broken my heart. Where is he?"

"He is gone," answered John Barnard. "He is not worthy ever to see you again. He has been sent away."

The comb dropped from her hand. Her face slowly crimsoned. "How could . . . ? How dared . . . ?"

He thought that her flushed cheeks and her inability to get the words out were caused by her confusion at Thomas's offence. He realized as never before the truth of the saying that it is the innocent who suffer for the guilty. "Oh, my poor child!"

She seized the blue ribbon of her dressing gown and dragged it between her teeth. As it was natural that she should feel confused, it was natural that she should feel indignant. This too was Thomas's work. It wrung his heart to see her so ravaged by fury, and he said hastily that it is a Christian's duty to forgive wrongs, and that time would help her to forget. "You are still very young. Your life is before you, and you have your child."

She beat off the hand that smoothed her hair. "How dare you send him away? What am I to do without a husband? I'm a married woman, and you want to make me into a nobody. How can you be so selfish? You think of no one but yourself. Why don't you think of me, why don't you think of my feelings? I don't want to live at Anchor House and be a nobody for the rest of my life. I detest it! I detest you all!"

"Silence! You have said enough. Do not disgrace yourself by

saying any more. That you, of all my children, should be the one—"

Julia, coming along the passage with valerian drops in case they were needed, halted in amazement at hearing John Barnard speaking to Mary as though she were one of his other children. If Barnard were to fall out with Mary—if Mary ceased to work— All that pleasurable sense of the spree underlying the calamity was shivered to bits by the sounds coming from the dressing room, sounds familiar enough and yet nightmarishly unfamiliar, since Mary was the offender and Mary was fighting back. The valerian drops being the nearest thing to hand, Julia swallowed them. The dressing-room door opened so unexpectedly that she scarcely had time to assume the air of having just got there; but he walked by her without a word. His mouth hung open; his face was livid and wore the bewildered expression that comes to the faces of the old. It was as though he were twenty years older than the man who had gone in ten minutes before. But twenty years are not so lightly achieved, as Julia knew. The true twenty years which would substantiate this projection of a bewildered old man extended before her, as orderly a perspective as the stairway descending to the ground floor. Down, down, down—every year of the same measurements, and resounding with the same admission of an accustomed tread. How many years must she descend before drunkenness overcame her and toppled her the rest of the way? In twenty years' time Mary would still be six months short of forty. Poor Mary! How long it takes to live if one is a woman, thought Julia.

That evening more fish-heads were thrown at John Barnard; but they had lost their efficacy, persecution had no fillip in it now. He heard with cringing relief that Mary had again been put to bed, and made no offer to go to her. He would have liked to go to bed himself. Instead he found himself closeted with Julia, who, making no reference to the events of the morning, told him that the first thing to do was to compose

212

Mary's mind. Mary must be brought to see that Thomas was no great loss. While Mary's outcries about being made a nobody still rang in his ears, he listened to Julia inventorying Thomas's composing defects. Thomas was idle, sickly, underbred, stingy —"I do not think he was stingy," her husband demurred, trying to end this inventory; and as Julia really could think of no evidence for stinginess unless she were to cite Darwell's comments on the way Thomas had left the house without giving as much as a penny to the servants, she hastened to shoot a surer arrow, saying that Thomas never showed an atom of feeling for little Johnnie. From start to finish, the marriage had been a miserable bungle, and Mary could thank her stars that she was out of it before worse befell.

"Could anything be worse than his offence?"

"I would rather not discuss that. In my opinion, too much has been said of it already. But there is no end to what Mary might not have had to endure from such a wretchedly weak character. Debts, gaming, going to races, intemperance, religious vagaries—"

A hiccup interrupted her, but she got the better of it and concluded, "Not to mention exasperating everyone they met. He was a selfish, worthless, cold-hearted, insignificant wretch, and Mary will do better without him."

"Yet it is a painful situation. She is bound to find it taxing."

"Stuff and nonsense! She'll be a married woman with none of the nuisance of it."

I don't want to live at Anchor House and be a nobody for the rest of my life, she had said. I detest it! I detest you all! And he, rushing out of the room, had exclaimed, I cannot believe that you are my daughter Mary! He spoke from his heart; at the moment when she should have been most his, when Thomas's depravity had undone her marriage and opened a rightful way for him to resume a father's possession, he found himself intimidating a repulsive stranger. There was a vase of jessamine at his elbow; he discovered that its fragrance was intolerable and moved to another chair, saying, "You are her mother. No doubt you know best how to deal with her. I leave it in your hands."

4.

Women conduct life as they conduct their needlework—with small stitches, with buttons and buttonholes, with reiteration of small stabbing movements that build up a smooth-faced untearable garment. Mary was a woman, he must leave her rehabilitation to Julia; and having sworn to himself not to interfere, he did not, though Julia's methods were not those he would have chosen. Surely it would have been more creditable if Mary could have been dissuaded from dwelling on Thomas without being encouraged to hate him; or, if hate were the unavoidable human expedient, at least could she not be brought to hate him in a more Christian spirit? And surely more use could be made of the child? Johnnie was now in the stage of being blandly noisy and refractory, and looked so like Simon Kettle that even Julia could not find much pleasure in him. Mary found none. He dirtied her and made her head ache. Everything made her head ache. Everything bored her. By day she fretted about her health, and at night she was afraid to sleep alone. After the shock of her rent ignorance had followed the shock of being scolded by Papa. She could not have been in a more propitious state to have her mind composed, and Julia, Darwell, and Euphemia, getting on with their female needlework, found her easy to work on. Hating restored her self-esteem; it was right and proper that she should resent an injury to herself that was also so strongly resented by her Creator. Hating imparted a sense of shelter; by attributing all the shock to her feelings to the husband who was gone, she was preserved from acknowledging a novel fear of the father who was extant. Finally, hating sanctioned her craving to talk

214

about Thomas. She had never talked of him so devoutly while still happily married to him. "Toast, Papa? I could never make out why Thomas was so fond of toast. I think hot rolls are so much nicer." "Now that Thomas has gone, I can enjoy singing again. He was such a cold listener—quite discouraging." "Johnnie said 'butter' this morning quite plainly. 'Butter.' It sounded so pretty. I feel so thankful that he will not remember Thomas, poor little darling!"

Autumn returned—the season of dinner parties. Julia appeared not to notice this, and John Barnard was driven to jog her memory. The thought of even one meal when Thomas's ghost would not sit at the table made him insistent on the obligation to compliment Crawley Blunt on his installation as rector. A small party, of course; no one from Prospect Terrace. If Mary did not feel equal to it she could dine upstairs. Mary felt quite equal to it. Her only proviso was that the dinner should not be given until she had a new dress; she could not wear the dresses of Thomas's epoch, the associations were too painful. The box did not come from the dressmaker until the day of the dinner party. At five minutes to five Mary came downstairs wearing black velvet.

A Raphael madonna in black velvet was beyond Crawley Blunt's scope, but it was easy to substitute Vandyke. Mary Kettle, grieving in her sables, kept him awake most of the night. Such sad, sweet dignity and such a youthful bloom—he had never seen anything like it. Paying his duty call a few days later, he ventured to hope that Mrs. Kettle might assist in a distribution of charity blankets. There was much distress in the parish, the times were hard; he was sure that Mrs. Kettle's heart would be touched by some of the cases he knew. Mrs. Kettle's heart was touched immediately, and he went off and churched Mrs. Hodds, thinking of Petrarch and Laura. Johnnie, wearing a blue pelisse trimmed with ermine, accompanied Mary to the blanket distribution. Crawley Blunt had revised his notion, which was that blankets should be taken to the

215

homes where they were needed. Something more graceful and with less risk of infection now seemed to him better. The distribution took place in the rectory dining room. Blankets, folded and ticketed, were laid on the table, and on the fireward side of the table chairs were placed for the ladies of the committee. Johnnie's pelisse was much admired, and so were the arrangements. The only thing that went a little wrong was the behaviour of the benefitees. Many of them did not attend, and those who did were the most disreputable of the Loseby poor, who either snatched their blankets and went away with no more recognition than benefited wolves, or stayed too long and made too much of their thankfulness. It seemed that these latter would never go. Indeed, why should they?—the room was so warm, and undistributed blankets lay on the table. But Mary continued to smile and condole and answer sad stories with hopes of better times, better health, and a change in the weather; and Johnnie crowed and babbled and took particular interest in Mrs. Ottaway's facial paralysis. "His first experience of ministration," said Crawley Blunt with tenderness, farewelling the mother and child. "So very young—but one cannot begin too early." Mary too, so very young, blighted in the bud, and worse than widowed. . . . He set his lips and went back to be polite to the remaining ladies, who were listing the remaining blankets.

Thomas was not even hated now, and Johnnie was everything. It was what John Barnard had hoped for, but he knew that Crawley Blunt accounted for it. Crawley Blunt's conduct was irreproachable. He did nothing to compromise Mary, even his attentions to the child were no more than what could be justified by a pastoral inclination towards a lamb who could claim no father except a heavenly one. Seeing him so much in love, growing thin and even growing grey in the climate of Mary's innocent attachment, John Barnard dreaded the next winter, when seasonal charities would throw them together. It was the first winter of the Hungry Forties; fever broke out in the lower town, and winter charities went beyond the bounds of anything Mary could share with Crawley Blunt, who only visited Anchor House to ask for soup and wine and Euphemia; for by age and character Euphemia was fitter for the sterner works of mercy, and had a particular knack with deliriums. At first Mary thought this nonsensical, but when she learned that Euphemia's knack was used for deliriums of either sex she became deeply concerned. Euphemia was not married, she knew nothing; she would learn the most dreadful things, things that the hardened Mary herself did not like to think of. Mary appealed on behalf of Euphemia's innocence to Julia, to John Barnard, to Crawley Blunt himself. Her parents were inclined to agree with her, but while Euphemia's cool Sunday-school manner was the only means to get a spoon between young Jimmy Baler's chattering teeth, Crawley held on to Euphemia. Then bug-bites were found on Johnnie, and Mary delivered her ultimatum: if Euphemia could not be kept at home, she and Johnnie must go away; her child was all she had, she could not endanger his life. Darwell thought so too, and would go with her. The ultimatum was delivered to her papa, and he accepted it thankfully. He had been in agonies of apprehension for her. Only a resolution to do nothing that his less fortunate neighbours could not do had prevented him from sending them both to Robina. His relief was so great that he hurried off to tell Julia.

"You have agreed? You mean to let her go to those people?"

"What people? I did not know she had anyone particularly in mind."

"The Kettles, of course. She had a letter from Sophie, answering hers, by this morning's post. Did you not recognize the handwriting?"

He could only say that he had not recognized the handwriting, and that he had given Mary his word.

The visit to Walton on the Naze outlasted the epidemic.

217

Simon's grandfatherly love and Sophie's solicitude could not be satisfied with less than a month, and when that month was out another two months were tacked on to it by little supplements and postponements. Mary came home looking the picture of serenity, and better dressed than ever in her life before. Sophie had embroidered her collar, Sophie had trimmed her bonnet, Sophie had given her a length of grey watered silk, and Sophie's dressmaker had made it up with the new-fashioned sleeves. As for the black velvet, it was quite worn out, and she had left it behind.

By provincial convention, a black velvet dress was tantamount to a wedding ring and should last a married woman for her lifetime. "I can only call it frenzy, " commented Julia. "And at a time like this, too, when honest folk haven't a rag to cover them."

"At least she might have sold it," said Euphemia. "Ladylike or no, she should have sold it." Assaying the velvet in terms of shawls and boots, she could not forgive extravagance and looked forward to Papa's indignation. She was disappointed. Having ceased to believe that Mary was perfect, John Barnard realized that she had discarded the black velvet dress because she could not have the gratification of openly discarding Crawley Blunt. It was the act of a foolish young creature. He could fathom it; he could almost partake in the reckless pleasure she must have felt in such an act. His love had been humbled by disillusionment, and admitted intuition. Euphemia noted that her papa was just as infatuated as ever.

Outwardly all Sophie, Mary was stuffed with Simon. She feared that Euphemia and Mr. Blunt, and indeed her dear, kind papa, were misled in doing so much for the poor of Loseby. If you gave people everything they asked for there would be no end to it. In Mary's opinion, it was dangerous. They might seem grateful now, but presently they would look on all these benefits as their right, and then, unless you con-

218

tinued to give way to them, there would be a revolution. Many very wise people—Mary included—felt that it was positively thwarting Providence, who sent these bad times on purpose to make the labouring classes more thrifty and more contented in their station, and also to make them think more of how to ensure happiness in the next world. Instead of weakening the poor by so much soup and flannel, would it not be more in keeping with God's intentions to leave them to learn self-help and resignation, and for Mr. Blunt to keep his strength for the pulpit instead of wearing himself out during the week so that one could scarcely hear a word of the sermon? At Walton there was a wonderful preacher, and a great many people in Walton, and in Colchester too, were expecting a Last Judgment.

The inefficacy of works presently failed her as a subject of conversation. But at Walton cream was served with the breakfast porridge, hothouse cucumbers appeared at least three times a week, and the puddings came from a pastry-cook in the town, who also supplied every kind of cake and sweet biscuit and ratafias. Johnnie always had a ratafia at bedtime, and after breakfast, an orange. Mary's revolt against the austerity of Anchor House (more pronounced than ever in these bad times) was conducted on Johnnie's behalf. Johnnie would not eat plain puddings; boiled mutton, however neatly minced, he pouched and spat out again; and he positively could not go to sleep without his ratafia. Johnnie was all she had, and she could not be expected to sit by and watch him dying of starvation; if, as Papa said, the mothers of other children were doing so, it was very sad; but it would not help them if Johnnie starved too. If Papa insisted on being so very inconsiderate, there was nothing else for it, she would have to go back to Walton on the Naze.

He knew this was blackmail, but he gave in. He even submitted to a weekly parcel from Sophie, containing those very special ratafias and other dainties for the nursery table. Wednesday was the day it came. Wednesday was the day he visited the workhouse. Among its inmates were men who had worked for his father, and for him. He could barely look them in the face, so great was his shame.

He had been in favour of Poor Law reform—another lost illusion, for what he saw of the new Poor Law institutions made him resolve to keep Loseby people out of them. Though trade was bad, he took more men into his employment and developed subsidiary industries, such as cooperage and brush-making. The business staggered under this extra load, and in 1843 he faked Daniel's share of the profits from his private capital. It seemed to him that he was fighting a losing battle, but from elsewhere he was assured that Loseby had escaped any real suffering, and that this was mainly his doing. He resented such assurances as though they were slanders, but he could not save himself from being voted onto committees and asked to advise and to draw up schemes. He discovered that inland there was a degree of misery which was in truth far beyond what he had fought in his native town. By then, Barnard of Loseby had become a name with a ring of hope in it, and as he rode from place to place, skin-and-bone creatures who had gathered to see him pass detached themselves like dead leaves from the hedgerows and uttered feeble hurrahs. But the committees were disappointed in their man. He was contentious and overbearing. Any other hotheads present always agreed with him, which held up proceedings and encouraged the notion that committees do nothing but talk. To cap all, he was a man from the coast, and in trade; he did not understand the agricultural interest. Possibly because he was a man in trade, he showed little patience with stopgap alleviations. This mercantile outlook infected a great landowner who should have been the stiffest representative of the agricultural interest, since he fancied himself as a Coke of Holkham and had turned a paternal enclosure of common land into a paradise for turnips. Struck by a remark on the futility of throwing dung over ground you neither ploughed nor seeded, Lord Andleby voted against the project in debate. It was a proposal to restore the income of a sixteenth-century bequest, which in the course of time had wandered into the banking account of a lay incumbent, to its original purpose of clothing twelve poor widows who lived chaste. Having voted, Lord Andleby said he was glad to oblige such a sensible man as Mr. Barnard. His gladness and Mr. Barnard's discomfiture were too entertaining not to be made a story of, and by this misunderstanding John Barnard became widely known as the man who unclothed the widows.

Loseby was angered when he took up with the people inland; though it suffered in no other way, it suffered in its pride. When the story of the widows reached the Bluefish, the Lord Nelson, and the Three Tuns, it was just what Loseby wished to believe of Grand Turk. After a day spent in arguing with an Ecclesiastical Commissioner's clerk in Norwich, John Barnard came back to find an array of shifts, petticoats, and bonnets dangling from the spikes along his wall. The gate was locked, giving him time to reflect on the display and also to observe several starred window panes. The insult must have been more than a piece of childish horseplay, for it would take a strong thrower to crack plate glass at such a distance. Euphemia came to unlock the gate. Her face wore an expression of disapproval, but such an expression was now habitual to it and so told him nothing.

"What is the meaning of this, Euphemia?"

"Some people came and made a hubbub, and Mamma had the gate locked in case they should come back again."

"But why are those garments hanging on the wall?"

Of course he'd be the only person not to know it, she thought.

"And why has not Tofts been told to remove them?" he continued.

"Mary needed him to get her trunk down from the attic. She was frightened, and wishes to take Johnnie away. She intends to go to Walton."

She snatches at any pretext to return to those people, he thought, and set his lips, feeling the wound reopen in him. He had tried to fix his mind on the misery of others and so forget his own. But it was in vain. He loved her irreparably, he had irreparably injured her, and his peace of mind was at her disposal.

5.

It was not much of a salve to his feelings to find that Mary had worked herself into real panic and was convinced that if she remained at Anchor House her head and Johnnie's would be paraded on pikes. On the following day she set off for Walton on the Naze. More, she insisted that he should accompany her as far as Norwich, and that he and the coachman should carry arms. Weighted with his ridiculous pistol, he returned to Loseby in a hired chaise, looking out on the brilliant harvest fields and wondering why his wall had been hung with ragged petticoats. Euphemia, always to be relied on for unpleasant truths, revealed the story about unclothing the widows, adding that it was very silly. Julia had the same explanation and added that it was very tiresome to be without Darwell, and that none of this would have happened if he had stayed in Loseby and attended to the business. But she spoke dreamily and seemed resigned to a state of things she resented. She had not become so dependent on Darwell that she could not uncork a bottle for herself.

Lord Andleby was bent on obliging Mr. Barnard. The remark about dung, working in his lordship's mind, had thrown up the word "slate." Slate affords no foothold for dandelions, thistles, nettles, and ragwort, weeds that grew on the thatch roofs of his disgraceful cottages and seeded themselves all over his exemplary acres. He decided to build half a dozen slate-roofed cottages, and invited the inspiring Mr. Barnard to pay him a visit of advice. John Barnard accepted the invitation with

222

particular pleasure; not only would some people live in decent dwellings, and others be paid for building them, but a visit to Felton Park would clinch the accusation about tearing the last rags off the backs of widows. Self-examination had shown him that he was incapable of any beatitude but the last beatitude: to be blessed when men reviled him and spoke all manner of evil against him falsely. He spent a week at Felton Park, as though in some odd variety of heaven—the rooms were so large and the voices so low, and the rightful inhabitants so blamelessly divorced from any realization of the common lot of man. He went out partridge shooting, admired pigs and Titians, admired Lady Andleby's water colours, and settled everything about the new cottages. Going home, he speculated as to what he might expect for this—his warehouses burned down, his horses maimed, and not a whole pane of glass in his windows. But everything was as usual. Euphemia was out among her poor, and Julia was lying down because of the heat.

Everything was as usual because they had taken such unusual pains to make it so. They were waiting to tell him that the day after his departure for Felton Park a letter addressed in Thomas's handwriting had come for Mary. Euphemia, with that disobligingness which was now daily more apparent, refused to share in the act of disclosure. It was Julia, primed but still unfortified, who drew the letter from under a cushion.

"From Malaga too," she sighed, breaking a silence she could endure no longer. "Could anything be more unfortunate?"

"When did this come?"

"Five days ago."

"The delay in sending it on is certainly unfortunate. Mary will wonder why it was kept here."

Julia's hopes that the letter would be paid for by nothing more protracted than a ceremonial burning vanished. "The poor child is more likely to be thankful for having been left in peace a few days longer. She will be ill again—worse than before, I daresay. If she were under any roof but Sophie's I would go to her myself. That wretched Thomas! Is there to be no end to him?"

"She is his wife. If he chooses to claim her, we can do nothing."

Julia bridled but conformed. She wrote off to Mary, begging her to do nothing without consultation and to bear in mind above all else the uncomfortableness of living with a husband who would not consider her feelings.

Burning of warehouses, maiming of horses and of reputation—how trivial his expectations had been in comparison with the reality! Yet do as he might to maintain a christian submission to God's appalling will, John Barnard could not quench a certain feeling which he was obliged to identify as a feeling of relief. He had done no more than his duty in expelling Thomas; Thomas, for that matter, had practically insisted on being expelled; yet he felt a guilty and tremulous hope at the thought of Thomas's return. It was as though he were being offered a second chance. But what second chance could be offered him, except to suffer more, seeing Mary and Johnnie carried away? Unless Thomas should be penitent?—at the thought of a penitent Thomas the sensation of that impending second chance immediately died away; there was no guilt in his hope, and no tremble of life in it either.

Mary's letter was addressed to Julia, and was sealed with a large black wafer. "A widow!" Julia exclaimed. She read on, and her next exclamation was that Sophie took too much on herself. An enclosure dropped from the letter; it was a printed form, filled out in a clerk's flourishing handwriting. John Barnard's mind was so much at sea that even when he unfolded the document and saw that it was in Spanish, and that the name in the flourishing hand was Tomás Kettle, the widow still seemed to him to be Sophie, and the dead man Simon. "Poor little Mary," said Julia in a voice of perfect resignation, and she handed the letter to him.

224

My dear Mamma,

I have some sad news. I am a widow! It has been a great shock, and I know I shall never get over it. I could not believe it, and at first Mr. Kettle could not believe it either and thought it was some trick. But now they feel sure it must be true, so I am going into weeds. *Grandmaman* is kindly seeing to it all, and I shall come home as soon as my clothes and Johnnie's are finished. I enclose the certificate and the letter, which made me cry, it is so sad!

But she omitted to enclose the letter, so they could not know what had made Mary cry or who had written it, or why it should have been directed in the handwriting of Thomas, who was dead.

"I really think Mr. Kettle should have written to you. It was the least he could do," said Julia. "Thomas gave you trouble enough, surely you are entitled to know why he died, and when, and all that."

"It does not signify."

He was halfway to the door when she looked up and exclaimed at his pallor and said he should take some brandy. But he repeated that it did not signify and went up to his dressing room and locked himself in. His intention had been to pray, but instead he walked to the window and looked out on the bright, trim lawn, strewn untidily with leaves that had fallen overnight. And he remembered how the leaves had rustled underfoot when he went searching for a chestnut to pleasure his dying son, and now he seemed to be walking through them once more, and in a like confusion of grief and belated love.

He had not long to himself. There was an outburst of screams and warbling sobs. The news of Thomas's death had thrown Ellen into hysterics.

By dint of baffling her family, Ellen had gone a long way towards baffling herself, and only occasionally remembered the conversation at the piano. Birthdays had seemed so many

225

rungs on a tottering ladder by which she would attain the height from which she could look back and see the events of that afternoon as something that had taken place when she was a child. Now Thomas was dead. Death was coffins, worms, the body turning blue, hairs sprouting like a demented harvest from the field of corruption; death was also hellfire, undying worms, and that Dreadful Day when everything is known and made public. An instinct of self-preservation commanded her to escape her own scrutiny by grieving as conspicuously as possible. John Barnard was carried from annoyance to acceptance: at last something had touched Ellen's heart. It was not the thing he would have chosen to affect it, but God's ways are not of man's choosing, and the work was done. Ellen's heart was touched. He stretched a protective sanction over her emotion, and Julia and Euphemia waited to be by themselves before openly speculating how Mary would like to come home and find Ellen chief mourner.

Mary did not like it at all. In a matter of minutes she dried Ellen's tears. "No doubt you are sorry," she said. "But it is too late now." The words were spoken mildly and were not in themselves remarkable for anything except Mary's usual good sense and candour; but her crape, her widow's bonnet, and the amount of room she appeared to take up by being so blackened and solemnified enhanced their effect. Ellen shrank back, swallowed her tears, and presently upset the tea-kettle. The phenomenon of Mary in her weeds was so vital that it put Thomas's death into the shade. It was as though Sophie Kettle kept an academy for teaching deportment to young widows, and Mary had come back from it, the prize pupil. She seemed so wholeheartedly widowed that her father was startled when she asked him if he really thought Thomas was dead.

It was the first time they had been alone together. Thomas's letter lay on the table. John Barnard had read it in silence and was still unwilling to speak of it.

226

"You do think it is true, Papa—that he really wrote this letter, and that he is dead?"

My darling, This letter will be sent to you after my death. A doctor, who seems a sensible man, tells me that I shall not recover. In two days, three at the most, I shall cease to reproach myself for having left you without saying good-bye. Forgive me for this, if you can. And if you can, remember that we were happy at Snipe Cottage, and loved each other while it was possible. But we could not take root under the shade of old trees. Now, and at last, good-bye, Mary.

"I suppose it was his lungs. The certificate said he died of *herida,* and Mr. Kettle made out that it was the Spanish for something hereditary. Thomas's mother died of a consumption."

She spoke in the voice of someone conscientiously examining every shred of evidence. He made no answer. He could see no reason why she should be told that Thomas had died of a wound. A wound got in a Spanish port inevitably leads the mind to drunken brawls and dancing-women.

"And though it doesn't look quite like his usual handwriting, whoever wrote it knew about Snipe Cottage and the trees in the park."

"A dying man has not much control over a pen, Mary. This is certainly Thomas's letter."

"Besides, who else in Spain would know my address? The address is written quite plain. He must have written it before he grew really ill."

"Or he might have taken pains to write clearly."

"Yes, of course. An address has to be clearly written. Thank you, dear Papa. I shall feel quite easy now. I am sure you are right. Mr. Kettle thought so too. At first he thought it might be a trick of Thomas's, but afterwards he changed his mind. He took a great deal of trouble. He was ready to write to Malaga to inquire. But when he showed the certificate to the Walton registrar, he was told it was certainly a real one. It was that that convinced him, not the letter."

"You showed your husband's letter to Mr. Kettle?" He could not keep the note of repugnance out of his voice, and she looked up defensively.

"Was that a wrong thing to do, Papa?"

"No, no! It was natural that you should. Take the letter, my love, and put it away."

"And the certificate?"

"Put away the certificate too."

For he could not justly blame her for exposing that pitiful letter for Simon's greedy malice to gloat upon. So young, and so perfectly candid, she would have shown the letter to anyone. She had shown it to him. Thomas would have felt that no less a betrayal into the hands of his enemies. Mary locked away her documents with solemnity and added a little key to the locket with Johnnie's hair which she wore on a chain round her neck. Such things could not be considered ornaments, any more than a wedding ring or a gold watch.

"These are my jewels," the lady in Roman history had said, exhibiting her sons. Johnnie was Mary's jewel—a fine well-grown jewel, full of fun and able to repeat any number of hymns by heart. She wore him—he was still in his black frock, with little black gloves, a touching spectacle—at Crawley Blunt's wedding. For Crawley Blunt had got married at last, to a second cousin, a platter-faced person, older than Euphemia, possibly even older than Crawley. Johnnie in his black frock and flaxen curls attracted much more attention than the bride. Shortly after this Mary paid another visit to Walton on the Naze, but it was the last for many years. There had been several small differences of opinion with *Grandmaman* about Johnnie, and Johnnie's Walton grandfather complained about being disturbed. The grandfather at Loseby was out most of the day, so it did not matter if Johnnie was noisy.

228

6.

"I cannot understand why our dear papa does not murder that brat," said Wilberforce, who had come home for the summer holidays. "You might well do something of the kind yourself."

"It is Ellen who has most to complain of. He's always tormenting her, and Mary sets him on. But as he's Mary's child, Papa can see no wrong in him."

"I haven't noticed him seeing much wrong in any of us. Do you know, I think his health is giving way."

"Do you?" said Euphemia placidly.

Five years earlier Wilberforce had won a scholarship to the Merchant Taylors' School, and the need for retrenchment compelled his father to be thankful for this. It was not a school he would have chosen; he did not like its situation in the heart of London, the boy would be exposed to the dangerous atmosphere of a great city, as well as the effluvia from Smithfield; but other men's sons would be fed by the money saved, and Hebrew was part of the curriculum. A second scholarship was about to take Wilberforce to Cambridge. This gave John Barnard unqualified pleasure. It was a classical scholarship, but Wilberforce intended to work at mathematics. He had confided this to Euphemia. She was still his only intimate in the family, and each time he came home she had greater pleasure in knowing it was so. But this time the pleasure was more carefully enjoyed, because she supposed it might be the last time.

Late in life—she was now thirty-one—Euphemia had found religion. Rational creatures, she opined, presupposed a rational Creator whose strokes were not dealt at random or in a confusion of misconceived good intentions, like Papa's. The succession of thwackings which had compelled her into a life of ungrateful servitude must have been laid on with a purpose.

And the purpose? She found religion in the moment when it darted upon her that the purpose must be to draw her slow attention to the God whose service is perfect freedom. It was not possible to serve both that God and Barnards. She must therefore join a religious community. Since Herrnhut was the only religious community she had any knowledge of, she decided to go to Herrnhut. It was not ideal. There was too much singing, and as a virgin she would have to tie her hair with a pink ribbon. But existence there was calm, purposeful, and thrifty. No lifetimes ran to waste, and it was in a foreign country, a landscape of no hope.

She began to prepare herself by improving her German and practising German script. Monsieur Tuggli wrote to her from time to time, but she did not intend to make use of him yet, in case he wrote of his approval to Papa. There were Moravians in Norwich, but that was too near home to be safe, so she entered into an illicit correspondence with a Moravian minister in Leicester, whose sermons were in print and could be praised by a grateful reader. As his replies could not be deposited under a tuft of grass by the family gravestone, she used a young woman in Loseby as a covering address. The young woman was one of her sick persons and suffered from bone disease. This was a common variety of tuberculosis in Loseby, and Euphemia's experience with similar cases made her pretty confident that Minnie Cheney would not die during the course of the negotiations. From appreciation to inquiries, from inquiries to doubts, from doubts to enlightenments, from enlightenments to further inquiries and a fresh cycle, she had led on the correspondence with much more skill than she had shown in the correspondence with Marmaduke Debenham. She was now ripe for conversion, and conversion waited only till she could overcome a worldly impediment of cash. It must be cash or consent; and as she did not suppose that her father would give his consent, she must somehow raise money for her travelling expenses, and some modicum of dowry to take in her pocket.

Ten years earlier she would have had money enough, put by from Aunt Robina's various guineas for buying herself something more becoming than what was provided by her parents; but the impracticability of bettering the independent poor without also bribing them had reduced her savings to three pounds, fifteen shillings and ninepence. It was tantalizing to see boats leaving Loseby for Hamburg and Lübeck. It was galling to hear (as she did from her poor) that Thomas Kettle had gone off on such a boat with a hundred pounds in his wallet. But she heard money jingling in Wilberforce's pocket without a shred of envy. It was there by right; not only was he a young man, he was well on the way to being a gentleman. Papa too was a gentleman, but with qualifications; he was a christian gentleman. Wilberforce would be a gentleman unqualified, neither held down by his birth nor hoisted up by his intellect. He would be a credit to her, long after anyone remembered that she had been his first teacher.

The rich August air, heavy with scents of phlox and cherry pie and lemon verbena, filled the walled garden and brought out the smell of mouldering wood which was the characteristic fragrance of the arbour where they were sitting. But Wilberforce, she thought, is scentless. Nothing emanates from him unsupervised or uncontrolled. It was as though he had grown up like a changeling, cool, detached, and, though wary, unafraid. Because of his wariness he was able to converse with his father almost as one human being with another. That same morning she had sat at breakfast as though at a circus, hearing Papa asking questions and Wilberforce unconstrainedly replying—the effect being even more striking, as they were talking about Cambridge, and Wilberforce was disparaging Jesus as rowdy. Wilberforce had no further need of her.

She was struggling with an impulse to tell him about Herrnhut when he remarked, "I have noticed another thing. I notice it with regret, as Papa would say. Darwell drinks."

"Yes, I know. But I don't think it matters. Most old servants drink, more or less, and Johnnie is looked after by the nursery maid."

"Darwell drinks more than less, Euphemia. The spicy breath of Joe's plantations almost knocked me down last night when she tried to kiss her Master Wilberforce. How is Joe? Any more little Joes?"

"Scarcely. The last one is not three months old."

"And how many does that make?"

"Five."

"I shall never get it out of my head that they are black—sooty little Barnards, trotting about in striped calico drawers, like the pictures in Kettle's *Juvenile Repository*. By the way, what became of that friend of Joe's—the one with the lake and the bulldog?"

"He's married too. Joe mentioned it in a letter."

The thought came to her, I must tell him how Bouncer was trained to attack Mary. The other confidence was put by, and she began her story. He listened gravely, his features relaxing slightly whenever he appeared in the narrative, and at the close he said with tenderness, "What an odious little marplot I was!" After further thought he said, "But you never revenged yourself on me. You have a very magnanimous character." It was plain that he gave not a whisk of consideration to her loss of a good kind marriage. He was really quite as selfish as Mary, but unlike Mary he had taken pains with his selfishness, and would do some good with it.

Euphemia was not the only person in the household to feel Wilberforce's charm. Darwell, whose patience with Johnnie had worn thin, was overcome by her dear Master Wilberforce looking such a young gentleman, and pursued him with maudlin tenderness, declaring herself ready to lick the blacking off his boots and offering him toast and dripping—he had always been such a one for toast and dripping. She went at it without shame or caution; being the oracle of Johnnie's constitution, indispensable to Mary, and in a position to blackmail her mistress

232

whenever she chose, Darwell innocently supposed she could behave as she pleased. Julia was of a different opinion. Since Darwell had become so emphatically a fellow drinker, Julia's former dependence had dwindled. Herself a capable drinker, she scorned a sloppy one. A great deal of feeling was released when she said, exasperated by Darwell's irruption into Wilberforce's bedroom, "Darwell, you forget yourself. Leave the room."

Darwell turned about. "Well, madam, if I forget myself, there are some things I don't forget, some things I could mention if I pleased to, that others might be sorry I remembered, madam. Especially in front of Master Wilberforce, the poor innocent that I—"

Though Wilberforce was cool-blooded, he could not endure an imputation of innocence. Before Julia could get her word in he exploded and said with the vigour of a schoolboy, "Shut up, Darwell, you silly old sot!"

They heard her go down the passage, boohooing. That evening she was absent from family prayers, and the nursery-maid explained that Mrs. Darwell had one of her bad headaches.

Darwell's bad headaches usually blew over in a matter of twenty-four hours. This was a more stubborn headache, and three days later the nursery-maid knocked on the morning-room door, saying that Mrs. Darwell looked at her so queerly that it made her nervous.

"Oh, thank you, Euphemia! I do not know how we should get on without you," said Julia perfunctorily as Euphemia began to free herself from the sheet she was darning. But Mary, who had been doing nothing, rose more quickly and with a flush of annoyance.

"It need not always be Euphemia, Mamma. I will go. I have been feeling very anxious about poor Darwell."

After the ministering angel's impetuous exit, Julia remarked, "Oh, goodness!"

"Yes, indeed," Euphemia replied.

Each knowing well what the other anticipated, they said no more, mustering their calm against Mary's disillusioned return. There was no need to do so. Mary came back reporting that Darwell's speechless gratitude was quite touching, that she had not wished to eat anything but had been delighted to have her head stroked, and that when Mary left her she was lying very peacefully, almost asleep, with Mary's handkerchief, soaked in eau-de-Cologne, laid on her forehead. Thanking God for a fool of a daughter, Julia thought no more of it. During the day, Mary made a couple more ministering flights, and came down from the last reporting that Darwell must be feeling better as she was getting up. Half an hour later the nursery-maid disturbed them once more. Mrs. Darwell, she said, was having fits. Would they please come to the foot of the servants' staircase, where they would be able to hear her quite easily.

There was no need to go so far. The house had become a sounding-board for Darwell. Rapid, thudding footsteps were interrupted by crashes, and Darwell's voice kept up an incessant rattling harangue. Just then Hester came downstairs, holding a key. Darwell, she said, had attacked her, saying that she was the devil, so Hester had locked Darwell in. Pat on this came Darwell's voice, screaming like a parrot, "Let me out, let me out, let me out, let me out!"

By this time Mary's wits had begun to move. Darwell must be in a high fever. The high fever was caused by something infectious, probably scarlet fever. Having nursed Darwell, she would be infected and would pass on the infection to Johnnie. Johnnie was in the garden, batting to Ellen's bowling, but the noise brought him in.

"Johnnie, Johnnie! You mustn't come near me!" she exclaimed. Johnnie, accustomed to associate the command with being either sticky or ill-smelling, was baffled. His sweets were exhausted, and he had not examined the dead rat since before breakfast. But he stopped in order to be on the safe side.

234

"Don't come near me!" she repeated. "You will die if you do. Oh, my darling Johnnie, my precious boy, you are all I have, and now I shall lose you."

Johnnie was bellowing in her arms when John Barnard walked into his home. As usual, Mary was the only member of the family who could give him a straightforward explanation of what was going on. Tofts was sent off to fetch the doctor, and during the interval, and when the doctor had been led upstairs by Euphemia, John Barnard sat holding Mary's hand, thinking that she was doomed and assuring her that she would most likely escape. But how could she? Only a few hours earlier she had been smoothing the brow of a case of raging scarlet fever.

The suspense had hardly had time to become intolerable when Euphemia and Dr. Bevan returned. Euphemia was pale, Dr. Bevan mopped a bleeding cheek with his handkerchief. "I must congratulate you, sir, on a very sensible parlourmaid. You would have had the woman among the ladies in a few minutes if she hadn't been locked in. Shocking affair, sir! Very distressing for a head of a family. She'd have had my eye out if I hadn't moved in time."

Euphemia, looking at her father, smiled reassuringly. His heart revived. "It is nothing infectious?"

"A plain case of delirium tremens. Hallucinatory stage. Phew! Wonderful woman for her age, though. Quick as a flea. Yes, she was within a hair's breadth of my left eye. I've had a very narrow escape."

"Thank heaven! Oh thank heaven!" said Mary fervently and showed signs of fainting.

The doctor gave her an unillusioned glance, said, "A little sal volatile," and took his leave, remarking he'd need a couple of stitches put in by the assistant. After that, he would send the apprentice, and a powerful midwife to put the patient in a tub of cold water and keep her there till she quieted down.

"Did no one suspect this?" asked John Barnard after the

doctor had gone out. It was a question that turned to ashes on his lips. He saw that everyone but Mary knew or suspected that Darwell drank.

"I knew, I knew! I've often seen her taking something out of a bottle," carolled Johnnie, springing from foot to foot. "I could have told you about it, Mamma."

"Then it was very naughty of you not to tell me," Mary retorted. "She might have murdered you, or set fire to your bed-curtains. I have never imagined such ingratitude, nor such slyness. I daresay she drank that eau-de-Cologne, for she asked me to leave the bottle. Papa! You must send her away. I can never be easy while she is in the house. I think she ought to go to prison."

She was rosy with excitement and ate enormously at dinner.

Many years afterwards, when Johnnie had become chaplain to a City company and took part in banquets, the noise of a particularly grand banquet would remind him of the first time he dined among the grown-ups against a background of Darwell's inexhaustible bellowings. This dinner also became one of Wilberforce's valued memories, partly because of Hester's majestic bearing, and partly because a shrimp sauce having been poured over a steamed blackberry pudding, and, his father eating it without comment, everyone else felt obliged to do likewise.

Dessert followed pudding, Mary had peeled a peach for Papa, when they became conscious of a change in the air. Darwell had left off shouting. Ignoring the peach, John Barnard got up and said grace. "For these, and all Thy other mercies, make us truly thankful." The words pinned him to his miserable responsibility as a head of a household. The tub of cold water having done its work, Darwell would begin to crawl back to her right mind. But to what purpose? Only to be dismissed, for a fault which was as much his as hers. She had been in his service for thirty years, she was older than he, and he had allowed her to go to ruin with as little concern as though she were a disused piece of furniture in the attic that the worm had got into. How much farther would his guilt extend, and how many others besides Darwell suffer by it? His household had learned to look on at intemperance, they were so hardened to it that Johnnie could boast about Darwell's bottle. From condoning, it is a short stop to practising; and Wilberforce was at Cambridge, exposed to the same temptations that had ruined Joseph. Conscience kept him awake most of the night, and whenever he drowsed he fell into a recurrent dream, in which he was climbing a flight of stone steps out of darkness, carrying something which was always the wrong thing—a barometer, a plate of strawberries, a ledger—while the thing he had gone to fetch was left behind On the fourth recurrence of the dream he came up holding a stuffed owl that was maggoty, but this time he also brought a recognition, for he knew that the steps he mounted were those leading up from his wine cellar. This recognition jolted him fully awake. A twilight of before dawn was in the room, and a gusty wind was blowing. As if he had pressed a hidden spring, a scene from the past shot out like a secret drawer with its suddenly unmysterious contents. On the day when the newly married Kettles were coming to dine he had gone down to the cellar for the best port and had noticed that great quantity of empty bottles. There he had stood, asking himself if it were not his duty to become a teetotaller; time-serving considerations obscured the bottles, and he had come up from the wine cellar with the right thing left behind.

It was not only Darwell who would have been saved. If he then had told his guests that he intended to give up strong liquors, conversation would have been about the temperance movement, and Julia's inquiry, eliciting the fact that Mutty had been sent away penniless and Thomas had taken her in, might never have been made. Even if it had been made, his mind would have had better things to do than to kindle with that wildfire indignation which swept him to London in search of

Thomas, and so brought Thomas to Loseby, and so married Thomas to Mary. Now it was too late. But if only because it was too late, and as an admission of being humbled, he would take the pledge and have his household do so too. Euphemia did not drink at all, Mary only for festivities and in winter to keep the cold out. For Julia the renunciation would be more difficult. Julia's need to keep her strength up was one of the considerations which had waylaid him in the wine cellar. But that was ten years ago. Julia's nerves were now much steadier, and she was over the age when women are said to need extra support. He would speak to her before breakfast.

The speech he had prepared in his mind came out pretty much as he had prepared it: responsibility to others who under Providence were less fortunately circumstanced to resist temptation; Wilberforce at Cambridge; Darwell a warning; thinking it over all night. The speech went on longer than he intended, but that was because Julia remained silent.

"I know what you are thinking—that I should have taken this step long ago. You are right, and what's more I delayed for a thoroughly petty reason. When I first thought of it Kettle was forever prating about a temperance movement in Loseby. I gave way to prejudice. I would not do a right thing because a bad man was in favour of it. And I was influenced by vanity too. I did not want to play second fiddle to Kettle in my own town. So I shut my eyes to the truth, God forgive me!"

"But now there is a scandal in the house, your eyes have opened?"

"If you choose to put it so, yes. As the world judges, it must seem so. I am sorry you do not judge me rather differently."

"But that is what people will say."

"I do not care what people will say. I have never let such a consideration influence me, and because I have not done my duty before is no reason why I should not do it now."

She turned the bracelet on her wrist. Her look was heavy and sullen, and for a moment she resembled the girl in Ro-

238

bina's lodgings. But when she spoke her voice had a forced triviality. "Well, Barnard, you must do as your conscience pleases—as you always do. But leave me out of it."

"Leave you out of it? You, my wife? It is out of the question. Whom God has joined, let no man put asunder. And I am sure your health would be none the worse for it."

"You must leave me out of it," she repeated.

"But why?"

"I drink. I am a drunkard. I have been a drunkard for the last twenty years."

The savagery of her words appalled him even before he took in their meaning. And it was as though to a lesser evil that he replied, assuring her that it could not be true, that she did not know what she was talking about, that he had never seen her the worse for liquor, that drinking in moderation and on medical advice is not the same thing as being a drunkard, that she did not understand, that he understood, that she was misled by her scruples, that she was making too much of it, that there was no habit which could not be overcome.

Infuriated by the egoism of his refusal to believe her, she waited for him to say what she was waiting for, and then struck. "Exactly! You've put it in a nutshell. *'Too painful to contemplate.'* You've had it under your nose all these years—but it was too painful to contemplate. You saw me worn out by bearing children, one after another as though I were a beast, and disheartened by your sulks and your fidgets, and grown fat and hideous and hypocritical—but you shut your eyes to it and went on calling me a model wife and mother, because I was too painful to contemplate. I suppose you are the most selfish person in existence. You are as selfish as Mary."

He flinched. "Julia! Does—does anyone know this?"

"You mean, does Mary know? I don't suppose so. If she did, it would be nothing to her. She is as cold as a fish, and as stupid as a barber's block—except that she has just enough wits to keep you doting. But you couldn't believe that either, could you? It would be too painful to contemplate. I've had to contemplate it, though. I've had to see my other children snubbed and ignored and mismanaged, because they weren't Mary. Do you know that when my poor Joe ran away—ran away because he was terrified of you—and you went after him to Cambridge, do you know what you said the evening you came back, the first words you said to me? 'Shouldn't Mary be in bed?' You're like the man in the French comedy. *'Et Tartuffe? Et Tartuffe?'* If Mary's not a Tartuffe, it's only because she's never needed to be; your infatuation didn't put her to the trouble of it. Do you ever look at Euphemia and see what she's shrivelled into? An old maid! She could have made a good match once, with that Mr. Debenham. He was very much taken with her, and she was quite ready to be in love with him. But you wouldn't let him come near her, you wouldn't let him come into the house because you thought he might carry off your Mary. But Mary had only to take a fancy for that miserable, ridiculous Thomas, and Mary's papa must give him to her immediately. And a couple of years later you snatched at a chance of getting rid of him, so as to have Mary all to yourself again. But Mary doesn't stay to be her papa's only comfort. She runs off to Walton to be a comfort to old Mr. Kettle. *'Et Tartuffe?'* Papa hopes the change of air will do her good. Mary can do no wrong, and none of my other children can do right. Do you wonder that I took to drinking, that I am neither more nor less than what Wilberforce called Darwell—an old sot? But you needn't trouble yourself. Mary is none the worse for it. Even now, you are more put about by hearing that your wax-doll Mary doesn't care a snap of her fingers for you than by hearing that I am an incurable drunkard."

She saw that she was flogging a dead horse, but scolded on. If he did not beat her, she must beat him. She too was suffering from shock, and violence was the only thing that could ease her. He sat on the edge of the unmade bed, tracing and retracing the capital B embroidered on the sheet, and tears fell from

240

him as though from an automaton. At last her temper ran out. But she felt neither triumph nor pity, only a sense of competence that came wearily back and acknowledged a situation that must be dealt with. She held her smelling salts under his nose, wrung his ears and slapped his hands, till with a deep sigh he came out of his stupor and fumbled for his watch.

"You can't go down looking like that," she said. He sat uncomplying and unresisting, while she applied the technique of cold water and toilet vinegar with which she was accustomed to revive her own appearance. A man's face is not so amenable to such aids as a woman's. Standing back to view the result, she commented, "You had best say you have got a bad headache."

That evening there was a public meeting in Loseby to raise funds for the sufferers in the Irish Famine. Those who attended it agreed afterwards that Mr. Barnard had never spoken so badly.

He knew himself that he went on too long, reiterating that we should not let our own troubles make us indifferent to the miseries of others; but while he spoke he kept his thoughts at bay. At last a round of applause, beginning politely in the front seats and deliberately prolonged at the back of the hall, forced him to give over. Even so, a brief respite remained to him, for he sat on a platform, where the conventions of public appearance stiffened his self-control, and among those who, whatever they might know of his circumstances, would not arraign him with them. Henry Powles would not turn on him with, "Your wife is a drunkard." Crawley Blunt would not lean forward to say, "Mary does not care a snap of her fingers for you." They would not even—so strong is the fellowship of the respectable classes of society—acknowledge that they knew anything about Darwell.

After the meeting he would have to walk home with his wife and his children. Even then, there would be a chink of mercy. People would stop to exchange a word or two about the meet-

ing and the probable amount of the collection. But then the
door of Anchor House would shut behind him, and he would
go into his study, where he had sat all day, and the devils sitting there would slightly stir to re-admit him.

7.

Darwell, handsomely pensioned and in a very bad temper,
was taken away by a niece, and a couple of days later
the nursery-maid gave notice, alleging that her mother would
not wish her to remain in a house where such shocking things
might happen at any moment. Julia reported this with an oddly
exultant look. Having discharged her fury on Barnard, she
felt much the better for it, sanguine and even frisky. It was
almost as though she had remarried him, and the pair whom
Darwell had joined together might be expected to live in something like amity. Commenting on her high spirits, Wilberforce
said that it showed how thankful Mamma must be to have got
rid of Darwell. Euphemia replied by asking if he supposed
getting rid of Darwell also accounted for the change in Papa.
She spoke tartly because she was afraid. Delirium tremens in
a servant is not worse than sodomy in a son-in-law; but neither
Thomas's affair nor Joe's ungrateful flight nor the deaths of
Samuel and Julius had kept Papa away from his office for a
week. At first she supposed that he stayed at home in case Darwell should become violent again and attack Mary; but Darwell
was removed, and still Papa sat all day in his study, in a condition of such black and frozen gloom that there was not even a
spark of irritation to be got out of him. The hypothesis forced
itself upon her that he had found himself attacked by some
mortal sickness. If so, she was lost. Mamma's gay enfranchise-
ment too, so much gayer than getting rid of Darwell could
warrant—could it be that she knew? It would be a shocking
way to behave, but comprehensible.

Presently Euphemia had further cause to be alarmed and perplexed. She saw that her father was going out of his way to approve of her. He seemed even to solicit her approval.

Flinching at every recollection of the interview with Julia, and unable to think of anything else, John Barnard fastened his miserable mind to the reproaches about Euphemia. His conscience barbed Julia's accusation, for Julia did not know that Marmaduke Debenham had asked him for Euphemia's hand and had been refused; but sharpened by this private indictment, the accusation was still tolerable because it offered a possibility of making amends. He would be kinder to Euphemia; he would do everything in his power to make her feel herself valued and indispensable—as indeed she was: if it were not for her sex, he would certainly have made her a partner in the business. He would tell her this, and he would make a point of asking her advice and consulting her before any major decision. He would put an end to her being at everyone's beck and call. He would check Wilberforce's tendency to overlook the respect owed to someone so much older than himself. He would suggest another visit to the Miss Binghams, whose lives, so quiet and yet so full, showed how happily Euphemia and Ellen might live on together after his death. And while he lived the term "old maid" should never be spoken under his roof. It was strange how Julia, frantically alleging that it was marriage and family life which had made a drunkard of her, should in the next breath bewail that Euphemia was an old maid; but drinking undoes reason, as it undoes honour and self-respect. He had said nothing to Julia about her disclosure, and he hoped he would never be driven to refer to it. In the course of rating him, she had called him a spoilsport, and the trivial prick rankled as a distinguishable smart among much deeper wounds. Spoilsport he might be, but whatever wretched solace she got by drinking should not be spoiled by his intervention; he could do nothing for her or against her. But he would be kinder to Euphemia.

243

He set himself to begin. Euphemia was either too busy or too reserved to respond. She looked coldly startled when he praised her. When he asked her advice she replied that he must know best. And at any attempts at fatherly confidence she ran away.

It was all part and parcel of his doom, he supposed. But he persisted, as a repentance, and also because Euphemia was the only person who promised peace of mind. Julia bewildered him by behaving much as usual. Having screwed himself up to expect her in delirium tremens almost immediately, he was at a loss. It intimidated him to realize that at this rate Julia might go on drinking too much for years to come. As for Mary, he scarcely dared look at her in case he should see what Julia had proclaimed. Presently she was not there to be looked at. Darwell had spoiled Johnnie, and Mary's inability to keep him either good or happy made her revert to thoughts of her widowhood. If Thomas had been spared, he would have known how to manage Johnnie. He would have loved the child, if no one else did. The mourning locket reappeared on her bosom, and she announced that she was going to visit Mutty and Hartley—poor Mutty was the only person who had really understood poor Thomas. Telling himself that as Mary did not know of his wretchedness she was not unkind in leaving him, John Barnard said that Mutty would be surprised to see Johnnie grown so tall. Mary replied that Johnnie would be left behind; he would be no trouble to anyone, as Euphemia could look after him.

"You put too much on Euphemia," he said. "I will not hear of it. It must not be."

It was. Mary went off to Dover exactly as she had proposed to do, without a smile out of place. He had antagonized her on Euphemia's behalf, and though Euphemia could not be expected to know this, and the evidence of Johnnie was against him, he looked for some reward. He took Johnnie for walks on the beach, and inexorably read aloud to him. But no reward came. He was driven back into thinking that though he would always do his duty by Euphemia, he could not hope to do more.

Before he had reached this conclusion Euphemia's alarm had grown desperate. Whatever had provoked her father's importunities, they threatened her with a further foundering in being essential. If she did not get away soon she would be trapped; and to get away she must raise money. On the evening before Wilberforce went to Cambridge she entered his bedroom, carrying a shirt which she had sat up most of the previous night to finish.

He looked up from his packing. "Bless you, bless you! If you roll it up it can just be squeezed in. I suppose I can send you my mending, as usual?"

"No. I think not."

"No? Well, I daresay you're right. I fancy my bedmaker is supposed to do it. I don't wish her to feel slighted."

"I wasn't thinking of your bedmaker. I was thinking of myself."

"You couldn't do better. Seriously, Euphemia, it's time you left off being the family slave. When will you assert yourself?"

"Soon, I hope. But first I must have some money."

He pulled out a sovereign, saying, "Can I, without immodesty, ask why?"

"No. And that is not enough. Wilberforce! Will you break open your pig?"

A pottery savings-pig, with two sixpences to jingle inside it, was given by Aunt Robina to each nephew and niece reaching the age of five years. The other pigs had, for various good reasons, been broken by their owners, but Wilberforce's pig was intact and believed to be well lined. It stood on the mantelpiece, its hide spangled with metaphorical bees. Now he wrapped it in a towel, laid it on the floor, and took up the poker. "This is a solemn moment," he remarked, disguising by a play-acting manner the fact that in reality he felt it to be such. The poker descended. On their knees, they unfolded the towel and sorted out coins from the shards. The coins amounted to three pounds and elevenpence halfpenny.

"I was afraid it would be a disappointment to you," he said.

"What on earth did you do with the rest?" she inquired. "How did you get it out?"

"Most of it never went in. I put my hand over the slit and shook the animal. But the coins stayed with me."

"What did you spend them on?"

"Oysters, mainly."

"Oysters, Wilberforce? You risked a Grand Finale for oysters? I thought I had taught you more sense."

"Do you remember the wholesome food that was set before me, Euphemia—the boiled rice and the boiled mutton, and the cabbage, and the good homemade jam? Do you remember that I was a delicate child, and that my digestion was weak? Do you remember that exercise in moderation was considered good for me and fresh air bracing, and that I was sent into the garden to walk briskly up and down while memorizing datives? I used to go down to the stables and into Back Lane and whistle like a young robin. And like the parent bird, old Granny Hewitt used to come hobbling along and sell me oysters. Cheap, too, because she was sorry for me."

"What did you do with the shells?" she asked after a pause.

"I did what everybody else in Back Lane did. I threw them over our wall."

She knotted the three pounds elevenpence halfpenny in her handkerchief. "You were a disquieting little boy," she said, "but I was very fond of you."

"*'Was,'* Euphemia? Did you say 'was'?"

But the door had closed behind her.

The pig was disappointing, and now, with a time limit before her, she wished she had taken his sovereign; for she had set fire to her boats, even if she had not burned them. By Christmas, Wilberforce would be home and asking questions. Though he would not betray her project, he would not approve of it, and since she loved him his disapproval would unsettle her. For many years of her life she had also loved her mother, but that was ended. Though Mamma's habit of drinking more than was good for her had never antagonized Euphemia, it gradually invalidated any warmth of feeling; for one cannot forever pursue with love a person whose life is concentrated on keeping appointments with a solitary gratification. Among the poor people whom Euphemia visited was a Mrs. Drusilla Hardcastle, who belonged to a sect so recondite that she went neither to church nor chapel, but stayed at home, waiting on the Lord. If you waited hard enough, she said, the Lord would begin to talk to you as plain as anyone could wish; and on several visits Euphemia had found her in such a trance of attention that there was nothing for it but to go away. Feeling at the time a considerable need to love someone, Euphemia hoped to find herself loving Drusilla; but it proved impossible, just as it had become impossible to love Mamma. With the one as with the other, love was an ineptitude. This realization gave Euphemia some sharp misgivings about going to Herrnhut. There too waiting on the Lord was practised. How awkward it would be to go to Herrnhut and find herself among people just like Mamma! She wavered, but not for long. One must take chances. Besides, it was not Mamma she wanted to get away from, but Papa.

Faced with a time limit, she began to panic. Mary came home, the autumn dinner parties began, she would be compelled to buy a fresh pair of gloves. She was wearing them for the first time, and their cheapness was glaringly apparent, when Crawley Blunt, looking across the table, said to her, "I have some sad news for you, Miss Barnard. Just as we were leaving the rectory, I had a message that poor Minnie Cheyney died this afternoon. But it is a merciful release."

She agreed. Conversation flowed on. Baldwin Cooper, on her right, asked her if she had noticed the unusual plenty of hawthorn berries, said to foretell a hard winter, and when that was dismissed, her attention was claimed by Mr. Lovell from the Terrace, who had some very confidential information as to why the *Royal Britain* steamship was bound to be a total loss. Her mind was occupied by a harder winter and a nearer degree of loss. Somehow she must provide herself with another address and another confidante, and yet avoid rousing any suspicions of not being perfectly aboveboard in the mind of her correspondent. She lay awake all night, tossing over expedients, each with something against it, till she seemed to be wading through discarded conjectures as through dead leaves; and by the morning she had achieved nothing except a respectable decision that while she was paying the visit of condolence she would say nothing about her letters.

On the wall of Minnie's room the text which she herself had illuminated so many years before caught her eye, just as it always did, but this time instead of regretting the smudged scrollwork in the left-hand corner, she read the words: "THE LORD WILL PROVIDE." The Lord had provided for Minnie. Euphemia looked with humble envy at the face of the dead woman who had escaped before her, and escaped completely. Her scheming suddenly seemed to her no more than a nuisance, a scrollwork on which she had wasted time and debased herself. Why go to Herrnhut rather than to the Bay of Naples, when all one had to do was to wait a little and then die? Minnie's brother stood in the doorway, and as she turned away from the bed he came forward and put an object into her hand, which she noticed only as being cold, and black like a coffin. "Minnie left you her respects," he said, "and her savings, if you will accept of them. She thought the world of your kindness." For the first time in her life Euphemia wept and was comforted in a man's arms. Minnie's savings amounted to over twelve pounds.

She unlocked the money box as soon as she had left off crying, knowing that to carry it off unopened would be a discourtesy to dead Minnie and kind Roger. "More'n you reckoned," he said. "I'm right glad it's so much. You deserve every penny of it."

His snarling voice and the emphasis of the dialect stayed in her ears as she walked back to Anchor House. She ought to have told him how the money would be spent. She ought to say good-bye to all her friends among the poor. It was disgraceful to slink away from Loseby without a word of farewell to those who had given her her only experience of loving-kindness. Rather than incur that reproach, she would tell her father and be damned to it. If he could intimidate her, she would deserve to stay in his house. If he could not, she would get out of it somehow.

When John Barnard came in, Euphemia was waiting for him in the study. Two months earlier, when he was trying to make amends, when he was craving for some sign of trust and even hoping that it might be possible to unburden himself of some of his cares, he would have welcomed her appearance there. But he had given up hope and could say no more than "Well, Euphemia?"

"Papa, I have come to a decision."

"A decision, Euphemia?"

"I beg your pardon. I should have said two decisions. The first is that I am old enough to make decisions for myself."

She saw him start and supposed it was in anger. In fact, he had flinched. Euphemia's voice resembled her mother's. In this last sentence it had just such a steel edge on it as Julia's had when she told him she was a drunkard. "You are cold. You are shaking with cold. You had better sit nearer the fire," he said gloomily. She did not move, and he said again, "Well, Euphemia?"

As she began to speak, he averted his face.

It was easier than she had supposed. Much practice in Sunday school had taught her how to speak plainly and consecutively, and after she had overcome her surprise at not being interrupted she went methodically through what she had to say, till in the end she had told him everything, even to the fact that until this last moment she had intended to leave home without informing him. By degrees the defiance died out of her voice,

249

but nothing like pleading replaced it. She owed him duty and truth, and would comply with that; but she could feel no obligation to admit love on his part or on hers. She would not posit it or sue to it.

She ended her statement and waited for him to speak. He remained silent, not turning his head. He is trying to frighten me, she thought. Silence was a gambit of his, and it always frightened her and sometimes drove her into an indiscretion. It did so now, for she said, "Well, Papa?" and instantly regretted it.

But nothing was dislodged. No thunder sounded. No skies fell. As she sat watching him it seemed to her that she saw something like relaxation taking place in that stern silhouette. He drew a long and somehow careful breath, as though some overhearing danger might still be within earshot. He turned and surveyed her with grave curiosity.

And is this how you choose to repay—? That was the kind of opening she expected, and she stiffened herself to stand firm. She heard him say, "You are going to Herrnhut? To Herrnhut? Strange."

Indeed it was strange and marvellous in his eyes, and the Lord's doing. So long ago, and dogged with sorrows even then, though not then caught and pulled down among them, he had stood listening to the parched winter hornbeams and had promised himself that in his old age he would revisit Herrnhut and die there. Now Euphemia was going, a fact which would make it impossible for him to go, since it was to escape him that she was going. The amends he had proposed to make were made for him, and all he had to do was fall in with them.

When he spoke again his voice was almost brisk. "How do you propose to get there? And have you made sure that you will be welcome?"

Still convinced that all this was a preliminary to wrath—for a stalking of the prey had often been part of his method—she answered that she proposed to take the boat at Harwich and go

250

on from Hamburg by diligence, that she had just sufficient money for this, and that as for being sure of a welcome, Monsieur Tuggli had got permission for her to be admitted on trial. For the rest, she hoped to give satisfaction and to remain.

He said that for a lady travelling alone on the continent just sufficient money was insufficient, and asked if she had thought about warm underclothes. Too late to thank him, she realized that he had given her permission to depart. As he was incapable of acting gracefully—as incapable as she—the magnanimity in the situation was bricked up between them by a discussion of practical details, during which he expressed nothing beyond a cautious anxiety for her welfare, and she a mistrustful anxiety to give as little trouble as possible.

"You will wish to say good-bye to Wilberforce?"

"I would rather not."

"He will wish it. So will your mamma. And Euphemia, you will please leave it to me to tell your mamma."

Thanking him for this, she came her nearest to spontaneous gratitude.

Julia, as he had foreseen, was furious. She renewed the tirade of Euphemia's wrongs. Thwarted of marriage, ignored and treated as a beast of burden, Euphemia was now to be bundled off to end her days in Germany among Moravians. Why not send her to the knackers?

"I am thankful to see any child of mine go out of this house," he said.

"Then you will be glad to hear that Mary met a Mr. Eustace at Dover," she retorted.

She had met a Mr. Eustace at Dover? And this was the first he had heard of it? But in such things a young woman would turn to her mother. In any case, what he had said remained true. If he could not be glad to see Mary go out of his house, yet he would be thankful. The idea somehow lodged itself in his head that Mr. Eustace was a schoolmaster, a somewhat strict schoolmaster who would undertake Johnnie.

251

In the end it was decided that Euphemia should sail from the Port of London, and in January, on the coldest night of the winter, he saw her go on board. The next morning he went to Tooley Street, where Daniel and he were to meet and discuss business. Basil Cook had died in 1844, his successor had mismanaged several contracts, and John Barnard wanted to close the agency. Daniel objected. Trade, he wrote, was improving; he expected the next ten years to be years of increasing prosperity, and a foothold in London was too valuable to be given up. He suggested that Dobson should be dismissed and replaced by a better man—"someone who will take an interest in it," he underlined. What this meant was made clear when Daniel arrived accompanied by his second son, Alexander. Alexander was the first military Barnard. He had lost a toe by gunshot in the China War, and by subsequent treatment in a military hospital he lost a leg by gangrene. So much was known and condoled with at Anchor House, but it was news to his uncle that Alexander had always wanted to join the family firm.

"There's a song about the one-legged man of Tooley Street," said Daniel, who had gone very grey and talked more than ever at random. "I can't recollect how it goes, but I know I've heard it. Or else it's a joke. Anyhow, there you are! Type and ante-type that Beenie's old uncle was always preaching about in St. Giles's kirk." This indication of Daniel's habit of attending the largest church of a locality, quite irrespective of its doctrine (in Rome he would have attended St. Peter's), did not forward his case; but with Alexander before him, John Barnard could not raise much opposition, and he had made up his mind that the present clerk must go. He had come early in order to go through the books. It was a foggy morning, and the peculiar loneliness of London had weighed on him. It was as though the fog were thickened by the cares of innumerable men, and all of them unknown to him. Thomas's specimen cabinet was still in the room, its glazed doors dulled and sticky with grime. Ingenious in self-torment, John Barnard had called for

252

the ledgers of 1836-37, and looked long at Thomas's handwriting. He noticed several mistakes in Thomas's arithmetic. They had escaped and could not now be put right. Nothing could be put right. And so, when Daniel and Alexander walked in, he was ready to agree to almost anything that would take him out of that room and away from his thoughts.

Alexander went off in a cab, having an appointment to keep, and the two brothers walked over London Bridge. Here the fog was so heavy that the river was invisible, but, habit being stronger than reason, they stopped midway and looked down into the Pool. It resounded with noises of water and shipping. And suddenly, from almost beneath them, a woman's voice said, "Have a cup of tea, dearie?"

"I've often thought I should like to live on a barge," commented Daniel. The thought of living on a barge led him to ask questions about his brother's family. He thought Wilberforce was still at school, he confused Euphemia with Ellen. Excusing himself, he said, "Julia don't write as often as she used to." Alone with Daniel, wrapped up with him by fog and the voices of strangers, John Barnard felt a childish impulse to confide in his brother. Daniel's ungloved hand, resting on the parapet, caught his eye, and he thought how it and his own had been shaped in the same womb. Staring into the fog, Daniel said, "Robina's got a cancer." The words scattered the illusion of intimacy. The nursery brothers were two ageing men, each meshed in his own net of calamity. While he was stammering for words of condolence, Daniel interrupted him with, "Don't tell Julia. Robina means to write to her later on." By the time they reached the north bank Daniel was twitting him with living in a district of England so backward that even now there was no railway to Norwich.

"I have no great wish to travel by steam," said John Barnard.

Daniel, laughing like a cockcrow, replied, "You'll do it sooner than you think. I'm taking you on a trip by railroad this afternoon. We'll go down to Brighton and dine there."

253

The wish of a man whose wife is dying is almost as sacred as the wish of a dying man, so John Barnard went down to Brighton and found that he enjoyed the new way of travelling. Unaccustomed to talking with anybody who effortlessly contradicted him, he also enjoyed Daniel's conversation at dinner. It gave him a sense of exhilaration and release, which he attributed to the Brighton air. The thought stole into his head that when Daniel was a widower they might go for some little jaunts together, to the Lake Country perhaps, or to the Shetlands, scene of Scott's novel *The Pirate*. Minna Troil had always seemed to him the most ideal of Scott's heroines. There would be no wickedness in it, for a man has blood ties as well as family ties, and the earlier relationship is often the more profound. It would be reviving to see more of Daniel, who now, by so much more knowledge of the world, seemed like the elder brother.

Robina died a month later, but no little jaunts followed. Daniel, disgusted by what he called the poltroonery of the Bank of England over the Three per Cents, went to visit Joseph and Grizzie. Before the year was out, he had married Grizzie's cousin, sent in his retirement, and bought an estate. "I am the luckiest dog in the world," he wrote, "for I have another charming Scotch wife (Elphinstone on her mother's side), and West Indian cooking is glorious, especially sucking pig. Leave the business to Alexander and come for a long visit. There is something for all tastes—*fêtes champêtres* for the young ones, and a whist table on the veranda for us fogeys."

John Barnard remembered that Joseph had never invited him to Mount Indigo; but, swallowing this first thought, he wavered towards acceptance. Mary was in a very low state; she suffered from palpitations, and since that fellow Eustace she had had another disappointment of the heart. *Fêtes champêtres*, as even Daniel now called picnics, and a warm climate would be good for Mary. Ellen had never been farther than Ely. The trip to Brighton had stayed warm in his memory, and he would like to see Daniel again. If Julia could be persuaded to stay at home? But he knew that Julia would not be persuaded. She would seize on this chance of seeing Joseph again, regardless of what Joseph could scarcely fail to see in her, and what Joseph's wife would see at a glance. While they lived quietly, she fuddled quietly and without open scandal; but to let her loose in a strange, bright society and abandon her to gaieties and excitement would be to expose her to shame. He kept Daniel's invitation to himself. Replying to it, he said that it was not possible to accept for the whole family, but that Mary, if a suitable escort could be found for her, might be very glad of an invitation. Apparently Daniel found it too much trouble to find the suitable escort. He answered with a letter of general regret, and said nothing of Mary.

He had acted for the best, he had put by his own wishes in refusing Daniel's invitation; and yet his conscience troubled him. Mary moped, Mary did not marry. The jaunt which could not be taken with Daniel was remodelled, and he offered Mary the choice of a tour to the Highlands, to Paris, or to the Lake Country. Without enthusiasm, she chose Paris. They arrived in Paris on February 20, and two days later the Revolution of 1848 broke out. John Barnard was interested, his spirits rose, he was happy to know himself an Englishman; but Mary was terrified and insisted on being taken away. The journey to the coast was full of delays and impediments, the Channel was rough, and when they reached Dover Mary declared that she could go no farther and must spend a week or so with Mutty to compose her nerves after such frightful experiences. Knowing that the excursion had been a dead failure, he was not sorry to travel on alone, and, arriving, he found himself positively glad to see Julia. She declared that he smelled of gunpowder; she was in excellent spirits and related a long circumstantial story about Mr. Lovell's buying ten mattresses to put in the windows when Number 4 Prospect Terrace was attacked by the Chartists.

255

PART SIX

1.

On the morning when she refused to take the pledge Julia became a new being. For years she had alternated between expecting her husband to discover that she drank and scorning him for not discovering it. Discovery would entail disgrace and an odious perspective of being preached at and attemptedly reformed. To remain undiscovered was equally mortifying— for could anything be more humiliating than to live in dread of a husband who persists in not finding one out? By springing the truth on him she had at one blow established herself in a freehold vice, and was quit of any further obligations to be discreet and to conceal. Concealment was now his responsibility. She could drink, and Barnard could deceive. Like other women in the period of childbearing, Julia had assessed with indignation the disproportion between getting a child, and carrying it, giving birth to it, and suckling it. The boot, she considered, was now on the other leg. Emancipation had the effects that emancipators attribute to it; if Julia did not actually drink any less, she drank more disposedly. Her temper sweetened, she left off pitying herself and sank a good deal of conjugal rancour in a new relationship of being a fellow grand-

256

parent and jointly groaning under the yoke of that tiresome child Johnnie. Released from fear of betraying her secret, she became talkative and sometimes amusing. This made the secret so much less obvious that Loseby society, observing these changes and that they dated from about the time that Euphemia went to Germany, discovered that poor Mrs. Barnard had been shockingly intimidated by that spinsterish daughter, and that they had been thinking so for a long time. In fact, if Euphemia's going had not so nearly coincided with Julia's freehold installation in drink, Julia would have missed her badly. Euphemia had been oddly standoffish for some little while, she was no longer such good company as she used to be; but in her heart Julia knew that, in the event of the worst, Euphemia would not be frightened and would be kind. That need was over; the worst had been precipitated and had turned out to be very much for the best. What remained was to miss Euphemia when a joke fell flat, or some chasm yawned in the household; when all the linen pillowcases simultaneously had holes in them; when there was no one but his mother to manage Johnnie; when no one had remembered to order more wine vinegar; when the room grew cold and her shawl was upstairs; when Euphemia's poor people kept coming to the house and neither Mary nor Ellen had time to attend to them; when letters had to be answered, when birthdays should have been remembered, and above all when Hartley and Mutty came to stay. This was an invitation of decency, for Mary had paid three visits to Dover, and something had to be done in return. Julia, writing the invitation, pinned her hopes on Mutty's implacable resentment at Thomas's ill usage, but it happened to be one of the times when Simon Kettle and not John Barnard was the villain of the piece, and the invitation was accepted. They came for a fortnight. Hartley was now seventy-eight, stone deaf, and a military Munchausen. He talked incessantly about his experiences in the Peninsular War, the nuns who fled to him for succour, the advice he had given to Wellington. John

Barnard chafed with embarrassment, and presently with rage, remembering that during the years when Hartley represented himself as storming Badajoz and rescuing whole convents from worse than death he was in fact living comfortably at Anchor House with Hannah and Selina. But it was vain to protest. Hartley was deaf, and Julia and his daughters indifferent to any sufferings other than those they endured from Mutty. Towards the close of this frightful visit Mutty quarrelled violently with Mary. Mary, it appeared, had slighted her by inattention to a crochet-work in progress. But it was all of a piece with Mary's usual behaviour, Mutty had seen through her pretences long ago; Mary cared nothing for her and only went to Dover in order to run after the officers.

After this it came as a shock to John Barnard to hear that Mary was proposing to travel back with them for another little visit. At first he could not believe it. Dislodged from disbelief, he would not hear of it. Against an inner voice that told him not to meddle, he found himself debating with Mary.

"I do not like this scheme at all. You must not go."

"But I have promised Mutty. I cannot disappoint her."

"You should consider your dignity as well as Mutty's pleasure. I do not wish you actually to bear resentment, Mary. But you have been too ready to forgive."

"Yes, I daresay it is silly of me. But it seems dreadful to bear resentment. And I know she has written to the butcher already, to order sweetbreads."

"That can be easily undone. She can write again. But what cannot be undone, my love, is the insult to your character. I cannot have it said that you only visit her in order to run after officers."

Mary flushed. Her eyes looked at him through an increasing brilliance of tears. "I do think it is hard—very hard—that you should believe such a thing. Nothing would induce me to run after an officer."

"Mary, you misunderstand me. I did not for a moment sup-
258

pose that you ran after officers. That is why I feel obliged—"

"And I don't want to marry again. I often wish I had never married, but you were bent on it. And worse than anything is to be treated as though I had never been married at all, and suspected of running after officers as though I were a chit of a girl. Surely as a widow I can decide whether or no I go to Dover?"

"Mutty insulted you. That should be reason enough."

"Mutty is so silly, she will say anything. And it would be ridiculous to take offence over such a trifle."

"Your good name is not a trifle."

"I really cannot understand why I am to be denied such a very small pleasure. You used not to be so unkind. You used to say you liked to see me happy."

He was silent from despair.

"Dear Papa!" There was a chuckle of triumph in her voice, though she had tuned it to no more than hopeful wheedling.

Furious at the situation, he said, "You are not to go to Dover. I forbid it."

"Oh, very well!"

He had feared that she would defy him. She had given in, but her submission only replaced one fear with another, and that of longer tenure, dating from that day when he told her that Thomas was dismissed, and she had cried out, "You think of no one but yourself. I detest you!" Now she turned a rusty knife in his wound with her "Very well." He knew that she would not go and that she would add this grudge to the secret hoard of grudges she stored up against him, and he also knew that she had been running after officers.

He soon began to find excuses for her, and reasons for blaming himself. There was no crime in hoping to find a husband; it was Mutty's vulgarity that put such a vile complexion on an innocent intention. If Mary, like other young women, could go about with a mother for a chaperon, there would be nothing to take exception to; indeed, since she was a widow, she could have gone to some respectable watering-place with Euphemia to companion her. He should have thought of this while Euphemia was at home. Euphemia was settled at Herrnhut, Robina was dead, and though Alexander had a wife, Mary had taken a strong dislike to her. Daniel had not answered his hint, and he could not cheapen Mary by hinting again. Wilberforce had friends, but they were friends of his own age, and Mary was in her thirty-first year—though thirty, he assured himself, embarrassed at the calculation, is young for a widow. With an embarrassment that was nearer shame, and with despairing pity, he looked on while she negotiated a visit to Walton on the Naze. The following year things improved. Johnnie entered Harrow school and caught the mumps, and Mary on a visit of maternal anxiety made such a pleasing impression on the wife of Johnnie's housemaster that other invitations followed. One of these included a day at the Great Exhibition. John Barnard was thankful to see her depending for her pleasure on something superior to Hartleys and Kettles, and as, beyond paying Johnnie's bills, he had no hand in the development, he hoped it might prosper.

And yet he craved for new calamities, feeling that a week in which he had not pressed himself to some sharp disillusionment was time wasted, and it was with something like intolerance that he watched the extremely gradual process of Julia's ruin. He had nerved himself, if not for delirium tremens like Darwell's, at least for scenes of total intoxication. Instead he saw her becoming shakier in the hand, shorter of breath, and considerably more slovenly in her person; but at the same time assuming a kind of implacable serenity. There were hours when he almost enjoyed her company—it gave him such a sense of liberation. But that was a feeling he did not dwell on. It could not be true. No man who was not a villain could find rest for his soul in the company of a drunken wife. Julia, who had brought the intuition of the slave into her epoch of freedom, knew exactly when Barnard took another fit of moral ague, and that when he was through with it he would come back and bask in her sunset glow. She did not warrant herself to last much longer—another two years, three at the most. But with life so nearly over, only a fool, she thought, would spoil the last of it by fretting and remorse. She certainly had not expected to find so much sugar at the bottom of the tumbler; and when the fear of death came up and gave her that little premonitory tap on the shoulder, as of one who says, "Your turn presently," she drove it away with talk of her youth and her childhood. Garrulous and somnolent, falling asleep in the present and waking up with some freshly remembered mishap or scandal from the past, she seemed to be declining into a lower walk of life instead of into the valley of the shadow of death. John Barnard told himself that she had a wonderful constitution, and took to reading aloud in the evenings.

They were in the spring of 1852, and midway through the seventh chapter of *Old Mortality* when Julia sat up on the sofa and exclaimed, "Murder!"

"Murder, Mamma?" inquired Ellen, whose thoughts had been far away and hovering round a cloister—for at that time Ellen was cherishing an imaginary idyll with Dr. Pusey.

"Did you have a bad dream?" John Barnard asked.

"Murder!" Julia repeated with even greater emphasis. "It is past my powers of endurance to listen any longer to your notions of a Scotch accent. Give the book to me!"

He spoke of not exerting herself. Mary said why not skip over this part and go on from where the story began to be English again. But Julia had possessed herself of the book and began to read. After a couple of pages she was taken with a violent coughing fit, and again she was begged not to overtire herself. She fought the cough to a finish and read on to the end of the chapter.

"I don't suppose you understood two words of it," she said when they thanked her for making it so interesting and lifelike. It was plain that she did not care, either. She sat upright, flushed and elated with performance, and the garnet brooch winked on her bosom as it rode in and out of the light. "Well! That was very enjoyable," she said, addressing her crony self. "When I've got my breath back we'll have some more. Mary! Be a kind child and mix me a rum toddy. I'll take it hot."

Mary went to the tea-table, where tumblers and decanters now appeared brazenly with the tea things and the hot-water urn. She had witnessed Julia's performance with nothing but disapproving indifference, and she expressed her indifference by pouring in considerably more rum than usual.

"Goodness me, girl! You've made it strong. I suppose you've helped me as you love me."

She stirred briskly and drank meditatively, her glance travelling from her husband to her daughters, and from them to the furnishings of the room. Uncommonly shabby, she thought, and decided that there should be a new carpet. Carpets, at any rate, can be got new when the colour and substance are worn away from the old ones. It should be bought before Wilberforce next came home. It would be agreeable for him to find something changed, if only a drawing-room carpet. John Barnard asked Mary for another cup of tea and commented on the loquacity of the garden owl. He hoped, by making a little conversation, to avert more reading aloud and so get Julia safely off to bed. She lumbered off the sofa, she appeared to be making for the door. He rose and gave her his arm and found himself supporting her to the bookcase. It was the *Works of Robert Burns* she pulled out.

"Now I am going to read you a little poetry," she announced, depositing herself on the sofa. "There's not enough poetry in this house." Her speech was clear, but the manner of it warned him not to meddle.

There was an Address to the Deity which did not take much time and would be admirable; there was an Address to a Mountain Daisy, and another to a shrew-mouse, which would be well enough. He saw her turning over the pages, pausing sometimes to read and smile, as though she were licking her chops. There were some very painful poems by Burns, but surely, even in her present state, Julia would not choose one of those for reading aloud in the family circle.

> "When chapman billies leave the street,
> And drouthy neebors, neebors meet;
> As market days are wearing late,
> An' folk begin to tak the gate;
> While we sit bousing at the nappy,
> An' getting fou and unco happy . . ."

It was *Tam o' Shanter* she chose.

She must have known it almost by heart, for she read it headlong, snatching a breath here and there, breaking off with dramatic suddenness and then rushing ahead into the next burst of narrative. The noise roused Ellen from her colloquy with Pusey. It was as though a fire had been kindled in the middle of the drawing room, a fire of dried furze, spitting, crackling, and hallooing. Mamma went so fast that even if it had not been all in Scotch, she could not have followed the sense. Something about a landlady; and then about a poppy; and then lightning, tomahawks, garters, and queens. The words flew by her, burning in the air like the lit twigs the fire casts away from itself. There went Satan—if anything so swift and godless could be Satan; but she let him go with the rest, for her wits were deafened by the incessant crackling gibberish that galloped out of Mamma. As if peering through the smoke of a furze-fire, she saw glimpses of Mary and Papa, Mary muttering like a witch as she counted her stitches, and Papa stirring his tea with a steadfast, shaking hand. How extraordinary! It bore no resemblance to poetry, so perhaps it was like Scotland. Scotland was a romantic country, claymores flashed, tartans fluttered, waterfalls leaped from the mountainside. Land of the mountain and the flood! . . . She felt a mad impulse to leap to her feet and declaim *Land of the Mountain and the Flood* to the accompaniment of the extraordinary noises that were galloping from Mamma. Pusey was nothing to her. Oh, she would ten thousand times rather fly unknown to the Highlands than join a sisterhood! All of a sudden Mamma began to read at a slower pace, the pace of a moral.

Yes, it was a moral.

> Think ye may buy the joys o'er dear;
> Remember Tam o' Shanter's mare.

Why? thought Ellen. But perhaps it was all about horse racing. Mamma shut up the book. No one said a word. The bonfire was extinguished. Ellen felt the room going round her, but slower now, lumbering unsteadily into repose. Hearing her name spoken, she jumped as if she had been shot.

"Look at Ellen," Mamma was saying. "D'you see Ellen? Look at her! She's the only one of my children with a spark of poetry about her."

Cloaked in a sense of fallen majesty, Julia got up from the sofa, sat down again, and remarked that she was going to bed.

2.

For the last five years John Barnard had slept in his dressing room. This night, anxious about Julia, who must have put a great strain on herself by so much reading aloud, he went twice into her room. Each time he found her sleeping just as usual, a minute vein flicking in one of her purple eyelids, her breath puffing through her half-open mouth. She must have died—so the doctor said—about four in the morning, dying blamelessly in her sleep, her position not altered since her husband last saw her, except that her right hand clutched the string of her nightcap.

It was a small family party that followed the portentous coffin into church. The most strikingly blackened member of it was Johnnie. He had come from Harrow, and before his arrival

Mary had alternately wondered if he would be given sandwiches to eat on the journey and how he could be fitted with a mourning suit in time for the funeral. Johnnie, however, had the foresight to get himself fitted out by the school tailor in the most superfine inconsolability. He had remembered sandwiches, too, and brought a note of condolence from Dr. Vaughan, the headmaster. It was his first funeral, and he was determined to do it justice.

"If he patronizes Papa much more, I shall tear him in pieces," remarked Wilberforce to Ellen. With Mary, Wilberforce took the line of seeming surprised that she proposed to allow her boy to attend the funeral, as though attending funerals were a form of not going home till morning, and Johnnie no more than a blackened infant. Wilberforce was in a bad temper. His conscience reproached him because for eighteen months he had not seen his mother; his ambition fretted him because by attending her funeral he would forfeit a meeting with the Astronomer Royal; and Euphemia, whom he had expected to meet, and who would have soothed both his conscience and his ambition, was not there. Since he must have a confidant, he turned to Ellen, and found her better than he expected.

Alexander Barnard and his wife were the only people from outside Loseby present, but the church, when the mourners entered it, was full to the doors. It was many years since Julia had gone about in Loseby; but her charities, and the strength of the soups and jellies, were still remembered, and to have lost so many children made her sympathetic and respectable. When the coffin was borne out of the church the whole congregation followed, and stood massed and silent while the committal sentences were said and the coffin lowered into the grave. The handful of sandy earth had fallen, lightly hissing, on the coffin lid, and Crawley Blunt was reading the last prayers when there was a sound of feet stumbling and hurrying along the path, and a loud, blubbering voice was heard, saying, "Stop, stop! Wait for me."

The crowd stirred; there were mutters of reprobation, whispers of "Send her away. Keep her off." Struggling and posturing, a figure out of a farce writhed its passage through the crowd to the grave's edge, a figure in a dirty nightdress dabbled with blood, bareheaded, with grey hair in a wagging pigtail, and bedizened with a crape streamer. It was Darwell. Her niece, in order to attend the funeral, had left her locked up, but she had broken out by a window. Having achieved her purpose, she forgot it and stood smoothing down her nightdress and dropping curtsies to Crawley Blunt till the niece took her away.

Crawley Blunt went home and asked for a pot of strong tea to be brought to him in the study; he was not through with Mrs. Barnard yet. Customs died hard at Loseby, where any attempt to change what ancestors had enjoyed or tolerated was resented as impiety to the dead; and a funeral sermon, preached on the Sunday after a burial, was a Loseby custom. Fortunately a sudden death is always a good cut-and-come-again theme, and he made the most of it, thus avoiding an undue discretion about Julia's failings—in a small parish like Loseby discretion can look positively glaring. But on Saturday night a set of roisterers from the Lord Nelson raided the rectory pigeon-cote, and Crawley Blunt, hurrying to the defence of his fantails and tumblers, tripped over the yard dog's chain, fell, and broke his nose. There was nothing for it but to give the manuscript of his sermon to Peter Culver, the new curate, and charge him not to depart from it. He did not depart from it, inasmuch as he read every word, but a new-brooming fervour moved him to add embellishments, and, the text being "They were taken away in good time," his major embellishment was to stress how mercifully God had removed Julia before she could have been pained by such manifestations of intemperance as had desecrated her funeral and chosen the quiet Sabbath eve to rob the pigeon-cote. Titters broke out at the back of the church. In the foremost pews silence was even more explicit. Wilberforce, glancing along the family pew, realized that Mary had no idea why this extempore passage was so appalling. She was listening with unaffected attention—basking in it, he said to himself, basking being of all mental states the one he was most out of sympathy with. A moment later he saw his father also glance at Mary, and saw a look of relief settle on his face. Jealous on his mother's behalf, scorning a man who could so entirely dote on a fool, Wilberforce thought without mercy, I shall tell him this afternoon. What he had to tell was that he intended to abjure the family business. Since it is best to get disagreeable things over quickly, he would speak that afternoon and go away the next day.

He saw his father go into the garden, and presently he went after him. He was not there. He was not in his study, nor in his dressing room. Mary was writing letters, Ellen was reading. The house, full of spring sunshine, seemed oddly empty and unconcerned. Having screwed himself up for the interview, Wilberforce could not settle to anything else, and a whim took him to explore the house as though it were the empty one it so nearly was. The dining room, with its long table where the three would sit together day after day; the drawing room, which Ellen would enter in order to practise her unachievable *Rondo brilliante;* the study, with the maroon curtains framing the view of the wall. His mother was dead, but it was Euphemia he missed—her unemotional kindness, her profound adequacy. It was she who had domesticated the house, and without her it would turn into a formal madhouse. Still exploring, he went upstairs and looked at his old nursery, where someone had thrown a dust-sheet over the rocking-horse, and into the room where he could just remember his brother Julius coughing in a bed, and a bird dashing itself against the closed window. Going back to the first floor, he looked with a stranger's curiosity into Mary's room, and into Ellen's, and then, with a sense of intrusion not aroused by these, into Euphemia's. It told him nothing of her, except that she was gone. Opposite this was his mother's dressing room, lined like a bird's nest with her former plumage, and still seeming to exhale a blood-warmth. There was her sofa, sagging from her weight, and the sofa-table beside it, marked with tumbler rings, and the sheepskin rug and the eared easy chair. Behind the sofa was the glass-fronted cabinet, its shelves crammed with nursery relics: Susan's dolls and the puppets Uncle Daniel had brought from Burma; a squirrel skin that Julius had cured for Mamma; the shoes Joe had worn as a baby; Euphemia's first kettle-holder; Samuel's stuffed owl; the long robe tied with pink ribbons that Robina had worn for her christening; and two of Mamma's own dolls, with dark leather faces and high waists—all sunk into one epoch of antiquity behind the polished glass. Above the cabinet hung the long browned copperplate of Guido Reni's *Aurora,* which had come from Aunt Maxwell—severe in its pagan sensuality above the clutter of hopefulness and bereavement and sentiment and forgetfulness below.

> *Lucifer antevolat. Rapide fuga lampada solis*
> *Aurora umbrarum victrix ne victa recedas.*

He read the motto for the thousandth time, compassionately remembering the days when the only word to which he could attach any meaning was the first word. The person in the char-iot, therefore, was the Devil, drawn by a rather incompetent artist who had forgotten to give him horns and a tail. I shall ask for that, he thought.

The door between the dressing room and the bedroom stood unlatched, and he pushed it open and looked in. Lying on the bed was his father. He breathed; he was asleep; but so profoundly asleep, so much a castaway in sleep, that Wilberforce, after the first start of alarm at finding his father in anything so like a state of nature, remained and considered him. There he lay, the author (under God, as he would be the first to point out) of Wilberforce's being, and of the being of four other sons and five daughters, five of them dead, two self-exiled; and of untold mischief, fear, and discouragement: a man who had

268

meant no harm, who had done his best for his family, who had been faithful to his wife and obedient to his God and loyal to his country, and a model of commercial integrity, and who had spread around him a desert of mendacity and discomfort. A residual smell of taproom stole from the room behind, and it was as though his mother's ghost had whispered dryly into her son's ear, Do you wonder at it? He did not; of all his father's children, except his father's waxen idol, Mary, he had suffered least under that tyranny of fidget, scruple, censure, and mistrust; but he had had enough of it to know what it was to be one of his father's children. And she, poor soul, had been his father's wife. Of all men on earth, John Barnard should never have married, never come between the sheets of that conjugal bed, to which he had now crept back like some sorry instinct-ridden animal. As a bachelor, as a quaint great-uncle, who was very fond of babies and would leave thumping legacies, he might have been well enough— perhaps even contented with his lot, perhaps even happy. He should not have married. Aunt Maxwell, that distant arbitress, should have known better and put a stop to it. She should have read the indices of that high, narrow forehead, and of those querulous eyebrows, starting up like hares at the least alarm; but probably she saw regular features and an air of Englishry and refinement, and, looking no further, gave her blessing and the Guido Reni and all the household linen.

Lucifer antevolat. Stirred up by the *Aurora* motto, another piece of Latinity came to his mind, rising heavily, like some great boding, brooding pike.

> *Nunc ratio nulla est restandi, nulla facultas,*
> *Aeternas quoniam poenas in morte timendunst.*

Afraid of living because of the unknown horror and eternal suffering that may be the price of that enforced and dubious pleasure, his father could never have known happiness or dispensed it. Lucretius was right.

269

But for the moment hell had no power over him. He slept profoundly, his body was relaxed, his features had fallen into a look of astonished gratitude. So why, thought Wilberforce, stir up needless vexation by an interview? He was leaving the next day. When he had picked up the routine of his ordinary life he would write a letter.

The letter came ten days later and was acknowledged by return of post. Signing the reply, "Your affect. Papa, John Barnard," and addressing it to Mr. W. Barnard, M.A., it seemed to John Barnard that it was little more than an ordinary business letter. A customer was going elsewhere. It was regrettable, and he must think it ill-judged, since the firm of Barnard & Son was prosperous and deservedly well thought of in the trade. But these reverses happen in business, and after replying to Wilberforce he answered a customer who wished to double a previous order for linseed because the first consignment had been of such superior quality: if the two replies did not actually counterbalance each other, still, they were much of a muchness, and all in the day's work. Gratifying, regrettable; as he wished or as he did not wish—these distinctions had recently become insignificant to him, and distinguishable rather as Tuesday is distinguishable from Wednesday. At Julia's death he had entered a new state of being. Ambition had released him—moral ambition, the most painful of all ambitions.

At first he supposed that what he was feeling was relief at the manner of her death. Not one of the horrors he had foreseen had come to pass. She had died without pain, without distress of mind, without scandal. She had not even directly died of drink. So encompassing was his relief that Darwell's appearance at the graveside, the pillorying sermon, and the titters from the back of the church, seemed no more than the clatter of the storm that rises behind the traveller but does not break till after he has reached his own fireside.

But the feeling of relief continued long after the manner of Julia's death could warrant it. It crept into all his acts and sen-

270

sations, it was as much present when he shaved as when he prayed, it established itself as part of his life; so much so that he became accustomed to it and did not feel obliged to give it any particular examination. This was just as well; for examination would have obliged him to admit that it was the fact, and not merely the manner, of Julia's death which caused it. For over thirty years he had been trying to turn a silk purse into a sow's ear by extending that flimsy article, a young man's fancy, into the durable zeal of the family man—trying to be patient when in fact he was bored; to rule, when he wanted to run away; to compound by concern over his children's upbringing the half-heartedness with which he had begotten them. Only Julia knew how discreditable to them both those occasions had been; how little love there had been on his side, how much unwomanly prompting on hers to rouse that little love into a brief lust, and how difficult it had been afterwards to conceal the resentment felt by both parties. He had done his best, no man can do more, and now it was over. God's hand had brought him safely to the beginning of his old age. He was in his sixty-third year, and not far from the time when the eyes of those who look out of the windows shall be darkened, and the grasshopper shall be a burden and the almond tree shall fail, the silver cord be loosed and the pitcher broken at the fountain. The majestic lament of Ecclesiastes rang in his ears like bells ringing for a victory. Julia was dead, Wilberforce did not wish to come into the business, the London office was now handling a larger volume of trade than the parent office in Loseby, he had lost the power of hearing in one ear—all these were intimations that it was time he turned himself away from the things of this world and prepared to humble himself before eternity.

3.

The terraces and the better-class parts of Loseby remarked on how suddenly Mr. Barnard had aged since Mrs. Barnard's death. She must have meant more to him than anyone supposed, for he seemed quite lost without her, not the same man at all. The taverns, the skittle alley, and the fishing streets said that Grand Turk had lost most of his feathers now, anyone might have more than half a mind to be sorry for the old bastard. In fact, the two years which followed Julia's death were the happiest years of John Barnard's life. He was himself, and yet he lived like a new man. It was as though, at the end of a long day's march, he had gone into the sea for a bathe; fatigue and purpose and footsoreness remained on shore, along with his put-off clothes, and his body floated in horizontal lightness and ease and could direct itself with no more effort than a kick or a flip of the hand.

But in this sea too, there was a current—just such another as the current that wrecked boats on Rigby Head—and presently his love for Mary reasserted itself and swept him towards her. While Julia lived, those frightful words, "Your wax-doll Mary doesn't care a snap of her fingers about you," constrained him to live as though they were true. Because they might be true he never dared to put them to the proof, warning himself that just as he had not seen that his wife was a drunkard he might not see that his daughter had no love for him. Indeed, why should she love him? Since none of his other children loved him, why should Mary do so? In his fumbling zeal to serve her, he had spoiled her life and made an untimely widow of her, and exposed her to the accusation and perhaps even to the act of running after officers. But as time absolved him from the discomfort of being a husband, and gently assured him that he was an old man with nothing more to fear from life but death, the appointed portion of all men, he began to turn tremblingly towards her and to hope.

Because for so long he had not allowed himself to look at her with his heart in the gaze he saw her almost as a new being. What he had abjured was a girl, a girl whom circumstances had fixed in a false immaturity as pins fix a butterfly in a specimen cabinet. Now she was a woman, the lady of the house, the mother of a son almost as tall as herself. Maturity suited her, and so did the mood of the time—the fashion for richer colours, more elaborate ornamentation, and fuller curves. She began to improve the look of the house. Bird's-eye maple, ebony, and satinwood replaced the rosewood and mahogany. Ornaments sprouted on surfaces which had formerly been bare, little fanciful tables stood about like pages, and on the walls mirrors and genre paintings in oils elbowed the old plain-faced portraits. With each innovation she asked him if he were not pleased with it, and because she had introduced it he was pleased: did not all these changes show that she was happy at Anchor House and felt herself the mistress of it? At her wish, gas lighting was installed in the principal rooms. One day she came in with a little dog—pressed on her, she explained, by Adelaide Culver, who of course could not know that Papa was not fond of dogs; and Adelaide had taken so much trouble to get it that Mary had not known how to refuse. It was a white, fluffy little dog, with a shrill bark and a pedigree. At first he tolerated it because it gave pleasure to Mary, and afterwards he came to feel an esteem for it because it was so devoted to her. She named it Fritz—a name in fashion for such little dogs. Fritz was the most victorious of Mary's innovations, but she was also responsible for the spikes being taken from the wall and the wall's uniformity being remodelled into battlements. She no longer felt any fear of Loseby's common people. They were good simple creatures, she said, who had known her since she was a child.

Through the brightened and enriched interior of Anchor

House, Ellen fluttered like some dark ungainly waterfowl, peering with her shortsighted eyes and knocking over the little tables. This led to recriminations. When Ellen took up charitable works and parish visiting, John Barnard was thankful for the ensuing peace, and thankful that Ellen seemed at last to have fluttered into independence. The poor too were thankful. Ellen was not Euphemia, but she was better than Miss Adelaide Culver, she did not, being Loseby born, flinch at whelks or confuse the Madagascar Mobbses with the Waterloo Mobbses. After a month or so, Mary began to feel scruples; they were similar to the scruples she had felt on Euphemia's behalf during the outbreak of fever, but they were more serious and more insistent. Euphemia had gone too far, but Mamma had then been alive, so that people could not talk so very ill-naturedly. The motherless Ellen was in a much more delicate position, and Mary felt the responsibility keenly. She felt it so keenly that one evening she confided to Papa how very uneasy she was about Ellen's headlong ministrations. Would it not be better to put a stop to them before she quite set the parish by the ears? He said that Ellen would learn by experience. Mary doubted this. She would never know an easy moment while Ellen was out of the house.

Seeing her look so extremely grave, his heart melted to a little levity. "You do not always know easy moments when Ellen is in the house, either."

Not looking at him, and becoming an emotional pink, she said, "Papa, I must speak quite openly. I have thought a great deal about Ellen. And I seriously consider the best thing would be for her to become a nun."

"A nun?" he said, turning pale; for it was as though the feet of Dr. Newman and Dr. Wiseman were in the basement. "A nun? My dear, have you taken leave of your senses?"

"But, you know, one can be a Protestant nun nowadays, Papa. They are called sisterhoods, and quite well-bred people go into them. If you could let Euphemia go off and be a

274

Moravian, you could not really object to poor Ellen being a Protestant nun. And I know it is what she really longs for."

"Mary, the circumstances are not the same. Euphemia took no vows. She could come back to us tomorrow if she wished to."

"I don't believe Ellen would be expected to take that kind of vow. I fancy that if she wanted to get out, all she need do would be to ask a bishop. What I feel myself is that she should be allowed to try it, say, for a year. After a year she might think differently. In fact, I'm sure she would. Ellen never knows her own mind for more than two days running."

He thought this a poor argument, and did not reply to it.

"If you don't approve, I'll say no more about it. But I feel quite sure that Ellen should not visit ruptured old men alone, so I shall make a point of always going with her." She spoke amiably, and he reproached himself for the moment when he had dreaded an altercation.

Mary was as good as her word and went parish visiting with Ellen, and presently found that she liked it of all things, so that scarcely a day went by when Mary was not out on some charitable errand or other. Nothing more was said of Ellen's wish to become a nun, and by the end of 1853 Mary's words about Ellen's changeable disposition were proved true. Now it was Ellen who received him when he returned from the office, coming down from her bedroom with dazed eyes and inky fingers. Ellen, according to Mary, was busy writing a historical novel, which of course would never get finished, any more than Ellen's other fads.

Ellen's receptions were not so comfortable as Mary's; but he could warm himself by thinking that when Mary returned it would be his part to receive her, to hear her exclaim, "Dear Papa! Here I am at last! I thought they would never let me go," to watch her careful hands untying her bonnet strings, and to put the footstool under her feet. Then, with the exact truthfulness which had always marked her narratives, she would

275

recount what had been decided at the Ladies' Committee, where she had visited, whom she had met, and what had been said. Nothing very interesting had been said, nothing at all out of the way decided, and sometimes, it seemed to him, her understanding of a situation had been superficial, for her very candour inclined her to judge by appearances; but to look and listen was pleasure enough, and the sameness of these conversations was half their delightfulness, showing him that she was happy, that she had no wish for change, no dissatisfaction with her lot, nor with him. Not since her childhood had she been so confidently filial, so sure of being loved. The last vestige of grudge had melted away, the last small colouring of discontent; and the exercise she took in going about the parish had restored her bloom, and fined down her shape (she had been growing rather stout). She is the picture of contentment, he thought—till one day in November, when the sound of her voice told him that this afternoon, at any rate, he would not have to depend on Ellen for a welcome. As he opened the drawing-room door she sprang up and came towards him, a picture of such triumphant contentment that the previous picture of contentment was as nothing in comparison.

"Papa! How glad I am to see you! We have been waiting for you to come in."

At the same moment, and in a voice equally emotional and equally elated, Peter Culver exclaimed, "Mr. Barnard, you must wish me joy! Mary has made me the happiest of men."

"An hour and five minutes ago," said Mary, making sure by a glance at the mantelpiece clock. "But I wouldn't tell anyone till I had told you."

"That was very considerate, my dear."

He could brace himself by this nip of irony, since Mary had no ear for irony; but, having spoken, he recollected that Peter might not be so happily obtuse. He need not have troubled. Peter immediately assured him that Mary was considerate to everybody, which was one of the reasons why he had loved her from the day he first met her. That day being nearly three years before, Mary might have had reason to complain that Peter had been somewhat tardy in seizing on his prize, but it was plain that no such thought crossed her mind, just as it was plain that now, at any rate, Peter loved her to the top of his bent, piously, enthusiastically, and adhesively. He was younger than she, and a younger son, but his behaviour made it impossible to suppose that he was marrying her for her father's money or her father's position, or anything but herself.

There was, indeed, no hope of faulting Peter over anything. He was a fool but by no means such a fool as he looked. His ears stuck out, and his lips were like slugs, but he was six foot high and a fine figure of a man. He had made Julia a tittering-stock in that funeral sermon, but he was a newcomer and did not know what he was doing; and as Mary then and now considered the sermon a very touching one, he could not be judged impertinent for assuming she had no objection to him. When he first came to Loseby he was disliked and ridiculed, but he had stuck it out and so achieved a sort of bruiser's popularity. He paid his bills, he was kind to old women and wary with young ones, his tenets were evangelical, his health was flawless, his temper was even, and though he seemed a vulgarian, the Culvers were a respectable West of England family, fervently religious and devoted to field sports. If these merits had been the blackest depravities, he would still have been irremovable, for Mary loved him.

Knowing him her own, she was generous with him. She offered him to her father as a son, and to Ellen as a brother, and knew he would be a father to Johnnie. Though she could not quite dispense him to the firm as a partner, she knew that he would be just the person needed if Papa had any difficulties with the work-people. The wedding was to take place early in the new year, but there were moments when John Barnard wished it might take place immediately. Then his annoyance would vanish like smoke, and he saw nothing but the fact that in the new year she would go away to live under another man's roof. It was hard to conceive this—harder, perhaps, because she would not be far away; he would see her come into church and go to a different pew, he would meet her in the street as though she were any other person who lived in Loseby. Meanwhile, nothing had been said about where the roof would be. Peter, expatiating on what he chose to call domestic bliss, went into details about slippers warming and curtains cosily drawn, but did not specify where these proceedings would take place beyond an airy reference to a little nest. Number 1 Prospect Terrace stood empty—but the Terrace seemed rather old-fashioned now, perhaps Mary would prefer Gothic Lodge, which also was vacant. One day in December, John Barnard saw that the "To Let" board had gone from Gothic Lodge, and that Unwin's men were going in and out with ladders and buckets. He did not care to think that Mary would have got so far without telling him, he did not care to question Unwin's men either. A lady in a sealskin coat came out of the house and spoke to the foreman, and he realized that she was the new tenant. He spoke of this to Mary, mentioning it casually, in case he might destroy her private hopes. She looked up from a list of people who were to be invited to the wedding, and told him that the people coming to Gothic Lodge were called Bowen, and Peter fancied that they might be Bowens who were somehow related to his aunt in County Down, where Adelaide Culver had gone to be a companion now that Peter no longer needed her.

"That is a relief to my mind," he said. "I had thought that you might be considering Gothic Lodge yourself."

She looked at him blankly, her pen poised above the list of names.

"For when you come to leave me, my dear."

"Leave you, Papa? Leave my dear home? No such thing! Nothing would induce me to leave you, and until the Bishop calls Peter to a living we shall live at Anchor House. Everything

278

will go on just as usual, and Peter will keep an eye on the stables and see that the horses are groomed properly. It is so very good of him not to hunt. It costs him a great deal, I assure you."

If his gratitude for this and all other mercies sounded rather breathless, she did not notice it. She repeated once or twice that they would all be happy together in dear old Anchor House, and then reverted to the wedding list, debating whether or no the Kettles should be invited. Theirs was a January wedding too.

The Kettles were invited, and came. Peter was determined to show nothing like malice to the father of the young man who had been such a wretched husband to Mary; this determination was not put to any strain, for the two men immediately found each other congenial, and presently they began a contest of mutual adulation, like two snails cohering in one slime. Peter had been reared on Mr. Kettle's publications: the hymns, the Negroes, the Protestant Orphans, the Young Button-Makers, he knew them all. Simon had corresponded with Peter's uncle, a light among the Bristol Evangelicals. Peter had often heard his uncle speak of Mr. Kettle; his name was a household word at Maple Grove. Such homes as Maple Grove, said Simon —it was only by a series of unfortunate accidents that he had never actually enjoyed its hospitality—were beacons indeed. Neither Puseyism nor laxity, there. While abhorring Puseyism and laxity, Peter and Simon were in agreement about the need for a living and contemporary faith which could make wise use of the marvels revealed through science. Religion, they agreed, had nothing to fear from science (Simon, in fact, had found that, discreetly sprinkled, it had, like salt on an asparagus bed, a most renovating effect on his sales), and biblical exegesis could positively do good; it removed, like plate polish, old misunderstandings and stumbling-blocks. But it was Mary who called out their richest gushes. Mr. Kettle had known her in the bud, and now the younger snail proposed to crawl all over the accomplished rose. Turning away from this conversation, John

Barnard caught sight of his daughter's face. She had been listening too. The face expressed unflawed satisfaction.

Once again, as in a dream, he saw her going away with a husband—a different husband, a different bonnet, a solider bulk in his parting embrace. But this marriage was none of his doing and gave him not the minutest foothold for self-condemnation. He disliked the bridegroom, that was all. The white satin favour was untied from Fritz's neck, the remains of the wedding cake was put in an airtight box. He was alone with Ellen in a house full of wedding presents, waiting for Mary's first letter. It came. She wrote that as she and Peter would now naturally occupy Mamma's bedroom, and Mamma's dressing room would become hers, it would be best if Papa moved into the spare room, so that the dressing room in which he now slept could be Peter's dressing room. As all three rooms would need doing up, she had written to Unwin, telling him to start at once. This was followed by directions about getting rid of the smell of paint, which might upset Peter's throat, and a list of the furniture which was now to be put away in the garret. As Ellen read she broke into a cold sweat. Papa moved out of his dressing room, Peter in Mamma's bed, Mamma in the garret—she did not know how she could even discuss these sacrileges with Papa, still less carry them out; and yet if they were not carried out Mary would be offended, and that too would displease him. She gave him back the letter in silence, and he read it through again, saying only that the cat must be shut in the garret from time to time to keep down the mice.

"I should think we had better be put in the garret too!" she exclaimed with crushing irony. He turned on her with something like his old formidability, and rebuked her for envy, pertness, and small-mindedness. She had put into words what he so nearly felt himself, and he disliked the sound of it.

The smell of new paint was still pervading the house when Ellen's anxieties were transferred to what might or might not go wrong with the dinner of return. This also had been the subject of a letter from Mary, who wrote explaining about Peter's liver, which must be borne in mind, and his constitution, which needed to be watched. John Barnard had endured the rearrangement of his house without flinching, but Peter's liver sent him into his study to become a prey to forebodings. At this stage he could still preserve himself by his old expedient of running down a side issue, so, evading the admission that Mary had turned him out of his dressing room without consulting him, he decided that her letters, so cold and perfunctory except where Peter's welfare was concerned, showed that she was already feeling the consequences of marrying a man who was younger than herself and had so much in common with Simon Kettle. Peter's constitution depending on veal and a special sort of arrowroot biscuit, Simon's digestion almost miraculously benefited by asparagus—the parallel was obvious, and he asked himself how he could endure to see Mary's face changing as Sophie's had done, and ultimately wearing, as Sophie's did now, the look of one who wearily and contemptuously acquiesces in the fate of making the best of a bad bargain. But the arrival of Mr. and Mrs. Culver blocked up that route of escape. Mary was beaming with contentment. Peter was the light of her eyes, and Mary's slightest wish was Peter's law.

4.

"My Mary is always right." "My Mary has the disposition of an angel." "My precious, my devoted, my own Mary." "Mary is naturally my first and only thought." Henceforward John Barnard was to hear, in season and out of season, these gross reverberations of his own idolatry, and to hear them responded to with equally outspoken vows. There was no hypocrisy about it. Mary and Peter were made for each other, and indefatigable in acknowledging it. Their love was virtuous and shameless; they wept in each other's arms and toyed with each other's noses. He could not understand how his daughter, sheltered by his and Julia's decorum from witnessing a single instance of conjugal familiarity, should now behave as if she had been brought up in a bawdy house. She had never, for all the force of her youth, behaved so with Thomas. Even when lying on Thomas's bed, though she had disgraced herself, she had not degraded herself, and in his extremity of hating her for it, he had hated her as an equal. To see her fondling with Peter made him feel at once abashed like a child and affronted like a patrician. For some months he continued to find pretexts for getting Ellen out of the way at such moments as he knew to be climacteric—wet mornings when Mary would insist on putting on Peter's galoshes, having first dropped kisses inside them to keep his feet warm, or the afterglows of Peter's more emotional sermons. But one day when Peter said, "I'm afraid we shock your Papa," Mary's answering laugh, so carefree and condescending, struck away his power to disapprove. He realized that he was an old fogey. He had grown up in an England which had the precision and balance of an engraving: good and bad, heaven and hell, Whig and Tory, Queen Charlotte and Queen Caroline. In that world modest women behaved modestly, and what they might lack in ardour was supplied by women who had ceased to be modest. But something, he did not know what, had happened to society, and he moved in a world where his judgments were outdated.

Self-satisfaction was part of this new order of things, supplanting the self-righteousness of his own day. His self-righteousness often assured him that he was in the right and Peter in the wrong; but as it is mortifying to be conscious of superiority while afraid of asserting it, there was no comfort in this. Peter was given to boasting of deficiencies as though there were some agreeable merit in them. He delighted in owning himself a smatterer, and used his ignorances as a platform from which to display his personal worth, as though saying, See how well I

282

can get on without such things! The bookcases in John Barnard's study held not only the gentlemanly equipment of Latin and English classics, but some French classics too. Peter would run his fingers along their backs and wonder that anyone should trouble to read such musty old stuff. "The-aitre dee Raycine," he would say. "What does that mean?" Hearing his father-in-law's stiffly careful pronunciation, he grinned. Peter was by way of sharing the study, writing his sermons there, or making out the balance sheets which seemed to be increasingly vital to religious life. Presently a large easy chair was introduced for Peter to relax in. Placed in front of the fire, it made an effective firescreen. Naturally, Peter read prayers. He also carved at table.

Yet in a sluttish way Peter was amiable—others, at any rate, found him so. He was seldom out of humour, he did not take offence, he was not censorious, and in a base way he was modest. He was almost always civil to Ellen, who was contemptuous and sullen to him. If he never failed to mention an act of charity, it was because he enjoyed performing it. His sermons were shoddy and perfectly sincere. Crawley Blunt, who had begun by thinking him an oaf, now praised his efficiency and said that marriage had been the making of him. The truth was, Peter was happy, and a happy man can never be much in the wrong. One thing qualified his happiness. No children came of the marriage; he was so large, so florid, and so naturally philoprogenitive, it shook Peter's faith in himself that he could not beget a family as that skinny old gentleman his father-in-law had done. He reimbursed his feelings by thinking that Mary was spared the pains and perils of childbirth, and by being a devoted stepfather to her son of another man's getting. High among Peter's excellences was the fact that he had been the making of Johnnie. Mary had not pleaded the usual remarrying widow's excuse: that her child stood in need of a father; she had married for love and made no bones about it. But she was delighted to admit that Johnnie had been a spoiled child, shockingly wilful and sly—for to take advantage of his grandmother's funeral in order to obtain three hats from the school hatters could only be described as sly, and when the bill came in she had scarcely dared show it to poor Papa. She did not mention that Papa had paid for the hats without a word of complaint. He had not told her—and how could she guess? —that he had paid for them almost with tenderness. The purchase, so haughtily incompetent, reminded him of Thomas, whom he had wronged, and the payment seemed a token of the amends he could never pay. There was no other sign of Thomas about the boy. In looks he was all Simon, and in manner a lustrous copy of Peter. To become an even closer copy of Peter, he intended to become a clergyman.

Johnnie's resemblance to Simon was re-ascertained twice a year, when the Kettles regularly visited Anchor House. John Barnard came almost to look forward to these visits. Nothing could make Simon palatable to him, but in Sophie he found, if not a friend, at least a protector. Her hypocrisy would not allow her to triumph openly over a fallen enemy, and in the lassitude of having been for so long Mrs. Kettle the only thing she now really cared for was appearances. To keep up the appearance of a harmonious gathering of old friends, she talked to him as though he were not old and negligible, and spoke of him with deference, as though he were still the master of his house. He knew well enough that there was no truth in her kindness, that she was, as she had always been, cold-hearted and self-seeking, and that whatever she did was done in pursuit of her own private and limited ends; but she was polite, she was decorous, and she reminded him of old times without rubbing reality into the wound of the present by feeling concerned about it. He had a further reason to be grateful to Sophie for her policy of keeping sepulchres nicely whitened: she took no part in abusing Thomas. On the grounds that Thomas was too abominable to be mentioned, and that Johnnie must know of him only as the wicked man who broke his mother's heart, Simon mentioned Thomas whenever possible, condoling with Mary and his worthy friend Mr. Barnard for having been so shockingly deluded, and flicking Peter into a lather of manly excitement. Time after time John Barnard's conscience started up. But he said nothing. It would be waste of breath to speak in Thomas's defence, but it was not that which kept him silent. It was fear.

From the days of Mary's infancy he had been afraid: afraid for her health, afraid for her happiness, afraid lest she should catch cold, afraid lest she should be led into sin, afraid lest his excessive tenderness should do her harm, afraid lest he should lose any particle of her love. He feared on her behalf and with a father's protective authority until the morning when he had to tell her that Thomas had been sent away; then he conceived a passive fear, a fear that he might somehow become afraid of her. The notion appalled him, but he had come to terms with it and lived with it as a possibility, similar to other possibilities such as a cancer or a bankruptcy. With her second marriage the possibility seemed about to go into a perpetual abeyance, since one does not usually fear a person who is demonstrably inattentive to one's existence. To be sitting with her and see her jump to her feet when Peter came into the room was proof enough that her filial love had never been more than habit and complacence. To retain that love, such as it was, he had only to keep in with Peter and be cool towards Ellen—for Mary's filial love had one element of the other kind of love: she was jealous of her sister and would be agreeable to her only at the price of no one else's being so. Though to spend the rest of his life observing these conditions might be painful, he supposed it would not be difficult, for he had never loved Ellen, and Peter was willing enough to be kept in with. Thus computing with himself, John Barnard forgot to include the disabling effect of unhappiness. Just as Peter's happiness kept him pretty much in the right, John Barnard's unhappiness kept him pretty constantly in the wrong. Out of the house, he lived by false pretences, enduring congratulations on his happy lot. At home, he moved in a cloud of uncertain, unaccountable guilt. Presently a more explicit guilt was added, which fastened on him every morning when he went to his office. The Crimean War had put an end to imports from Russia. The check to trade was more apparent than real; though the raw material had to be bought elsewhere, and at a higher price, the firm was doing more business, and the sidelines which he had started in the early forties as expedients against unemployment were now important and profitable in themselves. But none of this consoled him for the rising costs of imports and the loss of the Russian market for salt herring. The business was not what it was. The profits were bound to become less. A day would come when he would have to tell Mary that she could no longer go on living as a rich woman.

This thought finally broke down his sense of the paternal. Authority, pride, responsibility, all gave way. Nothing was left but to love and be afraid. An accident of fashion enhanced his fears. During the decade of the fifties women began to wear crinolines, and Mary prided herself on having the most imposing crinoline in Loseby. Every year more yards of silk and velvet were required to drape the structure, and a more elaborate system of flounces and outworks was festooned about it. With her stiffly corseted body, her necklaces, bracelets, and earrings, she seemed to be an idol rising from some peculiar dome-shaped altar, and looking calmly and negligently down on the offerings that had been laid around her. "The best," said Peter, "is not too good for my Madonna!"—for in the playfulness of family life Peter addressed Mary as his Madonna, and Mary called Peter "Pugsie."

Pugsie was hospitable, his Madonna liked entertaining, and both of them, in compliance with the fashion of the day, felt that hospitality called for pomp and expenditure. An Archdeacon without a pineapple was unthinkable, or a luncheon without truffles for a Bishop—and to do Peter justice, when his undistinguished relations came to stay they were treated as lavishly. The Bishop's chaplain, to whom the deprecating old gentleman in shabby black was introduced as "My father-in-law, Mr. Barnard," could scarcely believe his ears. Coming of a Norfolk family, Frank Gosling had heard many accounts of John Barnard of Loseby—according to some, the man of miracles who carried his town through three starving winters, and according to others, that intolerable stiff-necked fellow who rode roughshod over committees. Being himself of a chivalrous, meddling disposition, Frank Gosling admired the second achievement as much as the first, and he tried to talk to the old gentleman. After a few minutes he was whisked away by his hostess to a Lady Angelina, whose white whiskers were disagreeably relieved by her sallow ermine; but something in the manner of the whisking, and in the old man's flinching anxiety not to be troublesome, stuck in his memory. A few months later, being in his London club, he heard an undersized man, who was laying down the law about Wagner, addressed as Barnard. A surname, an aquiline nose, and the recollection of that legendary riding roughshod were not much to go on, but on the strength of them he inserted himself in the conversation, invoked the name, and wondered if they were fellow East Anglians. Discovering that this Barnard was the old gentleman's son, he asked him if he had seen his father lately. Hearing that he had not, he let loose the chivalrous and meddlesome disposition, and told Wilberforce that the sooner he went down to Loseby the better.

It was the summer of 1856, and less than a fortnight before, Wilberforce had come back from Russia, where he had gone in the autumn of 1853 to tutor the brilliant only son of a wealthy family. His pupil died eighteen months later, and during the remainder of the Crimean War Wilberforce had lived on his employers' estate in the Tver district. He had intended to visit Loseby at the end of the season, but now, rather than be bored by feeling guilty, he put by some engagements and went at once. During the journey, in between admiring the trinket-box richness of the English landscape, Wilberforce entertained himself by thinking the worst of Mary and Peter and preparing injurious remarks. The change in his father's appearance shocked him so greatly that Mary and Peter escaped his intentions. They seemed no more than footnotes to a tragedy. If they were the footnotes, Ellen was a preface by an editor with a bee in his bonnet. Intoxicated by having at last this opportunity to speak out her hatred of Peter, she could speak of nothing else; everything from her father's dilapidation to the new gong was Peter's fault. Instead of getting any sense out of her, he was drawn into arguments, asserting that Mary's selfishness was as much to be blamed for John Barnard's decay as Peter's usurpations; to which Ellen replied that between Mamma's death and Mary's marriage Papa had been well and happy— No! it was all Peter's doing; Mary was no worse than she had always been. The servants had been replaced, and a visit to Hester produced nothing more to the purpose than that everybody had noticed the change in Mr. Barnard and did not know how to account for it. Unwillingly Wilberforce broke through the reserve which since he could first remember had preserved him from anything so dangerous as intimacy with his father, manoeuvred him into the arbour, and began to ask questions. Was he unwell? Was the racket of all this entertaining too much for him? Did he not find Peter very tedious? Was anything wrong with the business?

John Barnard looked up. It was as if a door had opened before him. He began to speak about the cost of living, the need to retrench, unforeseen liabilities, a time when expenditure, quite excusable expenditure, would exceed income. He talked in general terms only, except when he spoke of various personal economies, and of feeling obliged to cut down his subscriptions to local charities. It would be painful, but he saw no alternative. For the cost of living, the need to retrench—he rambled through his generalities again, repeating himself and seeming almost doting, till again he branched into his private commitments, the annuities to old servants, the number of small pensioners. He reckoned them up. He had them at his fingers' ends, it was clear that he constantly went through these calculations. Then, with a change of voice, he said, "But Will Thurtle is over eighty, and so is old Parker, and Jane George has been tapped three times at least." It was clear that these also were familiar calculations. To hear him speak like that showed Wilberforce, as nothing else could have done, through what agonies of transmutation John Barnard of Loseby had been compelled.

But by then Wilberforce had spent four nights under his father's roof, and whatever spontaneity of feeling he had arrived with (at Arkadino he had often found his emotions quite surprisingly limber), the climate of Anchor House had frozen it. Everything in the home of his childhood admonished him to be on his guard, every familiar sound, the squeak of a chair pushed backward, the rattle of a drawer handle, warned him to take cover, while the personal integrity which he had so jealously preserved stood like an angel in his path, telling him that he had no love for his father and could not summon it up just because an occasion called for it. Wool doesn't grow on a snake's back, he said to himself, smelling the familiar dry decay of the arbour and watching an ivy leaf twist in his father's restless hands; he left me no option but to go my way on a cold belly and be more subtle than all the other beasts of his menagerie. That I don't wish to bite his heel, that is already something. I can feel no warmth for him. Even if I felt it and could express it, it would not be the comfort he wants. It is Mary he loves. Let her assuage him. Though he had no doubt that his father's unhappiness was genuine, he did not doubt either that Mary's sham affection would console it. Her shammings had always done the trick, and, as Euphemia often pointed out, the family was under a real obligation to Mary for contriving to remain Papa's only comfort, however shabbily and scantily they might

289

think she filled her useful role. But now she was not filling it, or even pretending to. Consumed by an authentic love for her husband, she was behaving just like those nursery-maids who leave the baby squalling for its pap and its rattle while they run after a guardsman.

She was a mature nursery-maid, moreover; her notions of love's young dream soared above muslin and bread-and-butter, and her guardsman had expensive tastes. They must be spending a great deal of money, and any man who had to tell Mary she must retrench would take his life in his hand. It was no wonder if John Barnard dreaded being that man.

And yet, looking back on the conversation in the arbour, it struck Wilberforce that the confidences, however true, were not the truth of the matter, and that his father had developed this delusion of poverty as a safety valve for some more profound sickness of the mind. He wrote noncommittally, hoping the business had not suffered by the war, to his cousin Alexander. Alexander replied that the business was doing very well; Uncle John's income had almost doubled in the last ten years. So it was as he supposed: the obsession about money was a safety valve. He could think of nothing he could do to the purpose, though for his own peace of mind, he would talk to Mary. He did so—it did nothing for his peace of mind—and before leaving Loseby he posted a letter to Euphemia, in which he described how their father was going to pieces under the stress of living in Anchor House as a nobody, and defined his own inability to mend matters. Only Euphemia would know how to do that, and he hoped she would return and set about it. He had never known Euphemia to fail. But now she failed him. Throwing away her letter, he summarized it by remarking crossly, "Moravian for 'better fish to fry.' " For Euphemia had refused to come back. Thinking it over, he came to the conclusion that Euphemia was right in her decision, though wrong in expressing herself so priggishly about her duty to Herrnhut. "I could do nothing," she wrote, "to alter the fact that Papa's whole heart

290

has been given to Mary, so that now he feels left out and forsaken. Old age is not a happy time of life."

Even if Wilberforce had not tried to guarantee his peace of mind by an altercation with Mary, his visit would have made life harder for John Barnard. Peter, resounding with patriotism like a drum, considered that Wilberforce's stay at Arkadino was tantamount to betraying his country; at least he might have made his way through the enemy lines and gone to the help of Miss Nightingale. And then to lounge home and tell Mary, who had quite exhausted herself knitting woollen comforters and making black-currant jelly for the brave soldiers before Sevastopol, that she was neglecting her father! "I do not think I can let him come here again, my pet!" Mary, who sometimes perceived as a tiny flaw in Pugsie that Pugsie was inclined to look on Anchor House as his own property (she felt that it was Pugsie's wife's) overlooked this error of speech. It was delightful to feel protected by Peter's strong will and superior mind. She submitted enthusiastically to the decision that Wilberforce should be banned from the happy home where he had done so much mischief, exciting Ellen and unsettling Papa, and she promised Peter that she would do her best to wipe out the effects of his visit. She did so; and John Barnard and Ellen sat, whenever they could, in the garret.

It was Ellen who invented the garret, and for some months she kept it as her secret domain, as much a refuge from Papa's sighs and silences as from Mary's requirements and Peter's merriment. When the house was full she could sometimes contrive to spend as much as a couple of hours there, uninterruptedly hating and grieving. As Papa had his study, she had her garret. But the analogy could not be maintained. Peter worked in the study, rested in the study; then he began to receive parishioners there, at which stage the rather too classical—aha!—Flaxman engravings were taken down and replaced by wholesome Landseers. One day, seeing Papa stand hesitating outside the door and then turn away, she yielded to an impulse and beckoned him to follow her. As he did so, the old look of mistrust and reprobation crossed his face, and she wished with all her heart she had not been so rash. When he saw her arrangements, he would disapprove. He would tell Mary, and her refuge would be lost.

John Barnard had never before set foot in his garret. It ran the whole length of the house, segmented by transverse partitions of lath and plaster. In his father's time the women servants had slept in it. He followed Ellen past the lead cisterns which he had himself installed, and past accumulations of old travelling trunks and broken furniture. The farthermost chamber had a curtain rigged up over the doorway, and entrance to it was seemingly blocked by a cheval glass whose mirror was cracked and partly broken away. Ellen slid round the cheval glass and held back the curtain for him to pass. As though in a dream, he found himself in Julia's dressing room. Just as the broken looking glass had reflected him imperfectly approaching—his legs and his face and no middle to him—the reconstruction of the dressing room was splintered and fragmentary. The sofa was there, its stuffing trailing from it, and the sofa-table, and the deep armchair; but the glass-fronted cabinet, too high to go against the wall, stood in the middle of the room, and the Guido *Aurora* dangled from a rafter. One corner of the room was taken up by a rusty iron kitchener. It was too heavy for Ellen to move, but she had thrown a red tablecloth over it. He sat down on the sofa and stared about him, and presently Ellen put a footstool under his feet. The noise of the sea was more audible here than downstairs; and though downstairs it had seemed a windless day, the garret windows rattled lightly in their frames, and cold airs wandered about the room, proffering a faint vinous smell to his nostrils. Ellen fidgeted to and fro, taking up ornaments and blowing dust off them, polishing the glass panels of the cabinet with her handkerchief. Neither of them spoke until he asked her why she

292

did not keep a duster at hand, rather than misuse good cambric. By that she knew he would not speak to Mary.

Though they shared a hiding place, they had very little to say to each other. The fact that she had done her father a kindness made no difference to Ellen's fear of him. It was as though she had been kind to a sick but dangerous dog. At any moment it might bite. And he, in his last holdout of loyalty, was on his guard not to get into an intimate conversation, in case he should say anything to Mary's discredit. Perhaps it was on his own account he was careful. It would be so very easy now to discover that the loyalty had withered from its object and was nowhere attached but to himself. Ellen, having a weak back, usually lay on the sofa. He sat in the armchair, with the red tablecloth round his legs. She was not Julia, nor did he try to imagine her so. But someone was on the sofa, and he was back in his old place, which no one grudged him or disputed with him. In winter the garret was cold as the beach; sometimes they found snow lying drifted in on the windowsills. In summer it was hot and airless. It was the dearest thing in their lives. It was so dear that they did not resort to it very often, in case they should be found doing so.

5.

Ever since the accident to his nose, Crawley Blunt had been growing deaf. He made light of the disability, averring that it even had advantages. For by this date Loseby had so far caught up with the rest of the world that he had several Puseyites in his parish, and one of them was so far advanced that she demanded auricular confession. Consenting to this rite, provided it took place in the vestry, he confronted her with an ear-trumpet and was not troubled again. In 1858, being stone-deaf and liable to attacks of vertigo, he wrote to the Bishop, saying that he wished to give up the living (it was a family living and in his gift) and suggesting that Peter Culver, his faithful curate, might very suitably succeed to it. His Lordship replied that Peter would do excellently—but would he and Mrs. Culver, that hospitable pair, be willing to exchange Anchor House for Loseby Rectory, a smaller and less convenient dwelling?

To Peter the rectory was as welcome a prospect as the rectorship. A man should not merely be master in his own house. He should be master of it. The smallness of the rectory was a positive advantage. By a little inflation of Culver requirements —spare rooms, and why not a bathroom?—it might become too small to contain the Barnards. Later on it would be easy to throw out a wing.

But for the first time in his life Peter found himself opposed by Mary. "What? Leave my papa behind? It is out of the question. He would break his heart." It was a most natural and exemplary state of mind for a daughter, and he had no doubt that he would soon persuade her out of it. He was mistaken. Mary was unpersuadable. Peter thought this very strange; for would they not be much happier, and ultimately of much more benefit to society, if they were not hampered by the presence of that ghostly old man and Ellen's port-wine stain—quite apart from the dimensions of the rectory, where they would be most inconveniently on top of one another? Mary continued deaf to the size of the rectory, deaf to the claims of society, deaf to the wish of a husband. It was out of the question, she repeated; Papa would break his heart. It was her instinctive first reaction, and, clinging to it, she overcame not only Peter's persuasions but the second thoughts of her own bosom. However uncomfortably, Papa must be retained. She had spent her life in the position of Papa's indispensable daughter; all her self-esteem, all her self-satisfaction were somehow nourished from that fact. It might not appear to have much to do with them on the surface, but neither does the taproot of a plant. And

294

Ellen too was necessary. Suppose Papa should become senile? Where he went, Ellen must go too.

Though she had no intention of yielding, Mary thought that someone else's obstinacy would add respectability to hers. She told Peter that she could decide nothing without consulting Papa. Peter groaned; he knew well enough what John Barnard would say. Mary also supposed that she knew what John Barnard would say. It was disconcerting to find him actually considering the alternative, and rather more than considering it; after getting his wits back, he seemed positively inclining towards it.

She gave a little twitch to the reins. "Of course, there is the question of expense."

"Yes?" he said, not even attending to that vivifying word, and seemingly absorbed in some mysterious calculations of his own.

"If you don't wish to come to the rectory with us, if you would prefer to live with Ellen instead of with me, naturally I won't press you, dear Papa. But one thing I must insist on. I should not know an easy moment if you were to leave Anchor House."

"No?" he said; but still he had not attended.

"No, Papa! You must stay at Anchor House, and you must live just as before. It would break my heart not to see the dear old house going on just as usual, the garden kept up, and the stables, and the house looked after by a proper number of servants. As for the extra expense—well, that can't be helped."

She paused; but before he could speak she went on. "So I will tell Lady Angelina that it can't be done. She was thinking of renting it. She would have been just the tenant I should like. But we won't think any more of that. I will write her a little note, explaining that I was mistaken, and that you would prefer—"

He cried out, interrupting her. For a minute he had hung, fascinated, over the extraordinary, the abyss-like possibility

295

of living without her. It had even seemed an easy thing to do, a smooth bridlepath to ultimate dying. That she should think of it so calmly jolted him back into his real life. He was in terror lest he might have spoken too late, and that in some unexplained way it had been decided to leave him behind. Satisfied that the appeal to his penuriousness had done the trick, Mary said with a tinge of pardon that if he really wished to come too she felt sure she could find room for him, and then she went to tell Peter that Papa insisted on going to the rectory.

In point of fact, the rectory was not so cramped as Peter had represented it to his hopes. But it could have been a great deal larger, and still there would have been no place in it for John Barnard and Ellen. There was no garret, and naturally the study was entirely the rector's. This was worse for Ellen. She had not an office to go to, as Papa had. Yet with the perversity of old age, Papa, though he went to his office, didn't stay there but came back early in the afternoon, complaining of fatigue. For a while he lay down, and then he went out and sat in the churchyard. Apparently the churchyard served him as another garret, though there was a public footpath across it, and houses all round.

Loseby was accustomed to old men sitting out of doors. The low wall in Ship Street, the bench outside the Lord Nelson, had regular frequenters, and when one of them died another was elected to his place. These were old fishermen, and John Barnard was a gentleman; but the observance of class distinction was satisfied, because the fishermen always sat in company, whereas he sat alone, and in the churchyard, which was genteel. People using the footpath or trimming up family graves came to accept his presence as a matter of course, and stepped aside without constraint to have a few words with him about his health and the weather. In a less traditional community he might have been triumphed over, being so obviously come down in the world, or pitied for being turned out of doors like an old leaky dog. But no one supposed that the Reverend

Lovey-Dovey had the stamina to turn Grand Turk out of doors, even if he should want to; while as for triumphing, there was no cause for it: John Barnard was only behaving as other very respectable persons did. To see him observing a Loseby custom made Loseby feel well disposed towards him, and he had never been so near popularity as now.

His fine-weather seat was a low altar tomb, sheltered between two buttresses on the south side of the church. Wearing a tall hat, and holding his silver-knobbed walking cane across his knees, he presented a well-to-do, respectable appearance, so perfectly prosaic that not even the most speculative summer visitors thought of him as a faithful mourner or an eccentric. When it rained he sat in the porch, looking out on the flagged path and the gravestones, numerous as ships in a harbour. His gaze, rambling among them, always came back to the Barnard stone, and always with a degree of surprise that it was not so tall nor so recent as he thought. It remained new in his mind, he supposed, because it had been so often made new to him by the deaths it recorded and by the youthfulness of those he had seen lowered into its pit. Their ages added together fell far short of the last-comer's.

Also Julia Barnard, Mother of the above,
Born March 21, 1794. Died March 30, 1852.

Also John Barnard. His name would follow theirs on the obelisk, as the shepherd follows his sheep into the fold. Another stone, shaded by some unsurmisable tree, would be inaugurated by Joseph Barnard; Euphemia could not, Wilberforce would not, lie down in the family grave, and Mary, though she might be buried in Loseby churchyard, would lie elsewhere and as Mary Lucinda Culver. These thoughts had become habitual to him, they were paths down which his mind could travel without risk of stumbling or having to turn aside from the unbearable. One afternoon, as he was thanking God for allowing him such resignation in his old age, he realized that for half a year at least he had been thinking of Mary's death as a matter of course.

It was as though an iron skewer on which for forty years his entrails had been spitted were smoothly withdrawn. Mary's death, that agonizing preoccupation, had lost its potency. His love, which since her second marriage had existed only as an acquiescence in the bondage of loving her still, hopelessly, apologetically, and in vain, had predeceased her. He felt an anguish, but it was only a momentary anguish. The pedlar going up Church Street, and calling out on his melancholy questioning intonation, "Old clo'es, old clo'es," had not added on a lower, more confidential note, "or rab-bit skins," before the realization was accepted and assimilated. Mary's death would mean no more to him than any other death. He felt the need to move about, as though it were a need to make sure that he was still alive and John Barnard still. He left the porch and began to walk through the churchyard. Light as air, casual as thistledown—it was only his feet that remained heavy and akin to the earth he walked on and the stones he walked among; the rest of him felt insubstantial and, as it were, abolished; the rain falling on him had more reality than he. The pedlar continued to cry his way up Church Street, someone was hammering, a smell of baking meat came from one of the houses that abutted on the churchyard. John Barnard walked among the graves, stopping to read each headstone as attentively as though he had never read such inscriptions before. He was among the older stones, which laconically presented him with their antitheses of having lived and being dead, and were eloquent only in their emblems of mortality: their hourglasses, their coffins, their crossed bones, their bitter cherubs composed of skulls and bats' wings. It seemed to him that these men and women who had lived out their days before he was born had lived more really than he, and that there had been more reality in their deaths. It was as though he could hear rough, substantial voices arising out of their graves, assur-

298

ing him that they were their very selves, and that death was no less actual and no less inexhaustible than herring. Vaguely comforted, he raised his head and looked towards the politer part of the churchyard. There was the obelisk. Something moved behind it, a quick dart of movement; it was a rosemary bush which had been planted on a grave near by, wagging at a gust of wind. He knew this perfectly, but meanwhile the sudden movement of the bush had become Darwell, bobbing curtsies beside Julia's open grave. On that day, seeing her so vile, so ludicrous, so degraded, he had known that she was only the outdoor picture of a sheltered Julia. Julia was no better—only more fortunate. Darwell was no worse—only more violently ripened by circumstances. Then, he had thrust down this knowledge and smothered it under consideration of the mercy of God, but he could admit it to himself quite calmly now. Now that it was too late, everything was clear. He saw his past life, springing like some malformed tree from where he had planted it in a bad love. Every branch of it was twisted awry, and from the branches hung calamities like dismal fruit. There was Julia, who had drunk herself to death with very little pleasure in it, and Darwell, who had followed her mistress because his bad love had rendered him a careless master. There was Euphemia, who had vindicated her estate of drudge by going away to drudge superlatively in a foreign land. There was Ellen, a drudge unvindicated, who flinched if he spoke to her. There was Thomas, snatched into marriage and tossed out of it. There was Wilberforce, with his unknown cold heart. Everything, down to the kitten which had been drowned because it scratched Mary, had suffered by his idolatry. And he had suffered too.

He heard someone speaking to him. It was Penny Bullen, whose husband, Crusoe, had been drowned some years ago. She had flowers in her hand, she had come to dress a child's grave. She was telling him that it was too late.

"Yes, Mrs. Bullen. It is too late; it is indeed too late."

299

"A nasty cold evening, and not fit for a man of your age. Mrs. Culver will be worrying about you. Go you in, Mr. Barnard! And take something hot, for you look very pinched."

The gawdy autumn marigolds in her hand were like a fire. Her words gave him a sudden picture of comfort in such a home as hers. He would have liked to be going back to a kitchen and to something hot, and to be warming his hands on the mug. But he did not suppose her kindness to him was more than a woman's habit of laying down the law. Her husband had always disliked him and been surly towards him, and she was a loyal wife.

As he walked back to the rectory he thought sharply, I shall see Mary. He would be seeing her with new eyes, a Mary whose death would not end his world. But she had gone out, and her absence was a relief to him. He was very wet, and his boots were muddy, and this would have displeased her. Suddenly asserting himself, he told the parlourmaid that he felt chilled and was going to bed; he would have the fire lit in his room and some soup brought up to him. Love had gone, and as the flames ran up the chimney he realized that when love goes, fear goes with it.

A tree of forty years' growth cannot be shivered by lightning without some difference in the landscape becoming noticeable. Mary presently observed a change in her father. It was a change for the better: he had left off bothering her. Mary having drawn his attention to it, Peter also noticed that there had been a change. Indeed, there were two changes: not only had his father-in-law become almost totally silent; he had taken to falling asleep during Peter's sermons. They must expect a gradual decay, said Peter charitably.

Yet at no time in his life had John Barnard felt such an urgent desire to speak. He wanted at once to accuse and to clear himself—to make plain that he had been a bad father, yet not a malevolent one. Ellen was the natural confidante. She was at hand, they had shared the garret, she had been trained in filial obedience and would not refuse to listen to him. He need only say, "Ellen, there is something I wish to tell you,' and she would put by whatever she was doing. But at the same time she would put by any capacity to hear him; she would become half-witted, unable to conceive that he could have anything to say to her which was not a reproach or a rebuke. If he were to begin, "Ellen, I have something to confess," an undenominational sense of guilt would make her incapable of understanding him. Even if she could be brought to understand that he was blaming himself, her anxiety to keep him at a safe remove would hurry her into assurances that he was good and Peter to blame for everything. So perhaps he would do better to put his confession into a letter. Joseph, his first-born, was so nearly a stranger that he might have a stranger's tolerance, even a stranger's compassion. Joseph had children too; he might understand how fatally the favourite child can become the Moloch to whom the other children are sacrificed. For some days John Barnard thought of the letter he would write to Joseph; but no letter could be a full confession of how he had sinned if it did not include his guilt towards Julia, and it was not possible to make that plain without telling Joseph that Julia had become a drunkard. Should his letter be written to Euphemia? This thought was no sooner entertained than he realized its futility. Euphemia knew everything already. She had judged him and gone away. Wilberforce, the last child of the story, had been born into such an established tradition of Mary's monopoly that he had never seemed deprived by it. It was a measure of how truly John Barnard yearned to accuse himself and clear himself that twice he began a letter to Wilberforce. But neither letter was finished; the thought of Wilberforce was too styptic.

His mind turned to another letter and another expedient. It dwelt increasingly on the visit to Herrnhut, but always as though he were remembering some story he had read, or rather a scene in that story which had remained with him though he had forgotten the rest of the book and the name of the author. He saw the travelling Englishman, walking in an alley of clipped hornbeams. A feeling of reverence for the man towards whose tomb the alleys gathered made the Englishman take off his hat, and the wind ruffled his hair. Dusk was gathering, but the time was going on so slowly that it might have been the oncome of winter and not merely the oncome of night. He walked to and fro, saying to himself, "I am here. I have found where I mean to die." And a dream of a later date seemed to validate the words, for in that dream the travelling Englishman was lying in a narrow white bed, it was night, and somewhere a choir was slowly singing a hymn. But the travelling Englishman had neither wife nor child, and that was why it was possible for him to feel so deeply at peace.

If he could overcome the awkwardness of appearing to pursue Euphemia (and in fact she need have nothing to do with him), perhaps, after all, the dream could become fact. For now he had no wife, and to all intents and purposes no children. At Herrnhut there was an infirmary, where they were kind to the aged—impersonally kind, and without indulgence, a valedictory kindness to free the soul from earthly ties. If they would admit him? The other letter began to shape itself in his mind, and in his office he made several attempts to write it. But lately, from talking so little, he had lost command of words, and any letter except a letter of business was almost beyond his power. So the letter to Herrnhut was still unwritten when Mary at breakfast opened an envelope, read something, and looked angry.

"Wilberforce is coming to Loseby! Could anything be more tiresome?"

"Tell him there is no room for him," said Peter scripturally. But she replied that this was no good, as Wilberforce had engaged a room at the Half Moon.

This time Wilberforce was back from South Africa, where he had gone to see for himself the stars of the Southern Hemisphere—an ambition of his boyhood, first aroused by an article in Kettle's *Juvenile Repository* which described the Southern Cross as being more brilliant and devotional than any other constellation. An astronomical friend at the Cape Town Observatory had been inclined to question the accuracy of Wilberforce's reporting, and Wilberforce had undertaken to copy out the exact text as soon as he got home. He had made the promise confidently, seeing in his mind's eye the row of *Juvenile Repositories* in the bottom shelf of the bookcase on the upper landing; it was not till some days later that he bethought himself that Anchor House had been abandoned, and that there was no saying what Mary might not have thrown away in the move. No doubt there would be a great many other changes too, predictable or unpredictable. Among the predictable would be Peter and Mary, as much brighter as a rector is brighter than a curate; Ellen, correspondingly more heated; and his father—Wilberforce did not care to forecast too exactly what changes might be expected in his father. He had not allowed—indeed, short of special revelation, he could not have done so—for the variation due to Ellen's having compiled a birthday book. The birthday book had been sold for five pounds to a London publisher, who had done so unexpectedly well with it that he paid her another five pounds and commissioned another birthday book. Ten pounds and fame had made a new being of Ellen. She sported a lorgnette, and Peter consulted her about his sermons—a tribute to intellectual achievement, thought Wilberforce, not likely to be extended to him. As for his father—he was four years older, that was all. The move to the rectory had not affronted him, he seemed, if anything, rather the happier for living in a house where he had not even a formal claim to be considerable. Peter had been at some trouble to explain that if Mary's papa might appear to spend a large part of his time in the churchyard, it was entirely by his own wish, and because he had such a wonderful constitution and liked his little chats with old friends.

303

Gentle exercise, said Peter; and Wilberforce agreed. The weather was fine, the churchyard a great deal better than Mary's drawing room, and when he had run down the *Juvenile Repository* (it had been transferred, together with Robertson's *Scripture Characters* and *The Compleat Angler,* to the Boys' Club) Wilberforce availed himself of the churchyard also, on the plea of keeping his father company. It was not an onerous kindness. For the most part they walked in silence, or talked desultorily about changes in Loseby. The old man had been talking about steam trawlers when suddenly his grasp tightened on Wilberforce's arm, and he began to drag him towards the obelisk. Trembling violently, he halted before it. For some minutes he seemed unable to discover what he was snuffing for, what quarry had suddenly excited him. Then he said in a whisper, "That is not all."

Stooped with age, he was still almost a head taller than Wilberforce. He seemed to be addressing something in the air.

"That is not all," he said again. "That is not the whole of my guilt." There was no answer, and he cried out desperately, "Wilberforce! Are you listening?" The words, and the tone of voice, carried Wilberforce back into his childhood. He felt the familiar impulse to escape before anything else was said, and almost looked round for Euphemia. Euphemia would know how one dealt with fits.

"The word 'guilt'——" he began, thinking that abstract discussion might apply to fits as usefully as it did to other turbulent subjects. But his father was now asking him if he had ever thought of marrying.

"On the whole, I think I may, though not yet. I should like a couple of children, because——"

"Give not your heart to idols! That is what I did, Wilberforce—your sister Mary. I know it at last. I loved her inordinately. Inordinately, Wilberforce. Everything has gone wrong because of that. Everything that came between me and her was an impediment. I trod it down or thrust it away. All of you, and

304

your mother too—I have sacrificed everything to an inordinate love. You might say that I deluded myself, but I deluded myself deliberately. I plotted with myself to remain deluded."

He paused, and added solemnly, "I have been a bad father."

Staring at the Barnard stone, Wilberforce said, "We are none of us perfect."

The old man sighed heavily and went on. "For a long time —longer than you will suppose—I tried to do my duty by you all. But my heart was not in it—my unhappy, doting heart."

Mechanically reading the names on the stone, Wilberforce had come to, *Also Julia Barnard, Mother of the above;* and the best he could muster up was "There must have been many worse fathers. I should not make too much of it, if I were you."

"I wanted you to know. That was all."

The savage humility of the words shocked Wilberforce into compassion. With no notion what to say, he knew he must say something. For a confession is a gift, one cannot receive it, however thrust upon one, without giving something in return—sympathy, if one is a woman; if one is a priest, absolution. The weathercock creaked overhead as the light wind veered, and he became conscious of the surrounding gravestones. It was as though a hundred prompters had sprung up in the wings, mutely holding out appropriate cues. *Repent; for the Kingdom of Heaven is at hand. . . . God is Love. . . . Thy will be done.* He began to speak of the consolations of religion, asseverating that no one could be better aware of them than his father—he was too prudently truthful to pretend to any personal experiences. Life, he said, was such an unmanageable thing that it is demonstrably the creation of some supernatural energy. A man with any intellectual candour must admit to a lack of control over his own existence, and probably David had something of the sort in mind when he wrote "It is he that hath made us, and not we ourselves," adding immediately afterwards, "O go your way into his gates with thanksgiving, and into his courts with praise"—which seemed a genuinely religious acceptance of the situation, and an example which his father should find consoling. Becoming embarrassed by all these pious conditionals, Wilberforce scrambled out on *The Pilgrim's Progress,* and fell silent. His father had not said a word and did not reopen the question.

The conversation with Wilberforce had shown John Barnard that he could arouse no interest—perhaps a little repulsion, but nothing else. He did not reread *The Pilgrim's Progress,* as his distinguished son had recommended him to do. He had no pleasure in religious reading, nor in going to church. Meditation was nothing but a doorway into vainly remembering and vainly regretting, and he had forgotten how to pray. The mercy of God had once been real to him, a rainbow which would appear among clouds and on which he could walk, a passage between the fatherhood of God and his own fatherhood; but that was while he loved Mary and invoked it on her behalf. Loving being at an end, mercy had departed; it was no longer an attribute of God. Very soon after the discovery that he no longer loved Mary, he had begun to ask himself how much of God was left to him now that Mary was relinquished. There was not very much. Listening to Wilberforce's bleak ramblings between nescience and making the best of it, he realized that he had no substantial impulse to know better, or to believe more. He could not attach any love to God, or feel any trust in God, and the fear of God was now barely more than a convention—a husk of fear. Presumably in the hour of death that husk would be filled; he would die in fear, knowing that after death comes the judgment. He would die, too, a plain Deist. The Jesus of the Christians was no longer a person to him; at most he was a person who had been known and loved a long time ago and in happier days—as if he had been known at Cambridge. Yet a tenderness for lost love and faith still trembled in his disfurnished heart and was irritable. Mutilated into a plain Deist, he still was outraged when Peter, coming home after the celebration of the Holy Communion, recounted the number of those who had partaken of it as though he were reckoning up the bag after a partridge shooting. But he was no longer one of Peter's partridges.

Now that he had ceased to occupy his mind with the question of how and to whom he should confess his fault, and had no religion of a kind that can be practised, time hung heavy on him. His health was decaying—but in a gradual, insignificant way, as dust accumulates in an empty room: there were no sharp pains to intimidate him, no symptoms to watch or to avoid watching. On his seventieth birthday he gave up going to the office. A clerk replaced him, and the workers in the Loseby branch of Barnard & Son made him a presentation of an eight-day clock. It was the Loseby branch now. The bulk of the business had shifted to the London office, and Alexander and his boy Daniel would perpetuate the title of the firm; for John Kettle, inheriting nothing else from his father, had inherited Thomas's unmercantile mind and was reading for Holy Orders. Cricket was his other devotion, and he intended to become a clerical headmaster. Codicils, which had brightened the declining days of Johnnie's other grandfather, did not interest John Barnard. His will had been redrawn after Julia's death—the orthodox will of a father of a family, and he made no alterations to it, except that recently he had doubled all the charitable bequests. The fret about money had left him. When he knew he no longer loved Mary, his eyes were opened to the truth of his estate, and he knew he would die a wealthy man. From time to time he exchanged letters with his brother Daniel, and at Christmas and for Joseph's birthday he wrote to Joseph and received in reply a letter from Joseph's wife, giving him messages from Joe, who was too busy to write himself, and telling him about the grandchildren he had never seen and would never see. Sometimes it seemed to him that there were two sets of these West Indian grandchildren, those who were infants and had a black woman for their nurse, those who were grown up and travelled to the old country, though not to Loseby. He had a few local cronies; but his life had never extended into friendships, and the cronies were too well known and bored him; he preferred the conversations of his churchyard acquaintances. Once or twice he found himself fancying that he would enjoy a talk with Sophie, who was in her second widowhood. Hypocrisy did not offend him now as it had done in the past, when he too lived in a pasteboard castle, and during the period of visits to Anchor House she had been kind to him. But after Simon's death Sophie had gone to live at Chantilly, and nothing more had been heard of her.

In the spring of 1863 he seemed to be in the way of making a new friend. Lady Angelina had never intended to rent Anchor House; it was on behalf of a nephew that she put out feelers. The nephew, an ageing fast man, had got into the London papers because of a habit of beating little girls, and had been advised to go and live somewhere out of the way, with the plea of ill health. He and his silly, devoted wife put up a pretence of settling in, stayed just long enough for the scandal to follow them and inconvenience Peter, and then left with the last quarter's rent unpaid. After that Anchor House stood empty for several years, and when new tenants took it Mary elected to find them disagreeable and not worth cultivating— venting on them the annoyance she had not been able to vent on Lady Angelina. They were three maiden sisters, reputed to be horribly learned; during the holidays the house was filled with nephews and nieces. The eldest sister was a cripple, and it was she that he was shown in on when, instead of delivering a message about a bazaar to the servant, the sight of his own door opened to him drew him in through it. Announced by the servant, he entered his own study, became aware of a mingled smell of fish and oil paint, and saw a lay figure, and then a lady who was painting a crab and some seaweed with extraordinary minuteness. Conversation developed out of the crab. The sad-faced old gentleman who would have made such a fine portrait by Bellini knew a great deal about crabs, about fishing, about tides, and told her that in parishes where there is a lifeboat the parson is *ex officio* a member of the crew and goes out in her. "Our Saviour must like that!" she exclaimed— and for a moment John Barnard was not a Deist. During the summer he went again and again to see Miss Walcot. The crab was replaced by a tangle of rusty ships' chains, and that by an old net, thrown over the arm of the lay figure, and though he could not conceive why she should paint such everyday objects, it pleased him to see them rendered so exactly and as though no one had ever set eyes on them before. He was not required to talk of art. It was Loseby she liked to hear about. Talking of old ways, and of characters who had taken their crust while he was still a schoolboy, telling of superstitions and extraordinary adventures, explaining the Norfolk dialect and how its tune varies from place to place, he felt the pleasure of bestowing, and it was sweet to him. Nothing could give him back his heart, which an error of love had eaten out as a worm eats the hazel kernel, but Miss Walcot's attention made him feel that he was not altogether negligible; at least he could interest a lady. Something like artistry awoke in him. Not only did he ferret through his memories for things that would interest her, but he considered how best they could be presented, and where, and where not, he should introduce the dialect. But one afternoon a sister came in, bringing a phial and a wineglass, and saying that it was time for Frances to take her tonic. She sat down, and as a listener she was more enthusiastic than her sister, so that he exerted himself to please and stayed too long. As he left the room he heard her say, "Whew! My dear—" and Frances Walcot reply, "No, no. It pleases him."

Walking back to the rectory he reasoned with his pride, telling himself that if Miss Walcot chose to be kind to an old man he should not thwart her. He went once more to Anchor House and stayed a moderate while, asking questions about modern painting. After that he did not go again.

He supposed he could relieve them of his visits without seeming uncivil; for the autumnal equinox was past, the weather was cold and stormy, and they would not expect him to venture out in it. He still had the churchyard. He was no worse off than before, except that he could not go there with his old freedom, as Mary had begun to object, saying that he would make himself ill and that she would be unjustly blamed for it. This did not stop him, but from policy he sometimes delayed until she had gone out herself. Ladies now had a fashion of going out to tea parties at an hour when their grandmothers had gone out to dine. Mary went to many tea parties, and when he was fortunate the tea parties were in places beyond Loseby, so that she went in the carriage and started early. Tea parties in Loseby, when she did not set out till four, curtailed his span of daylight and sociability, for no one frequented the churchyard after sundown, and to sit staring through the dusk at the unmoving gravestones made him drowsy. There was a seat in the porch, but it was only a narrow plank, and he often looked at the church door, thinking of the warmth and the padded pews within, and sometimes of the popish churches, gaudy and kindly and open all the week, which he had explored with Julia when they went to Paris. Julia had much enjoyed the smell of incense. Paris was a fine city. Leaving the Place de la Concorde, one came to the Tuileries, and thence . . . A clatter roused him. It was the silver-knobbed cane falling out of his sleepy grasp. The noise of the sea came rolling solemnly through the dark, and he thought how all his life it had been in his ears and yet he had seldom been much aware of it. When he listened it was almost always for some practical reason, a storm or the forecasting of storm, a shift in the wind, the state of the tide. In the same way, the domestic voice of a clock is

310

always admonishing one of the nature of time, but one listens to it thinking of hours and appointments. And so he had never given ear to the true voice of the sea, the waves travelling to the shore, languidly, or with a light gaiety, or confusedly and in violence, but always to break, uttering the word *"Now!"* Walking with his nurse on the beach, he had discovered that the waves said, "Now!" and had remarked on it, asking her what they meant by it. Why should they say, "Now!" and then go away again? She replied that, on the contrary, the waves said, "Hush!" and that little boys should take a lesson by it. "Now! Now!" If only he had heard the admonition of the waves, if only he had obeyed that bidding and at some now or other had forsworn his idolatry and lived out his life as a man and not as a votary, though he should now be an old man, and sorrowful, it would be with a ripened old age and a justified sorrow. But the real sorrows which one by one had fallen upon him he had invalidated; bereavement after bereavement had left him Mary, the waves had said their *"Now!"* unheeded and gone away again. He lived under the same roof with her and was completely alone, and his final bereavement, the death of his illusion, had cost him so dishonourably little that it was like one of those foiled waves that spread themselves up the shore with no sound except a little hissing of foam.

The stick fell to the ground, but this time it did not wake him. He was dreaming, and in his dream he was reading the names on the obelisk by the light of a handful of phosphorus. It was a slender light; he could see only one name at a time, and he moved the light up and down, looking for a name that should be there, that had a right to be there, and yet he could not find it. He knew the place where it should be, between Julius and Julia. But what was the name? He had forgotten it.

He woke up suddenly, and the name was on his lips.

"Thomas!"

It was quite dark; he could see nothing of the man who had

come along the flagged path, but he knew the footfall. It was Thomas. And he could tell Thomas, and Thomas, for all his pride and all his injuries, would understand.

Thomas had entered the porch. But a different voice spoke to him, and a heavier hand settled on his shoulder. "Grandpapa! Don't you know how late it is? You'd better come home quickly, before Mamma notices you're not in, or you'll be in her black books."

It was kind of Johnnie. "Thank you, my boy. I think I must have fallen asleep." Sleepily he took the young man's arm, noticing how full and strong it was within the sleeve. "Do you know, your step is just like your father's."

"Like the Pater's?" Johnnie's voice was umbraged. "Well, I shouldn't have thought that. He's got a heart of gold, but he walks like a hen."

"I don't mean your stepfather. Your father."

The arm stiffened. "I'm sorry if I resemble him in any way."

"I should like to tell you about your father. He was a most unfortunate young man."

"I won't hear a word about him! He was an unmentionable scoundrel and broke my mother's heart. I know that about him. I don't need to know more."

In his anger Johnnie walked so fast that John Barnard had no breath for speaking. Even when he went to bed the sensation of breathlessness persisted. During the night he woke several times and noticed, as though it were something happening to another man, that he was feverish and in pain. In the morning he could not get up. People came and went—the housemaid, Ellen, Mary, the doctor. The pain grew worse. They gave him brandy and beef tea, and put a mustard plaster on his back. There were now two pains. In a surprisingly short time it was night. The doctor came a second time. A creosote lamp was brought into the room; he was given something in a spoon which made him sick. He was burning hot, he was icy cold. Julia sat by his bed. Sometimes Julia became Ellen, and

312

then he knew that Julia was dead and that he was dying. Suddenly, instead of the sea fog and the squawking of gulls which for so long had filled the room, it was a midday, and a clear, keen sunlight streamed through the window and fell on a little table by his bedside that had a white cloth on it and had not been there before. The door opened. Peter came in, wearing a surplice. He had the air of a complete stranger, a grave and rather impressive man. Mary, Ellen, and Johnnie followed him, and John Barnard understood that he was about to receive the communion of the dying. It gave him considerable pleasure; the words were full of beauty and serenity, and Peter remained a reassuring stranger. When it was over, Peter, Johnnie, and the table went away. Mary and Ellen were still on their knees. He supposed they too would soon go away. He shut his eyes; for the moment he was feeling much weaker and also much easier. He knew that the death agony would come presently, but for the time being he was at peace. The bed rose and fell with an easy motion, it was as though it were riding on a calm sea, and if the wine were not giving him heartburn he would have tried to fall asleep. Instead, he went out of the house on his way to the quay, and saw a fishing boat being pushed up the street to the sound of organ music. But he felt his hand clutched, and kisses were pressed on it. It was Mary. He was obliged to open his eyes. They had all come back; Peter was only Peter, and Mary was fondling his hand and crying over it. "My dearest, dearest Papa! What shall I do without you? What will we all do without you? No one has ever been so kind, no one has ever been so good. The best of men! The best of men!"

It was horrible. Only her tears had any truth in them, being paid to death. Everything else was completely false. He tried to move his hand away. She took a firmer hold of it and went on with her weeping flatteries. Now there was falsehood even in her tears.

"Listen," he gasped.

"No, no, dear Papa! Don't try to talk. It will only weaken you. I know how you love me, there is no need to tell me. Just lie quietly till you are stronger."

"Listen, all of you," he said, wrenching his faculties back into life. "Attend! Only my name, and after that, 'Lord, have mercy upon me, a sinner.' Do you hear? Nothing else. It is my dying wish."

They promised him it should be so. He shut his eyes and tried to compose himself, but after a few minutes he began to hiccup. He covered his face with his hands to veil his agony. In due course, Johnnie, at a nod from Peter, went out to order the passing bell to be rung.